ALEX SHAW spent the second half of the 1990s in Kyiv, Ukraine, teaching Drama and running his own business consultancy before being headhunted for a division of Siemens. The next few years saw him doing business for the company across the former USSR, the Middle East, and Africa. *Cold Blood*, *Cold Black* and *Cold East* are commercially published by HarperCollins (HQ Digital) in English and Luzifer Verlag in German.

Alex, his wife and their two sons divide their time between homes in Kyiv, Ukraine, Worthing, England and Doha, Qatar. Follow Alex on twitter: @alexshawhetman or find him on Facebook.

Also by Alex Shaw

Cold Blood

Cold East

Cold Black

ALEX SHAW

ONE PLACE. MANY STORIES

HQ
An imprint of HarperCollins*Publishers* Ltd
1 London Bridge Street
London SE1 9GF

This paperback edition 2018

First published in Great Britain by
HQ, an imprint of HarperCollins*Publishers* Ltd 2018

ISBN: 9780008310189

MIX
Paper from
responsible sources
FSC® C007454

This book is produced from independently certified FSC™ paper
to ensure responsible forest management.

For more information visit: www.harpercollins.co.uk/green

Typeset by Palimpsest Book Production Ltd, Falkirk, Stirlingshire
Printed and bound in Great Britain by
CPI Group (UK) Ltd, Melksham, SN12 6TR

To my wife, Galia, and my sons, Alexander & Jonathan.
To family in England and Ukraine.

Prologue

Harley Street, London, England

Aidan Snow sat on the examination table wearing only a pair of black boxer shorts. Dr Durrani poked Snow's left leg with a gloved index finger, his large, bright eyes focusing intently.

'Hmm. The incision seems to have healed nicely; the reduction in scar tissue is what we would have hoped for.' Turning his attention to the right leg, Durrani continued. 'I'm not as happy with this one, but then you did leave it rather a long time before coming to see me.'

Snow nodded. It hadn't been his idea to visit the doctor, but a direct command from Jack Patchem, his handler at SIS. Patchem's view was that no undercover operative could 'blend in' if he was riddled with scars. Snow saw no reason to complain.

'Now the shoulder. Hmm. If you would just raise your arm for me… that will do fine. Any pain at all? Any discomfort?'

'No.'

'None?'

'None,' Snow lied. He got the occasional twinge from all his old injuries, especially those caused by bullets, but letting the SIS-contracted doctor know that wouldn't help with his operational status.

Snow was fit – above average, even by army standards – but by the ripe old age of thirty-six, he'd had one leg crushed in a car crash and the other punctured with a round from an AK74. This was in addition to a recent bullet to the right shoulder. Ten years separated the first and second set of injuries, but they had been caused by the same ruthless former Spetsnaz member.

The first injury had led to Snow prematurely leaving the SAS and the second set had caused him to be recruited by Her Majesty's Secret Intelligence Service (SIS), or as it was more widely but inaccurately known, 'MI6'. After rehabilitation of his injuries and a refresher course in the Welsh mountains, competing against the newest SAS Selection hopefuls, he had been passed fit for service.

'Medical over. You can get dressed now.' Durrani walked to the sink, removed his gloves, and unnecessarily washed his hands. He straightened his blood-red bow tie. 'How's Jack these days?'

The question took Snow by surprise. 'I'm sorry, Jack who?'

'Good, good, just checking – "loose lips sink ships" as they used to say.'

'They also make for very bad saxophonists,' Snow replied as he quickly dressed.

'What? Oh, very good. Mind if I use that one?'

'Not at all.'

'Thank you.' Durrani smiled and opened the door. 'Well, all being "well", I'll see you this time next year. Goodbye.'

Snow knew better than to shake the doctor's hand. For a plastic surgeon, Durrani had a strange phobia of 'personal contact'.

Snow exited Durrani's examination room and couldn't help but glance at the pretty receptionist, dressed in her pure white uniform; he could make out the line of a black bra beneath. She smiled at him as he self-consciously looked away and left the building.

Harley Street was busy with lunchtime traffic, businesspeople and a few lost tourists being given directions by a pair of

Metropolitan Police officers. Snow headed north towards Regent's Park and the nearest tube station; he had a meeting with Patchem at their Vauxhall Cross headquarters. Snow cared little for London, although living there was a necessity. It was too noisy and too scruffy, especially compared to some other capital cities. But not Paris. Snow remembered his friend, Arnaud, half-French and always defending the homeland of his mother.

Arnaud had argued that Paris was the 'capital of Europe' with its grand architecture. Snow had retorted that the 'grand architecture' didn't make up for the pavements littered with dog shit and the stench of cheap cigarettes. He still blamed himself for what had happened. The events of eighteen months before, in Ukraine, had hit him harder than he had thought possible. Snow's mental scars, too, had been 'cosmetically repaired'. Involuntarily he touched his shoulder and felt for the bullet wound, now almost invisible but still aching. Snow had tried to save the life of a friend and failed.

A noise from behind broke his train of thought. A scream. Snow turned. A figure was standing outside Durrani's building, Middle Eastern or Asian. A voice inside his head tried to tell him something. Snow retraced his steps back towards the doctor's surgery, his eyes on the entrance. Another scream. Snow broke into a jog. Two men left the building in a hurry; one had his face obscured by bandages. They joined the first, who had now moved from the building and was holding open the door to a waiting Ford Mondeo. There was an object in the hand of the last man to exit the surgery: a handgun.

The gunman looked directly at Snow, who was still running towards him, and pulled the trigger. There was a 'thud' as a suppressed 9mm round left the weapon and raced towards the SIS operative. Snow instinctively dived left, down the basement steps of the nearest building, crashing into several bins.

A car door slammed. Winded, Snow raised his head. The Mondeo was now 'four up' and pulling away south into traffic.

Snow sprinted to the surgery, straining his eyes to see the registration number of the Ford. He had a decision to make: follow the X-rays or check the building.

Snow took the steps up, two at a time. The door to the communal hall was open, as was that to the surgery. He'd hoped beyond hope that he wouldn't find what he did. The receptionist lay sprawled back on her chair, her dress ripped open to expose her breasts. There was a neat bullet hole in her forehead and an explosion of blood on the cream wall behind. Snow swore, fury rising within. He kicked open the doctor's door and found that Durrani had also been executed. Lying at an acute angle across his desk, he had been double-tapped in the chest then shot once through the skull for good measure.

In a flash, Snow was back out on the street, mobile phone to his ear as he waited for the emergency services to connect him. There was a loud honking from further up the street. The Mondeo was still there, caught up at the traffic lights at New Cavendish Street. Snow had to reach it. He ran faster than before, switching his phone to video-capture mode. Snow heard raised voices from behind and turned. The two Metropolitan Police officers. One saw the open door and went up to investigate, the other followed Snow.

'Excuse me, sir... sir, excuse me,' the officer shouted.

Snow continued to intercept the car, while the policeman quickened his pace, one hand on his helmet in what looked like a scene from the 'Keystone Cops'. Snow drew level with the Mondeo and looked in. Four men, Middle Eastern. The one with the bandages was now removing them; another held a handgun. As Snow aimed his cameraphone at them, a hand grabbed Snow's shoulder. Snow pivoted and flung his unknown attacker to the ground, his phone dangling by its carry cord. The police officer hit the pavement with force, his helmet spinning off into the traffic.

'Security Services,' was all Snow managed to get out, before a

4

round zipped past his face. He fell to the pavement, the lights changed, and the Mondeo moved off. Snow tried to get to his feet but was forcefully pushed flat by the second officer, who had now caught up.

'Secret Intelligent Service. You're stopping the wrong person.' The second officer attempted to place his knee on Snow's chest. 'Stay still!'

'For the love of God...' Snow twisted and, using his right leg, swept the officer's legs out from under him. He sprang to his feet. The first officer, now standing, had extended his folding truncheon and was holding it in his right hand.

'Get down... down!'

'Get out of the bloody way!' Snow lurched forward and ducked inside the officer's advancing arm. He kicked the man in the back of the knee before ripping the truncheon from his hand and hurling it into the street.

Snow sprinted to the end of the road and at the junction reacquired the Mondeo, fifty metres ahead on Wigmore Street, stopped this time by a taxi. He heard sirens now, from Harley Street behind him, an armed response unit arriving on the scene given the sensitive Central London location. As Snow watched, the target vehicle raced off, mounting the pavement and breaking the speed limit. Snow turned and was met with a cloud of CS gas...

'You... sodding... idiots!'

Hands again tried to clamp him. Eyes streaming, Snow fought back, kicking out at the blurred shapes. One officer went down swearing, the other landed a punch. Snow lost control completely and shoulder-barged the second officer before delivering an uppercut to his unprotected jaw. Both officers were down, hurt.

'Listen to me!' Snow yelled. 'There's a kill team out there getting away. We need to call it in!'

'Armed police! Drop your weapon and lie on the floor, face-down.'

Snow shut his still-streaming eyes in disbelief. He slowly placed his phone on the pavement and lay down beside it. A black tactical boot kicked the phone into the gutter.

'That's HM Government property. You'll get a bill!'

'Be quiet now, please, sir.'

Gloved hands grabbed Snow's and pulled them behind his back. His hands secured, Snow was searched before being hoisted to his feet. The tight plasticuffs bit into his wrists. The two 'beat bobbies' were looking none too happy.

'My name is Aidan Snow, I'm an SIS operative. Call Vauxhall Cross – they'll confirm who I am.'

'I'm sure we'll do that at the station,' the CO19 member mocked.

'Come along, please, sir,' a second added.

'An SIS officer is down and the shooter is getting away. Call it in!'

'Move!' The friendly tone evaporated.

Arriving at the secure police station, Snow was led to the front desk for processing. The duty desk officer looked up, unimpressed. The CO19 officer placed a clear plastic bag on the desk. It contained the contents of Snow's pockets, wallet and phone.

'Name?'

'I'm an operative for SIS. Call them.'

'Your name?'

Snow took a deep breath; they were only doing their jobs, all of them, if badly. 'Aidan Snow.'

'Right then, Mr Snow, if you'll just press your fingers there for me, we'll scan your prints.'

There was little point in resisting. Snow put his fingers on the scanner. He wasn't a fan of anyone having his personal information, let alone his fingerprints.

The desk officer looked at the screen and frowned. 'OK, we're going to put you in a holding cell until we can confirm your identity.'

Snow shrugged. He had no idea what had been on the scanner screen or even which database had flagged up, but he knew either way he'd be in for a wait.

'Any chance of a cup of tea?'

'Sure. How do you take it, shaken not stirred?'

Chapter 1

Shoreham-by-Sea, UK

A victim of the credit crunch they would call him, an unavoidable casualty of an unseen enemy: the recession. Paddy Fox swallowed his pint bitterly. He was no one's victim. He looked at the jobs page for the third time before screwing it up in a ball. The anger he felt towards them hadn't lessened in the six weeks since it had happened, the rage he had for his former boss. He had nothing to prove. He was James 'Paddy' Fox, a twenty-year veteran of the SAS and worth something. If no one saw that, then sod 'em.

Fox's mobile rang and he grabbed for it. 'Yes?' His guttural Scottish hue hadn't been lessened by years of living in Hereford and then Sussex. There was a pause, which instantly told him it was a company trying to sell him something, before a voice reading from a script spoke.

'Can I speak to Mr James Fox?'

'You could.' He cut the connection.

Take, take, take! The world seemed to want something from him, but not him. He flattened out the paper and circled another job, the 'Dymex' logo blurring in front of his eyes. Tracey still worked for them, but why he had kept a corporate ballpoint pen he didn't know. Was it his sackcloth?

Fox downed his pint of bitter and wiped his lips on the back of his hand. Just the two for now; more later when he already knew he'd storm out of the house after arguing with Tracey. It had become an almost daily occurrence since he'd become, as he saw it, 'redundant'. He looked across the Crown and Anchor's dingy, deserted bar. Burt, the jowl-heavy landlord, was the only other person in the room, with the exception of 'old Dave', who sat in the corner like a fixture, with his paper and pint of Guinness. Fox shook his head; what a miserable pisshole of a pub. It was the only bar in Shoreham that had yet to be 'neoned', as he called it, to have a bit of paint slapped on, fancy lights added, and the price of the drinks doubled. As such, it was the only place where the average age of the punters was over twelve – in his mind anyway. He stood, placed his empty on the bar, and nodded at Burt as he left the pub. Outside it was rush hour, cars cutting through the narrow streets of the old town in an attempt to miss the traffic. In a way, the SAS veteran was glad he wasn't part of the corporate world any more – the 'rat-run rat race'. Nevertheless, he was still angry at how he had left it.

Summoned to a glass-walled meeting room, Fox had looked across with disgust at the younger man in his designer suit and signature dark-blue shirt. The man spoke as Fox's stare remained locked onto his eyes.

'I'm sorry, Paddy, I really am, but as you were made aware at the start of the consultation process, cuts have to be made. We've been as fair as we can.'

There was a pause as Leo Sawyer waited for Fox's reply. Unable to bear the awkward silence, Fox's line manager, Janet Cope, coughed to clear her throat.

'James, we really are sorry to let you go but it's been decided we need two sales engineers, not three.'

Fox stared at each of 'the suits' in turn. 'What about the position in Saudi?' Fox's voice was loud in the small, glass-walled room.

Cope flinched and Sawyer nervously straightened his tie

'You weren't suitable for the role. Sorry,' Sawyer replied, in what he seemed to think was a sympathetic manner. He felt Fox's green eyes bore into him.

'But I speak Arabic! Can any of the other candidates?' Fox had started to turn a shade redder than normal.

Cope gasped. 'Now, James, I understand that you're upset, but we don't need to shout.'

Fox cast her a contemptuous look. 'Only my mother calls me James.'

Cope herself turned a shade of pink and looked down.

Sawyer pushed a sheet of paper across the table to Fox. 'If you have a look at this you'll see we're paying you in full for your unused holiday time, three months' redundancy pay – as per your contract – and an additional bonus for all your hard work over the last five years.'

'Six years. I've been here since 2002.' Fox picked up the sheet and scanned the thirty-eight lines.

'Of course, six years. My mistake.'

'Your redundancy is effective immediately, as of the end of today. That means you can start looking for work from tomorrow. We wouldn't want to stop you from finding another job. We really are truly sorry.' Cope smiled that 'monkey smile' Fox had hated ever since the day she'd become his boss six months earlier.

Fox folded the letter, placed it in his shirt pocket, and stood. He stared again at both suits. Sawyer was about to speak but Fox held up his hand.

'Thank you for your sincerity.'

Heads turned as Fox crossed the open-plan office to his desk; some tried not to make eye contact, others tried to look sympathetic. Either way, to him they were just pathetic. His two sales colleagues, those that weren't being pushed out, were, unsurprisingly, nowhere to be seen. He reached his desk and started to empty its drawers into his pilot case. Fox had always disliked

11

Sawyer. Ever since the last Christmas do, when Tracey had let slip he'd been in 'Desert Storm', the man had constantly quizzed him about his past. Sawyer – a member, he claimed, of the 'territorials' – had then tried to take the whole of sales and marketing on a team-building paintballing weekend. As marketing director, Tracey had gone and according to her Leo was 'such a laugh'. At the next work event, Fox had caught him staring at her and given him the nickname 'Eagle-eyed Action Man'. In fact, the only real action Fox could envisage Sawyer getting was from behind at the local gay bar.

Looking up, Fox saw the security guard leave the MD's office with a clipboard in his hand. He bore the man no ill will.

'Hi, Mick. Are you going to march me off the premises? '

'Sorry.' He put the clipboard on Fox's desk. 'I'm going to need the car keys and your signature here.'

Shaking his head, Fox took the keys to his BMW three series and dropped them into Mick's outstretched palm. 'Of course you are, and I'm going to walk three miles to the train station.'

'Thanks.' Mick cast a glance around before saying, almost in a whisper, 'I don't suppose Mr Sawyer has offered to drive you in his Z4?'

'I'm not queer.'

Mick suppressed a smile. 'It's my break in ten minutes – I'll take you to the station.'

'That would be good pal, thanks.'

It was the way of the world. Mick had more decency than all of them. He patted Fox on the shoulder and left him to finish his bags. Fox continued to shove his personal papers into the pockets of his case. Sawyer and Cope remained cocooned in the meeting room, eyes glued to documents, pretending to look busy and hoping he would leave. Fox closed the case and walked towards the stairs. As he passed the meeting room he tapped on the window, causing both occupants to snap their necks to the right. Fox smiled and held up his middle finger.

Fox tried to forget that awful day as he crossed the road towards the river and used the pedestrian bridge to make his way home. The tide was out as usual and the river had turned into a thick, muddy smudge. Bloody awful if you asked him, but then Tracey hadn't when she'd bought the house that overlooked it. As he reached the opposite side he could hear them already, the local kids from the flats out again on their 'mini motos', zipping between cars. Jim would be outraged. Jim was always outraged.

'Get off the bloody road! I'll call the police!' Jim Reynolds, retired decorator and moral voice of the street, yelled after the miniature motorbikes.

Fox laughed. 'Good evening, Jim.' He liked his neighbour, even if he made fun of him.

'Is it? I've had them effing kids tormenting me for the last hour! Shouldn't they be at school?' He waved his hedge scissors.

'Jim, it's almost six.'

'Oh, well, at work then, or doing their homework. At their age, I was painting houses.'

'So are they, with spray cans.'

The area had been touted as the latest urban development for professional people with two point four children and a BMW. The truth, however, was that the kids from the local council flats saw the quiet, pothole-free roads of Shoreham beach as their private racetrack.

The old man removed his gardening gloves and scratched his head. 'Any more news on the job front?'

Fox shrugged. 'Who wants to employ an old soldier like me?'

'That's the problem – no gratitude. They should have given you a medal.'

Reynolds knew that, as a member of the SAS, Fox had been sent into Iraq. Fox hadn't been a member of Bravo Two Zero, as all those who knew the truth of his past seemed to think, but a deep-penetration mission which had never been publicised. It had been their job to recce the approach to Baghdad in advance of the coalition's arrival, an arrival which hadn't come, at least not for ten years. This mission, he never talked about. Reynolds, himself a veteran of Suez, had great respect for Fox.

'Maybe when we're both dead they'll put plaques on our houses?' Fox smiled.

There was the sound of bass-heavy music from behind them and Tracey Fox, his wife of five years, raced up the road in her convertible Saab.

'Here she comes, Ghetto Gertrude!'

Reynolds chuckled as Tracey pulled up onto the drive. 'Hello, love.'

'Hi, Jim.' She smiled warmly then changed her face when she spoke to Fox. 'The sooner you move that old heap of yours out of the garage the better. I don't know why you keep it!'

'It's a classic, love.' It was the conversation they had each evening when she was forced to park her new car on the drive.

'Help me with my bags then.'

'Yes, ma'am.' Fox winked at Reynolds and made for the car.

Reynolds picked up his hedge scissors and continued to trim his already perfect shrubs.

Fox followed his wife inside with her laptop bag, which she complained was too heavy to carry. He found her looking through the mail.

'So, tell me, what have you been up to today while I've been out at work?' It was a daily question, thrown at him with growing disdain.

Fox placed the bag on the floor and took a breath. 'I went online, put my CV on Monster, checked my email, and fixed the tap in the kitchen.'

Tracey nodded. 'And?'

'And what?'

'Did you call any of those agents I gave you details of?' Her hands were now on her hips.

14

He looked at the gap between her blouse buttons and the red of her bra. She had a great pair of tits. 'No. I'll do it tomorrow.'

Her expression grew sour. 'You've been saying that for the past week, Paddy!'

'I know, love, I know.' Here came the lecture.

'You're not going to get a new job sitting on your arse all day long.'

'Then how can I use the computer?'

She ignored his attempt at levity. 'It's been almost two months now.'

'It's been six weeks.'

'Exactly. When the redundancy money runs out, what then?' Her eyes narrowed.

Fox sighed. They had met at Dymex, where she at least still worked. 'I've got enough saved and, besides, you earn twice as much as I did.'

'What? You want to live off me; you, a man, want to live off me?' The argument wasn't new and their lines were well rehearsed.

'Don't be sexist.' He loved to goad his oh so PC wife. 'I'm not going to "ponce" off you. I'll find something.'

She turned and headed upstairs. 'I'm going to have a shower.'

Fox watched her arse twitch beneath her tight skirt; even when she was angry he still fancied her. He spoke beneath his breath. 'Hi, dear, how are you? Have a nice day? Don't worry...' He smirked to himself. Right, he'd bung a risotto into the microwave and uncork a bottle of the Chilean Merlot she liked, that'd calm her down for a bit.

Paddington Green Secure Police Station, London

Snow signed for his belongings at the front desk. 'Should I be honoured you came in person?'

'Yes,' Patchem said flatly.

The desk officer gave Snow a stern look. 'You're free to go.'

'Much obliged.'

'In future, for heaven's sake, if someone says they're an SIS officer, call us to ask.'

'Very well, sir.' The desk officer showed no sign of accepting Patchem's reprimand. 'Don't let me keep you.'

Outside they got into Patchem's Lexus and drove away.

'Thanks, Jack. So why did you come?'

The Secret Intelligence Service section head looked over his shoulder as they pulled into traffic. 'I didn't want to waste any more time. Something is happening, Aidan. GCHQ has picked up increased chatter referring to some sort of attack and soon. MI5 have been going through possible targets but as yet with no success. According to my counterpart at Five, it's like looking for a grain of salt in the desert.'

'So why is Six interested?'

'We're interested because most of the chatter is emanating from Saudi Arabia. This impacts us because, in addition to my role at the "Russian Desk", I've just been assigned caretaker of the "Arab Desk" until the boss appoints a permanent replacement.'

'Congratulations.'

'I don't need your congratulations, I need your help.' Patchem paused as they exited a roundabout. 'Look, I'm a Russian specialist; our Director General knows this but she insisted. Aidan, to be candid, I know bugger all about the Middle East, that's why I need operatives I can rely on. I brought you into Six because I was impressed by what you did in Kyiv and how you did it.'

'Thanks, Jack, but I'm no Middle East expert either.'

'The "Arab Desk" is in a mess and I don't know who I can trust there.' Patchem had yet to fully assess the desk staff. 'I need my own team.'

They arrived at Snow's flat. 'So what's my assignment?'

'There isn't one, yet.'

Patchem brought the Lexus to a halt. There was a silence. He stared into the distance.

'Are you OK?'

'Durrani was a friend.'

'I'm sorry.'

'What? Oh, I see. Yes. It's been a trying day.'

'Thanks for the lift.'

'Thanks for listening.'

'Do you want a drink?'

'Want, yes. Allowed, no. Jacquelyn is expecting me home.'

Riyadh. Saudi Arabia

There was a strange noise in the air and a familiar smell in his nostrils he couldn't quite place. Burning oil! The Saudi whipped off his thin bedsheet and rushed to the window.

Flames were leaping from his garage; worse still, they were moving towards his Rolls Royce Phantom! Struck dumb, he was unable to call out to his security guard as the flickering flames reflected hypnotically off his bedroom window. He opened completely the French windows and nervously moved onto the balcony, the heat like an oven on his face.

Finding his voice, Al Kabir yelled for his guard. Two shadows darted beyond the perimeter wall towards a pick-up truck. Without lights, the truck moved away into the darkness of the desert. There was a rushing sound and suddenly an explosion from the garage, quickly followed by another. A wall of flames raced towards Al Kabir's newest car. His hands gripped the railings on his balcony but before he could move or utter another word the Rolls Royce was engulfed.

Fouad Al Kabir awoke from his mid-morning snooze with a start. It hadn't been a dream. The fire had caused over a million dollars' worth of damage. In addition to the Phantom, two much more expensive vintage Rolls Royces had been destroyed. The oldest had wooden wheels and had belonged to his grandfather. He stood. They were irreplaceable; this was why Prince Fouad Al

Kabir was so angered and saddened. He had already ordered a new Phantom, but the others! Fouad kicked the remaining wall to the garage in despair. This was terrible on a personal level but an outrage on a national level. He, Prince Fouad Al Kabir of the House of Saud, had been attacked! It was unprecedented. He wasn't fearful – the concept had never entered his head – but he was upset.

Twenty more members of the Saudi Arabian Royal Guard Regiment, the unit with the task of protecting the Royal House of Saud, now patrolled his 'palace'. His brother had said he'd been foolish to stay at his small place in the desert, but security wasn't a concept Fouad could fully understand. He was royalty, so why should he be in any danger? Unlike his brothers – especially Umar – Fouad didn't like to leave the Kingdom. He was happy to stay within its borders and play at being a businessman and scholar…

There was a buzzing from under his robes. Puzzled, he retrieved his Vertu and answered. 'Yes?'

'Your Highness, peace be upon you. I hope you are well?' the voice asked in classical Arabic.

'And you. Who is this?' Fouad noted the number was withheld.

'I am a humble servant of God.' The voice had a lyricism.

'As I am. And?' Every Muslim was a servant of God; the caller was stating the obvious.

'He instructed me to burn your English cars.'

'What?' Fouad couldn't have heard correctly. 'You burnt my cars?'

'That is correct, Your Highness.'

Fouad was incensed. 'Then you will be punished.'

'If it is "His" will.' The caller paused; he could hear the prince breathing heavily on the other end. 'Burning your precious cars was a way to get your attention. Now, do I have it?'

Fouad held onto a palm tree to steady himself. He couldn't

18

understand what was happening. 'What do you want?'

'You sit on the board of directors of Saudico, the world's largest supplier of oil.' The caller paused again.

Fouad didn't know how to react; here was a stranger, speaking to him in a very impertinent manner. 'Yes, I do.'

'You must order the company to immediately cease supplying oil to the infidels.'

Fouad paused then started to laugh heartily. 'If you were not going to die for destroying royal property, I would find you a very funny man.'

The caller grew angry. 'Do not mock me, you fool.'

'What!' Fouad ended the call. He had never been so insulted in all his life.

Fouad walked towards the terrace and snapped his fingers as a signal that he wanted a cold drink. Could he have the call traced? He would ask the police chief. Just as he was about to sit, the phone vibrated again.

'Yes?'

'That was unwise, to end the call in such a way.'

Fouad's thumb hovered over the cancel button. 'Any leniency I may have shown towards you has just been withdrawn. You will be executed for both your actions and your remarks.' That would surely make this unknown person repent.

The caller was again calm. 'Stop supplying oil to the West or your daughter will be the one to be executed.'

Fouad dropped his glass. It smashed on the tiled floor. Immediately a servant hurried to clean it up, but the prince pushed him away. 'What did you say?'

'Princess Jinan...'

'Don't you dare mention her name...' He was redder than he had ever been before.

'Princess Jinan is no longer at her school. We have her.'

Fouad felt dizzy. He spluttered with rage and waved his arms to attract the attention of his guards. 'You lie.'

The line went dead; the caller had disconnected at his end. The prince's brain tried to process the information. He had several people to call but didn't know who to contact first. The commander of the guards arrived and bowed.

'Call your men who protect my daughter! Immediately!'

The man bowed again and vanished into the house. Fouad dialled his brother's number from memory and held the phone to his ear. As he did so the military officer reappeared holding a different handset.

'Your Highness.'

Fouad snatched the Nokia and looked at the screen. What he saw made his heart stop. It was a picture of his daughter with a gun to her head. The prince could feel his heart racing; he clutched his right hand to his podgy chest... he couldn't breathe. He slumped into a chair. His Vertu had now connected with his brother in England, who was calling his name. Panic set in as the prince's entourage rushed to revive him.

'Your Royal Highness.' The voice of the commander of the guards was clear and precise as he spoke to Fouad's brother, on the other end of the line in London. 'Prince Fouad is unwell.'

'How?' Prince Umar was concerned for his favourite younger brother.

'He has fainted, Your Highness, from learning of some bad news.'

'Which is?'

Major Hammar didn't quite know what to say. 'Someone has kidnapped the princess.'

'Kidnapped? But she is in Brighton, at Roedean.' The prince in the Saudi Embassy was suddenly anxious.

Shoreham-by-Sea, UK

Fox checked his watch. The job interview in Central London had been a complete waste of time, in and out in less than an hour. The interviewer – some hair-gelled kid in his twenties – had attempted to grill Fox about his suitability for the job. A job he was overqualified for. The boy had seemed offended when Fox had refused point-blank to elaborate on his military career. His CV mentioned only his parent unit, the Gordon Highlanders, and not 'the Regiment'.

On Fox's way out he'd seen the other applicants, ten years younger and twenty pounds fatter. He had no chance and didn't give a... He turned into his street and saw a familiar car. The dark-red BMW Z4 of his former boss, Leo Sawyer, parked four houses away on the bend – complete with a number plate that did indeed confirm he was a wanker: LE07 SAW. Fox frowned. Why would the jumped-up salesman be here? A dark thought struck him, and an anger of the type he hadn't felt for years, deep inside. Fox stopped and retrieved his mobile. Dialling Tracey's number, he continued up the street then saw her car in the drive. A mini moto buzzed past him from behind, making him flinch. Silly old git, getting jumpy.

'Where are you?' she answered.

'Just getting on the train at Victoria,' he lied, eyeing her car in the drive. 'And you?'

'Still in the office. Should be home when you are, though. I'm just seeing to something.'

Fox almost threw the phone but managed to control himself. He snapped it shut. 'Eagle-eyed Action Man' was shagging his wife. He walked down the path, dropping his jacket and briefcase on o the grass, then tried to open the door. It was closed from the inside – the key still in the lock. He could feel the anger rising as he pressed the bell. There was no answer. He started to bang, then pound with his fists. 'Open the door!'

There was movement inside, a twitch from a curtain. Fox took a step back and was about to shout again when another mini moto shot past. He turned in the direction of the noise just as two saloon cars swept into the road. Both were going too fast for the bend.

As Fox watched, it felt as though he were seeing everything in slow motion. The first car swerved to avoid the youth on the mini moto. The bike bounced up onto the kerb and carried on, but the car hit the opposite kerb and the wall to the garage compound.

There was a heavy crunch and shrieking of metal as the Ford Mondeo hit the wall. The second car, some fifteen metres behind, slammed on its brakes and stopped sideways on. At the same time, there were noises and movement from his house. Fox ran across the road to the Ford; joyriders or not, they needed help. The driver's side had hit first and what was left of the screen was covered in blood. Fox's eyes scanned the vehicle; the driver was dead, he was sure of that, but the passenger was moving. He was reaching down to pull at the door when he saw a weapon in the footwell. There was a whimpering from the back.

Fox peered in. Lying half on the seat was a girl, an Arab-looking girl, with duct-tape over her mouth and arms fastened behind her back. A man was lying under her; he tried to push her off. Fox saw the second weapon, this one a semi-automatic. The girl locked eyes with him and Fox recognised the pleading look of fear.

Without hesitating, Fox grabbed the handgun from the front of the car, took a step back, and shot the passenger though the ear. The sound was like thunder in the enclosed space. Momentarily deafened, he pulled the rear door and the girl half-fell out. The second male passenger opened his eyes and reached for his weapon. Fox dragged the girl clear and put a double tap directly into his temple. His head exploded.

Shots from behind. Fox threw himself over the girl and pulled the door in front of him. It was the only protection they had. More rounds and now shouts. Fox sprang to his feet, weapon held in both hands, instantly acquiring a target. A passenger from the second car was running at full sprint towards him, with what looked like an assault rifle in his hands. Fox fired the first round, hitting the assaulter in the chest, and then a second, aimed at the head. The man span sideways and crashed to the ground.

Movement from his right. Another X-ray, this one using the houses for cover, was heading his way. Both men fired. Fox ducked again and looked at the girl. She was shaking beneath him. He took a breath and sprang back up. He let off a single shot at the target. The man was moving now, back towards the car as the driver shouted at him wildly. Another target came into view, blocking Fox's line of fire to the retreating car; this figure was wearing a dark-blue shirt and was racing directly towards the Z4. Taking a millisecond to decide, Fox fired a round into the man's back.

The second car spun its wheels in a 'J-turn' and screeched away. Fox, out of rounds, had no time to grab another weapon as he tried to catch the number plate. All around he saw curtains twitching. Two teenagers wearing hoodies were standing stunned, next to their mini motos, holding up mobile phones, videoing the whole event. On seeing Fox staring at them, they both legged it, carrying their toy bikes.

Fox bent down and pulled the girl to her feet; he spoke to her in Arabic. 'You're safe now. I'm going to take the tape off.'

The girl let out a moan of pain as the tape was removed, then started to sob as he undid her bonds. She was about seventeen and beautiful. She held her hands to her face.

'Come with me.' Fox reached out gently and took her by the arm. He walked her up his neighbour's path. Reynolds opened the door, a shocked expression on his face. Fox pushed the girl at him.

'Jim, look after her.'

Without waiting for a reply Fox moved back to the street and, bending down, checked the nearest X-ray for a pulse. There was none. He kicked the assault weapon away to the side of the road and then moved towards the man with the dark-blue shirt, his former boss, Leo Sawyer. The sales director lay on his back, eyes open, breathing laboured. Fox's single round had ripped through him, puncturing a lung. Fox aimed the empty weapon at Sawyer's head and let him hear the 'dead man's click'.

Fox felt no remorse; the man had tried to screw him and had screwed his wife. It had been a split-second but conscious decision, his anger and the urge for revenge manifesting itself in the single bullet. He didn't care if Sawyer lived or died.

Fox didn't need to check on the two X-rays in the car – he had drilled them at point-blank range; half their skulls were missing. He knew they were dead. Fox took out his mobile and dialled 999. The operator confirmed his mobile number and asked him which service he required, then transferred him. Before he could speak he heard sirens nearing. Fox sat on the kerb and waited to be arrested. He had once again demonstrated to the world that he was only good at one thing – killing.

Chapter 2

Presidential Dacha, Minsk Region, Belarus

Dark hair patted down, burgundy tie, crisp white shirt and dark-blue suit. Sverov admired himself in the mirror. It was important he make the right impression; he was, after all, going to be the first ever head of the Belarusian Intelligence Service – the KGB – to be interviewed by the BBC.

When the BBC had contacted him via the embassy, his initial reaction had been to refuse the journalist an entry visa into the country. However, after a moment's thought, he'd decided that the potential positive publicity would greatly help the image of Belarus. So he'd replied yes and got his hands on the most recent reports filed by the same journalist to check his credibility.

It was going to be a full half-hour interview for the BBC World programme *HARDtalk Extra*. Sverov had read with much interest the list of former interviewees, some of whom he greatly admired, while others he would have shot on sight if they ever entered his country. He had advised the President of the benefits this interview would bring and then made him believe it had been his own idea all along. Megalomaniacs like the President, although he never would have admitted to anyone that he thought his leader was one, were easy to manipulate.

Sverov exited the bathroom in the presidential *dacha* and took his seat in the study. The BBC make-up girl had already applied his, something he found effeminate, but a necessary evil. The sound recordist clipped a microphone to his lapel, a 'backup', he had said, to the furry grey sound boom suspended out of shot above his head. The BBC journalist, Simon White, lived up to his name. He was possibly the pastiest individual Sverov had ever met. His thin frame actually looked bigger onscreen but his eyes had a dark intensity.

Sverov had demanded a list of questions a month in advance and made it clear he wouldn't answer any new ones unless they'd been faxed and agreed. Sverov spoke, in his own opinion, 'good English', but had said that, for the actual interview, he would feel more 'comfortable' speaking in Belarusian. The producer, however, had asked if the interview could be in English, as this was the style of the *HARDtalk* series. Sverov accepted his reasoning that, to 'woo the West', one must speak their language. For the past month he had been practising with the KGB language instructors. His English was more than 'good' – he was in fact fluent – but he wouldn't have passed for a native speaker. He still had an accent and sometimes paused to find the most appropriate words.

As the crew readied themselves, Sverov noted White's professionalism, a trait lacking in all Belarusian journalists. This was with the exception of those, of course, who worked for the state-owned *Golas Radzimy* (Voice of the Motherland) and *Narodnaja Volya* (The People's Will). The BBC crew were ready, he was told, to start taping the interview. Sverov nodded and composed himself. He knew in which order the questions were to be asked and had already rehearsed his replies, but he was still sweating and not because of the harsh TV lights. The director gave the cue and White started with his piece to camera.

'Speaking in 2005, the then United States Secretary of State, Condoleezza Rice, identified six "outposts of tyranny" around the world. These were Cuba, Iran, Burma, North Korea,

Zimbabwe, and Belarus. My guest today is someone who was not at all happy with this statement. Ivan Sverov, Director of the Belarusian State Security Service, the KGB. Director Sverov, thank you for agreeing to speak to *HARDtalk*.'

Sverov nodded. He wasn't happy with the introduction, either, but had his prepared response to it – the Americans would turn red.

'Thank you for the opportunity to let me correct the lies perpetuated about my country by the former Bush administration.'

The reply was what White expected. 'If I may start with what has been said about your President. He has been accused, allegedly, of crushing dissent, persecuting the independent media, political opposition, and rigging elections.'

Sverov frowned. 'By whom? Certainly not credible governments. President Lukachev has led Belarus for more than fifteen years. He has given us more than fifteen years of stability. Can any of our former Soviet neighbours boast that? Indeed, President Lukachev came to power on his promise to "stop the Mafia", to root out corruption in the former government. To make accusations of illegal activity against the President is a nonsense!'

Although impressed by the formality of his interviewee's English, White cut in. 'What about Secretary of State Rice's comment labelling Belarus an outpost of tyranny?'

'Secretary Rice's assessment was very far from reality. We invited her to see our country for herself. These completely false stereotypes and prejudices were a poor basis for the formation of effective policy in the sphere of foreign relations. On behalf of my government I would like to invite her successor, Mrs Clinton, to visit. Now let us look at the word "tyrant". What is a tyrant? A tyrant is an individual holding power through a state, a ruler who places the interests of a small group over the interests of others. In this context, President Lukachev has placed the interests of the Belarusian people above the interests of the rest of the world. Let us look at the original meaning of tyrant. In ancient Greece, tyrants were those who had gained power by getting the support of the poor by giving them land and freeing them from servitude or slavery. The word "tyrant" simply referred to those who overturned the established government through the use of popular support. President Lukachev has the popular support. Secretary Rice did not choose her words with care. Perhaps she did not fully understand them?' Sverov folded his arms. He was very pleased with that reply, especially the wordplay.

White was not perturbed. 'If I may? The 2007 referendum, which the President won, allowing him to run for a third term, was criticised for being rigged.'

Sverov shook his head in disbelief. 'Observers were present and they say to the contrary.'

Sverov continued to set out the policies of the Belarusian government and their hopes for wider cooperation with Europe.

White nodded. He was no fool. He had seen the information on the subsequent demonstrations in Minsk, which had been violently dispersed by heavy-handed riot police. 'Why did the Committee to Protect Journalists describe Belarus as one of the ten worst places to be a journalist?

'Again, this is based on lies. Let us look at the facts. Since 1994 the President has doubled the minimum wage and combated inflation by reintroducing state control of prices. Is this a bad place to be?'

'Freedom of the press, is that not important?'

'All freedom is important. My purpose is to preserve freedom. The state security services exist to preserve freedom.'

White didn't give up. 'So why is there no independent press or media in Belarus?'

Sverov tried not to show his anger; the journalist was attempting to lead the interview away from the agreed parameters. Perhaps he had been too hasty to judge White as different from the activists who attempted to attack his government and their achievements? He calmed himself and answered the question.

'We welcome the media in Belarus; you are evidence of this. Our book-publishing industry is another example of this; it is thriving and we export many Russian-language books to other CIS states.'

White looked at his notes for a moment; the answer had been as expected – evasive. No mention had been made of the many independent newspapers forced to close due to 'bureaucratic irregularities', including failure to keep to regular publication dates. He tried a different tack. 'Is it not true that the problem in Belarus…'

'Problem!' Sverov had started to lose his composure.

'If I may continue? The "problem" is not official censorship, which is explicitly forbidden by your national constitution, but the volume of legislation used to curtail freedom of expression and silence internal dissent?'

Sverov fixed the journalist in the eye, a move the camera did not miss. 'Such as?'

'"Discrediting Belarus abroad" and "insulting the President". These are criminal offences punishable by up to two and five years in jail, respectively.'

'Yes, they are.' The KGB Director nodded. 'These laws protect the reputation and good standing of our country.'

White tried to come in. 'But…'

Sverov held up his hand. 'If I may finish? Let me cite one of your own UK laws, "Incitement to racial hatred". This law makes it illegal to "deliberately provoke hatred of a racial group by distributing racist material to the public or making inflammatory public speeches, creating racist websites, inciting inflammatory rumours about an individual or an ethnic group, for the purpose of spreading racial discontent".'

There was a pause. Sverov was happy he had remembered the lines word for word. 'This is exactly what our laws protect against. Inciting racial hatred, against Belarus and its President.'

'But these laws are being interpreted in a very sweeping

manner. Take, for instance, the case of Mikolai Markevich, the editor of the *Den* newspaper. He was sentenced to eighteen months forced labour in 2002 for allegedly insulting President Lukachev…'

Sverov leaned forward in his seat. 'Our laws dictate that, for national security reasons, I cannot comment on individual cases.'

'But would you like to hear what Mr Markevich himself had to say on the matter?'

'I do not think your audience would want to hear the ranting of a convicted criminal.'

Sverov was on the brink of cancelling the interview but feared the repercussions from the President. He had started well, made some good, persuasive points, and now had to ensure he continued in the same manner. White wasn't going to make him look small or weak.

White pursed his lips before continuing. 'The EU has shut its doors to you. Are you not the lonely man of Europe?'

'Since 1998 we have been an active member of the Non-Aligned Movement, which has some 116 member states. This is the majority of the world community. Belarus, as a NAM member state, is not alone. Belarus has an active economy. We export more than 55% of our gross national product and 80% of our industrial production. There are not many countries in the world with the same coefficients of the export share. By "shutting the door", the EU is losing a huge amount of trade with us. Therefore, while I would favour Belarus working more closely with EU member states, I believe we would not have much to gain by becoming a member – rather that the EU would gain more.'

'Surely you can't mean that?' White was surprised. This response had been tantamount to Belarus turning her back on the EU.

'Belarus is fortunate. We have old friends, such as Russia and Ukraine, new friends, such as the other NAM member states, and those whom we are not averse to becoming acquainted with, the EU and the US. However, we are perfectly happy at the moment and certainly not "lonely". "Our dance card is full," as you would say.'

'What about the standard of living in Belarus? Is it not lower than in the West?'

'By what measure? The number of US-imported goods?' Sverov shook his head and smiled in what he thought was a scholarly manner. 'Let us look at the findings of the "Save the Children" report, which compared 167 countries. Belarus has the highest rating for quality of life for women and children among all countries in the former Soviet Union. This is higher even than the new EU member states. Belarus is the leader, in the post-Soviet era, in the production and supply of agricultural goods per person, the GNP share for education, and the share of students of further education among the population. Belarus exceeds all CIS states in the generalised index of human development calculated by the UN. How can we have a "lower standard of living"? Is the UN incorrect?'

White nodded. The Belarusian had an answer for everything, which would make for amusing, if not politically astute, television. He wanted to move the interview on. He would ask about tourism next, then bring up the government ban on certain 'rock groups' performing in Belarus.

The interview over, the sound man removed the mic and thanked the Belarusian. Sverov stared at White, who was exchanging words with his unit director. They had far more people than he would have thought necessary recording this programme, but then they were the BBC and, he surmised, must be experts at what they did.

Riyadh, Kingdom of Saudi Arabia
Fouad Al Kabir held his diamond-encrusted Vertu mobile phone in his right hand and counted his worry beads with his left. The call had come directly from his brother, the Saudi ambassador

in London. His eldest daughter, Jinan, was safe! Al Kabir gazed out over the city from his high office window and thanked Allah for his daughter's deliverance.

'But what of those who took her?' They had to be punished.

'Two escaped, the rest are dead,' replied Umar Al Kabir.

'You are certain she is not in danger?' The younger brother wanted the elder's reassurance.

'Fouad, it was Jinan who called me herself.'

The sun reflected heavily off the window as it set in the desert sky, a mixture of reds and gold filling the room. Fouad finally let himself relax as Umar relayed what Jinan had told him about how she had been snatched from school and how a man had come from nowhere and saved her.

'This is a man of honour, brother. He must be rewarded.'

'I agree,' replied the ambassador.

'Where is my daughter now?'

'She is safe. I will personally collect her, brother; as her uncle I will not leave that to another. I will be with her in an hour.'

'Thank you.'

'Do not thank me, brother. We are family.'

Flanked by two large bodyguards on each side, Umar Al Kabir entered his diplomatic Mercedes and ordered the driver to head for Brighton as fast as he could. They would pay no heed to speed limits, enforcement cameras, or traffic police. There had been an attempted kidnapping of a member of the Saudi royal family! Sitting comfortably in his leather seat, Umar Al Kabir dialled a Whitehall number very few people had, and was immediately connected to the British Foreign Secretary.

'Robert, this is Umar. I have some strange and worrying news to tell you. Someone has tried to kidnap my niece.'

Paddington Green Secure Police Station, London
Left alone in the cell while his details were checked, Fox tried to make sense of the day's events. He had killed three men, wounded

a fourth, saved a child, and ended his marriage, all in the space of a minute. The police had arrived and cordoned off the street, forming a barrier. Arms raised above his head, Fox had approached them and given a description of the remaining X-rays and the Mondeo; however, they seemed more concerned with arresting him, the man responsible for the bodies on the ground. Now, three hours later, he sat in the secure police station being treated like a criminal.

His thoughts again wandered to Sawyer as he relived the scene in his head. Fox had seen the man's face, had recognised him, and in that moment all his anger, all his frustration, had shot down his arm to his trigger finger. It wasn't an accident; it had been a conscious decision. However, that would be difficult to prove. Sawyer had been in the way – in his line of sight during a firefight – and was an unfortunate victim of crossfire.

What about the kids' videos? The fact that Sawyer had decided to run, to leave Tracey, proved he wasn't a real man. What of his Tracey? This, he regretted – losing her. He could never be with her again, not now she had betrayed him, even if she forgave him for shooting her lover. It was his code: loyalty. Fox wasn't a man to forgive betrayal; he hadn't done in the past and he wouldn't now. Shooting Sawyer was rough justice but in his mind was just that – 'just'. Tracey would have to accept this and move on.

Fox shook his head and chuckled to himself demonically. Shit, he had felt more alive in that minute than at any other time since leaving the Regiment. Like a boxer making a successful comeback for the world title, he had felt elated. He had killed but more importantly he had saved. Saved the life of an innocent school-girl. In the Almighty's book of 'good and bad deeds', he was sure saving her cancelled out ending the life of a terrorist or even a philanderer. Sawyer, a pathetic little man who hadn't only cheated on his own wife, but taken another's?

Fox felt bad for Sawyer's wife, that was all; the man had no children. Fox wasn't religious but in situations like this, after he had killed, he would sit and reason it out. This, however, had been the first time he had shot a man who wasn't endangering his own life, an unarmed civilian. His first attempted murder? Perhaps Sawyer was dead; he had been told nothing.

The cell door opened, breaking his train of thought. A uniformed police officer, with greying temples, pointed at Fox. 'Get up and follow me.'

Fox rose and walked out of the cell; the door was shut behind him by a second officer. The three men walked down a harshly lit corridor to an interview room. The door opened and he was ushered inside. A further two officers were sitting at the metal table.

'Please take a seat, Mr Fox.' DCI Mincer was fifty-five and had a round face that tended to put those he questioned at ease. These were enviable traits in a member of the anti-terrorist squad. Fox sat and Mincer started the tape recorder.

'Interview with James Celtic Fox. Officers present, DC Flynn and DCI Mincer.'

Fox smirked at the second name; Mincer gave him a look that said, 'I've heard it all before'.

'Interviewee has declined the offer of counsel.' Mincer started the interview. 'Mr Fox. Can I call you James?'

'Only my mother calls me James. My name's Paddy.'

'Can I call you Paddy?'

'Knock yourself out.'

'Paddy, we've checked the information you gave to our desk sergeant and I have a couple of questions.'

'Fire away.'

Mincer ran his right index finger down a page of text. 'You were in the army?'

'Correct, man and boy.'

'The Gordon Highlanders? You left the service in 2004.'

'When I turned forty.'

'Right, but after looking further at the army records you left the Highlanders in '85 after serving four years. How do you account for this?'

Fox rolled his eyes. 'I'm afraid that's classified.'

'Classified?' Flynn snorted. 'What do you mean?'

Paddy shrugged. 'I've signed the Official Secrets Act. I can't discuss that with you. I could tell you but I'd have to shoot you.'

Flynn blanched. 'Is that an appropriate comment?'

Mincer placed his hand on Flynn's shoulder. 'Well, let's move things on a bit. Ray?'

Flynn nodded and took over the questioning while Mincer listened. 'You shot four men. Did you know them?'

'No.'

'What about Sawyer?'

'Yes.'

'So why did you shoot him?'

'I didn't know it was him.'

'But you shot him.' Flynn folded his arms.

The scene flashed in his mind. The cars, the girl, the X-rays, and then Leo Sawyer. 'Yes. He was running, I thought he had a weapon.'

'But he didn't.'

'No.'

'You shot an unarmed man. An innocent man.'

'I also shot three X-rays. I thought Sawyer was the fourth. I made a mistake.'

'You murdered three men and attempted to murder a fourth.'

Fox's eyes flashed. So Sawyer was alive? 'I rescued a girl. A girl who was the victim of a kidnapping. Where is she now? How is she?'

Mincer spoke. 'She was taken away by her uncle. She's safe.'

'Who was she?'

Flynn undid his top button. 'A schoolgirl studying at Roedean. Now back to you...'

'What about the other two, in the other car. Are they in custody?'

Flynn took a deep breath but Mincer, playing 'good cop', spoke. 'No.'

Fox shook his head. 'If your officers had listened to me first, rather than arresting me, there wouldn't be two terrorists running free on the south coast!'

Flynn was breathing deeply. Fox could tell this wasn't a game to him; he really was 'bad cop'. 'You shot an innocent bystander who was your former boss. Coincidence?'

Fox smiled; he would not rise to the bait. In the jungles of South America he had been interrogated by people with no rules and was now being snarled at by a man wearing an M&S machine-washable suit. He spoke slowly. 'Yes, Mr Flynn. It was a coincidence and an accident. I didn't know it was Sawyer when I pulled the trigger. It was a decision I took, but it was wrong. Unless you've been in a firefight, Mr Flynn, you have no frame of reference.'

Flynn fumed. 'This was Shoreham beach not bloody Baghdad!'

'But the guns were the same,' Fox replied.

'OK, OK.' Good cop again. 'Now, let's go through your statement from the beginning.'

Residence of the President of Belarus, Minsk, Belarus
Crushing the sheet into a ball with his fist, the special adviser to the President of Belarus bellowed, 'No… No… NO!'

Having never seen him so angry, the head of the Ministry of Energy shook as he spoke. 'Eduard Alexeievich, what will be our response?'

Eduard Kozlov put his left hand on his hip and held the crushed memo up in his right. His eyes were burning with fury, his fist trembling as he spat. 'Our response? They dare to prevent the nation of Belarus from receiving its gas? Our response will be to demand that they continue to supply us!'

36

Kushnerov hardly dared speak further but forced himself to do so. 'I understand, Eduard Alexeievich, but what of the $500 million we owe them?'

'They are thieves, Yarislav Ivanovich, thieves! Nothing more. When we were one country it was our shared gas, but now they expect us to pay $100 per 1,000 cubic meters! Our "strategic partner" wants to bankrupt us!'

Kozlov sat heavily at his desk. Kushnerov remained standing while the presidential adviser rubbed his eyes hard with his fists before gesturing that his visitor should take a seat. There was an uneasy silence. Both men had been part of the brokered agreement late the previous year that had fixed the price of gas for the next. Russia had already attempted to increase the price for several of her largest customers, including neighbouring Ukraine, stating that all such prices were based on 'outdated Soviet agreements'. The result: Russia had turned off the supply to Ukraine for several days in late December. Deliveries to Russia's largest European customers fell in turn as Ukraine allegedly 'skimmed' the gas it needed from an export pipeline transiting its territory.

Belarus, too, faced the taps being turned off. Under immense coercive pressure, and minutes before ringing in the New Year, they had hastily agreed a price: $100 per 1,000 cubic meters of gas – a massive increase from the previous price of $47. To soften the blow, however, Russia agreed that Belarus would pay just $55 per 1,000 cubic meters for the first half of the year, then make up the difference of nearly $500 million by the end of July.

It had been a delaying tactic – both sides knew this, but Russia had a further objective. Concerns were voiced in the EU parliament about the union's reliance on Russian fuel; RusGaz supplied a quarter of Europe's gas. Member states were starting to get nervous, looking into the possibility of finding alternative suppliers. In the Kremlin, worried words were exchanged. This was exactly the opposite image that RusGaz wanted to promote. In order to secure the transit of gas, thus allaying the fears of the

Brussels 'Eurocrats', Russia threw Belarus a bone: sell half of your national pipeline company, Beltransgaz, to our gas company, RusGaz; your bill will then be paid and we will guarantee no more price increases. More importantly, the Russians didn't need to add that the EU's fears would be dismissed.

The ultra-nationalist President of Belarus was loath to sell off his country's assets until told by his own people that they couldn't afford to run them. Feigning indignity in public, but realising his lucky escape in private, he agreed. RusGaz purchased a percentage of Beltransgaz for $2.5 billion and, to show good faith, made initial instalments totalling $625 million. Yet by the due date for the Belarusian 'gas bill', the country had defaulted. RusGaz's money had been transferred to the Belarusian Ministry of Finance and the $500 million went unpaid.

Kushnerov broke the silence. 'We must ask the finance minister to pay up.'

Kozlov opened and closed his red-rimmed eyes. 'That is what I shall advise the President.'

Kushnerov, by nature a timid and nervous man, clasped his hands tighter. He didn't like this double-dealing and trickery. For him, a price was a price and a deal a deal – the old Soviet way – but now everything was skewed by capitalism, the need for greed. 'So what is our response?' The conversation, as he feared his lunch just might, had come full circle.

Embassy of the Kingdom of Saudi Arabia, London, UK
The international reporters and journalists sat and waited for the press conference to start. The ambassador's press secretary had just finished going over the rules they must abide by: not to interrupt His Highness while he was speaking and not to address him unless he invited questions. The Saudis did press differently to almost everyone else. In their opinion the press were there to listen, accept, and report. The crews from the BBC and Sky News exchanged looks and rolled eyes.

His Highness Umar Al Kabir, Saudi ambassador to the United Kingdom, entered the conference room and sat. Behind him on the wall was a large banner emblazoned with the Saudi national emblem, the crossed swords above the palm tree. He looked at the amassed reporters from the international press and started his statement to them.

'At approximately 11 a.m. today, my niece, Princess Jinan, was abducted from her place of education by a group of unknown men.' There were deep intakes of breath around the room and camera flashes. Prince Umar continued. 'She was gagged, bound, and placed in the back of a car. Her father, my brother Prince Fouad, was contacted this morning by the kidnappers, who made ridiculous demands.' He paused and looked around the room, the flashbulbs of innumerable cameras painting his face. He nodded then continued. 'I am happy to say that, as of 1 p.m. today, Princess Jinan is safe.'

There was a muttering around the room and several reporters threw up their hands, while others attempted to ask questions. Umar reined in his annoyance and instead addressed them directly. 'Yes, you. Please ask your question.'

The reporter from Sky News started to speak. 'Your Highness, can you please tell me if she was rescued or returned?'

Umar nodded. 'She was rescued by a very honourable British citizen who happened to see her with the kidnappers.' His lips curled up to form a smile; he was about to play his trump card. 'You have video footage of the rescue already; you have been showing it on your networks for the past three hours.'

The room exploded as hands were thrown up; others left the room, retrieving mobile phones in order to call their networks.

Umar held up both hands. 'Gentlemen, and ladies, on behalf of the Kingdom of Saudi Arabia I wish to personally reward and thank my niece's saviour. I will be meeting with him here within the next two days. All of you are invited.'

Prince Umar stood, nodded, and left the room. The press

secretary was mobbed by reporters and camera crews wanting more clarification.

In Whitehall, Robert Holmcroft slammed his fists on the desktop and swore out loud for the first time in years. His friend, Umar, had just bamboozled him. He had publicly thanked a murder suspect for saving the life of Princess Jinan, a man who was currently being held pending charges! The deaths had been playing on international TV screens all afternoon. As Home Secretary he had the power to issue a 'DA-Notice', an official 'request' to news editors not to publish items on specified subjects, for reasons of national security. This story should have come under DA-Notice 05: United Kingdom Security & Intelligence Special Services. But he had been too late. The cat was well and truly out of the bag with this story thanks to a pair of juvenile delinquents with 3G mobile video telephones using YouTube.

The light on his desk phone flashed and he glared at it before pressing the answer button. 'Yes!'

There was a pause; his secretary was taken aback by his angry tone. 'The Prime Minister is on the line.'

Holmcroft let out a sigh. 'Put him through.' This was going to be a very difficult conversation.

Minsk, Belarus

The man with no official title was the first passenger to step off the Belavia flight from Moscow. He was greeted by a large black government sedan and driven away without completing any form of customs formalities. Maksim Gurov was the deadly hand of the Premier Minister of the Russian Federation.

A former member of the Russian KGB, the FSB as it had become in 1995, he had been in the First Chief Directorate, responsible for foreign operations and intelligence gathering; within this, he had commanded the 'Vympel', the most secretive and deadly of all the KGB Special Forces groups.

He didn't appear officially on any staff list. He was known

only within the Russian Premier Minister's very small and select circle of advisers, the powerful and the deadly. This meeting was to be with Ivan Sverov, head of the Belarusian KGB. No official records would be kept; to all intents and purposes, the meeting wouldn't have taken place because Gurov didn't officially exist. He hadn't done so since 1995.

Gurov sat in silence in the back of the sedan as they sped towards the presidential *dacha* in the Minsk woods. He had a simple proposal to deliver and expected a simple answer. He would be back in the air within three hours, the last passenger to be let onto the plane.

The Mercedes paused briefly as the heavy iron gates were drawn back, before continuing on into the grounds of the *dacha*. A light rain had started to fall, obscuring what was left of the weak daylight that attempted to penetrate the heavy tree cover.

Inside the *dacha*, Sverov stood by the fireplace, enjoying the warmth from the burning logs. Behind him on the wall, the eyes of the President seemed to peer from the large oil painting. It was August and the *dacha* felt unseasonably cool; a severe winter was expected for the people of Belarus. He heard his security team open the front door and straightened to receive his guest, the man from Moscow.

Gurov wasn't a memorable man in terms of looks or stature. At just under six feet he was of average height, weight, and build. He had the look of a middle-level banker, except for his eyes, which were an unnerving dull grey that did little to hide the seriousness of the mind behind them.

Sverov extended his hand. 'It is a privilege to finally make your acquaintance.' The handshake was firm and he fought the urge to shiver. 'Please take a seat.'

Gurov nodded and sat. 'Director Sverov, thank you for agreeing to meet with me.'

'My pleasure.' There had been no choice; his President had been informed that this man was coming but Sverov saw no

41

reason to be impolite. He sat opposite his visitor, a low table separating them. A pot of coffee sat in the middle.

'It has been brought to the attention of my Premier Minister that your country has certain unpaid debts relating to the supply of gas.'

Sverov blinked but said nothing. This was not his area of expertise. The KGB had nothing to do with the Ministry of Energy.

Gurov continued. 'It was necessary for RusGaz to terminate your supply. I am not here, however, to speak of unpaid bills or to collect payment. Please do not see me as an enforcer. I am here to deliver a suggestion, a proposal to you, which could write off the $500 million that your country owes mine. I have sent your President only the outline of the proposal. It is you, as Director of the KGB, who would implement it.'

'I see.' He didn't. Who did this Russian think he was?

Gurov handed him a large envelope. 'In here you will find detailed plans, methods of contact, and timelines.'

Incredulous, Sverov placed the contents on the table. 'Forgive me, I do not quite understand. I report directly to the President of Belarus and it is from him that I take my orders.'

Gurov looked into the Belarusian's eyes. 'Once this meeting is over, call your President. Until then, accept what I say.'

Sverov folded his arms. He had nothing to lose. 'Carry on.'

'You have a man we need to use. Voloshin. Konstantin Andreyevich.'

Sverov's eyes opened wide. Voloshin was one of the Belarusian KGB's most closely guarded secrets. A Spetsnaz member trained to carry out international covert operations and acts of sabotage in his country's name. A 'deniable operative' as the West liked to call them.

'Do not be surprised that I know of this man, Director. Our paths have on occasion crossed. It is a tribute to you that I wish for this agent to be used.'

42

Sverov looked down at the papers. 'You say that everything is laid out here?'

'That is what I said. I do not have much time to brief you, Director, therefore I believe it would be advantageous if I were to speak while you listen.'

Sverov nodded, said nothing, and poured himself a cup of coffee.

Embassy of the Kingdom of Saudi Arabia, London, UK
Paddy Fox pulled at his shirt collar in an attempt to loosen it slightly. He hated being dressed like 'a monkey' and had always managed to have his top button undone when working for Dymex. Now, however, in the Royal Embassy of the Kingdom of Saudi Arabia, it had to be buttoned. Ironically, he was dressed as though he were attending a job interview. In the waiting room next to him sat DC Flynn, acting as a minder from Scotland Yard. Fox was under arrest for murder and attempted murder, even though there was a campaign in the media to have all charges dropped. *The Sun* had even nicknamed him the 'Desert Fox' for saving the Saudi princess. They had interviewed his neighbour Jim, who, without mentioning the Regiment, had implied that Fox had been a 'special' soldier.

On the advice of the Home Secretary, the press hadn't been invited to the embassy a second time. There had been a group of 'paps' outside, but Fox's minder and the embassy's security detail had managed to shield his face. The media was desperate for a recent picture as the videophone footage had been pixelated too much for their liking. It was all fuss over nothing as far as he was concerned. He had done what he was trained to do: rescue hostages and neutralise X-rays. He hadn't known at the time that the hostage was royalty and, frankly, it wasn't impor-tant. He might have fought for 'Queen and Country' but he wasn't particularly in awe of the first. Fox pulled at his shirt again – he was sure the police had bought him a size too small.

As he hadn't left the cells on bail, a shirt and suit had been 'acquired' for him.

The large double doors at the far end of the waiting room opened and a member of the embassy staff beckoned for him to follow. They turned a corner and walked down a long corridor which had various portraits hung on the walls: Saudi royals, camels, and racehorses. They reached another set of large double doors. The man knocked, opened them, and retreated back the way he had come.

Prince Umar stood and left his desk. He was dressed in an impeccably tailored dark-grey business suit, white shirt, and old school tie; his hair and perfectly kempt beard were jet black. He smiled broadly and stretched out his hand to take his visitor's.

'Mr Fox, I am extremely honoured to finally meet you.' The handshake was firm.

'Thank you for the invite, Your Highness.'

'And this is?' Umar looked at the minder.

'DC Flynn, sir.'

Umar seemed puzzled but shook his hand nonetheless. 'Please both take a seat.'

The three men crossed the room to an ornate fireplace where Umar sat in a large burgundy leather chair. Fox and Flynn sat on the matching settee opposite him. Umar clapped his hands and a servant brought in a tray of dates and a pot of black coffee. The two guests were given a cup each.

'Mr Fox, on behalf of my brother Prince Fouad and the House of Saud, I want to thank you for rescuing my beloved niece, Princess Jinan. You are a man of honour and courage. You were unarmed yet you managed to stop four armed men and save Jinan. We will forever be indebted to you.' He bowed his head, a mark of great respect for a Saudi royal.

Fox tried not to look too uncomfortable. Like most Regiment men he found it hard to take praise. 'I just did what anyone would have done, Your Highness.'

'Anyone with Special Forces training, Mr Fox.' Umar smiled widely and showed off a set of perfect white teeth. 'You were in the SAS, if I recall?'

Fox momentarily looked down. 'I'm sorry, Your Highness, but I cannot confirm or deny your assumption.'

Umar moved his hand as if batting away a fly. 'You do not have to.'

There was an awkward silence as the prince drank his coffee and his guests did likewise. An embassy staff member entered the room carrying something resting on his arms but covered by a ceremonial cloth. The prince stood abruptly. Fox and Flynn rose also. The man bowed, held out his arms, and Umar took off the sheet to reveal a large ceremonial sword. He held it up with both hands, took a step forward, and offered it to Fox. 'On behalf of the House of Saud.'

'Thank you, Your Highness.' Fox took the sword into his own hands. It was heavier than it looked. The scabbard was ruby and emerald encrusted; the actual metal was a highly polished greyish white. Platinum.

Prince Umar continued to smile and picked up a booklet that had been lying on the table. 'This is from my brother and me.'

The servant took the sword while Fox studied the booklet. It constituted details of a bank account in Zurich in the name of James Fox. He read on; the balance was two hundred thousand pounds. 'Your Highness, I can't accept this.'

Flynn looked over his shoulder. 'It is the law, Your Highness. A criminal cannot legally profit from his crime.'

Fox felt his face burn. Flynn was a fool. That wasn't what he'd meant.

Umar's eyelids flickered and he slowly turned his head to look at Flynn. 'What crime is that, officer?'

Flynn felt his own face flush. 'Three counts of murder and one of attempted murder, Your Highness.'

Umar stared for several seconds at Flynn, who dared not move his eyes. 'Mr Fox has not committed a crime in my country. Let me remind you, Mr Flynn, that you are in the Royal Embassy of the Kingdom of Saudi Arabia and, as such, on sovereign Saudi soil. If Mr Fox would like to, he could remain here and claim asylum, but I am afraid that you are no longer welcome.'

Inside Flynn bristled, but knew he was powerless. 'But Your Highness... I...'

Umar held up his hand. 'Officer Flynn, Mr Fox has committed no crime and he will not be prosecuted.'

Flynn had started to feel resentment. 'I think that is up to the Crown Prosecution Service to decide.'

'No. Mr Fox will not be prosecuted. Mr Fox, would you like to remain here?'

For a moment Fox couldn't decide if the prince was joking or being serious. 'Thank you for your kind offer but...'

Umar lowered his hand; his face had creased into an expression of reassurance. 'Do not worry, Mr Fox. The CPS will not bring charges. And now I must take my leave of you.' He held out his hand once more. 'Mr Fox, we shall remain forever indebted to you.'

Umar ignored Flynn, turned, and moved towards his desk. The double doors opened behind them and both Englishmen were ushered out of the embassy, but not before Fox had been reunited with his sword. On the street outside, the 'paps' had multiplied and now a gang of twenty jostled to get photographs as Flynn, not too delicately, pushed Fox into the waiting unmarked Special Branch BMW 5 series.

'Go,' Flynn told the police driver. He turned to Fox, now making no attempt to hide his anger. 'I suppose you found that funny?'

'Hilarious.'

Before Flynn could reply his phone rang. He answered it and his jaw dropped. 'He's done what?' In shock, Flynn stared blankly at the back of the driver's seat for several seconds before closing the handset. 'You're free to go.' Flynn looked like he was choking. 'The CPS has dropped all charges.'

Fox started to laugh. 'Drop me off at the nearest bank.'

Flynn spluttered, his face redder than ever. 'You're carrying an offensive weapon!'

'So arrest me.' Fox held out his hands, ready to be cuffed.

Flynn had no reply; he balled his fists as shock once again gave way to anger.

Chapter 3

Maidan Nezalejsnosti, Kyiv, Ukraine

Dudka stood with his dog on the edge of Maidan Nezalejsnosti and watched as Kyivites went about their daily routines of shopping, drinking, and falling in love. A hot August lunchtime on Kyiv's Independence Square, and all those who could manage it were away on holiday or at their *dachas*. Those who stayed behind, however, enjoyed the sunshine.

Maidan Nezalejsnosti was the heart of the city and had been home to innumerable national celebrations. Every New Year's Eve it was crammed with over a hundred thousand people waiting for the clock to strike midnight. Dudka had been at the festivities in London once, and been most unimpressed. Independence Day was another great celebration, as was Victory Day, the only hangover from the Soviet Union he enjoyed. In recent years, however, the square had been home to many political gatherings.

As the home of the Orange Revolution in 2004, well over two hundred thousand Ukrainians had camped and protested until they caused a rerun of the presidential election. One year later it became the home of those wishing to cause a rerun of the parliamentary elections. The ironic aspect to Dudka was that in the first event the then Prime Minister had illegally won the election while in the second he claimed he had illegally lost. And now? Well, now he was the President of Ukraine.

Such were the politics of Ukraine. In the past Dudka had tried to keep out of it all and had 'supported' the right person, regardless of his personal preferences. He had initially been appointed by Ukraine's first President in 1992, and again kept his views to himself when promoted by his successor to the position of Deputy Head of the SBU, head of the Main Directorate for Combating Corruption and Organised Crime (Director). However his boss – he hated to think of him as that – Yuri Zlotnik, was a highly political beast.

Zlotnik's position as head of the Security Service of Ukraine (SBU) was a parliamentary appointment, upon recommendation by the President. Directly under Zlotnik were deputies who were appointed, in turn, on *his* recommendation, again by the President of Ukraine. In normal circumstances this process would have resulted in a fair, impartial, and dedicated security service; however, in a government where the President and Prime Minister had been at war, problems arose.

Zlotnik was a compromise candidate, the President's initial recommendation having been boycotted by the parliament, led by the then Prime Minister. It had been a bitter time as the two sides played a game of chess. Finally, as a 'compromise', Dudka took delight in remembering, Zlotnik had been confirmed as head of the SBU. Zlotnik then attempted to clean house by putting pressure on the President to appoint men close to him who were, no surprise to anyone, supporters of his sponsor, the Kremlin-favoured Prime Minister. Now, two years later, the former Prime Minister, originally a mechanic from the eastern city of Donetsk, had finally become the President of Ukraine. Zlotnik and his pro-Russian cronies were now cemented in power, the President's men.

Zlotnik had decided to keep Dudka in place. Dudka was the oldest and most respected Director in the SBU, with years of distinguished service prior to that with the Soviet KGB. With age, however, Dudka had become less subtle and it was no secret that he wasn't a fan of the new President and his men from Donetsk. If asked, Dudka no longer held back with his honest and sometimes blunt views.

Dudka reached down to stroke his dog, a grin on his face. He remembered how Zlotnik had turned red when, at an office party, Dudka had shared these views with him. Zlotnik had slammed his vodka glass down on the table and stormed off. As such, Dudka was, in essence, the enemy within. He was constantly butting heads with his boss but he had got results, more so than Zlotnik's cronies. He was, as Zlotnik had told him to his face, 'an oxymoron – a convenient inconvenience'.

Dudka turned and headed home, back up Karl Marx Street, or Horodetskoho Street as it had now been renamed, to his flat two minutes away on Zankovetskaya Street. Both streets, the first named after a political activist, the second after an apolitical actress, were busy with locals and tourists alike, shopping at the overpriced boutiques. No doubt his colleague and head of the SBU's Anti-terrorist Centre, Pavel Utkin, would be looking at the summer crowds and worrying. He saw danger in everything.

Dudka and Utkin also did not see eye to eye. They were constantly colliding with each other over who had jurisdiction, his own Directorate for Combating Corruption and Organised Crime or Utkin's Anti-terrorist Centre. Nowadays the distinction wasn't clear; organised crime seemed to be increasingly carried out to fund terrorism. For his part, Dudka wanted things to be smooth. It was Utkin, the younger man by twenty years, with an eye on the top job, who wanted to take over. The problem was that Utkin, too, was one of the President's men.

Dudka found himself working with the 'Bandits from Donetsk' – as the press, not he, had labelled them. The consensus had been that January's presidential elections would oust the bandits.

Consensus had been wrong. The election had given them the most powerful position of all, that of President of Ukraine.

Dudka reached his building, entered the lift, and rose to the third floor. His official lunch hour over, he settled his dog back down and left for his office. He would walk, not bothering to use his car, an advantage of living in the very heart of the city. He'd be there within sixteen minutes, taking a circuitous route to bypass the crowds on the central square. He put his tie and jacket back on, both bought from the state-owned central store, Tzum, and shut the front door.

Since secession from the Soviet Union, Ukraine had changed greatly and yet not at all, he mused as he journeyed back down Zankovetskaya. The shops lining the capital's streets were full of expensive imported goods and the city bustled with a tenfold increase in traffic, but beneath the surface many of the same people were running the country. They might have renounced communism but they were still Soviet in mentality. The faces hadn't changed either. It was the new generation that would really change the place and he feared that, at seventy-two, he wouldn't live long enough to see his dear country become fully grown. His day had gone and all he could do now was ensure his homeland didn't implode before he could hand it over. His own protégé, Blazhevich, was one of the people who would shape the future of the SBU. He was young, not yet thirty-five, and untarnished by the Soviet past. He had first proved himself to be a worthy officer two years before, when, working together, they had halted an international arms trading network. If Dudka had to name one good man in the nest of vipers that the SBU had become, it would be Vitaly Blazhevich.

Dudka crossed Kyiv's main boulevard, Khreshatik, by means of the underpass and puffed as he walked up Prorizna Street. The hills kept him trim. He thought of himself as solid. Certainly not fat. Yet his late wife, the ballerina, had always been putting him on a diet! Two American businessmen passed him walking downhill. One was gesticulating to the other, who was nodding and looking serious. Dudka took this in his stride. Fifteen years ago all foreigners would have been stared at, but today, although still undiscovered by international tourism, more and more foreign businessmen were in Ukraine.

The criminal element, too, seemed to understand the value of 'foreign business diversity'. In the early days his caseload had been heavy with instances of attempted or actual extortion on and against foreign business interests. Now these were few and far between as the criminals themselves tried to expand abroad. This, however, caused new headaches as he laboured to improve ties with foreign agencies and Interpol. But Dudka's current caseload was surprisingly light. Not much had happened in the last two months; perhaps the bandits were watching and waiting for the political situation to settle before deciding on the most profitable type of 'business'? Or perhaps, he mused once more, they, too, were just on holiday?

SIS Headquarters, Vauxhall Cross, London, UK
Snow climbed the stairs to stretch his thigh muscles. Sitting for too long in traffic, his left leg had become stiff. He reached Patchem's floor, his thighs gently warmed, crossed the open-plan section, and pushed the door that led to the reception area for the 'Soviet Desk', as it was still affectionately called by the longer-serving officers. Patchem's overly serious secretary nodded that he should enter. Patchem gestured for Snow to sit. Through the large thick glass window, the Thames below reflected the mid-morning sun.

'Paddy Fox.' Patchem didn't waste his words.

Snow nodded. The dramatic rescue footage, which some over-excited journalists were saying was the most sensational since the Iranian Embassy siege, had made Fox something of a media sensation. The royal endorsement of Umar Al Kabir had only added to this. It had been leaked that Fox was an SAS veteran of both Iraq wars. The media, who liked nothing more than a real-life 'action hero', clamoured for more information and pictures like a pack of feral dogs. Even Britain's most well-known former SAS member turned author had commented on Fox's actions in his newspaper column.

'I know you were in different squadrons, generations, but you must have met over the years?'

'We have met.'

Snow didn't mention the freezing nights spent in a hedgerow in South Armagh's 'Bandit Country' while on attachment to 'The Det', the Royal Ulster Constabulary's intelligence unit. The pair of them had been deployed to relay information on a suspected new IRA cell.

'What do you think of him?' Patchem's bright-blue eyes burned into Snow's. 'Liked by most, respected by all, I assume?' Patchem continued, with mild sarcasm.

'Yes.' What was he getting at?

'But in possession of a short temper. He wouldn't get past the psych test in today's Regiment selection. Six weren't interested in him either, even though he spoke Arabic. Here, have a look.' Patchem removed a buff-coloured file from his briefcase on the table in front of him.

Snow took the file and opened it. It was a censored version of the military record of one James Celtic Fox. A boy soldier in the Gordon Highlanders, he had passed selection at the age of twenty-one and into B Squadron 22nd Regiment Special Air Service. Mobility Troop. Specialist: demolition. The file listed some of the campaigns he had undertaken, many not known outside the confines of Whitehall and Stirling Lines. Large areas had been blacked out when the file had been photocopied.

'Fox made corporal in the Highlanders but was demoted back to private.'

Snow looked up from the page. 'Oh?'

Patchem spoke, matter-of-fact. 'He threw his sergeant major out of a window.'

Snow wasn't surprised; he'd believe anything of Paddy.

'Evidently he found the bugger in bed with his wife. Luckily for both men the room was on the first floor! So, to business.' Patchem held his hand out for Snow to return the file. 'As the media has been so keen to broadcast to the world, an unknown terrorist organisation attempted to abduct the daughter of a member of the Saudi royal family. Fox stopped them, shot three of the kidnappers, and rescued the girl. Unfortunately he also seriously wounded a bystander – you'll have seen all this on TV'

Snow nodded.

'Well, this person, the "innocent passer-by", happened to be having an affair with Fox's second wife.'

'Quite a coincidence.'

'That's exactly what the CPS thought. However, it has been decided, though not made public yet, that he's not to be charged with attempted murder. It turns out the Saudis have some friends in very high places. These people "persuaded" the Home Secretary to drop all charges against Fox.'

It would be put down to the 'special relationship' between Saudi and the UK, which in reality had far more to do with arms contracts. Patchem had heard that Saudi Arabia had threatened to nullify the latest contract if Fox were prosecuted. Al Kabir was the Saudi signatory.

'What's more, Fouad Al Kabir is to offer Fox a position in Riyadh, as head of security, to show his gratitude. What I want you to do is persuade Fox to take it.' Patchem pressed a button on his keyboard and an image was projected on the blank, light-blue wall behind Snow's head. 'Recognise him?'

Snow swivelled in his chair and saw an image of a dead body. The picture zoomed in and Snow recognised the man. A second image, this one a still from Snow's mobile video footage taken in Harley Street, appeared next to the face.

'The same person.'

'I agree. He has yet to be identified, but this is one of the abductors Fox neutralised. The attack on Durrani and the abduction are linked.'

Snow frowned. 'Are you saying that Dr Durrani had links or dealings with terrorists?'

'Absolutely not. He had a higher security clearance than you. He'd worked for us for years and was fully vetted. He trained in the UK but was a Pashtun, originally from Quetta. His family came to the UK when the Soviets invaded neighbouring Afghanistan. Due to his contact with us, we monitored all his patients. We know they included members of the Saudi royal family. With regard to whoever perpetrated these two acts, to be candid, we have no leads whatsoever. Furthermore, the media and the PM are asking "why". The last thing we need is someone putting the desert wind up the Saudis.' Patchem half-smiled at his play on words; it hid his sadness at the loss of a colleague. 'If Fox takes this job it would also get him well and truly away from the media. Whitehall are very keen to kill the story. Everything you need to know is in here. Any questions?'

Snow shook his head as Patchem handed him a second file.

'Good. Call me with your progress. You have three days.'

Snow stood and left the office. He would have to be careful. Fox would be drawing much attention from the media and Snow didn't want his face in print beside his old comrade's.

Shoreham-by-Sea, West Sussex

A disgruntled DC Flynn had the police driver drop Fox off at Cabot Square in London's banking hub, Docklands. Fox easily found the only branch in London of his new Swiss banker and, after passing their security process, was allowed to withdraw cash against his generous payment from the Saudis. After buying wrapping paper, with which he covered his sword, Fox entered Canary Wharf tube station, taking the Jubilee Line to Westminster, where he changed to the Circle Line for Victoria.

Now safely ensconced in his Southern Central train to

Shoreham, he sat back and watched as the scenery outside the carriage changed from the bustle of London to Surrey suburbia, then the green of the Sussex countryside. Finally reunited with his mobile, he had made several calls home – none of which had been answered. There was no response from Tracey's mobile either. It wasn't that he wanted to talk to her, but that he wanted to let her know he was on his way home. Having relished his walk from Shoreham station, he stopped short on seeing the 'For Sale' sign in his front garden. He felt the anger bristle inside him but had to admire his wife's spirit. She was wasting no time. The house was in her name, she had bought it, so she was going to sell it. He walked up Jim's path and knocked on his front door.

'Paddy.' His neighbour's face registered shock but also relief. 'You OK?'

'Yes, thanks, Jim.' Fox nodded at the sign. 'What's all this about then?'

'She's left, gone to her sister's place, but I didn't tell you that. Sorry.' He looked at his feet.

'Don't be.'

Jim swallowed. 'You know I spoke to the papers? Someone had to say what kind of bloke you were.'

This newspaper interview had angered Fox at first but no longer. As pensioners, any extra cash would make their lives easier. 'Jim, you've got nothing to be sorry about, mate, and if it earned you a few quid or paid for that cruise Maureen wanted… well, just buy me a pint sometime. Is Maureen in?'

'She's out doing a bit of shopping. Didn't want me to get under her feet at Tesco; you know what women are like.'

Jim hadn't meant to be ironic. 'I do indeed. How is she?'

'Fine. She was a bit shaken at first but then she started telling all her friends about it. I think she'll be telling that story for years!' Jim smiled. 'She got her best china out for that girl. And then when we found out who she was! Well, talk about all her dreams coming true – meeting royalty and that.'

Fox shook his head. 'As long as you're both all right?'

Jim nodded. 'Paddy, there were a lot of paparazzi hanging around. One asked me to give him a call if you came back.'

Fox reached into his pocket. 'How much did he offer you? I'll match it.'

'No, I didn't mean that. There's been a couple of them hanging about. I just wanted to warn you.'

'Thanks.' The last thing Fox wanted was his face in the papers.

'That bloke, the one you...'

'Shot?'

'I'm sorry. I saw him before but I didn't feel I could tell you. Not my place.'

Fox tapped the old man on the shoulder. 'Not my place either, by the look of it.'

Sharm el-Sheikh, Egypt

'Sharm el-Sheikh is known as the City of Peace, referring to the large number of international peace conferences that have been held here.' The fat man's voice carried on the breeze from the next boat. He continued reading from his guidebook. 'Sharm el-Sheikh remained under Israeli control until the Sinai Peninsula was returned to Egypt in 1982 after the Israel-Egypt Peace Treaty of 1979. A prosperous Israeli settlement had been created there in the Seventies under the name "Ophira", derived from biblical Ophir. Some of the buildings erected at the time are still in evidence.'

'Is that where we're going this afternoon, Dad?'

The boy, the Chechen guessed, was seven and still at the age where he hung on his father's every word, even if he didn't understand.

'No, we're going out on this boat to see the fishes.'

'Can we eat them?'

'Some of them, but some could eat us!'

The boy laughed. 'Dad, that's silly.'

The Chechen drank his iced tea and looked back at the shore. The cornice was crowded with cafés. Tourists took up tables, chatting loudly, eating ice creams, and getting sunburnt. On the sea, power cruisers and yachts mixed with day launches, glass-bottomed tourist barges, and fishing charters. It was the perfect place to have a meeting without being noticed. The neighbouring boat moved off, taking the British holidaymakers out of earshot.

'I am listening,' Khalid said quietly.

The Chechen smiled, although what he was about to say was not a joke. 'We are in a position to be able to help each other. There are many true believers in your country who fear that the Kingdom is too lenient on the infidels; that the Kingdom is governed by those who seek to line their own pockets.'

'This is the view of a growing number. It is not a secret.'

'But what is a secret is that, among these true believers, there are those who are ready to take direct action.'

There was a pause as the Saudi sipped from his glass, his mouth suddenly becoming very dry. 'There are such people.'

'I would like to help them.'

The bluntness of the Chechen's reply caused the normally composed Arab to frown. He had never met this man before; the meeting had been set up using a Soviet-era KGB sleeper channel. A channel that Khalid thought he would never have to answer again. 'You are a believer, a true believer?'

The reply was in Arabic. 'I am Chechen.' It was a lie, but he had learnt his Arabic in Chechnya. 'I know firsthand what it feels like to have one's own beliefs subjugated by an occupying infidel force. I represent a powerful group who will no longer stand by and watch our Muslim brothers in the Kingdom mocked by their own rulers.'

'And what could you offer, my brother?' The Saudi did not switch his Oxford English for Arabic.

'If certain targets were to be presented, I would be able to assist in both the funding and equipping of any attack.'

'Training?'

'Special Forces training, my brother.'

There was a pause as the wash of a jet ski caused the launch to rock. Khalid looked the man in the eye. 'This is an interesting proposal.'

'One that you should accept.'

'How is it that you came to know of my beliefs?' Khalid was still not completely trusting of this Chechen. He could have accessed his handler's file to entrap him, part of the Christian crusaders' war against the true believers.

'Alexander Williamovich wanted me to say "my love for my country is as pure as the vodka that has replaced the love of my wife".'

Khalid grunted, reassured. The odd sentence was confirmation that this man had indeed come from, or had the blessing of, his former Soviet handler. An amateurish and clichéd device which was effective for that very reason.

'How is the vodka-soaked fool?'

'Dead. He was murdered by the very Russians he served. Did you know that his grandfather was also Chechen?'

Khalid was saddened. It had been this man who had recruited him out of Oxford, masquerading as a fellow undergraduate. 'My brother, I should like to accept your kind offer of assistance.'

The Chechen nodded and smiled briefly. 'We can make immediate preparations, my brother. I have a list of targets that I assume you would want to attack.'

'I have my own target list.' Khalid frowned. He didn't like taking orders and wanted to make it quite clear that he, even if funded by this man and his people, would be in charge.

The Chechen had expected this. The Arabs were a proud race, much like the Russians, he mused, but both were easy to lead, if hard to control. 'I assure you, my brother, that I only suggest my targets because I have intelligence on them and it could be that some of our targets are the same.'

'Perhaps then we should compare lists?'

'I see you have already targeted the Al Kabir family.'

Khalid's eyebrow twitched with surprise. 'An unfortunate mistake caused the girl to be rescued.'

'I am here to prevent unfortunate mistakes. Next time we may meet in Dubai, in a more fitting environment.'

'Insha'Allah'

Shoreham Beach, UK

A shiny green Mini Cooper, plastered with company decals, pulled up outside Fox's house and the driver got out.

'Mr McDonald?' The estate agent was young, suited, and eager.

'Aye, that's me.' Fox, now wearing a baseball cap, shook with his right hand, a small carrier bag of shopping swaying gently in his left.

'John, John Edgar.'

'Thanks for coming at such short notice, John.' Fox had made his accent thicker than normal.

'That's no problem at all, Mr McDonald.' Edgar twiddled the keys on his finger nervously. 'Well, as you can see, it's a nice, quiet street. What brings you to the area?'

'I'm looking for somewhere nearer to my work.'

Edgar nodded, to show his understanding. 'Good. Well, it's a new development, just over three years old, I believe. Shall we go inside?'

'Let's.'

The man from Andrews & Son opened the front door and stepped back to let Fox inside. As Fox passed, he swiped the keys from the door.

'Thanks. I'll take it.'

Edgar was confused but smiled nevertheless until the door closed and he was locked out. Fox winked at himself in the hall mirror as he made for the kitchen, ignoring the doorbell, which the bemused estate agent now rang. Reaching under the sink he turned the water back on then opened the understairs cupboard

60

and did the same with the electricity supply. The doorbell had stopped ringing. Fox filled the kettle with water. Edgar's face appeared at the back window; Fox held up the kettle and gave a 'thumbs up' before lowering the roller blind.

Tracey had really done a number on him. The house was bare except for the odd items that had been left strategically to 'sell it'. The kettle in the kitchen, expensive cooking utensils hanging on their pegs, and magazines, of the type they never read, on the coffee table in the lounge. Luckily, both the TV and three-piece suite had also been used for staging.

A thought suddenly occurred to Fox. He moved quickly to the internal garage door and opened it. There she was, his beloved Porsche, stubbornly standing stock-still and refusing to move until she had been fully restored. She was where he had left her but was now surrounded by boxes. Fox opened the nearest one to find it full of clothes – his. He was relieved; at least she hadn't thrown them away. Picking up the box he made his way upstairs and took a shower, again ignoring the front door, and now his mobile.

Riyadh, Kingdom of Saudi Arabia

Khalid stared at the desert. Was there no greater example of Allah's greatness? He was doing His work on earth, carrying out His divine will. It was time to start the new jihad against the infidels, who, in league with the corrupt royals, would defile the house of Islam.

Khalid had received a target list from 'the Chechen' and some suggestions. He had found them most acceptable. His men had been instructed and soon, Insha'Allah, the Kingdom of Saudi Arabia would be cleansed of the infidel plague and become the true house of Islam.

Wellness Fitness Club, Brighton Marina, UK

The three 'meats' were in again, pumping themselves up to ridiculous proportions. Fox shook his head. What a trio of tits! Each in their early twenties, one was well over six foot, the second just under, while the third – who Fox had nicknamed 'mini-meat' – was scraping five. As they passed, Fox kept his eyes on the monitor in front of his treadmill and the main report on Sky News, some sort of demonstration in Ukraine. Looking down again he saw that the two larger meats were now loading up the leg press machine for 'mini-meat', who as usual was making grunting noises as he pushed the plates away from his body under the ever-increasing pressure.

The guy really was comical, thought Fox. He was square. His shoulders were broader than Fox's and his chest fuller; the sad thing was that this actually made him look shorter. Meat One and Meat Two egged him on and threw him a bottle of water when he had finished his set.

Fox had seen all sorts in his time, from the wiry types who were happy to run all day to the meatheads who thought they were invincible. These were usually Paras, huge, hulking men who ran into bullets like they were rain but died none the less. Strength was a great thing to have but flexibility and speed were just as important. Fox reached the five-mile mark and slowed down the machine before stepping off.

At forty-five he was in as fine a shape as he had been at twenty-five, or so he claimed. Not for him the beer belly and saggy skin. True, his joints ached more now, but he took a perverse pleasure in confronting the pain and battling through it. He drank greedily at the water fountain before heading for the pull-up bar directly in front of the leg press station and 'the meats'. Resting between sets, they gave the older man sideways glances. Fox knew they were watching so decided to show off. He jumped up for the bar and, pausing only for a second to get his grip, snapped off ten very fast pull-ups. Dropping back to the floor he noticed their stunned expressions.

'Bit tired today,' he said in their general direction as he made for the bench press.

Snow showed a member's pass and was let in. He followed the signs for the gym. Mid-afternoon and the place was busy with young mums and those who, he supposed, worked shifts. He looked around before spotting the man he wanted to talk to, pumping his arms into the air.

'Is that a warm-up set?' Snow looked down at Fox.

It took a second for the old soldier to register the face, then his own creased into a broad smile. 'Wouldn't be for you, you English poof!' Fox rested the weight on the stand and rose to his feet, extending his hand. It had been more than fourteen years since he'd seen the young trooper he'd shared a cold ditch with.

'It's good to see you, Paddy.' Snow shook the large hand.

'You too, mate.' Fox jerked his head and implied they should move.

Snow followed him to the personal trainer area in the corner, away from the other gym users. They both sat on different pieces of exercise equipment.

'So, what are you doing here?'

'I came to see you.'

'Well, you see me.' Fox took a gulp of water.

Snow gave a quick look over his shoulder to see that no one was within earshot. 'I need to talk to you about something.'

Fox wiped his mouth on the back of his hand. 'You still Regiment?'

'Not quite.'

Fox raised his eyebrows; he knew better than to question any further here at the gym. 'Listen, let me get a shower and meet me outside. You got a car?'

Snow nodded.

Snow brought his Audi round to the entrance. Five minutes later, he and Fox were leaving Brighton Marina and heading back to Shoreham.

'You're a celebrity.' Snow cast Fox a wry look as they pulled out into the seafront traffic.

'Apparently I'm very popular on Al-Jazeera.'

'So what happened?' Snow wanted to hear it firsthand.

'Who wants to know?'

'Just me, Paddy.'

Fox folded his arms and leant back in the seat. It was a relief to recount the story to someone without fear of either prosecution or publication. He trusted Snow. As they headed towards Shoreham, Fox gave a full account of his actions on that eventful afternoon.

'Did you see it was Sawyer before you pulled the trigger?'

Fox kept his eyes on the road. 'He was in my line of sight.'

'But did you see it was him?'

'Yes, I saw him.' Fox gripped the leather armrest. 'He was shagging my wife.'

Snow slowed as they reached the outskirts of Shoreham. 'You didn't get the job then?'

'What?' Fox chuckled. 'No, I did not.' He pointed ahead. 'Take the next on the right; you should be able to park at the Co-op.'

Snow turned and within a minute eased the car into a space.

'So, who are you working for?' Fox was blunt.

'Six.' Snow had no need to hide the fact.

Fox nodded knowingly. 'I could tell.' He tapped his hand on the dashboard. 'Has this got machineguns and rotating number plates?'

'No, but it's got an ejector seat especially for passengers of the Scottish persuasion.'

Fox held up his middle finger in reply as they exited the car.

Snow followed Fox out of the car park and onto the narrow high street. Both men stayed quiet until they'd reached the pub and were sitting with a pint. As usual, the Crown and Anchor was empty except for Burt and Dave. Burt pointed to the newspaper in his hand and gave a thumbs up.

'So what can I do for you?' Fox had an idea what his old comrade in arms had been sent to ask.

'I heard you got offered a *big* job?'

Fox nodded. 'Aye, I did that.'

'I think you should take it.' Snow sipped his lager.

'You mean "Six" thinks I should take it?'

'Yep.' Patchem had known all along about Snow's operational relationship with Fox, which was why he had chosen him to make the approach.

Fox downed his pint. 'Training makes me thirsty. You'll have to persuade me.'

Snow took the hint and got Fox another pint of bitter and a Diet Coke for himself.

'What, you become bent or something? Where's yours?'

'I'm driving.'

'You are not. I said you'll have to persuade me. Now get yourself another. You're staying the night at mine.'

Snow returned to the bar; he hadn't needed much encouragement. This time, in addition to his pint, he plonked two double whiskys on the table. 'If we're drinking, we're drinking.'

Fox lifted the spirit glass. 'Up the arse, no bebies!'

'You'd know.'

Fox narrowed his eyes. Not many could get away with saying that to him. They both downed the whisky. Dave looked up from his newspaper but said nothing. Fox sipped his pint. 'So what've you been doing for the last decade and a bit?'

Snow recounted his own story, from his return to the Regiment after his assignment with The Det, to assisting the Ukrainian SBU, getting shot, and then 'joining' Six.

Fox whistled. 'Me? After the Regiment I worked for a bunch of tossers for six years, got made redundant, and then, I nearly forgot, killed three bad guys and saved a princess.'

Neither story was the usual 'reacquainting yourself with your mate' chat, but then neither man was a normal 'mate'. Although of different generations, they had worked and almost died together in the SAS. Snow thought back to the night in Armagh when they'd been dragged out of the ditch by Jimmy McKracken, the IRA's newest and, by reputation, hardest 'hard man'. Fox, having an Irish father from whom he had inherited the nickname 'Paddy', had played the local trump and claimed to be from another cell. He had knocked Snow about with blow after blow to give his story credibility, while using his best Ulster accent.

After McKracken's men finished planting the roadside bomb, Fox and Snow were taken back to a farmhouse, where, in a world before mass mobile phones, the IRA cell leader wanted to corroborate Fox's story. Snow was thrown – bruised, head covered in a Hessian sack – into the barn, while Fox was marched to the kitchen. Neither man knew where the other was but both acted as one.

Snow pretended to be more injured than he was and, just as his IRA guard was removing his sack, he lunged out with his leg, sweeping the man to the floor. The young Irishman was winded and dropped his handgun. Snow rolled on top of him and using his head as a weapon, broke the Irishman's nose before clamping his still-bound hands around the youth's neck. He had only meant to render him unconscious but the adrenaline of the situation meant he'd pressed too hard.

This was Snow's first kill, a hard kill, but he had had no time for remorse. Using the volunteer's knife, he cut through his bonds, collected the gun, and made, as stealthily as possible, for the farmhouse.

In the kitchen, Fox wasn't tied to the chair but had the eyes of two men on him, while McKracken had moved away to make his call. Having spent his summers with his grandparents, who hadn't lived far away, Fox was regaling his watchers with stories when one of them sensed movement outside. Fox sprang to his feet and kicked the nearest man in the groin. The first terrorist crumpled and Fox grabbed his assault rifle. As he did, Snow sent two 9mm rounds through the window and into the skull of the second. Fox ventured further into the house, as Snow moved through the door, pistol trained on number one, lying on the floor clutching his groin.

Fox heard shots but McKracken hadn't stayed to fight. He had taken his Cavalier and was making good his escape. The night had been a success. The bomb was defused and the remaining IRA cell member turned 'grass', delivering valuable intelligence. Fox and Snow had made an effective team.

Fox stood. 'Come on, let's get some grub.'

'What about here?' Snow fancied the homemade steak and kidney pudding.

Fox looked at him as though he was mad. 'Do you enjoy living?'

Dave, who was collecting the glasses, stared at Fox. 'Think about me. You get to walk away, but the missus insists on cooking for me every bloody day!'

They exited the pub and moved down the high street. 'You wanna move the car?'

Snow shook his head. 'No, it's a pool car. If it gets towed I'll get another.'

'"MI6 takes on clampers" – that'd look good in the *Evening Argus*.' Fox enjoyed his own quip. 'Right, I fancy an Indian.'

Fox marched the pair of them around the corner to the Indian Cottage restaurant, a sixteenth-century cottage converted to become Shoreham's best Indian. The fact that, like most Indian restaurants, it was owned and staffed by Bangladeshis was lost on the two former soldiers.

*

The noise of a seagull outside the bedroom window woke Snow with a start. Head throbbing, he unzipped the 'maggot' Fox had lent him and rolled off the mattress. Wearing only his boxers and T-shirt, he walked to the window and looked out. The house had a view of the street opposite and, if he craned his neck to the left, Shoreham beach and the English Channel. The early morning sunlight danced on the surface of the sea. Snow pulled on his jeans and made his way downstairs in search of ibuprofen, aspirin, or paracetamol – anything to avert the hangover which would soon fully manifest itself.

The sound of a kettle boiling and the smell of bacon met him halfway. As he reached the bottom Fox greeted him with a broad smile. 'Have a nice lie-in? You must be getting soft in your old age.'

Snow checked the time on the microwave: it read 7:15. Fox grabbed the kettle and poured the scalding water into a pair of mugs. 'Here, regulation brew. Milk's in the fridge.'

'Cheers.' Snow poured a measure then handed it to Fox. 'You got any…'

Fox cut him off. 'Second cupboard. Still got some horse tablets they gave Tracey for her back.'

Snow took two painkillers and gulped them down with hot tea. 'How are you feeling?'

Fox cracked an egg. 'Me? Right as rain, but then I'm not an English poof. Sunnyside up?'

'Yeah,' Snow nodded, although truth be told he was still full from the previous night's curry.

'What time are they expecting you back at spy central?'

'It's flexible.' Snow took another swig of tea. 'So?'

Fox spread his arms. 'You want me to give up all this for a fistful of sand?' Snow remained silent as a smile spread across Fox's creased face. 'Did you think I'd actually say no?'

'No.'

'Eat.' Fox slapped two eggs, three rashers of bacon, and a pair of sausages onto a plate. 'For tomorrow we may die.'

Arizona Bar and Grill, Kyiv, Ukraine
Gennady Dudka was looking forward to seeing his oldest friend,

Leonid Sukhoi. He crossed his arms and smiled, reminiscing about times long ago. They had been conscripts together in the Red Army before being selected for the KGB Border Guards, where they had both stayed and risen through the ranks until Sukhoi transferred back to his native Belarus and Dudka returned to his homeland of Ukraine. They had met up as frequently as work would allow over the years and had enabled as much collaboration as possible between their two KGB divisions.

Then, however, 1991 happened and the mighty Soviet Union imploded. The two friends found themselves working for different countries, Sukhoi now employed by the Belarusian KGB and Dudka by the Ukrainian SBU, Ukraine having dropped the Soviet name but not much else. As the Nineties and the new millennium passed, Ukraine had gradually stepped out of the shadows of the former Soviet Union and was walking, if slowly, towards the West and the EU. Belarus, on the other hand, had tried to rebuild the Union and sought to create, first, a 'Belarusian and Russian Union' and then a 'Greater Slavic State' with Russia, Yugoslavia – as was – and Ukraine. Yugoslavia had crumbled into civil war before they had a chance to sign up, and Ukraine hadn't answered the door to their neighbour; they were busy entertaining their new visitor – the West. Now isolated by all but the infamous 'Axis of Evil' and Russia, Belarus was alone and mainly ignored, a remnant of the Soviet Union that neither fitted into the past nor the new democratic future of Europe.

Dudka hadn't seen his friend for… he counted on his fingers… close to three years. He frowned. Had it really been so long since Leonid's granddaughter married her own ambitious KGB officer from Minsk? Time had passed in an instant; now both in their early seventies, Dudka had started to realise that Leonid and he didn't have all that much time left. Dudka was in as rude health as ever, but he feared for his friend, who, although taller, had always been 'delicate'. He made a resolution to keep in touch more, in future, with those who mattered to him most.

The restaurant had started to fill up with early Sunday customers; it was just after twelve and Leonid was due any moment. The waitress again asked Dudka if he was ready to order, and for the second time he told her he was waiting for someone and could she just bring him a glass of water and turn the air conditioning down? He shivered; outside it was a balmy, early September day, but here it felt like the midst of winter. His water arrived, complete with ice cubes – an American idea. He gave the waitress a withering look. Not taking the hint, she left as he noticed his old friend enter the room.

Dudka smiled broadly and held out his arms, shook Leonid's hand, and then embraced him. 'My dear friend. How good it is to see you!' He meant it; he loved Leonid like a brother.

Sukhoi also smiled but not quite as warmly. 'You too, old rogue.'

Dudka took a step back and regarded his friend; he had put on some weight, his shirt and jacket seemed a bit tight, and he did not seem at ease. They sat.

'I trust it was a good flight from Minsk International?' It was a joke; neither the airport nor the airline were truly international.

Sukhoi smiled half-heartedly.

Dudka frowned. 'What's the matter?'

They paused while the waitress brought more water and ordered quickly before she had a chance to leave.

Sukhoi drank his water then mopped his brow; he was sweating. 'Genna, you are the only one I can speak to. You are the only one I trust.'

Dudka's expression turned serious. 'Whatever I can do to help, I will – you know that, Leonya.'

The head of the Belarusian KGB's third directorate nodded. He was in a dangerous position; so dangerous, in fact, that he had had to leave the country he commanded and enter Ukraine to seek help. He glanced around the restaurant. He had initially chosen it at random but was later happy to find it was an ex-pat favourite – not many old Soviets.

'There are certain elements in my government that would seek to destroy my country.' Sukhoi's tone was serious. His words hung in the air as their soup arrived, Borsch being one of the only Ukrainian dishes on the menu.

'Lukachev has done a good job so far; I say let him finish.' Dudka dipped his roll then took a soggy bite; his comment was laced with sarcasm.

Sukhoi noticed a crumb fall onto his friend's tie. It was no secret between them that neither was enamoured of the Belarusian leader. The problem was that like-minded men in Belarus were hard to find. All those of their age had too much to lose and the younger generations had been indoctrinated during the overlong years of Lukachev's rule.

'Something terrible is being planned, something that would almost certainly bring about the destruction of the Belarusian nation.'

Dudka's spoon stopped and its contents fell back into the bowl, splattering his tie. His friend was being even more alarmist than usual. 'What is this about?'

The KGB man swallowed hard. The restaurant was fine for making contact but he couldn't take any more chances. 'Is there somewhere we can go that is secure?'

Dudka narrowed his eyes. 'Yes. You are serious?'

Sukhoi nodded. 'I need help, Genna.'

Dudka knew not to push the matter any further. Both men sat in silence and finished their soup, neither having an appetite for a main course.

Dudka paid and they left. He had parked his government-issue Volga outside. The SBU's younger men had been given new Volkswagen Passats but he preferred his Volga. He nodded at the restaurant's security guard, who, dressed in full urban grey and blue camouflaged fatigues, looked more like a commando than a glorified doorman, and unlocked the car parked just outside. Traffic rumbled past them along the Naberezhno-Khreshatik, the riverside highway that neatly dissected Kyiv.

Sukhoi looked around nervously as he opened the passenger door. Suddenly he groaned and fell forward onto the bonnet before sliding off and onto the asphalt.

'Leonya!' Dudka moved swiftly, for a man of his age, around the far side of the car. He heard a sound like heavy hailstones and saw Sukhoi's body convulse. Dudka threw himself to the floor. Someone with a silenced weapon was shooting at them! Lying flat on his face, he reached out to grab Sukhoi's hand. Something hit him and there was a sharp, stinging sensation on his face. Dudka winced but reached out again. He couldn't feel a pulse. Raising his head, he saw an Audi 80 parked on the other side of the road pull off in the direction of the new bridge and the city's left bank.

Moving with more speed than he had done in twenty years, Dudka was up and firing his service-issue Glock 9mm at the disappearing target. The shots were wild except for one, which smashed the rear windscreen. Dudka turned back to his best friend, who lay motionless at his feet; there were specks of blood behind his head.

Chapter 4

King Khalid Airport, Kingdom of Saudi Arabia
For the past ten minutes the passengers around Fox had formed long queues for the toilets on the Riyadh-bound Boeing 747. Once in the tiny cubicles they removed their Western clothes and replaced them with Arab robes. The cabin changed from a sea of coloured shirts to an almost monochrome of men in white thobes and women in jet-black abayas. The only flashes of colour now came from the red-chequered headdresses of the Saudi men and the few remaining Westerners.

Just before they entered Saudi airspace the chief flight attendant announced that, to comply with the law of the land, the bar would now be closed. The cabin crew would collect all miniatures and empty glasses. Unlike other flights, no one here dared hide a bottle in their pocket for later. Alcohol was strictly forbidden in the Kingdom of Saudi Arabia. It was a good job the content of the passengers' stomachs wasn't scanned, Fox thought to himself. He had never seen so much booze being put away on a commercial flight; it had been like a knees-up at Stirling Lines!

Thirty-five minutes later, his seat upright and tray stowed, Fox braced himself for landing. He didn't fear flying; he feared crashing. As the plane touched down there was applause from the locals returning to the Kingdom; the ex-pats, however, didn't look pleased. No sooner had the aircraft come to a halt than the Saudis were standing and removing their bags from overhead lockers. The flight crew asked for all passengers to remain seated once, then a second time, then gave up.

Fox collected his rucksack from the overhead locker and exited the plane. He looked wistfully at the grinning cabin crew, realising this was probably the last time he would see female flesh for a while. Stepping out of the fuselage, the heat hit him like a wall. The temperature was in the forties and he immediately felt drowsy. Alcohol, heat, and tiredness did not a good mix make. The short drive to the terminal was cramped and hot. The terminal was also crowded, but cooler, as innumerable air-conditioning vents spat at travellers.

At passport control there were several long queues, each for a different counter, one for KSA residents, another for diplomats, yet another for VIPs, and finally the one for the rest of the world. There had been another desk for 'tourists', meaning the Hajj pilgrims, until all Hajj flights had been redirected to Jeddah and a purpose-built terminal. Millions of the faithful, dressed in loincloths, would descend upon the Kingdom annually for the ritual of circling the pillars and throwing stones or something – Fox didn't care for the facts; to him it was daft, pure and simple. The world's largest and most dangerous pyjama party where, each year, hundreds were crushed to death. These thoughts, however, were highly offensive to Muslims and would get him arrested, if not worse, if he were to voice them. Fox joined the nearest and longest line. To his right was the sign for the toilets. It had two signs, one showing the head of a bearded man wearing robe and headdress and the other a woman's veiled face. It looked like a prop from Monty Python's *Life of Brian*.

'Any women here?' Fox muttered to himself as he replayed the stoning scene in his head.

The queue moved slowly forward and eventually Fox produced

his passport. His visa was examined by a uniformed Saudi, whose eyes opened wide on seeing that he was to work directly for the royal family. It was stamped and returned. Just through the gates, Fox was greeted by an immaculately dressed military officer. He held out his hand.

'Welcome to Saudi Arabia, Sergeant Fox.'

Fox cringed and shook the proffered hand; the grip was firm. 'Paddy will do fine.'

'Paddy.'

The eyes of the young officer gleamed. 'His Royal Highness sent me personally to collect you and speed your entrance into the Kingdom. Now, if you will follow me, we shall expedite your luggage. I hope your flight was agreeable? I am Captain Barakat.'

'Nice to meet you, Captain.'

'Basil.'

Fox looked amused and the captain shrugged. 'I know that in your country it is a funny name. Basil Brush, Basil Fawlty, yes?'

'Yes.'

'But in Arabic it means "brave".'

'I meant no offence.' Fox spoke in Arabic.

Basil smiled broadly. 'Your Arabic is excellent.'

'So is your English. Sandhurst?'

'That is correct, Paddy; I believe your language skills stem from Hereford?'

Inside, Fox swore. Who else knew he'd been in the Regiment? 'Correct.'

They walked along a corridor and reached the customs hall. The four conveyor belts were empty but the hall was packed with passengers from earlier flights, patiently waiting.

Basil put his hand on Fox's arm. 'Stay here a moment.'

The officer disappeared through a door and two minutes later the nearest conveyor belt started to whir, luggage from the BA flight tumbling down the chute. Fox saw his dark-red Samsonite case, always easy to spot, and grabbed it.

Basil reappeared and took the handle. 'Allow me.'

Basil led Fox towards the customs area. The officials, on seeing Basil, waved them past and within seconds they were pushing through the swarms of taxi drivers, eager relatives, and chauffeurs, all waiting for their pickups. Fox fumbled inside his rucksack for his Ray-Bans and put them on as they exited the terminal building and were again assaulted by the heat. Basil seemed unaffected, even though he wore a uniform jacket, and strode towards a white Bentley Continental Flying Spur. He raised his arm and the boot popped open.

'Nice.' Fox was again taken aback. The car in front of him was the world's fastest four-seat production car, capable of 0–60 mph in 4.9 seconds and a top speed of 195 mph. Basil lifted Fox's heavy case and, showing an unexpected level of strength, swung it into the boot. He held his hand out for the rucksack and, once this was inside, closed the lid.

'Shall we?' Basil opened the front passenger door and Fox climbed into a world of cream leather, burnt oak, and walnut. 'A good company car, yes?'

'Your army pay must be better than mine ever was.'

Basil nodded as he eased the large sports sedan away from the kerb. 'Prince Fouad is a most generous employer. The car is, of course, his but I am to use it for important errands.'

'Tell the prince I am most grateful.'

'You will tell him in person when you arrive.'

'Of course.' Fox had momentarily forgotten he was due to meet his employer on arrival. Uncharacteristically, he now felt shabby in his brown Merrells, sand-coloured cargo trousers, and check shirt. Sod it. He dressed like a lackey for no one, royal or no.

The car joined the Riyadh highway and was soon cruising at over 100 mph. Basil flashed his lights at anyone who dared drive slower. There were speed limits in the Kingdom but not for the royal family or, indeed, important officials.

'Have you read *Bravo Two Zero* or *The One That Got Away*?'

'Yes.' Fox knew what was coming.

'You were in Iraq in '91?' Basil had read all there was to read about the legendary SAS and was thrilled to have a former member as his passenger.

'I can't tell you, Basil.'

'I'm sorry – operational security, I expect?'

'No,' replied Fox dryly. 'I'm an old man. I can't remember.'

Basil laughed loudly in the soundproofed interior of the Bentley. 'That English sense of humour. That is why I like the English more than the Americans.'

'The English are a funny lot.' Fox didn't bother to mention that he was actually Scottish.

'For me, I prefer slightly the writing of Chris Ryan to Andy McNab, but that is just my personal preference. I have all the books of both men. Do you have a preference?'

Fox shrugged. He didn't want this subject to continue further.

'Perhaps you should write a book also, Paddy?'

'What would I write about? Gardening?'

'Again the English humour.' Basil's laugh became a tone higher.

There was a sudden wail of Islamic music and Basil reached into his trousers to retrieve his phone, all the while the Bentley continuing at over 100 mph. Basil spoke in Arabic. Fox listened to the conversation but was more interested in their progress. The car swerved slightly as Basil replaced the phone in his pocket. 'That was the prince. He is glad you have arrived safely. '

'Insha'Allah,' Fox replied dryly.

'Yes. God willing. We should be at the palace within the next ten minutes or so; it depends on the traffic.'

'You mean how fast they can move out of our way?' The needle had started to climb higher.

'Yes. Exactly.'

Twice more in the next ten minutes Basil received calls, not from the prince. Twice more Fox became a nervous passenger, which, for a man who loved fast cars, was rare. They pulled off the highway and headed into the desert along a road which led to a high wall, with steel gates and a security box on the outside. Basil sounded his horn and the gates opened without the occupants of the car being checked.

Immediately inside the walls, Fox's eyes became wide. In complete contrast to the desert outside, inside was the greenest grass he had ever seen, several fountains, and a large, white, Mediterranean-style villa. The Bentley glided up the mirror-flat granite drive and stopped in front of the house. Basil got out and quickly moved around the car to open the passenger door. The warmer air entered but this time it was moist and bearable. A man in a white jacket appeared and was handed the keys. Basil then gestured that Fox should follow him and they walked around the house and into a large area at the back. To the left a huge, white, single-storey building sat apart from the rest of the house, and on the right a large swimming pool nestled perfectly amidst a landscaped garden. Basil ushered Fox towards the canopy to one side and the portly, robed figure who sat there.

'Your Highness.' Basil bowed.

Prince Fouad Al Kabir rose from the lounger and extended his right hand.

'Mr Fox. How pleased I am to welcome you here.' His English was accented, but not Sandhurst, unlike both his brother's and Basil's.

Fox took a step forward and bent at the waist to meet the royal hand. The grip was limp, as though Fouad didn't quite know how to shake hands. 'It is an honour to be invited, Your Highness.'

'Sit, please, Mr Fox.'

Fouad sat back on the white linen lounger and Fox sat on a lower one to his left while Basil remained standing. 'That will be all, Captain Barakat.'

Basil bowed and headed back to the house as members of the serving staff appeared with a pitcher of fruit juice, trays of fruit and pastries, dates, and an urn of Arabic coffee. A coffee cup was filled and presented to Fouad then a second was handed to Fox. The staff retreated out of earshot. Fouad leaned forward.

'I really am very grateful for what you did for my daughter. I will forever be in your debt.'

'I did what anyone would have done, Your Highness.'

Fouad held up his finger. 'Now, I know that is not true. You are a man of honour and of discipline, Mr Fox. My brother speaks highly of you.' He drank his coffee and Fox did the same. 'So, what do you think of my humble home?'

Fox let his eyes wander before answering. 'I like it.' He could think of nothing else to say; as far as houses of the Saudi royal family went, it was the first he had been in.

Fouad stood and Fox hastily followed.

'I like it here because there is a lesser need for air conditioning than the city. We have our own micro climate thanks to my very clever gardener.' Fouad gestured towards the many palm trees lining the walls before he started to walk towards the other building. 'This is not your first time in the Kingdom? I believe you were here when there were troubled times for our neighbours?'

'Yes, your Highness.' Fox didn't want to elaborate but knew what the prince was alluding to. He wiped his brow with the back of his hand and followed his new employer. Between the heat, alcohol, and sheer fatigue, he was finding it hard to stay polite, however grateful he might be.

The prince abruptly stopped and turned. 'Mr Fox. What happened to my daughter in England was outrageous.' He turned back and continued along the path. He waved his arm. 'What happened to me here in my own home was also unacceptable. This is something that I have not experienced before. Allah be praised, you were my daughter's saviour, but now I also need you to ensure my continued safety.' At the door to the building he again faced Fox, as if to express the severity of the matter. 'Much damage was done to my most prized pieces but my general collection was untouched.'

Fouad pushed the door and stepped into the building. Fox entered behind him and could hardly believe what he saw. The room was vast, like a giant aircraft hangar, and full of rows upon rows of cars. Fouad smiled like a kid showing off a new toy to a friend as he watched Fox look around. 'Do you like cars, Mr Fox?'

'Yes, Your Highness, they are a hobby of mine.'

'Indeed?' Fouad was happy and clasped his hands together. 'How so?'

'When I left school I wanted to be a mechanic like my dad; that's why I joined the army.' He had, however, been placed in the infantry and not the Royal Engineers as requested, so had had to learn the inner workings of the internal combustion engine in his spare time. A knowledge that had served him well in the Regiment's Mobility Troop.

'What car do you drive in England?'

'I have a Porsche 930 Flachbau.'

'What is that?' Fouad looked earnest.

'It's the 930 with a 935-style "slantnose" conversion, Your Highness.'

The prince nodded enthusiastically. 'Of course, yes. You must forgive me, my German is not very good – I did not know the word. If I remember rightly, that had the uprated 330 bhp performance kit?'

'Yes.'

'Ah, I can see you ask how I would know such things? Well, I am one of the founding members of the Porsche Club of Riyadh. Porsches are a particular fondness of mine. Let me show you.' They crossed to the other side of the room, passing as they did so a 'Who's Who' of twentieth- and twenty-first-century sports cars.

'Here!'

With a flick of the arm he unfurled a dustsheet that had been covering a silver Porsche Carrera GT, the fastest road-going Porsche yet built. Fouad glanced back at his new employee to gauge his reaction. Fox was smiling and shaking his head slowly from side to side.

'Each year we have a race from Riyadh to Bahrain. I fly out three engineers from Porsche Germany in Stuttgart to check the cars before we leave. The race starts at 3 a.m., when the tarmac is coolest, otherwise the tyres would not be able to cope. I hold the current record at three hours and five minutes.' He smiled conspiratorially. 'But then I do have the fastest Porsche in the race.'

Fox leant forward and looked in the 'cockpit'. He was beginning to like his new boss. 'You have great taste, Your Highness.'

'True. Some collect art, but to me this is art. Working art.' The prince suddenly clapped his hands. 'We shall speak at another time. I see you are tired after your journey. I fear first class is not what it once was. Captain Barakat will take you to your rooms. You shall start work tomorrow.'

Basil appeared at the door and the prince bade Fox farewell. In the Bentley once more, they made swift progress back towards the city suburbs. Fox's driver was, he knew, eager to make further conversation but sensed that Fox was beyond speech. Fox started to nod off, despite the speed they were travelling at, but within twenty minutes they had reached a residential area. The Bentley slowed at another high wall and gate combination; again it was ushered in unchecked.

They stopped and Fox looked around. They were inside what looked like an upmarket holiday park made up of one- and two-storey villas, some terraced, some detached, which were built in two horseshoes, the two-storey buildings making up the outer ring. In the centre was a swimming pool and what looked to be a barbecue area. To one side were three tennis courts and land-scaped lawns. At the barbecue area the residents were cooking or standing drinking.

'This is where all the Riyadh-based foreign employees of the Al Kabir Group live.'

'How many are there?'

'In Riyadh there are about one hundred or so. There are many more in Dammam, of course, for the oil refineries, and in Jeddah. The Al Kabir Group is one of the Kingdom's largest and most successful employers.'

'Really? That's interesting.' Fox didn't add that, as it was owned by a branch of the royal family, of course it would be successful.

'Let me show you to your house.'

Basil unloaded the car and headed for the larger outer row of villas.

'This one, Paddy.'

He pointed to a two-storey villa at the end, nearest the gates. The villa, as did all the others, had a three-feet-high white picket fence around it and a small, very green lawn. It was painted brilliant white and Fox took a guess that the interior colour would be the same. On entering he wasn't disappointed. Basil heaved both case and rucksack with ease up the flight of stairs and into the front bedroom.

'I hope you will feel happy here, but if you need anything please don't hesitate to call me.' Basil flashed him a large smile with brilliant white teeth that matched the paintwork, and produced a business card from his inside pocket.

'Shukran.'

Basil shook Paddy's hand – again the strong grip. 'You will be collected at 8 a.m. tomorrow. Have a nice first night!'

Basil left the villa. Fox looked around the very white room. It had an American-sized double bed, two walk-in wardrobes, an en-suite shower, and a balcony. He looked at his watch – still on London time, two hours behind Saudi. It was early afternoon in the UK but mid-afternoon here; if he had a nap now he wouldn't be able to get a proper sleep later on. Fox shook his head. 'Come on, you old git, only two bloody hours difference,' he muttered to himself as he unpacked his case, took his washbag, and entered the shower.

Central Moscow, Russian Federation
The office was in an unassuming riverside residential apartment block within walking distance of the Kremlin. From the exterior, the balcony looked like any other, but the glass in this was an inch thick and bulletproof. The double doors that led from the communal hallway to the flat were also armoured, made from heavy, reinforced steel designed to withstand a direct hit from an RPG.

In his high-security Moscow residence, Maksim Gurov spoke over the secure phone to Ivan Sverov in Minsk. Both men had been monitoring the Ukrainian news channels. The report of a shooting was high on the schedule, just after the most recent exchanges from the 'President vs opposition leader' battle. However, the reports couldn't confirm who the victim had been; the Militia had yet to release details. This was what Gurov had expected of the Ukrainians.

'Your man saw the ambulance crew arrive?'

'He also saw the body being loaded onto a gurney.'

'Was the face covered?' Gurov needed to know if the old man was dead.

'He could not see. He was stopped from getting any closer by the Militia.'

'Was the target neutralised?' Gurov was infuriated.

'Voloshin stated that he fired an entire magazine into him.'

Gurov now had no doubt. He viewed the Belarusian KGB Spetsnaz operative as among the very best. He had, after all, once been his commanding officer in the Soviet Red Army. 'Good. I will send you further instructions.'

'How?' Sverov didn't like being ordered about, but before he received an answer the Russian had ended the call.

Central Kyiv, Ukraine

Sukhoi opened his eyes and focused on the white roof of the ambulance. He felt a stabbing pain in his chest and his head was spinning. He heard a familiar voice.

'Why did you not tell me you were wearing a Kevlar vest?' Dudka had been angry at his friend's omission but relieved he wasn't dead.

'Did you think that I had got fat, Genna?'

'As a matter of fact, yes.'

'On a Belarusian diet?' Sukhoi winced as the ambulance bounced over a pothole.

'You have at least two broken ribs and a severe concussion.'

'Where are we going?' Sukhoi felt groggy.

'To a secure hospital, where we take the politicians and members of the SBU.'

'Fix up the spies?' remarked Sukhoi ironically.

Dudka looked at his friend. 'Do you know who shot you?'

'Yes.'

Dudka wasn't surprised, 'Do you know why?'

'Yes.' Sukhoi turned his head and looked up at the Ukrainian. 'We have to stop them, Genna, or mine won't be the only death…'

Sukhoi felt his eyes close as the world around him started to go black. Just before it did he heard a concerned Dudka ask the medic if the patient would be OK; then he lost consciousness.

Riyadh, Kingdom of Saudi Arabia

Fox, dressed in a pair of cargo shorts and white, polo-style T-shirt, neared the barbecue area. An ex-pat wearing a tight, lime-green T-shirt with a faded sun-godlike face logo and denim shorts intercepted him.

'Hi, I'm Paul Clements, head of the Escape Committee.' He extended his podgy hand.

'Paddy Fox.'

'Welcome to Stalag 17, Paddy. I bet you could do with a beer?'

'You read my mind.'

Clements took a bottle from a cooler and handed Fox an opener.

'Cheers.'

Fox took a long swig of cool beer. 'Real?'

Clements nodded. 'We do, from time to time, get the real stuff. The label says it's non-alcoholic but then not all shipments in from Bahrain are tested.' He tapped his nose conspiratorially.

Alcohol was available in all ex-pat compounds but was highly illegal. It was smuggled in from various embassies and sources, usually via the Bahrain Bridge. However, the supply and quality varied. Several years before, the police had made an example of a couple who made and sold home brew. Their wine, although tasting nothing like Tesco's finest, had been in great demand.

'You join us on a happy occasion when we have the real stuff; otherwise we rely on home brew. You get a taste for it after a while.'

Looking around, Fox could see that most of the compound's residents had now descended on the pool and barbecue area. 'Friendly lot?'

Clements nodded. 'Yep. We've got about fifteen different nationalities here as well as a few "tame" Saudis who come for the parties. We all put a few quid into the kitty monthly and have these events every weekend. There's always something to drink to: birthdays, promotions, and... err... the weekend. So how long are you here for then?'

Fox took another sip. 'A year, but the contract is open-ended.'

Clements looked surprised. 'Just you or are you bringing your wife?'

Fox nearly snorted his beer. 'My wife, I imagine, will be contacting me only via her solicitor. We're getting a divorce.'

'Oh. Well, I'm afraid this isn't the best place to be a bachelor. Unless you like camels?'

Fox replied deadpan, 'They're OK for the occasional hump.'

Clements slapped Fox on the back. 'I can see you'll fit right in.' Both men drank. 'So, just you in the large villa then? Unusual – the boss must like you.'

Fox didn't want to explain any more than he had to. 'Scottish charm. What brings you to this place then?'

'This, the Garden of Eden?' Clements took another swig. 'Fashion.'

Fox blinked.

'I know I don't look like a Versace catwalk model…' He pulled at his T-shirt. 'But I am in charge of the Al Kabir Clothing Group.'

'Nice.'

'I'm responsible for bringing international fashion brands into the Kingdom and selling them to the locals to wear when they travel abroad or lounge about at home. Our biggest sellers are handbags and shoes.'

'Is Saudi a hotbed of fashion?' It wasn't something Fox had ever paid much attention to.

'Ah, you'd be surprised. Next time you see a woman walk past in her abaya, have a look at her shoes. Chances are they'll be designer, French or Italian, and she'll have a matching handbag. When they meet at their girlfriends' houses, off come the abayas to reveal the latest Paris collection items. I was at a friend's place, local guy, and I thought I'd wandered onto the set of Fashion TV!'

Two more residents approached them. The younger of the two held out his hand. 'All right? I'm Lordy…' He pointed to his chest. 'And this is Franklin.'

'Frank.'

Fox shook both men's hands. 'Paddy.'

'You the security guy, then?' Lordy's South London accent was soft on the 't's.

'That's me.'

'What's yer background? Army or summit?' Frank's own accent was strong, Newcastle.

'I was in the Highlanders a while back.'

'Could 'av guessed. No offence.' Lordy held his bottle up as a salute.

'None taken,' Fox replied, deadpan.

'So, why do they call you Paddy then, seeing as you're a Jock?' Lordy smiled innocently.

'My father was from Belfast.'

'Right.'

There was a pause as they all took a swig of beer. Clements spoke first. 'It was a hairy time a few years back – before your time, lads. We could have done with you then, Paddy.' Clements addressed the others. 'The compound attacks had us all worried.'

Lordy and Frank nodded; they had heard the stories. Fox himself had been briefed on the Riyadh compound bombings.

In the early hours of 12th May 2004, three cars, a pick-up truck, and a 4x4 had driven through Riyadh. Three of the vehicles were car bombs while the other two carried armed assault teams. Their targets were three expatriate compounds: the Dorrat Al Jadawel, owned by the London-based MBI International; the Al Hamra Oasis Village; and the Vinnell Corporation Compound. Vinnell, a defence contractor at that time, was training the Saudi National Guard. All three compounds contained a large number of Americans and other Westerners. Each compound was, therefore, a high-priority target for the Khawarij insurgents, their goal being to drive the infidels out of the Kingdom and topple the Saudi monarchy.

The terrorists failed to gain entry to the Jadawel compound, blowing themselves and the gate guards up in the process, but the other suicide bombers successfully gained access to the remaining two target compounds. Both were devastated. Al-Qaeda later claimed responsibility although they hadn't had a direct hand in any of the acts.

The response from the Saudi authorities was swift and ruthless. The Saudis arrested in excess of six hundred terrorist suspects and seized bomb-making equipment and thousands of weapons cached around the Kingdom.

Clements finished his beer and reached into the cooler for another. 'I was scared shitless, I won't lie.'

Part of Fox's brief was to advise and update the security of the compound, a job made all the more difficult as it was a new position.

'What was the plan in case of attack?' Fox deliberately stayed away from military terms.

'Bugger all.' Clements wiped his lips. 'They put a couple of extra blokes on the gates but didn't give us any instructions. I took to sleeping in my clothes and had an escape plan laid out in my mind, but a lot of others left. The embassy was in a difficult position; it couldn't order everyone to leave as it didn't have the authority. Also, it would have offended the royal family. So it "recommended" that, unless it was vitally essential to remain, all British nationals should leave immediately. Some of the old sweats, including me, decided to stick it out. Mind you, it turned out all right in the end. The prince rewarded our loyalty.' Clements shook his wrist and the diamond-encrusted gold Rolex that adorned it.

'It's amazing what them knock-off shops can do nowadays.' Frank gestured with his chin.

'I'd have gone home. I'm here to build things not get demolished myself!' Lordy chuckled at his own joke.

'So, Paddy, you gonna make us all safe then?' Frank looked at their new neighbour.

'Starting tomorrow.'

'We'd better get you fed then. Grab a plate from the pile and enjoy some of Frank's finest cooking.'

'I hope you brought some Rennies,' Lordy said, smirking.

Military Hospital, Kyiv Oblast, Ukraine
The strapping prevented his ribs from moving too much and the morphine stopped the pain. Physically Sukhoi was feeling better,

if slightly lightheaded. He had been at the centre overnight and had slept well for the first time since recent developments and learning of his agency's plans. This was, however, due to the morphine, and not the fact that he was out of danger.

Dudka sat next to the bed in the large room and ate a fresh roll and butter with a glass of sweet black tea. 'You are sure you don't want to eat, Leonya?'

Sukhoi slowly waved his hand. His appetite had all but vanished four days earlier. 'No, you go ahead.'

Dudka shrugged, 'If you insist.' He was anxious to know what his friend had to say but didn't want to drag it out of him. The concussion had been such that the doctors thought he should be left to sleep sedated overnight to avoid any potential swelling, which might have caused concern in a man in his seventies. Dudka looked down at his friend with the bandaged head. 'You look like a war hero.'

Sukhoi pointed to Dudka's own face. 'Did they hit you?'

Dudka self-consciously felt his cheek and forehead. 'From the kerb – a couple of chips of concrete hit me, that's all.' He continued to look at Sukhoi, waiting for him to talk.

Sukhoi motioned for the glass of water that stood next to his bed. Dudka passed it to his longtime friend.

Sukhoi sipped. 'The Russians are not happy with the new world order and take great offence at the Americans' claim that they are now the world's only superpower. The Chinese are growing in importance all the time and have already surpassed Russia. They have more money to spend on their military, manufacture most of the world's goods, and have been a member of the WTO since 2001. As we know, Russia and Belarus are not. In the Middle East the Arabs, led by the House of Saud, are holding the world's economy to ransom with their oil. In essence Russia is no longer a first-league player; they have been relegated.'

Dudka finished his tea. He hoped there was more to hear than a modern history lesson. 'So what have you learnt?'

'Two weeks ago I learnt of a meeting between representatives of my President and Russia's Prime Minister.' Dudka leant forward and Sukhoi continued. 'Prime Minister Privalov wants to use force to stop the Russian slide, to once again make Moscow a force to be feared…'

Dudka cut in, unable to control himself. 'How? Military action against China and Saudi Arabia? That would be complete madness.'

Sukhoi wagged his finger slowly. 'Not directly. Russia has the world's largest known oil reserve.'

Dudka knew this. 'They have a name for it, "Cold Black". In ten years the West will be their largest client.'

'That is the point, Genna; Russia cannot wait for ten years.' Sukhoi drank again. 'For if they did so they would not be in charge of their own reserves. Russia has asked her "friends" to do her bidding. They need the West to be reliant upon Russian oil much, much sooner.'

'How?'

'Russia wants to destabilise the current oil supply. If the West cannot get oil from the Arabs, they will look to Moscow. Moscow will fill the immediate deficit and then offer the West terms they cannot refuse. China already uses some Russian oil as a fuel and raw material; they, too, would become dependent.'

Dudka leant back and let out a sigh, trying to imagine the magnitude of such events. 'Such a coup would be all but impossible to achieve; hands would point at Russia. When will all this start?'

Sukhoi shrugged. 'It already has, Genna.'

'What!' Dudka nearly fell off his chair.

'They know that I know, my friend; that is why they tried to stop me from telling you.'

'Who are "they"?' Dudka wanted it made very clear.

Sukhoi looked deeply into his friend's eyes; it weighed heavily on his heart. 'The KGB, my KGB.'

Dudka shook his head. It was the craziest thing he'd ever heard. But he had seen the evidence – his friend of over fifty years shot in front of him, a man he knew had never lied to him. 'How did you find this out? You have a source?'

'President Lukachev's *dacha* is bugged.'

'What!' His friend was very crafty. 'But is it not swept regularly?'

'It is, but the officer in charge of the sweeping is also the officer responsible for placing the bugs. He turns them off, sweeps, and then he turns them on.'

Dudka nodded. 'Who is watching the watchers? You have tapes?'

'Don't be so old-fashioned. I have a memory card.'

Dudka had heard the term but didn't quite understand. He left the 'technical stuff' to his subordinates. 'Where is this device now?'

Sukhoi looked around the room. 'Where is my phone?'

'You need to call someone – is that wise?'

'The card is in my phone.'

'Oh.' Dudka frowned and then bent sideways, placed the empty hospital plate on the floor, and brought his briefcase up and onto his lap. Flicking the catches open he removed Sukhoi's phone. 'Safekeeping.'

Sukhoi held out his hand. As Dudka watched, Sukhoi's shaky hands opened a slot on the side of the Sony Ericsson and retrieved a thin piece of plastic less than the size of his thumbnail.

'An M2 memory card. This particular one can hold over one and a half thousand photographs or two hundred minutes of video or three thousand minutes of audio.' He pushed it back inside, switched the phone on, and pressed play on the media menu. 'Listen.'

Dudka took the phone and held it by his ear. The sound quality wasn't great but he could hear the unmistakable voice of Ivan Sverov, head of the Belarusian KGB.

Sukhoi watched as his friend listened intently to the conversation. He held out his hand and Dudka returned the phone.

'You have it all on this chip?' This really was incredible.

'Yes.'

For the first time in his career Dudka had no answer.

Sukhoi broke the silence; he couldn't bear his grief alone any longer. 'The intelligence officer was my son-in-law, Shidlovsky. They found his bugs. They shot him.'

Dudka's eyes flicked open. 'My God. What about Masha?' He suddenly felt concern for his goddaughter.

His old friend shook his head as his eyes started to water. 'The Militia found her… she had been… strangled.' His head slumped; he held his hands over his face and started to sob.

Dudka felt powerless. How dare they! His own eyes were wet but anger stopped him from breaking down. He stood and placed his hand on Sukhoi's head as images from the wedding danced before his eyes, then much earlier ones of Masha picking flowers with him, her godfather, in the woods. He started to shake, so removed his hand and paced the room. His fists were clenched. He was no longer the seventy-two-year-old SBU Deputy Director; he was once again the Red Army soldier with revenge on his mind. He would personally kill the men responsible for his goddaughter's murder. 'Who knows that you have come to Kyiv?'

Sukhoi raised his head, his eyes wet and red. 'I told no one – they presumed I was at home crying. But I travelled on my own passport; no use giving them extra ammunition if I am under surveillance.'

Dudka thought aloud. 'And they let you board the plane because…?'

'They wanted to assassinate me on foreign soil?'

'To make it look as though it was someone else.' The two directors were thinking alike.

'But there is nobody.' Sukhoi paused and wiped the last tear from his eye. 'How did I get here, Genna?'

'What? You don't remember our conversation?'

'No.' Sukhoi shook his bandaged head slowly.

'Ambulance staffed by SBU medics.'

'How many people know I am alive?'

Dudka totted it up on his fingers: the ambulance staff, two doctors, several nurses, and Blazhevich. 'Less than ten. They can be spoken to. But we cannot fake a body. There were witnesses; their weapons were silenced but mine was not. I have a feeling that your embassy and the KGB will be knocking on my door very soon, wanting to know where you are.'

'I cannot go back, Genna. I now have nothing to go back for. You must hide me, at least until we can act on this information.'

'Agreed. But we must keep this quiet. You know that my SBU has its own problems, like your KGB? There are some in the agency who are not as dedicated to independence as I.'

'Chief Zlotnik and Director Utkin?'

'How did you know?'

'I am KGB, remember?'

Dudka let his mouth curl into a thin, humourless smile. He pointed at the phone. 'I need to listen to that. We have to take you somewhere anonymous, off the radar.' Dudka retrieved his own phone. He would summon Blazhevich.

Riyadh, Kingdom of Saudi Arabia

Fox gulped down the water as though he'd not had a drink in days. He had forgotten how vicious the heat of the desert was. This time he was finding it much harder to acclimatise than before. He didn't want to admit it, even to himself, but now he was older. He was, however, relishing the role that lay ahead.

Prince Fouad had given him full autonomy in the implementation of changes to the security setup and training of personnel. Fox's role was very much like the tasks he had carried out in the Regiment, training private armies and carrying out threat assessments. In his first two days he had drawn up contingency plans

93

in case of a terrorist attack on both his compound and Prince Fouad's palace. Training of the security guards at the compound had started. Most were also expatriates from the subcontinent and it hadn't been easy for them to grasp that they needed to be proactive, i.e. to actively assess all possible threats and implement protocols. They were used to being told what to do by their Saudi masters.

The military personnel guarding the palace, however, were a different story. The usual lacklustre attitude to work that most Saudis displayed had been drilled out of them by the Americans. The Saudi Arabian Royal Guard Regiment, having received training from both Delta Force and a 'private security company', were, so far, among the best units Fox had worked with. He had complimented both Captain Barakat – 'Basil', as he insisted Fox call him – and his commanding officer, Major Hammar. Fox hadn't detected the usual arrogance associated with officers when asked to take instructions from a non-commissioned officer, as Fox had become in the Regiment. Once his protocols for the palace and compound had been fully implemented he would move onto the other compounds, offices, and facilities owned by the Al Kabir Group. It was a large job and he knew a lot was expected of him. He felt valued again.

It was just after midday and, across the Kingdom, everything had slowed as the day's first 'shift' was over. The Saudi working day was dissected in two to account for the heat, much like a Spanish siesta. Most workers returned to their jobs in the mid-afternoon, working until late at night. Fox hated the idea of this disruption, the daily 'stop start'.

'Mad Dogs and Englishmen, Mr Fox?'

Fox turned and was surprised to see Prince Fouad himself standing next to him. 'I'm sorry, Your Highness?'

'Mad Dogs and Englishmen go out in the midday sun!' The prince had a mischievous expression on his face.

'I'm not English.'

'And you are not a dog.' For a Muslim, to be called a dog was an insult indeed.

'I agree, Your Highness, so that leaves me just mad.'

Fouad waved his finger. 'We are all born mad, Mr Fox, and some remain so. I fear that I am one of the some. Come, Mr Fox. I have something truly wondrous to show you!'

Prince Fouad headed abruptly towards the large, climate-controlled building that housed his collection. Fox followed. Once inside, Fox was again stunned by the number of cars and the sheer value of what sat before him.

'Here. Please remove the dustsheet.' Fouad stood by his latest acquisition.

Fox reached down and pulled back the cover. What he saw shocked him. 'What is she?'

Prince Fouad could hardly contain his glee. 'She is a 918 Spyder. Please, please, take a closer look.'

Fox crouched, something he would never have done in front of the prince without his direction, and peered closer. 'But the 918 isn't in production, it's a concept car.'

'That is correct, at present. However, when you are willing to pay, let us say, a princely sum, anything is possible.'

Fox looked at the shape. The car clearly displayed classic Porsche lines, resembling from certain angles both the 550 Spyder and the Carrera GT. It was, in his opinion, the best-looking car he had ever seen. He shook his head. 'Your Highness, I'm stunned.'

'And this is why I say I am mad, Mr Fox. You realise that this car is an electric hybrid?'

Fox straightened up, a broad smile on his face as he registered the irony.

Kyiv Oblast, Ukraine
Blazhevich kept his eyes on the road and tried not to think too hard about who his passengers were. He was proud to be called

on so often by his boss, Gennady Stepanovich, for special assignments. Although looking and sounding like an old communist at times, he admired the Deputy Director. Blazhevich was now Dudka's most trusted officer, but this hadn't always been so. Boris Budanov had initially been Dudka's choice, the star of the SBU who Dudka had nurtured and trusted. However, Budanov was also the same officer who had been passing intelligence to a Kyiv-based arms smuggler that had resulted in the abduction and murder of a British citizen. Blazhevich had uncovered the mole. Dudka had felt humiliated, and then angered; however, Budanov's folly had been Blazhevich's fortune.

Dudka finished skim reading Blazhevich's report. 'The vehicle was found on the left bank?' Dudka referred to the newer part of the city with Soviet tower blocks that had been erected in the Sixties and Seventies.

'Yes, Gennady Stepanovich. The person driving the car claimed it wasn't his, that he found the key in the ignition.'

'As a model citizen, he was taking it to the nearest Militia post?'

'Yes, Gennady Stepanovich, but he was heading in the opposite direction.' Dudka was being sarcastic but Blazhevich played along. 'He is not a suspect; he was seen taking the vehicle by several witnesses who knew him. There were full prints of three different people in the car and partial prints of eight others.'

Blazhevich had seen the car. It was a silver 1993 Audi 80. Originally sold in Germany but imported into Ukraine in 1998 and re-registered, it didn't look as if it had been washed since. A forensic investigator's nightmare.

'No trace of our would-be assassins. Any leads at the airport?' That was the quickest way out of the country, after all, Dudka reasoned.

'None as of yet. We have finished checking the flight manifests and CCTV footage but have seen no one suspicious.' It was like looking for a needle in a haystack – to use an expression he had learnt in his English lessons.

'And you won't.' Sukhoi spoke for the first time since entering the car. 'Their escape route will have been well planned.'

Blazhevich knew who the passenger sitting next to Dudka was, even though he hadn't been introduced. 'Who are we actually looking for, Director?'

Dudka was about to speak but Sukhoi held his hand up to stop him. 'Belarusian KGB agents. My country sent them to assassinate me.'

Blazhevich looked in the rear-view mirror at the old man. The vehicle swerved slightly. Not knowing what an appropriate response would be, he replied, 'Oh.'

'They may be long gone or they may even be hiding in their own embassy.' Dudka folded his arms. 'But if they learn that Leonid Grigoryevich is still alive, they may try again.'

Blazhevich trusted Dudka above anyone else but couldn't quite believe what he had just heard.

Sukhoi, as if reading Blazhevich's mind, spoke. 'Yes, young man, that is correct. They view me as an enemy of the state.'

'Vitaly Romanovich, this is a very delicate situation. Only you and I are to know that Leonid Grigoryevich is alive; only we are to know of his whereabouts. Our beloved Director Zlotnik must know nothing of this.' Dudka wanted the situation to be clear to his subordinate. 'I would not put you in this position if I did not believe I could trust you.'

Blazhevich's mouth had gone dry. Again, not knowing quite what to say, he nodded. 'Of course, Gennady Stepanovich.'

Worthing, West Sussex, UK
Snow jogged along Worthing beach and breathed in the sea air of his hometown. Since leaving Ukraine and joining MI6 he had tried to come down as often as he could. He hadn't checked the tides, but was glad the sea had been gracious in retreating enough to enable him to pound the sand that lay just beyond the familiar pebbles. He was pushing himself, wanting to blast

away the cobwebs of London and the stress of working for MI6.

To Snow, running wasn't a chore but a necessity, not only for the sake of fitness but also his mental welfare. He reasoned out problems while he ran and had in fact made all his best decisions after a long run. He was sure the SIS psychologist would have something damning to say about that, even though he was running out his problems, not running away from them.

He ducked under a strut supporting Worthing pier and turned for home. The seafront had started to get busy with day-trippers, coach parties from the North and families. Snow moved from sand to pebble beach and pumped his legs harder before eventually transferring to the promenade where he increased his pace on the smooth surface.

Having been an embassy brat, his father a high flyer in the Foreign Office, Snow had spent much of his childhood and adolescence in various Eastern European cities, including a long posting in Moscow. The upside of this was that he was fluent in Russian and could pass for a Muscovite; the downside was that he had no real roots. For a brief two years, which coincided with his A-levels, they had been back in Worthing at the 'family seat'. Then, once more, Mr Snow senior was posted abroad. At this point, an eighteen-year-old Aidan Snow ignored his parents' protestations that he go to university and enlisted in the British Army. Turning down a chance at officer training, he went into the ranks, completing the minimum three-year service requirement before successfully passing 'Selection' for the SAS.

Snow had wanted to be a 'badged member' of the Regiment ever since seeing on television, as a nine-year-old, the live footage of the Princes Gate Operation Nimrod hostage rescue at the Iranian Embassy. His parents had laughed it off and bought him a black balaclava and toy gun, but as he grew older Snow's desire to join only increased. When he was forced to quit the Regiment and go back to the classroom, this time as a teacher, his parents were happier.

Snow thought back to his time in Kyiv and the carefree ex-pat teacher life he had enjoyed. He missed it and he missed his friends, those who were still there, and those who were dead. His life now was very different to that of a PE teacher, but deep down he knew that, although he had loved teaching, his body had craved the adrenaline rush of being a member of the SAS. Now, as an operative for SIS, or MI6 as he and the papers preferred to call it, the rush was back. The thing he missed now was the camaraderie of the Regiment.

Snow tried to push it from his mind as his feet hit the asphalt. It was Saturday morning and he was going to enjoy some real sea air. The fact that his parents were out of the country helped.

Three miles later, Snow walked the remaining few steps to the family house and fell through the door. He'd forgotten how much harder real running was than the treadmill he used in London. Snow headed upstairs, showered, and changed into some clean clothes before taking his company Audi and heading back into central Worthing. He was too lazy to cook and would find somewhere to have brunch. Being a bachelor meant he could do what he wanted, until Monday morning at least.

Orane, Kyiv Oblast, Ukraine
Dudka had been given the *dacha* while the mighty Soviet Union still believed it ruled the world. It had been allocated to him by the government. In those pre-capitalist times all property was assigned by the state. As a decorated officer in the then Soviet KGB, Dudka had received his flat on Zankovetskaya and the *dacha* near Orane, north of Kyiv on the Teteriv river.

He had spent many weekends there in summer, when his daughter was a child and his wife was alive. Like most Ukrainians they had grown fruit in their small orchard and made preserves and pickles. Dudka had seen himself as a bit of a farmer and had even become fond of making his own wine.

Nowadays he rarely visited the *dacha*. It held too many memories that caused him too much pain. He had lost his wife to cancer four years earlier but the grief was, on occasion, still raw. He hadn't dared let it cross his mind that the incident at Chernobyl might have been responsible.

The *dacha* had been their sanctuary from the outside world: his responsibility to the state and hers to her ballet students. For she had continued to teach into her sixties. Irina had loved to dance. That was how they had met – the young KGB officer who fell for the ballerina. It sounded like a Pushkin or Chekhov fairy tale but it was true. Katya, their daughter, had also danced at the *dacha*; they all had, in the summer. But summer for Dudka was over now and the snows of winter were fast approaching. His wife was dead and his daughter and granddaughter lived in Cyprus.

'Stop the car over there on the left,' Dudka ordered Blazhevich.

As the car stopped, Sukhoi's eyes fluttered open. He looked around, taking a few seconds to realise where he was. 'I haven't been here for years.'

'Since 1990.' When they had all belonged to the same Union, Dudka didn't need to add.

'Has it been so long?'

Dudka smiled. 'You've been busy.'

Dudka got out of the Passat and helped Sukhoi emerge from the other side; he was still unsteady on his feet. Blazhevich tried to help but Dudka pushed him towards the boot. Blazhevich opened the boot and hoisted the bags out. He then followed the two old soldiers into the summerhouse.

Inside the air smelt of polished wood and the unlit open fire. The floors were wood, as were part of the walls, the rest brick-covered with white render. The room was open-plan with lounge and kitchen forming one large room. The bathroom was through the kitchen. It hadn't been designed to be modern, just functional. Upstairs were two bedrooms and a balcony. Dudka indicated that Blazhevich should take the bags containing clothes upstairs, leaving the equipment. He did this as the old men sat in the worn armchairs by the fireplace. There was a moment of silence as both sat lost in contemplation.

Blazhevich returned and stood awkwardly by the dining table. 'Shall I bring in the food, Gennady Stepanovich?'

'Unless it can walk in here by itself, that would make sense.'

Sukhoi smiled thinly as Blazhevich left. 'You are too hard on that boy, Genna.'

Dudka waved his hand. 'I am sweetness and light.'

Sukhoi retrieved his phone and placed it on the low table in front of him. 'Are you sure this place is not being watched?'

Dudka laughed. 'Only by those who choose to steal my plums.'

Sukhoi nodded. 'You know what I mean, Genna.'

'It is secure.'

Blazhevich returned and placed a bottle of vodka on the table in front of the two directors. Dudka looked up at him quizzically. 'I did not pack that.'

'I know, Gennady Stepanovich. I did. I thought that it was an essential item.'

'Medicinal,' Sukhoi interjected.

'Yes, Director.'

'I am glad to see that you are finally using your initiative. Well done. The glasses are in the cupboard over there.' Dudka pointed. Blazhevich moved into the kitchen area. 'He'd make a good butler.'

Sukhoi shook his head slowly. 'Don't put that on his permanent record.'

Blazhevich returned with three glasses. Dudka raised his eyebrows at the third but poured a measure into each. 'To us.' He led the other two in the toast.

Blazhevich unpacked an SBU laptop from its case and set it on the table. He then removed the memory card from Sukhoi's mobile phone and placed it into an adaptor. Dudka looked on in awe; there were some things that were beyond him. When

101

Blazhevich was certain a copy had been made, he returned the card to the phone, opened the reader programme, and then pressed play on the laptop.

The three intelligence officers listened in silence. Dudka had his eyes closed to further enable his concentration, Blazhevich sat forward on a dining-room chair while Sukhoi tried to read both for a reaction. The recording lasted for almost forty-five minutes and outlined a plan to attack the oil refining and delivery capacity of Saudi Arabia. Exact targets and timelines, however, were missing.

There was a stunned silence. Dudka spoke first. 'This is a very dangerous piece of information to hold.'

There was no verbal reply. Sukhoi nodded while Blazhevich stared, transfixed, at the two directors.

'Who is the other man on the recording?' Dudka knew Ivan Sverov, Director of the Belarusian KGB, but not the other voice, the one with a Moscow accent.

Sukhoi shrugged. 'He is from the Kremlin but no one knows his name.'

'What?' Dudka was puzzled.

'There is no record of him either entering or leaving Belarus, but he was on a commercial flight.'

'I don't understand, Leonya.' Dudka leaned forward and refilled the glasses.

Sukhoi answered. 'There were eighty-nine named passengers on the inbound Belavia flight from Moscow but ninety passengers in total. Our man was not named.'

'Hmm.' Dudka raised his glass, nodding but giving no actual toast. This time Blazhevich drank only half. 'So this man is a ghost? He controls the PM behind the scenes, an unseen adviser?'

'That is my guess.'

Blazhevich found his voice. 'Was this the only visit?'

'As of four days ago, yes.'

'But this is not the entire plan. They must hold further

meetings to provide targets and mission updates,' Blazhevich continued.

'Have you an idea, Vitaly Romanovich?' Dudka questioned.

'We have this recording as proof but, unless we can name the other speaker, it may not stand up at an enquiry. We need to put a face and a name to the voice.'

'If we intend to play by the rules, yes.' Dudka was slightly scornful. 'So how do we get that, a face and a name?'

'We put Sverov under surveillance and we listen to his calls?'

'That would potentially also be an act of war, Vitaly, if it were to come to light.'

Blazhevich mimicked his boss. 'If we intend to play by the rules.'

'Regardless, we must find him,' Sukhoi stated.

'But first,' Dudka said, finishing his vodka, 'we need to announce your death.'

Chapter 5

SBU Headquarters, Volodymyrska Ulitza, Kyiv

The doors to Dudka's office opened and, without knocking or offering a greeting, Yuri Zlotnik addressed the older but less senior man. 'Where have you been?'

Dudka looked up from his papers, then at his watch. It was half past nine on this Tuesday morning in September. 'Here. Before that I was at home recovering from my injury and I may well be again later. Head wounds are complicated.'

Zlotnik placed his hands on his hips and continued to stare. This time, taking in the large plaster on Dudka's forehead. His tone, however, was still accusative. 'What happened on Sunday?'

Dudka paused on purpose, as he always did, to annoy his boss, then shook his head slowly. 'It was terrible. My dear friend was murdered.'

Zlotnik remained standing but nodded his head. 'Tell me about it.'

Dudka gave him a questioning stare; he was going to enjoy playing the victim. 'Leonid Grigoryevich and I had been friends since before you were born. On Sunday he and I had just finished having lunch when we were shot at. He was gunned down in front of me on the pavement.'

Zlotnik remained impassive. 'You will need to give a full report.'

Dudka stood, an act that shocked his boss, and took a step forward around the desk. 'I have just told you that my friend was shot dead in front of me. Stop wasting my time.'

Zlotnik blinked. 'Don't you forget who you are speaking to, Gennady Stepanovich.'

Dudka decided now was the time to lose his temper; he took another step forward and pointed at his boss. 'And you do not forget whom you are addressing.' Several drops of spittle flew from his mouth.

Zlotnik became flustered. 'I understand that you are upset, but certain procedures have to be followed.'

Dudka regained his composure. 'You are, of course, correct. That is why I have called a press conference.' He looked at his wristwatch. 'It will start in one hour. You should attend.'

'What?' Zlotnik's face reddened.

'As head of the SBU, it would, of course, be beneficial for international relations between us, Belarus and Ukraine, if you said something positive.'

Zlotnik opened and closed his mouth several times like a goldfish before the words came out. 'But you have not told me what has happened!'

'Then sit down and listen.' Dudka pointed at a seat.

Admonished, Zlotnik sat. Dudka returned to his own chair. There was a phrase for this he had read in a business journal: 'managing up'.

The television cameras of several Ukrainian stations, including Inter Channel, 1+1, and ICTV, jostled for position with those from Russia and the West. Flashes of light bounced off the faces of the men in suits as they entered. Dudka was the first on, followed by Zlotnik and the head of the Kyiv Militia, Kutsenko. They sat. Name plates had been put on the table, as had microphones. Dudka held up a hand and a silence fell among the assembled members of the press. He wasted no time with a welcome note or introduction.

'Yesterday, at approximately twelve-fifty, as I left the Arizona Bar and Grill restaurant, I was fired upon by a person or persons unknown. I was not hit but… my companion and longtime friend, Director Sukhoi of the Belarusian KGB, was fatally wounded.'

Dudka took a sip from the glass of water on the table in front of him and shook his head theatrically. Flashbulbs exploded around him but before he could continue, Zlotnik spoke.

'We are following up several leads and are working with the Belarusian security service to find those responsible. I have every faith that these killers will be brought to justice.'

In Moscow, the faintest of smiles crossed Gurov's lips. He had not predicted that the SBU would get so involved but nevertheless the result pleased him. The troublesome KGB Deputy Director was dead; this had yet to be confirmed by the Belarusian ambassador in Kyiv, but he didn't need further proof. Ukraine would now be forced to work more closely on security matters with Belarus, which would, of course, be outraged that such a key figure had been murdered on the streets of their sister state.

None of this mattered to Gurov. It would be a smokescreen to obscure the masterplan. Sukhoi was a security leak that had been plugged, and the tape's content could no longer be verified. Now the Director had been taken care of, Gurov could continue with his work. It was time to speak again to Sverov in Minsk. Further instructions now needed to be carried out. The man was a nuisance, but a necessary one if his plan was to work.

Gurov continued to watch the Ukrainian news channel with professional interest. The recent political situation in Ukraine had not been foreseen. Russia had backed the winner but their man's election victory was being jeopardised by Ukraine's former Prime Minister, 'The Witch', as she was known in Russian political circles. She was again the fly in the ointment. If she won a future election, Russia wouldn't accept her as the President of Ukraine. Russia needed Ukraine on its side, or she could pose a serious threat to Russia's monopoly on energy supplies. Ukraine was a huge potential source of the hydrocarbons, electricity, and bio-diesel that the EU was extremely keen to exploit. With 'Moscow's man' as President, Ukraine would not compete with their master.

Gurov had some ideas on how to achieve this. Perhaps that would be his next task: to finally banish 'The Witch'? The main event, however, was to take place shortly in the Middle East and it was his to direct.

Presidential Administration, Kyiv, Ukraine

Olexandr Chashkovsky, the President of Ukraine's chief of staff, shook the hand of Dmitro Nykyshyn, the Belarusian ambassador to Ukraine, and gestured for him to sit. They had met before and both were career politicians.

Chashkovsky spoke first. 'I am sorry, Ambassador, that the President could not meet you personally.'

Nykyshyn smiled ruefully; the President was in deep debate with his bankers from Donetsk. 'I am given to understand that he is currently a very busy man.'

Chashkovsky nodded and flattened his tie as he sat. 'What is it that I can do for you, Ambassador?'

Both men knew what the meeting was about but formalities had to be adhered to. 'Olexandr Ruslanovich, it has now been two days since your security services announced the death of our Deputy KGB Director, Sukhoi, but we have yet to see his body. We have yet to make a formal identification.' Nykyshyn folded his arms.

Chashkovsky paused and prepared his answer. 'Your Excellency, I do apologise for the delay. Our best forensic pathology team have been studying the body for any extra clues that might help the murder enquiry.'

'You are to be commended on this, but I cannot see why this has delayed me from seeing the body?'

'We have been awaiting the results of a specific test, and if the body were to be at all contaminated, the result would not stand.' This was what he had been told to say by Deputy Director Dudka and he hoped it made sense.

Nykyshyn frowned but, as he had no understanding of medical matters, seemed to accept this. 'Olexandr, if I may?'

Chashkovsky nodded at the use of his first name.

'I am just a man, like you, doing his job. I have been asked by my President to facilitate the identification and repatriation of Deputy Director Sukhoi's body as soon as possible. This is so we can give him a decent burial, as befits a man of such standing, and put this business behind us. Therefore, anything you can do to speed up the process would be much appreciated.' Nykyshyn gave a professional smile.

Chashkovsky responded with one of his own. 'Leave it with me, Your Excellency.'

Mortuary No. 2, Holosivski Region, Kyiv, Ukraine

The mortuary was cold and eerie. Nykyshyn shivered, despite his outwardly professional demeanour; he had never been in this situation before. He was a banker by education and not by any stretch of the imagination a law enforcement or intelligence officer. This was why he was accompanied by Investigator Kostyan, who was. Although, as ambassador, he was the senior representative of Belarus in Ukraine, Nykyshyn knew he was expected to defer to the KGB investigator.

They followed the chief medical examiner down the corridor, passing several large glass windows. In one, Ambassador Nykyshyn caught a glimpse of a corpse opened from neck to waist. He swallowed hard and felt nauseous.

'Just along here, comrades.' The examiner, who had no sense of occasion, was jovial; his blood-red tie shone out brightly from beneath his doctor's whites. He stopped abruptly and turned on his heels. Nykyshyn, who had been looking at the floor, almost walked into him. Kostyan caught his arm. 'Now, I must warn you, comrades, that this is not a sight for the faint-hearted.'

Kostyan answered. 'We understand, Doctor.'

'Good.'

The examiner opened the door and they followed him into the room. In the middle was an autopsy table covered with a white sheet.

'When you are ready?'

Kostyan nodded. The examiner removed the sheet. Nykyshyn's eyes went wide with horror and his hand rapidly rose to his mouth, complete with handkerchief.

'Is it him?' The ambassador could feel the bile start to rise.

Kostyan pulled an envelope from his inside jacket pocket and removed a photograph. He held it up so he could compare the face, or what was left of it.

'I think so.'

'Good…'

Nykyshyn suddenly clamped his hand over his mouth and started to bend at the waist.

'There is a bucket in the corner.' The examiner pointed.

'Have you X-rayed the teeth? I have a copy of the dental records here.' Kostyan continued to study the corpse.

'Yes. Let me get them for you.' He left the room.

'Can we please go?' Nykyshyn wiped his mouth.

'Not yet.'

'Why?'

'Because it is not him.'

'What?'

Kostyan pointed, 'That is not the body of Sukhoi.'

'But you just said…?' Nykyshyn was confused.

'I have been informed that he was not shot in the head.'

'Are you sure?'

Kostyan looked at the diplomat. 'I am a KGB investigator. I am never unsure.'

The examiner returned with an X-ray sheet. 'Here you are.'

'Spasiba.' Kostyan took the sheet and, pinning it to the light box on the wall, compared this to his own sheet. What was left of the jaw did indeed contain teeth which looked remarkably the same. 'I am satisfied.' He handed the X-ray back to the examiner, ignoring Nykyshyn's questioning gaze. 'When can we take possession of the body?'

Belarusian Embassy, Kyiv, Ukraine

'Someone has spent much time trying to make us believe that the body in the mortuary is Director Sukhoi.' Voloshin, at the Belarusian Embassy, was on a secure line to the man whose real name only he knew.

Gurov's eyes squinted as he looked at the Moscow River, the midday sun reflecting harshly off the surface. 'What are you saying to me?'

'I am saying that the body in the mortuary is not Director Sukhoi.'

'You have failed.' It wasn't a question but a statement of fact; however, the anger Gurov felt didn't show. He was a professional.

Voloshin retorted, 'I emptied an entire clip into the old man. I saw him fall.'

'Kevlar.' Another statement.

'That would be an explanation.'

A barge passed beneath the balcony: grey, ugly, powerful. 'You are to find Sukhoi and terminate him on sight.'

'Understood. What of the tapes?'

Gurov followed the ship as it disappeared round the bend in the river. 'Without him there is no proof that what is on the tapes is authentic. Any child can digitally record.'

'Understood.'

'Do not contact me directly again, Konstantin Andreyevich. Go through Sverov. I will find you if I need to.'

'Understood.' But the connection had already been broken.

Voloshin looked at the photograph he had taken of Dudka at the press conference. The meeting had been with this SBU officer. It was this man who had shot at him and this man who he was certain had tried to deceive him.

Presidential Administration, Kyiv, Ukraine

Ambassador Nykyshyn had been outraged when Kostyan, the Belarusian KGB investigator, had told him of the Ukrainian deception. In his view the Ukrainian authorities had obstructed justice, and now he was going to hold nothing back in making his views clear to their President. However, the problem was that he wasn't 'available' for an audience; this time he was en route to the city of Donetsk. Nykshyn felt his anger rise. How dare he be palmed off to an underling? As the representative of the President of Belarus he took this as a personal insult.

The meeting had been arranged hastily. The office of the Belarusian Embassy had called the office of the President of Ukraine, requesting a meeting regarding the assassination of Director Sukhoi. The President's chief of staff, Olexandr Chashkovsky, was again to meet the ambassador on the President's behalf. This time he had thought it wise to have Director Zlotnik of the SBU at his side to allay any fears the Belarusian party might have. Nykyshyn had brought Kostyan.

The four men stood uneasily in the ornate conference room. Chashkovsky was perturbed by the expression on the ambassador's face.

'I am sorry again, gentlemen, that the President could not meet you personally.'

Nykyshyn said nothing, his face grave. Chashkovsky continued, 'Let me introduce you to Director Zlotnik of the SBU. He will be able to answer any questions you have.'

Zlotnik shook hands with the ambassador. 'Ambassador Nykyshyn.'

Nykyshyn nodded. 'This is Investigator Kostyan of the KGB.'

Kostyan extended his hand. 'Director.'

'Investigator.' Zlotnik noticed the grip was military firm.

'Gentlemen, shall we?' Chashkovsky indicated that they should sit. 'What is it that we can do for you, Ambassador?'

'Do, Olexandr Ruslanovich? You can explain why the body of Director Sukhoi has been substituted for that of another.' He pushed a file across the table containing the hideous photographs, which, if he saw them again, would surely induce more vomiting.

'Substituted?' Zlotnik's back went rigid. 'I don't understand what you mean?'

Chashkovsky opened the file, a look of revulsion appearing on his face. Zlotnik grabbed the file and took in the contents.

'The cadaver you have shown us in the mortuary is not the body of Director Sukhoi, late of the KGB.' Nykyshyn stared in turn at each man.

Zlotnik furrowed his brow. 'Did the mortuary show you the wrong body, did they make a mistake? If that is the case, let me apologise.'

'No, Director. The body they showed us was made to resemble that of Director Sukhoi. But it was not him.' Kostyan fixed the SBU man in the eyes.

Zlotnik looked down, compared the faces, then the notes which had been added. 'The dental records are the same…'

Kostyan cut him off. 'The dental records have been made to look the same. However, while very convincing to a generalist, I can assure you that an expert would show you where changes have been made very recently to the enamel.'

'But DNA tests would prove the identity.' Zlotnik looked up.

Nykyshyn's finger pointed at Chashkovsky. 'Which I insist, on behalf of the President of Belarus, are immediately carried out.'

'Of course, Ambassador. But I still can't quite believe what you are saying.'

'Director.' Kostyan's tone changed. 'I believe that parties unknown have tried to hinder my investigation.'

'But Investigator, you have just arrived to file a report on the assassination, which I believe is protocol for the Belarusian KGB?' Zlotnik was puzzled.

Kostyan shook his head slowly. 'That was not what brought me to Ukraine, Director. My orders come directly from the President. What I am about to share with you is highly classified.' Kostyan retrieved a file from his case and gave a stapled set of papers to both Ukrainians. 'We have been investigating Director Sukhoi for some time as we believe he is attempting to sell government information to the highest bidder. The information would directly jeopardise the national security of Belarus and, as such, set off a domino effect into Ukraine and Russia. I use the present tense as I believe he is still alive.'

Zlotnik, although reading the papers, was listening intently. 'Please go on.'

'A month ago we arrested four former military officers on suspicion of treason. We had reason to believe they were spying for Poland. We know that Polish intelligence is eager to obtain information on the Russian anti-missile defence systems in Belarus, especially the long-range S-300 air-defence missiles. When questioned, the suspects gave us vital information about other serving personnel. This included a high-ranking Russian military officer, who was detained in Russia and has now confessed to the Federal Security Service. It is evidence from this officer that, I am sad to say, led us directly to Director Sukhoi of the Belarusian KGB.'

Zlotnik was now looking into the dark eyes of the investigator. 'That, if proved, would be a very serious situation. What evidence is there?'

'Director, I am sure you understand that I am not at liberty to discuss certain details of the investigation. However, the evidence is damning. The KGB officer who was despatched to bring Sukhoi in for questioning was found dead. He had been shot in the back of the head. Sukhoi's own daughter, who had been informed of the situation, went missing and was later found strangled. We believe that Sukhoi or his associates were responsible for these shocking acts. Director Zlotnik, Sukhoi was last seen alive with Director Dudka of the SBU. I believe that Dudka has been complicit in this substitution.'

Chashkovsky sat slack-jawed, eyes unfocused.

Zlotnik's nostrils flared. 'Director Dudka is the most experienced senior officer in the entire Ukrainian Security Service. Yet you say to me that you believe him to be involved?'

'He and Sukhoi are lifelong friends. I believe that Dudka is involved. Yes.'

'He must be questioned.' Chashkovsky had found his voice. 'Where is he now?'

'I believe he is recovering from the head injury he received during the assassination... attempted assassination.' Zlotnik's own head was spinning.

'I know that I have no jurisdiction here, but if I may make a suggestion? I would not contact Director Dudka. Why? If he is, and at this present time we have no reason to believe otherwise, a loyal friend helping another, we must not do anything that could tip Sukhoi or his associates off, thus endangering him. If he is guilty and on the inside, we must not tip *him* off. We must locate him and take him into custody in a covert manner.'

Chashkovsky had gone very pale; this was not the meeting he had ever imagined, even in his nightmares. He had met Dudka on many occasions when he had scheduled his 'quiet' meetings with the President. He liked Dudka; the thought that he was a traitor or helping one was too much for him to countenance. Zlotnik also wrestled with the idea that Dudka could somehow be implicated. He didn't agree with Dudka's views or politics but, although he would never verbalise it, had a grudging professional respect for the veteran. Yet in the past there had been the fiasco with Dudka's direct report – Budanov. What if Dudka had known about his actions all along? What if Dudka had been part of it? Selling secrets? Dudka was anti-Moscow and information about Russia's answer to the European missile defences wouldn't be that hard for him to obtain. Now Zlotnik thought about it, Kostyan's claims seemed more credible.

'We will have to pass this information to the President for his consideration before any action can take place.' Chashkovsky tried to keep his voice calm.

'No,' Zlotnik overruled. 'Investigator Kostyan, you will have my full support. You and I must now go to my headquarters and formulate a plan.'

Trying to regain some control of the meeting, Ambassador Nykyshyn stood. 'As the direct representative of the President of Belarus, I expect to be informed immediately of any developments. Gentlemen.' He took a step towards the door then turned, having a second thought. 'Investigator Kostyan, you should accompany Director Zlotnik.'

SBU Headquarters, Volodymyrska Street, Kyiv
'Where is Dudka?' Zlotnik's tone of voice was, as ever, accusative.

'I… I am sorry, Director, but I do not know.'

Zlotnik looked down at Dudka's long-serving secretary. She, like her boss, was dressed in the Soviet Union's finest. 'When did you last speak to him?'

'This morning, Director, when he had finished with the press conference. He said he was not feeling at all well and that he was going to have his head looked at.'

'Well, it sounds to me like he should have his head looked at.'

'I'm sorry, Director?' Dudka's secretary was puzzled.

'Nothing. Did he mention if he was going to return to the office or if he was going home?'

'He didn't say. Would you like me to call him for you?'

'No. No, thank you. I shall do that myself.'

Zlotnik walked towards his own office. Investigator Kostyan, who had been hovering behind him, listening, fell into step.

'And if he is not at home? Is there somewhere else he might be, perhaps with a relative or friend?'

'Dudka has no friends and his family, what there is of it, lives in Cyprus. Do come in.'

They entered his corner office, which was on the opposite side of the building to Dudka's. Zlotnik pressed a button on his desk phone and Dudka's mobile rang briefly before going to answerphone.

'Dudka, it is Zlotnik here. I need you to come to the office. Call me when you get this message.' He pressed end then looked up at the Belarusian. 'You have me worried, Investigator, and I am not too proud to say it. If Deputy Director Dudka is involved in this, you have my word he will be prosecuted.'

'That is good to hear.'

'However, my hope is that he is not. I need not say what a disgrace it would be to my country and my service.'

'As Sukhoi is to mine?'

Zlotnik spoke quickly. 'I didn't mean to imply that Director Sukhoi was a disgrace to your...'

'It is all right, Director. I am not offended. It is my job to investigate, to root out the rot in order for new wood to grow.' Kostyan's own organic metaphor gave him an idea. 'Does the Deputy Director have a *dacha*?'

'I imagine so.'

'Do you know where?'

116

Chapter 6

British Embassy, Kyiv

Vitaly Blazhevich stood in the foyer and again stared at the painting of a cricket match. Even after several explanations it still made no sense. Perhaps when he was next in England he would go and see a game to finally try to understand.

Soft footsteps sounded behind him.

'Vitaly. What can I do for you?' Alistair Vickers, SIS station chief in Ukraine, extended his hand.

'Alistair. I have a request.'

'Walk this way.'

Vickers headed back up the corridor to his office. Since working closely together two years before, the intelligence officers had continued to liaise. Vickers shut the door as Blazhevich sat.

'Go ahead.'

'I have a defector for you.' Blazhevich wasted no time

Vickers blinked. 'Defector?'

'Director Sukhoi, of the Belarusian KGB.'

Vickers leant forward in his chair. 'I know who he is, but he's dead.'

'Yes.'

While Vickers listened, Blazhevich related the events, as Sukhoi had described them, that had led to the murder of Sukhoi's daughter and the attempted assassination. Blazhevich didn't say, however, where the KGB Director was hidden or what exactly was on the smuggled recording. There was a silence as Blazhevich finished and Vickers digested the information.

'He's seeking to claim asylum in the UK?' Vickers wanted to be certain he had understood his fellow intelligence officer correctly.

Blazhevich nodded. 'Yes.'

SIS Headquarters, Vauxhall Cross, London, UK
'Hello "C".'

'Take a seat, Jack.'

Patchem sat in front of his boss, the Director General of the Secret Intelligence Service, Abigail Knight. Knight was the first female head of the SIS. She had risen through the service fighting for each promotion, offending many in the process but earning a reputation for being tenacious, to say the least. Knight had held the post for barely two years and was part of a reshuffle after the SIS had been criticised in a classified enquiry. The criticism wasn't warranted but had given Knight an opportunity she hadn't been too noble to accept.

The SIS somewhat lagged behind their sister organisation, HM Intelligence Service, who had appointed their first female Director General, Stella Rimington, in 1992. Knight's appointment hadn't been a PC move but it *had* been political in the sense that a new 'direction' was needed. Jack Patchem, a longtime friend and fellow case officer while she was in the ranks, was an important staff member now she was the boss. Behind closed doors they had kept their informality, and behind their informality was a close friendship.

'So, tell me what you have?'

Patchem folded his arms. 'I have a possible defector for you.'

Knight tried not to show her surprise. 'From where?'

'Belarus.'

Knight frowned. She had, of course, seen the reports from GCHQ that a senior Belarusian intelligence member had been assassinated in Ukraine. 'Who?'

Patchem smiled like a schoolboy with a secret. 'Leonid Grigoryevich Sukhoi'

Knight shook her head slowly; getting information out of Jack was sometimes like pulling teeth, she imagined. 'So he's not dead. The assassination attempt, was that real or staged?'

'It was real all right. He was lucky enough to be wearing a bulletproof vest concealed beneath his suit jacket.'

'So he was expecting to be assassinated?'

'Sukhoi had arranged a meeting with an old colleague, Director Dudka of the Ukrainian SBU. The attempted assassination happened as they left a restaurant.'

'Who else knows Sukhoi is alive?'

'You, me, our station chief in Kyiv, and Director Dudka's man. Certainly not the Belarusians.'

Knight drummed her fingers. Defections hadn't been common since the demise of communism, especially in the intelligence community. Most tended to be disaffected businessmen with dirty secrets, seeking sanctuary from Russian prosecution. Sukhoi could potentially be a prized asset.

'Why the defection?'

'Sukhoi has some very high-level intelligence that something major is planned, an international act of aggression.'

Knight leant forward, shocked. 'Sovereign aggression?'

'He will not tell us, until he is in our protection.'

'What do you think it could be?' Knight hated not knowing answers.

'My best guess, and that's all it is at the moment, is that it may well be something to do with Russia's reaction to the new European missile defence plan. Or perhaps, another push at Georgia via South Ossetia? But our officer at the Tbilisi embassy has heard nothing.'

Knight nodded. Belarus was the last European stronghold of old-style communism and anything they could learn about it was welcomed. She pondered for a moment. Diplomatic and trade relations with the Minsk government were all but non-existent so granting political asylum to Sukhoi wouldn't upset either her boss, the Foreign Secretary, or, perhaps more importantly, the Americans. 'Where is Sukhoi now?'

'I believe he's in a safe house somewhere near the capital. I'll send you all I have via email.'

'OK. I'll read it, speak to the Foreign Secretary, and then give you the yay or nay.'

Patchem stood. 'I'll be in my office.'

'I know.'

Patchem left the room and shut the door. Returning to his own office on a lower floor he called Kyiv.

'Vickers.'

'Alistair. I've just spoken to the Guvnor. We should have an answer by the end of play. Is our friend still safe?' The line was encrypted but Patchem didn't want to risk using any names.

'Yes.'

'Very well. I'll call later.' He replaced the receiver.

In Kyiv, Vickers sipped his Earl Grey. The exciting stuff was about to happen again. He held up the plate of custard creams. Blazhevich shook his head; he didn't like biscuits.

'We should have an answer for you later today. I'll send you a text as soon as I have anything more. Be prepared to move quickly.'

'That is good.' Blazhevich finished his own tea. 'I shall return to Director Dudka.'

Orane, Kyiv Oblast, Ukraine
Dudka answered the call. 'Tak?'

Blazhevich spoke into his headset. 'I'll be with you in a minute, Uncle.'

'Was all well with your mother?' Dudka replied, using the safe question they had practised.

'Yes. She is happy to help.'

The Passat was now visible from the inside of the *dacha*. Dudka stepped behind the window frame and peered at the approaching car. He noted that there was indeed only one occupant: Blazhevich.

'The boy is back.'

'Good. Good boy,' Sukhoi replied.

Dudka moved to the door and drew his weapon as Blazhevich walked from the car. Their eyes met and the younger man noted the weapon with some alarm.

'I am alone and I was not followed.'

Dudka beckoned him inside and placed the pistol back on the table. 'I had to be certain.'

Sukhoi was sitting by the fire, wrapped in a blanket. He looked up at Blazhevich expectantly and gestured to the second chair. Blazhevich looked at Dudka, who nodded.

'I have spoken to the British and explained the situation...'

'Get to the point,' Dudka cut in.

Sukhoi frowned. 'Continue.'

'They are to speak with London and advise me, but we must be prepared to move quickly.'

'Were they interested? Will they grant asylum?' Dudka's impatience was again greater than his friend's.

'Vickers was very eager. Yes.'

'*Dobrey*. We are packed.' Dudka pulled up a wooden chair and, without being prompted, Blazhevich gave up the more comfortable armchair.

'I never thought that I'd become a traitor,' Sukhoi grunted. 'But if I had stayed in Minsk, a traitor I would have become.'

'The only traitors are those in Minsk, Leonya – traitors to the people of Belarus.' Dudka folded his arms in an attempt to keep himself still. 'How is Vickers to contact you?'

'Text message. A simple yes or no and a time.'

'Time?' Dudka pushed.

'He will send us a time to meet him at the embassy.' Vickers and Blazhevich had used such methods before but never for anything so important.

The *dacha* was silent as all three men thought about what might happen next. There were several options for getting a defector out of the country. Commercial carrier – in this case British Airways – private jet, or border crossing by diplomatic car. The contents of the car would not be searched as it had the peculiar status of sovereign territory. In the past ships had also been used. Dudka stood and paced the room.

'Shall I make tea, Gennady Stepanovich?'

'Yes.'

Arizona Bar and Grill, Naberezhno Khreschatyska, Kyiv

The traffic was heavy along the riverside as Investigator Kostyan surveyed the scene of the attempted assassination on Sukhoi. He had already quizzed the staff at the restaurant. The waitress, young and large-breasted, had remembered the two old men. They had been happy to see each other and had not eaten much before leaving. When asked if she had heard what they were discussing, she said she had not. Music had been playing and she had been talking to the chef. Did she see either man pass a package to the other? Again the answer was no, she had not. Kostyan himself ordered an American-style burger, which he finished before leaving.

He crouched and surveyed the ground. There were some strike marks from the rounds on the kerb but otherwise nothing else to indicate that anything untoward had happened there. The guard who had been on duty was off, so couldn't be quizzed. The sound of the Belarusian national anthem started to waft from his pocket. It was a silly thing but amused him. Kostyan retrieved his Nokia. Only two men had the number and the second was calling him.

'Kostyan.'

'Investigator Kostyan? This is Director Zlotnik.'

'Director. What news do you have for me? Have you found Dudka?'

'Not quite, but he does have a *dacha*.'

'Where?' Kostyan listened intently.

'It is north of Kyiv, somewhere near Orane. We are to send a Berkut team there to apprehend him.' Zlotnik omitted to add that they didn't know exactly where it was.

'That is good news, Director. Can you please advise me as soon as he is in custody? With your consent, I should very much like to question him.'

Zlotnik, egg on face, couldn't, of course, withhold consent of any type. 'I will let you know the minute he is here.'

Orane, Kyiv Oblast

A shrill electronic tone sounded in the darkened *dacha*. Dudka rose from his bed and made for the landing. Blazhevich was standing at the balcony, keeping an eye on the path leading to the summerhouse.

'What does it say?'

Blazhevich's face was illuminated by the green glow of the screen. 'Yes. 5 a.m.'

Dudka grabbed the phone and peered at the screen to double-check. 'We have about six hours then. Get some sleep. I'll wake us all at four.'

'But Gennady Stepanovich, surely you need sleep more than I?'

Dudka handed back the phone. 'Vitaly, all the beauty sleep in the world will not help me at my age with this old face. You, however, can improve and, furthermore, must be sharp as you will be driving. Now go and lie down, that's an order.'

'Yes, Gennady Stepanovich. Good night.'

'I hope it will be, Vitaly Romanovich.'

Dudka waited until Blazhevich had entered the second bedroom before he leant against the wooden railings and let out a large breath. His heart had started to pound in his chest. Before the text message none of this had been real, but now it was going to happen. He was going to help a defector. Tomorrow would be long and dangerous. First, hand Sukhoi over to the British, and then, once he was safely away, deliver his news to the President. He had turned his own phone off. There had been three missed calls and three messages left on his voicemail. The first was from his secretary. She had left a message that Zlotnik had been asking her strange questions about him. The second had been from Zlotnik himself, asking him to return to the office, and the third had been his beloved granddaughter, Katya, asking when he was coming to Cyprus to see them.

Dudka understood the concept that the signal from a mobile telephone could be used as a tracking device, even when turned off. This was why he had removed the battery after Blazhevich had returned. Questions would be asked of him, of course; he had, after all, ordered dentistry on an unclaimed corpse. He smiled despite himself. Given time, he was certain that the President – he would ignore Zlotnik – would thank him. The cool night air hit his face and carried with it the scent of the orchard. Yes, he hoped all would be peachy in the garden.

*

The sky was a dark blue in places where the sun had tried to banish night but not yet succeeded. Blazhevich wiped the dew from the wing mirrors and the windows of the Passat; he would be driving for the first two kilometres without lights, using NVG goggles, and wanted to maximise his vision. Once they were on the highway lights had to be used; otherwise they risked colliding with a trucker. The bags were packed and he now waited for the two elderly men to hobble out of the *dacha*. Dudka moved well enough but Sukhoi was still troubled by both his head and ribs.

There was a sudden noise in the woods. Dudka pushed Sukhoi the remaining distance into the car and drew his pistol. Blazhevich had already drawn his and adopted a firing position, partly shielded by the front tyre. More noise now, the sound of birds being scared from their roosts. A sudden crashing. Blazhevich had sighted his SBU-issue Glock on the point where the noise came from when a wild deer leapt out of the forest and onto the road. It paused momentarily to take in the three men before bouncing off and into the darkness. Blazhevich let out an audible sigh of relief. Dudka stood.

'Why did you not shoot? He would have made a substantial lunch!'

Dudka's humour was as dry as ever, and Blazhevich's reply feigned ignorance. 'Sorry, Gennady Stepanovich. I was not ready.'

Unseen in the darkness, Dudka smiled the smallest of smiles; he appreciated Blazhevich for appreciating his jokes. 'Vitaly, once you have driven us to the British Embassy you must leave. I do not want to expose you to a potentially career-damaging situation. You are to say that you were acting upon orders and nothing more.'

'Gennady Stepanovich, I will not leave until I know that the two of you are safe. My career and any potential damage to it is not the most important aspect here.'

'Vitaly, do as you are told.' Dudka's voice was overtly firm.

'I hope the meter has not started?' Sukhoi's voice came from inside the car, 'I'm not paying a kopek more than ten roubles.'

Blazhevich shook his head and got into the driver's seat. When both he and Dudka were seated he started the engine, placed the heavy night-vision goggles over his head, and turned them on. The two-litre Passat was alarmingly loud in the pre-dawn but they had no other option. Blazhevich carefully edged the car off the *dacha*'s concrete parking space, past the fence, and into the

125

narrow lane. He kept the speed low and lifted his foot from the accelerator to coast on the downhill parts, all the while his eyes straining to make sense of the green-black world outside.

There was a distant rumble of tyres on the dirt track, then a shape emerged through the trees and turned towards the highway. In the green world of Voloshin's own night scope he identified the vehicle to be the pool car of Officer Blazhevich. He would strike immediately the Passat joined the highway. He had his orders regardless of the Ukrainians, who wanted the two old men alive. Voloshin floored the accelerator of the Lada Niva. The engine took a huge breath before launching the 4x4 off the grass and onto the road. The tyres bit into the tarmac and the Lada shot forward. Voloshin's plan was to ram the target vehicle and then terminate Sukhoi.

Headlights exploded behind Blazhevich, dazzling him. He saw a vehicle in his rear-view mirror accelerating towards him from the opposite side of the road. He pushed his right foot to the floor and felt a surge of power from the VW's engine. The Niva slewed behind him, just missing the boot. Blazhevich kept his foot firmly planted as the Passat accelerated, but the Niva, although a slower machine, had had a slight head start and swung back, slamming into the rear offside passenger door.

Glass smashed as the heavy Soviet 4x4 made contact with the sleek German saloon. Sukhoi was thrown to the opposite side of the cabin and cried out in pain as his belt dug into his broken ribs. In the front Dudka's head was jerked into the door. The tyres squealed loudly as the car was momentarily pushed sideways. Blazhevich struggled to keep control as the Passat headed towards the ditch. However, the tyres regained their grip and the Passat again started to accelerate.

The rear windscreen exploded as a round tore its way through. Blazhevich ducked and Dudka scrambled for his handgun; twisting in his seat, he shot back into the darkness blindly. Sukhoi remained down, holding his ribs. More rounds in return pinged off the Passat's bodywork. There was a junction on the right and, like a giant ship at sea, a fuel tanker swung slowly onto the highway. With the lights still switched off it didn't see the Passat. Blazhevich jinked left and narrowly avoided the cabin. He tried to control his breathing.

More rounds cracked against the Passat until they finally pulled out of range of the much slower vehicle.

'Leonya, are you injured?'

Sukhoi sat up. 'My ribs are hurting but I'll survive. What about you?'

Dudka felt his forehead. His wound had opened up again and blood had started to trickle into his eyebrows. 'Bloodied but not beaten.'

'I'm OK too,' Blazhevich added, concentrating on the road ahead.

'I would expect nothing less, Vitaly.' Dudka patted him on the shoulder.

They drove on in silence for several more kilometres, each alone in their own thoughts. Sukhoi had brought his dear friend into this business and now he, too, was being targeted. Dudka's own mind was trying to work out how the assassin had known where they were.

A warning light flicked on. 'No!' Blazhevich banged the dashboard. 'We have a puncture.'

'Can it be fixed?' Sukhoi was anxious.

'Maybe, but we can't stop.' Blazhevich's mind sought a solution.

'We'll take another car.' Dudka spoke matter-of-factly. He looked ahead. 'The Kyiv checkpoint is no more than four kilometres down the road. Find a Militia vehicle there and I'll commandeer it.'

'Simple,' Sukhoi added.

With the steering getting progressively heavier and unresponsive, they continued on until the checkpoint came into sight. A hangover from Soviet times, the Militia checkpoints served several purposes. They ensured that all heavy goods vehicles did not exceed their stated weight, served as visible 'speed-enforcement cameras', and had on occasion been used to extract bribes to subsidise the under- or non-paid Militia officers. They were, however, also used to prevent 'the wanted' from either entering or leaving the capital by road.

As they neared the raised barrier the tyre finally gave out and parted from the rim. The Passat lurched sideways and sparks flew from the wheel, flaming brightly in the still pre-dawn. The barrier went down and a young officer jumped out of the control booth holding up his hands. Blazhevich steered the Passat as best he could to the grass verge, the car lurching and trying to dig into the soft earth.

Dudka exited the car and straightened up, speaking before the militiaman could say a word. 'What's your name, officer?'

The militiaman gulped, taken aback. 'Plishko, Yuri.'

'Well, Plishko, Yuri. I am Dudka, Gennady, Director of the SBU.' Dudka held up his ID. 'Are you in charge here?'

'I am... not.' He indicated towards the booth. 'Officer Svinarchuk is but he is...'

'Asleep on duty?' Dudka shook his head disapprovingly. 'Officer Plishko. I am commandeering your vehicle. We are working on a matter of national security and our vehicle is damaged.'

'But you can't...'

'Officer Plishko, as you can see from the registration plate, the car is an SBU vehicle, I am an SBU Director, and the men in the car are SBU officers. Now hand over the keys. I will take full responsibility for this.'

Plishko frowned but did not argue. 'Follow me, Director.'

The two men walked towards the control booth. Dudka followed the young militiaman inside and was greeted by the smell of onions. Officer Svinarchuk was sprawled facedown over the desk, snoring drunkenly. Plishko reached for a hook and handed the keys to Dudka sheepishly. Dudka nodded and they exited the booth.

'I will need a receipt for those,' Plishko gushed.

Dudka spoke without looking back. 'I am always on the lookout for those with SBU potential, Officer Plishko, and unlike your colleague, I believe you may have it.' He reached the boxy blue and white Militia Lada and opened the door. 'Here is my card. Be sure to have your superiors ask for me personally.'

Dudka stood straight and saluted, something he hadn't done for a very long time. Plishko snapped to attention. Dudka started the car and drove it closer to the Passat. Blazhevich helped Sukhoi into the backseat before transferring the bags from the boot.

Dudka looked again at the bewildered militiaman. 'You have done an important thing today, officer. You have helped maintain the integrity of Ukraine.'

With Dudka now in the driving seat, they continued on towards central Kyiv and the British Embassy as all the while the sky around them was changing colour. Reaching Kyiv's old town – Podil – Dudka drove the underpowered Lada, illegally, lights flashing, up the very steep and heavily cobbled Andrivskyi Uzviz then took the first left onto Desyatynna Street, the home of the British Embassy. Outside there was another Militia booth, and the battered Land Rover Defender that belonged to Vickers, with its telltale red diplomatic number plates.

The militiaman got out of the booth and regarded the Lada suspiciously. The front door of the embassy opened and Alistair Vickers stepped onto the pavement. He held his hand up to the guard and spoke in Russian.

'They are with me.'

The militiaman shrugged and disappeared back into the booth.

Blazhevich looked warily both ways before getting out of the car.

Vickers held out his hand; Blazhevich shook it swiftly. 'Let's get them inside.'

With nods but not words, Dudka and Sukhoi were let into the embassy. Blazhevich led them to Vickers's office while Vickers himself shut the door behind them.

'Welcome to the United Kingdom, Director Sukhoi.'

'Thank you for your support, Mr Vickers,' Sukhoi replied, shaking the Englishman's hand.

'It is good to see you again, Director Dudka.' Vickers now shook hands with Dudka.

'You too, Alistair. I hear you are still speaking Russian.' Not yet Ukrainian, he didn't need to add.

Vickers didn't get the jibe. 'I am always trying to perfect it, Director Dudka.' Vickers's eyes moved to the blood smear on the old man's forehead. 'Please sit, you must all be tired.' Tea and croissants had been set on the meeting table. 'Director Sukhoi, on behalf of the government of the United Kingdom I would like to offer you political asylum. Do you accept?' It was a formality but Vickers had to ask.

Sukhoi cleared his throat before taking a sip of hot tea. 'Yes.' His voice was small and tense. 'The information I have is very important, more so than my life; indeed, my country has tried to prevent me from divulging it to anyone.' Sukhoi drank more tea. 'I must get this information to the UK safely.'

Vickers nodded. 'Director Sukhoi, you are perfectly safe here in the embassy. You will stay here until this afternoon when we shall take you in a diplomatic car to Boryspil Airport where you will board the British Airways flight to London. At no time will anyone be able to stop you. On arrival you will be taken to a safehouse and debriefed.' After this it would be a new identity and a house in a quiet location somewhere in England's South East, but Vickers didn't need to explain further.

Dudka looked at Sukhoi. What thoughts must now be running through his head? His friend of over fifty years. They had been young officers together, middle-aged family men together, and now old men, who had together betrayed their countries. For the first time since he'd met Sukhoi in the restaurant, Dudka thought of his own career and the consequences of his actions. He had deliberately lied to his Director, and by extension the President, about Sukhoi's death. He'd misinformed Belarus about the loss of a senior intelligence agent and now would take full responsibility for his defection.

Once Belarus found out about his role, relations between the two former Soviet republics would sour even more. Wars had been started for less. But friendship came first, before loyalty to one's country. A very uncommunist belief, yet one that, unintentionally, the Soviet Union had fostered by throwing together millions of servicemen from an amalgamation of autonomous and semi-autonomous republics. Sukhoi and his daughter had been family to him and Dudka wasn't about to let anyone or anything simply attack his family and walk away.

The realisation that his career was over and potentially his own life endangered didn't scare him. He had lived a charmed life, produced a beautiful daughter, and become a grandfather. He could ask for no more. He now had but two goals. Vitaly Blazhevich must not lose his career and his goddaughter's murderer must be found.

'Mr Vickers. I cannot thank you enough for your assistance.' Dudka stood and extended his hand.

Vickers rose and shook once again.

Dudka looked at his oldest friend. 'Leonya, I feel that this is goodbye.'

Sukhoi, eyes moist, replied, 'Perhaps, old friend, perhaps.'

There was the briefest of embarrassed pauses before the two old soldiers embraced. Dudka nodded and snapped his fingers.

'Vitaly, it is time we went.'

Dudka left the room without another word. A minute later he and Blazhevich were on the empty pavement in the early morning light. Dudka took a deep breath and turned right.

'So what now?' Blazhevich was a step behind.

'We're going to work.' The SBU Headquarters on Volodymska Street were a brisk five-minute walk away. 'I'm going to report the attack.'

'But what of Director Sukhoi?'

'Vitaly, in your desk you will find official orders, with the presidential signature forged by myself, stating that you are to provide a protective detail for Director Sukhoi. Once the forgery has been discovered I will admit to "misappropriating resources" and acting without remit. You will not be implicated, I will be finished, and dear old Leonya will be in Britain.'

They crossed Sofiyivska Square as the sun started to hit the golden domes of the cathedral behind them, then passed the central Militia headquarters.

'But Gennady Stepanovich, I cannot accept that. You have done what is right for Ukraine and the world!'

Dudka stopped and paused, a grandfatherly smile on his face.

'What is right for the world, Vitaly, may not be right for Director Zlotnik.'

SBU Headquarters, Volodymska Street, Kyiv

Yuri Zlotnik was far from happy. Dudka had arrived at the office, where he calmly sat at his desk opening the previous day's post and drinking black tea. Furthermore, he had point-blank refused to talk about Sukhoi. Zlotnik had resorted to putting him into a holding cell, where, to his dismay, Dudka slept for three hours. Now Zlotnik stared across his desk at Deputy Director Dudka while trying to control his breathing.

'You have been the subject of a nationwide manhunt!' He let the words hang in the air; Dudka, to his amazement, looked nonplussed. 'Furthermore, you have perverted the course of justice!'

'I was conducting an undercover operation.' Dudka's eyes showed no sign of fear or intimidation.

'On whose orders?' Zlotnik's nostrils flared.

'Mine. I am in charge of my own department.'

Zlotnik slammed his fist on his desk in frustration. 'Where are the mission briefing notes?'

'Under lock and key.'

'Where exactly?' Zlotnik pressed both palms flat against his desk in an effort to regain his calm.

'My office.'

Zlotnik stabbed himself hard in the chest with his index finger. 'I am to be briefed on all matters that pose a threat to national security. This is something which you failed to do.'

Dudka shrugged. 'I was going to.'

'When?' Zlotnik all but screamed.

'Today, when the operation was over. There is a magpie in our midst, a traitor.'

Zlotnik exploded. 'The traitor is you, Dudka! You have aided and abetted a wanted criminal!'

Dudka leant back in the chair in his boss's office to show his forced apathy. He wasn't impressed by how Zlotnik was handling this, but then Zlotnik was a buffoon.

'Explain.'

Zlotnik's anger had rendered him momentarily speechless. He grabbed at a glass of water, spilling a large part over his shirt.

'Explain? Oh, I am going to explain, "Director Dudka". I am going to explain to the President how you kidnapped a foreign intelligence officer and informed his country that he was dead.'

'I also commandeered a police Lada and broke the speed limit.'

This time Zlotnik did shout. 'You listen to me, Dudka. I don't know why you have done this but you are finished! Do you understand me? Finished!'

'I agree.' Dudka nodded calmly.

Zlotnik closed his eyes, exhausted by rage and beaten by his subordinate's insolence. There was a thick silence. Dudka nodded his head thoughtfully. Zlotnik made himself speak. 'Sukhoi is wanted for questioning by our partners, the Belarusian KGB. He is responsible for unspeakable acts of treason. If he is not stopped, these will have a devastating effect on our national security.' Zlotnik let his words trail away. 'Dudka, where have you put him?'

Dudka's eyes drifted to the antique Jungens clock Zlotnik had restored and installed on his wall, the only thing, in Dudka's mind, that showed Zlotnik had any taste or intelligence at all.

'He is no longer in the territory of Ukraine.'

Sipping now from his glass of water, Zlotnik tried to control his breathing. 'Where is Sukhoi?'

The Jungens struck midday; his friend would be on his way. It wouldn't hurt to tell Zlotnik now. 'He is in the United Kingdom.'

Zlotnik's hands balled into fists. 'Explain!'

Dudka did.

Moments later, Zlotnik sat, apoplectic. 'Do you understand what you have done? Do you understand the magnitude of your actions?'

'Oh, yes.' Dudka nodded. He had helped to halt a potential global catastrophe.

Zlotnik, unable to contain his venom any further, shot to his feet. 'You are hereby under arrest for treason and stripped of your rank and office. You will be taken to the holding cells where you will give a statement telling everything.'

Dudka's mind drifted. So, it had happened. He had lost everything. What did he feel? Emptiness, regret, fear, remorse? No. Relief. Relief and calm. He had saved a friend's life and perhaps the lives of thousands. The doors behind him opened and two junior officers, whom he did not know by name, placed him in handcuffs and led him out. He passed Investigator Kostyan waiting in the anteroom. Their eyes met and Dudka smiled broadly. The Belarusian KBG investigator stared back, steel in his eyes.

Zlotnik stood in the doorway and watched Dudka as his disappeared. He felt a sense of doom as he saw Kostyan's questioning look.

'Good afternoon, Investigator Kostyan. I am afraid I have grave news.'

'What?' Kostyan dispensed with pleasantries.

Zlotnik re-entered his room. Sitting behind his desk he at least felt a bit protected from the man who now sat opposite him. 'Director Sukhoi has been granted asylum by the British and will be on a flight to London later today.'

Kostyan's eyes fluttered; he didn't show the anger or indignation Zlotnik had anticipated. 'Where is he now?'

'The British Embassy. He is to be put on the British Airways flight at 14:15. I am afraid that, as he is officially on British sovereign territory, there is nothing further I can do. You must lodge a complaint with the British…'

Kostyan stood. 'I must contact Minsk.'

Zlotnik got to his feet but Kostyan had already started to walk away.

British Embassy, Kyiv

The diplomatic car was ready and awaiting its occupants in the walled courtyard at the side of the embassy. There was the sound of a lavatory flushing; Vickers waited outside the WC for Director Sukhoi to emerge. The Belarusian opened the door, now dressed in a shirt, pullover, cords, and a tweed jacket, courtesy of HM Government. Sukhoi's face was lined, not just with age, but worry. He nodded at Vickers. The two men exited the building and took the three steps to the waiting car. The Jaguar XJ was the ambassador's car and as such the most prestigious vehicle the embassy had. The ambassador himself was not in Kyiv. It was also the only car available at short notice with the exception of Vickers's own tatty Land Rover Defender.

As the compound gates opened Sukhoi sank nervously into the dark-red leather. Looking out through the tinted glass Vickers saw nothing to concern him. The street was relatively empty and the Jag soon turned onto Sofiyivska Square before heading towards Maidan and then the airport.

'It should only take us forty minutes or so, Director. Although he refuses to wear a seatbelt, Oleg is a good driver and, of course, the speed limits don't apply to our diplomatic plates.'

Sukhoi nodded and for the first time spoke in English. 'Thank you again, Mr Vickers, for everything.'

'Not at all.' Vickers replied in the same. 'Leonid Grigoryevich, I must ask you now if you can give me a hint as to what information you have? We, as you can see, have acted in good faith. This would be an act of good faith on your part.'

Without considering the request Sukhoi spoke. 'The Russians want the world to buy their oil. Saudi Arabia is in the way.'

'So what are they planning to do?' Vickers's phone rang before Sukhoi could answer. He had to pick up; it was Blazhevich. 'Vickers.'

'The Belarusians know you've got Sukhoi.'

Vickers froze. He knew Dudka would have to eventually tell the SBU but wished it hadn't been quite so soon. 'Zlotnik told the Belarusians?'

'A Belarusian KGB investigator was at the office when Dudka was led away.'

'Where is Dudka?

'He has been placed in a cell to await further questioning.'

'Thanks, Vitaly.' Vickers ended the call. He met Sukhoi's eyes. The old man had caught the gist of the conversation. 'We will get you there safely. You have my word on that.'

'I do not doubt your word, Mr Vickers, but I fear that my government will stop at nothing to prevent me from leaving Ukraine.'

'Director Sukhoi, this is a diplomatic vehicle, what can they do?'

Wearing a pair of leather driving gloves to prevent any finger-prints, Voloshin waited. His instructions had been succinct: 'Sukhoi must die. Use any available means.' His car was parked at a café overlooking the Boryspil highway, the only road that led directly to the airport and the route the British must take. He had acted fast; this was his last and only chance to complete this part of the mission. If he failed now he failed his country and his unit. Voloshin had never failed before but this old goat had somehow managed to elude him twice! There would be no third time. His car was now up to the task.

Voloshin watched the traffic. Large luxury sedans sped past, shaking the Soviet-era Ladas and Zaporozhets, reminding Voloshin of the giant yachts in Dubai that tossed the old dhows in their wake. Voloshin thought of what he'd do once this was all over, and of the beachside villa in the sun that he'd been promised. He focused again and pushed all thoughts of personal enjoyment or gain from his mind. He would be in Dubai soon enough but it wouldn't be for pleasure. Not yet.

Voloshin again refocused his mind on the passing traffic. He had been given a list by the KGB station chief of the cars kept by the British Embassy. They had to be registered with the Ukrainian Ministry of Internal Affairs so the list was easily obtainable. Of the five cars kept, they would most probably use one of the larger saloons, either the Audi A6 or the Jaguar XJ6. He had so far counted innumerable Audis – one was even diplomatic but carried the wrong country identifier – and an old XJ6. If he missed them here then his only course of action would be to board the plane, for which he had a ticket purchased under his diplomatic identity.

He blinked then checked through a pair of field glasses: the car had had a red plate. And the identifier? Yes, he had spotted the Jaguar, cruising just above the posted speed limit. He started the Mercedes and joined the flow of traffic. He would follow them for a while until he was certain he could attack.

*

Classical music wafted through the Jaguar's innumerable speakers. All was calm. Vickers glanced at Sukhoi, who was staring blankly out of the window. There was a sudden roar and then the car shook violently. Vickers span in his seat. A large black Mercedes was behind them, touching the rear bumper. It accelerated as if to overtake, but caught the rear panel. The Jaguar shuddered again. There was swearing from the driver's seat now as Oleg indicated right and started to pull over to inspect the damage.

'Keep going! Don't stop!' Vickers knew it was no accident.

Oleg looked back. 'But we have had an accident. We must report…'

A window exploded – Vickers didn't know which – and Oleg's head convulsed sideways. The Jag continued to decelerate and arc towards the side of the highway. Sukhoi shrank lower into the seat and held his hands over his face. Vickers lurched into the footwell before clambering over the front seat. Oleg was slumped on the gear stick, his arms in the spoke of the steering wheel. Vickers grabbed the wheel and pulled it left. The car jerked and Oleg's arms became freed. Unbelted, the driver fell out of the seat. Vickers held the wheel. He couldn't get to the pedals but he had to somehow control the car.

The Mercedes hit them again, the Jaguar lurched right, and this time Vickers was thrown forward, temple hitting the steering wheel. Everything seemed to dim and slow momentarily before the Jaguar left the road and bounced over the grass verge towards the trees. Vickers pushed himself back up and got into the driver's seat as two more rounds entered the car. The first hit the central console, shattering the satnav. The second hit Oleg. Branches scraped the side of the car and Vickers prayed these wouldn't set off the airbags and cut the ignition.

Gunning the accelerator, Vickers pulled the wheel right once again right and the Jag bounced up onto the tarmac of the highway. The Merc was no more than three metres behind and once again raced towards them. Just before it hit, Vickers caught a glimpse of flags fluttering on the bonnet and then a masked figure at the wheel. The impact eased the Jag along the highway and he managed to put some space between himself and the Belarusian Diplomatic Vehicle...

The red and green flag of Belarus snapped viciously in the wind. Two diplomatic cars, both with diplomatic immunity, both sovereign territories, involved in a high-speed chase! This kind of thing wasn't meant to happen; there were conventions. It was an act of war! Pushing these thoughts from his mind, Vickers reached for the belt and strapped himself in. Oleg had collapsed into the passenger footwell, his blood coating the leather and colour-matching the carpet.

'You OK?' Vickers shouted back.

'Da.' Sukhoi's voice showed more fear than ever.

'I will get you to that plane.' Foot now firmly planted in the carpet, he concentrated on the road ahead as the large Jaguar engine roared.

Behind them Voloshin, too, was focused. He dropped his Glock. He had an AK74 short barrel in the passenger seat with a full clip of ammo. He changed lanes and followed the British car diagonally, in the blind spot. Taking a second to position himself, he reached for the Kalashnikov and placed it on his lap with the stock resting on his left forearm. He pressed the button so that the electric window lowered and at the same time floored the accelerator.

The Merc drew alongside the Jag and he raised the rifle. The driver stared at him; they were no more than a metre apart. Under the mask, Voloshin pursed his lips and squeezed the trigger. Rounds entered the Jag instantaneously and it swerved. The Merc matched the manoeuvre and again the two were side by side. The driver now had fresh blood on his face. Voloshin didn't care who he was, just that he wasn't dead. The nose of the Jag suddenly dipped, taking Voloshin by surprise, disappearing behind him. The driver had stopped. Oblivious to the blaring horns, Voloshin, too, stopped, slamming the Merc into reverse.

Up ahead, blue flashing lights appeared. The Jag now shot past as the driver again reversed direction. Voloshin cursed and followed suit. A Militia car was in the middle lane, fifty metres ahead. The Jag squeezed past the police vehicle and into the fast lane. Voloshin now passed the same vehicle on the other side. Instantly the Militia vehicle attempted to give chase and momentarily drew up between the two diplomatic cars. The officer's mouth fell open as he realised that both vehicles had red plates; that both were diplomatic.

Voloshin squeezed the trigger and a line of rounds ripped into the police vehicle. The boxy Lada wobbled before falling behind and flipping over. That would stop them from being followed, for the moment.

Vickers was sweating profusely, his heart pounding like never before as he wiped the blood from his eyes. He had been hit – where exactly and by what he didn't know. For all the media and Hollywood hype, SIS were primarily intelligence gatherers, yet here he was under fire! He racked his brain for the defensive driving-course techniques he'd been taught years before. None seemed appropriate; all he could do was try to outrun his attacker.

The sign indicating that the airport turning was a mile ahead flew past. More blue flashing lights appeared in front now as several Militia vehicles pulled onto the highway. What would they do? What could they do, thought Vickers. Both he and the Mercedes had diplomatic immunity!

'The chip is in my phone…' The voice was weak but lucid.

'What?' Vickers looked back.

'If anything should happen to me, the chip with the intelligence is in my phone.'

'Director, we're almost there.'

Sukhoi nodded but was unconvinced. 'Whatever anyone says, Mr Vickers, you must know this: Dudka is no traitor. Myself? Perhaps.'

There was a thud and the shattering of glass. A sudden rush of air filled the car. An object landed on the seat next to Sukhoi. In a split second forty years disappeared as the KGB spymaster grabbed the grenade and, in a fluid motion, hurled it out of the side window. Less than a second later it exploded. The shockwave pushed Sukhoi down and took his breath, Vickers swerved as the Jaguar bucked. Almost at the airport exit they reached the two Militia vehicles. Vickers slowed to match their speed. Eyes wide, the nearest officer, radio in hand, looked into the British car.

Voloshin swore. He had backed off after the first grenade and would now catch up to throw another. He didn't like this one bit. Two Militia vehicles buzzing around the target vehicle and more certain to appear, but his orders couldn't have been clearer: 'Use any means.' He planted his foot squarely on the accelerator pedal and once again rammed the Jaguar. Suddenly he was forced to the right as the Jag turned for the off ramp and the spur that led to the airport. He yanked the wheel left, causing both vehicles to understeer into the grassy central reserve that housed the huge electronic billboard announcing 'Welcome to Kyiv'.

Wheels lost traction in the wet grass and the British car started to spin, coming to a halt facing the Mercedes. Airbags exploding, both ignitions were cut.

Seconds later, Voloshin's eyes flickered open. He shook his head and felt hammers of pain. He kicked open his door, grabbed his rifle, and reacquired the target. The Jaguar's rear door was open and the old man was awake. Blood seeped from his mouth. He tried to move; not to escape, but to sit up. Sukhoi was trying to die with honour. Still dazed, Voloshin's hand tightened around the pistol grip.

'What are you waiting for? Finish me!' the old man was yelling. 'Come on, do it!'

Voloshin's eyes caught movement: the driver. He now trained the rifle on the man. The brown-haired figure fell out of the Jaguar and onto the grass.

There were voices approaching from behind. Voloshin span round. Three Militia officers. Two holding up service pistols, one open-palmed. He had diplomatic immunity but they still wouldn't let him kill. He depressed the trigger and cut them down before they had chance to fire a single shot. Looking back around, he saw that the driver had pulled himself up to his hands and knees. The man looked up. Voloshin could tell he was English: not a driver, not an operative, but a spook. He trained the Kalashnikov once more on Sukhoi and pulled the trigger. Nothing. He dropped the rifle and felt for his sidearm… missing.

Vickers was on his feet and lunged, knocking the former Spetsnaz commando down. Vickers balled his fist and hit the man square in the face, feeling his knuckles bloody. He pulled at the balaclava to reveal the face. Voloshin, dazed, rolled and forced him off; scrabbling away, he pushed himself up again, facing the Englishman. Angrily he ripped off the mask and felt his split lip. The metallic taste of blood filled his mouth. Enraged, he pointed at the diplomat.

'This is not between you and me. Interfere again and I will kill you.'

The fear Vickers had experienced earlier was gone; now all he felt was adrenaline. 'You touch him and I'll kill you.'

Voloshin frowned and launched himself at Vickers. He felt the air get knocked out of the spook as he hit him. They went down, Voloshin on top. This time it was his fist that made contact. Vickers's head snapped sideways and his eyes rolled back. The assassin's hands tightened around Vickers's throat momentarily before he decided to let go.

Voloshin stood and strode towards the Jaguar. Sukhoi was hobbling on the grass. The younger man kicked his legs out from under him, sending his target crashing to the ground. Without remorse, without another word, Voloshin grabbed Sukhoi's head, pulled it back, and snapped his neck.

Chapter 7

Yuri Zlotnik drummed his fingers. Life had dealt him yet another undeserved blow. Not only had he now been forced to recognise that Dudka may well be innocent, but also that he, Director Zlotnik of the Ukrainian SBU, had been used in a plot to murder a fellow intelligence officer. He looked up from the photographic composite. 'Yes, this is Investigator Kostyan of the Belarusian KGB.'

The President's chief of staff, Olexandr Chashkovsky, agreed. 'This looks very much like the man we met.'

Vickers nodded. It hurt. His jaw had been dislocated, was badly bruised, and his right eye was almost closed. This was in addition to the flesh wound in his left shoulder. 'So where does this leave us, gentlemen?' He managed to ask.

Zlotnik spoke. 'Cards on the table? This man, Kostyan, told the both of us that Sukhoi was involved in the passing of sensitive information to the Poles about the Russian anti-missile defence systems in Belarus.'

Vickers grimaced then wished he hadn't as his reaction to pain only caused him more. 'What Sukhoi was bringing us wasn't about missiles. It was about an act of international Russian aggression.

My PM wants to brief your President within the hour.' He looked at Chashkovsky. 'Please arrange this.'

'Immediately.' Chashkovsky rose and left the table.

There was a silence. Zlotnik looked at Vickers. If he wanted one hundred per cent proof that Dudka wasn't involved, he couldn't provide it; but he knew deep down that the Deputy Director was not. 'You have a special relationship with Dudka, I believe?'

Vickers nodded, grimaced, spoke. 'Yes.'

Zlotnik reached into his suit pocket. 'One minute, Mr Vickers.' He pressed the speed-dial button on his mobile and was connected to SBU headquarters. 'Release Dudka and send him home.' He ended the call then sighed. 'If you had told me even five years ago that I would be sitting with a representative of MI6 and taking his government's side over that of Belarus, I would have laughed. But things have moved on, the world has changed. I am not going to lie to you, Mr Vickers; personally, I believe that Ukraine's best future hopes do lie with Moscow and not the EU. This aggression you have alluded to would drag Ukraine into a conflict it can ill afford. We are not Belarus; we are not a puppet of the Russians, but a partner. '

'Director Zlotnik, I agree with you on the second point but not the first. Ukraine must eventually join the EU.'

'On that point, then, we agree to differ?'

Chashkovsky re-entered the room. 'The conference call has been arranged. The President is very concerned. Director Zlotnik, he wishes you to remain here in order that you may be briefed directly afterwards.'

Internally Zlotnik fumed, but did not let it show. 'Of course.'

Vickers stood. 'If you gentlemen will excuse me, I must report to my superiors in London.'

10 Downing Street, London, UK
The British Prime Minister, David Daniels, looked up from his

coffee at the four other people in the meeting, a worried man. At the long table in the cabinet room sat Malcolm Wibly, the Home Secretary, and Robert Holmcroft, the Foreign Secretary, accompanied by Ewan Burstow, Head of the Intelligence Service, and Abigail Knight, Director General of the Secret Intelligence Service. What they were to discuss was classified as 'No Eyes', meaning that no record would be taken and no documents would leave the room. It was the highest secrecy level in the United Kingdom.

Daniels pushed a strand of hair away from his forehead, a nervous tick that the satirists readily exploited. 'I've just finished a video conference with the President of Ukraine. What we have discussed is incredibly shocking and, if verified, could be considered an act of war.' He paused to note the reaction from those he had called.

Knight knew the content of the tapes; the others were intrigued, except for Holmcroft, who looked distinctly annoyed.

Daniels coughed. 'Ms Knight, perhaps you could set out the situation more succinctly than I?'

'Very well, Prime Minister. We have come into possession of audio recordings of a conversation between the head of the Belarusian KGB and the special adviser to the Prime Minister of Russia. They set out the basis for an operation by Russia to destabilise the Kingdom of Saudi Arabia with the use of Belarusian agents as a catalyst. Their reason for this course of action is to destabilise the world's oil market in order that they may sell their own, thus taking market share from Saudi Arabia.'

Holmcroft exploded. 'What!'

The PM nodded. 'I'm afraid so, Robert.'

'That is an absurd notion. How on earth would the Russians expect to get away with this?'

'How do they envisage destabilising the Kingdom?' Wibly, who wasn't given to theatrics, asked.

'Through a series of as yet undefined terrorist acts.'

'Which they would have us believe is the work of Al-Qaeda? How are the tapes to be verified, Ms Knight?' Wibly continued.

'The actual audio is currently being analysed by a sound laboratory to test the authenticity of the voices. Coincidentally, the BBC conducted an interview with Ivan Sverov, Director of the Belarusian KGB, earlier this year.'

Holmcroft made no attempt to hide his annoyance. 'What about the authenticity of the actual intelligence? This could be a red herring, a ruse perpetrated at our expense.'

'As to the actual authenticity of the intelligence, Foreign Secretary, Director Sukhoi of the Belarusian KGB – the person responsible for supplying us with the tapes – was assassinated as he tried to leave Ukraine with a British diplomatic escort. If you remember, we granted him political asylum?'

Holmcroft looked abashed. It had been his decision.

'Robert, I stand by it. The man risked his life and lost it in order to expose this danger.' The PM nervously clenched his hands. 'Ms Knight, how long will it take for the laboratory to authenticate the voices on the tape?'

'We should have the result within the next few hours, Prime Minister, as to whether one of the voices is indeed Sverov. The other voice, however, is problematic in that we don't know who it is.'

'Didn't you say the other man was the Special Adviser to the Russian Prime Minister?'

'Yes, Home Secretary, I did, but that is the problem. The position is so "special" that we don't know his identity.'

Wibly scratched his nose. 'Without that, how can we know if Russia is in fact involved?'

'We can't, Malcolm,' Holmcroft snapped.

Burstow, who had watched the territory-marking, now spoke. 'We need to identify the second voice without question. I can talk to our UK assets within the Russian administration and see what they tell me.'

'What they want to tell you, Ewan.'

'Yes, Foreign Secretary – what they want to tell me.'

The PM rubbed his eyes. 'This is getting us nowhere. What we need to do is decide on how we interpret this intelligence and then on what actions we need to take to safeguard the United Kingdom, her allies, and of course Saudi Arabia herself.'

'Prime Minister, it may not be prudent to inform the Saudis until we have full confirmation and some details to give them.'

'Ms Knight, we must inform our strategic allies immediately. That should have been our very first action.' Holmcroft stared at the SIS Director General.

'Foreign Secretary, you know the Saudis far better than I.' She paused both to stroke his ego and to hint that she knew how close he actually was to the Saudi ambassador. 'In my opinion the Saudis would be enraged and launch a purge. This would cause panic and instability in the oil markets and the net result would be the same.'

'But Ms Knight, if we don't inform the Saudi authorities they will be unprepared. Attacks could take place and lives would be lost. We would have blood on our hands.'

'I concede that could possibly happen.'

'What timescale do the tapes set out for this plan?' Burstow again was being logical.

'The recordings were made two weeks ago and mention imminent action.'

'Is there any indication anything has happened yet?'

'No, Foreign Secretary, but GCHQ has picked up increased chatter to and from Islamic fundamentalist websites mentioning Saudi Arabia.'

'But no actual threats?'

'No.'

'Ms Knight, what assets does the SIS have in Saudi Arabia?'

'We have an intelligence officer at the embassy, a field officer at the trade office, and some locally recruited informers, Prime Minister.'

'Ms Knight, I'll await your news from the laboratory. If the voice is that of the Director of the Belarusian KGB I shall call Washington. In the meantime you have my authorisation to send in more SIS officers. We cannot be spread so thinly.'

'Prime Minister, this is not a wise step.' Holmcroft again voiced his doubts.

'Robert, this is the decision I've made. We must use every means at our disposal to learn more about any potential terrorist attacks in the Kingdom. That means men on the ground. As soon as we have any intelligence we shall immediately inform the Saudis.'

SIS Headquarters, Vauxhall Cross, London

The real impact of the intelligence was felt when the laboratory confirmed the voice on the tape to be that of Ivan Sverov. The digital voice print of the BBC recording was a ninety-six per cent match with the smuggled KGB tape. Patchem had been informed by Knight of this and of the request by the PM to get more assets into Saudi Arabia.

As he had protested to Knight when she had given him the caretaker role, the Middle East wasn't his bag. He didn't care for Arabs and had paid them the minimal amount of attention over the years. Of course, he had condemned them for backing the ill-fated war against Israel, but had also understood the great allies they had been in stopping Saddam from holding onto Kuwait and in halting the spread of radical Islam. The resignation of Dominic Maladine, former head of the Arab Desk (officially known as the Middle East section), had come as a surprise. Vauxhall Cross was a workplace like any other and, as such, not immune to the rumour mill. Rumour had it that Maladine, who was a confirmed bachelor, had been fond of cross-dressing and rent boys. Others had said his blunders had been covered up, including a same-sex, honey-trap-style operation conducted by a certain Middle Eastern security service.

Patchem didn't know what to believe, so ignored it all. What was of salient importance for him was to get up to speed. Maladine's swift departure had opened up a can of worms. The staff below Maladine had, as it turned out, run the section while Maladine drifted in and out of the office at will. Maladine appeared to have lost any interest in the service and had been waiting for his retirement. Now Knight was head of the SIS, dead wood had started to be cast aside and a new sense of urgency was present.

After taking the relevant files from the Arab Desk, Patchem returned to his own office, where he had called a teleconference with all intelligence officers based in and around the Kingdom. He could send perhaps two Arab specialists into the field immediately without arousing suspicion from the Saudis. These men had already been booked on the next available BA flight to Riyadh with diplomatic passports. What Patchem now needed was a covert operative.

Patchem looked across the desk at Snow. 'I've got an assignment for you. I need you to go and see Paddy Fox.'

'OK.' That meant a trip to Saudi Arabia, Snow knew that much.

'We now have reason to believe something major is being planned. We can't take it to the Saudis as we don't have a target list, and, from what I've gathered, the Saudi security forces would panic and lock down the entire country at the slightest whiff of trouble, leaving us with next to no chance of gathering intelligence. Aidan, I want to know the feel of the place. I've set up a meeting with an informant in Jeddah. A man I know, who can be trusted. He'll contact you in country. In addition to this, I imagine Fox has seen more than our embassy-based officer. I understand that his employer has facilities in various locations across the Kingdom. This has given him a chance to travel without question.'

'So, what's my cover?'

'I'm afraid it's a fastball. There's a trade mission leaving on Friday; you're to join it. You've got one day to prepare your legend.' Patchem pointed to a folder on the desk. 'Everything you need is in there. There's a man in Richmond expecting you.'

Snow reached for the folder. 'Thanks.'

'One more thing, Aidan; try not to get your pool car clamped again, there's a good chap.' The smile on Patchem's face was mischievous, causing Snow to grin.

Presidential Administration, Kyiv, Ukraine

Dmitro Nykyshyn waited in the room he had been in many times before. The Belarusian ambassador was happy that at last he was going to get an audience with the President of Ukraine. He was still owed an explanation as to the lies the Ukrainian SBU had told him regarding the body of the late Director Sukhoi. He was going to accept the apology in a dignified and professional manner, while leaving no doubt in the President's mind that, as Belarusian ambassador to Ukraine, he must never be misled again! Once again it was the President of Ukraine's chief of staff, Olexandr Chashkovsky, who appeared first and shook his hand.

'I am sorry, Excellency, that the President could not meet you personally.'

Nykyshyn's eyes narrowed. Was this some kind of a joke? 'When can I see the President?'

Chashkovsky sat and gestured for the ambassador do the same. 'That depends on you.'

'What?' Nykyshyn was puzzled.

The door opened and Zlotnik entered carrying a meeting folder. 'Ambassador.'

'Director Zlotnik. Have you come to personally apologise to me?'

Chashkovsky and Zlotnik exchanged glances before the SBU Director spoke. 'Ambassador, last time we met you introduced us both to Investigator Kostyan of the KGB.'

150

The ambassador nodded. 'Correct, and your agency hindered his investigation, in a most unprofessional manner.'

Zlotnik ignored the accusation. 'Where is Investigator Kostyan now?'

'I believe he is in Belarus submitting his report, which will include evidence of your irregular methods. Why do his whereabouts concern you?'

Zlotnik was going to enjoy putting the pompous diplomat in his place. 'The President summoned you here in order for me to inform you that Investigator Kostyan is the official suspect in the murder of Director Sukhoi of the KGB.'

Nykyshyn's mouth fell open; his eyes darted to Chashkovsky and then back to Zlotnik. 'What you are alleging is preposterous. Investigator Kostyan was sent here to investigate the murder of Director Sukhoi!'

'Ambassador, Director Sukhoi was very much alive when Kostyan arrived in Ukraine. We have evidence to suggest that it was Kostyan who murdered him, in addition to two members of the Militia and an employee of the British Embassy.'

Nykyshyn's mouth moved several times before he managed to say again, 'Preposterous!'

Zlotnik opened his folder and handed him a copy of the photofit image. 'This man was identified at the scene by a British diplomat. As you can see, this is Investigator Kostyan.'

Nykyshyn's eyes were glued to the print as he realised, with horror, that it was an almost perfect composite image of the man he knew as Kostyan. He swallowed and attempted to regain his composure. 'This is all you have?'

Chashkovsky now spoke for the first time since Zlotnik had entered. 'The President would be very grateful if you would help us with our enquiries by answering a few questions about Kostyan.'

Nykyshyn could feel his heart beating in his chest and was finding it difficult to breathe. 'I am not at liberty to divulge any information whatsoever about a member of the KGB.'

'This man, Ambassador, is an assassin who has killed both Ukrainian and Belarusian citizens within the territory of Ukraine. You have a moral and legal obligation to assist us in his capture.'

Nykyshyn didn't know what to say, didn't know what to feel. Was he outraged that the accusations had been made or was he outraged that, if true, he had aided an amoral assassin? He had been informed directly by the Director of the KGB to expect the investigator and offer him full support, which he had.

Nykyshyn finally found his voice. 'Any request for support, any allegation, any evidence must be submitted to me and I will then in turn submit it to the Prosecutor General in Minsk.'

'Your Excellency…' In Zlotnik's opinion the formal title was now risible. 'Will you, here, today, answer questions about Kostyan? Yes or no?'

'Director Zlotnik, I have given you my answer. Now, if there is nothing else you wish to discuss, I shall to return to my embassy.'

'In that case, Ambassador, I am afraid that you have left us with little alternative.'

Chashkovsky handed him an envelope bearing the presidential wax seal.

'You are forthwith expelled from the territory of Ukraine. Please leave immediately.'

Nykyshyn stood, face reddening and chest heaving. 'This is an outrage! How dare you issue such an ultimatum! I demand to see the President of Ukraine! I demand to see him now!'

Zlotnik took a step forward and Nykyshyn flinched. 'Would you like me to help you find the exit?'

Nykyshyn shook with rage, again unable to speak. His mind blurred and his heart beat erratically as two members of the presidential security detail entered the room. They stood by the open door.

'Please leave,' Chashkovsky asked in a reasonable tone.

Nykyshyn held up the letter and the photofit. 'You have disgraced yourselves and your country! This is an insult to the President of Belarus!'

'Escort the ambassador out of the building.'

Without a word the two security personnel advanced towards Nykyshyn. The first reached for his arm to usher him away. The ambassador jerked clear, held up his hands, and walked towards the door.

Zankovetskaya Street, Kyiv
Dudka opened the door. Zlotnik stood with a bottle of vodka in his hand.

'You've come to gloat?'

'No, Gennady Stepanovich, to apologise.'

'You'd better come in then.'

Dudka shut the door and gestured to a pair of slippers with his foot. It was a Ukrainian tradition that all guests remove their shoes and wear slippers when entering a home. Not for religious purposes but for the practicality of cleaning.

Zlotnik slipped them on. 'Thank you.'

'This way.'

Dudka walked along the hall and into the lounge. The room had once been impressive. Full-height, dark-wood cabinets lined one wall, a Soviet-era settee was against another, and an elderly television sat at the far end, next to a large, redundant fish tank. In front of the window, a dining table and four chairs were set out. Dudka deposited himself on a chair and pulled out another for his guest. Zlotnik handed Dudka the vodka but saw that an almost empty bottle sat on the table. Dudka removed an extra shot glass from a built-in drawer, filled it, and handed it to Zlotnik. He then filled his own glass.

'What are we drinking to, Yuri Ruslanovich?'

'To you, Gennady Stepanovich.'

Dudka nodded and they both downed the last of the semi-tepid

153

Nemirof. Dudka opened the new bottle and refilled the glasses. He looked at Zlotnik expectantly.

'While your actions were somewhat reckless...'

'Some apology!' Dudka cut him off.

'Gennady Stepanovich, let me finish. While your actions were somewhat reckless, you were right to take them.'

'How so?' Dudka was going to enjoy this.

'The Belarusian investigator, Kostyan, was the assassin.'

Dudka blinked. 'What!'

'He fooled us all.'

Dudka drank his vodka without saying a word, then refilled it. His hand shook with rage and some spilt on the tablecloth. 'You are telling me that I walked past the very same man who murdered my friend?'

'Yes.' Zlotnik necked his own drink, which Dudka did not refill.

Dudka closed his eyes and tried to control his grief and anger. It was probable that this 'Kostyan' had also murdered his beloved goddaughter, Masha, and her husband. Opening his eyes he stood and removed a Soviet-era photo album from a cabinet.

'See this? It is all that is left of them. Father, daughter – both dead. No descendants, a line wiped out.'

Even though he was twenty years younger than Dudka, the anger the older man displayed scared Zlotnik. 'I'm sorry. What can I say?'

Dudka sat and refilled Zlotnik's glass. 'The first thing you can say is a toast to absent friends.'

'Absent friends.'

Dudka opened the album, ignoring his guest. No words were needed, for the moment. Zlotnik took in the room. It hadn't been decorated since Soviet times. There was nothing to hint at the money he knew Dudka had made from his relationship with his old KGB comrade General Varchenko. Varchenko was now busy building his own luxury resort near Odessa. Why did Dudka

154

live like this? Why not join his daughter and granddaughter in Cyprus?

'I am putting you on compulsory paid leave for two weeks. You need the rest.'

Dudka looked up from his memories and nodded his assent, his anger spent. 'Perhaps I shall take a holiday, leave the country.'

'Cyprus?'

'Belarus.'

Zlotnik shook his head. 'Gennady Stepanovich, the murder will be investigated and we will find the man responsible. You have my word on that.'

'Oh, I have no doubt that he will be found; in fact, all we have to do is ask the Belarusian KGB where he is. But then what? Demand that they hand over to us one of their black operatives?'

Zlotnik conceded the point. He knew his words were meaningless. 'Gennady Stepanovich, let me talk frankly to you. Nothing would give me greater pleasure than to be able to march into the KGB headquarters on Skaryny Avenue with an international arrest warrant, but you and I are both wise enough to know that it'll never happen. So please, Gennady Stepanovich, for all our sakes, take your leave, but leave Minsk alone.'

Dudka grunted an acceptance. The man would not be arrested. He poured two more shots. 'I want any potential disciplinary action against Blazhevich dropped. He was following my orders.'

'Understood.'

Dudka raised his glass. 'The future.'

'The future,' Zlotnik echoed. 'Gennady, you and I are witness to information that is beyond classified. The Russian plans must not be spoken about by anyone. Do I make myself clear?'

Dudka met the eyes of his boss. 'Crystal.'

A clock in another room chimed; Zlotnik's ears pricked up. 'Gustav Becher?'

'No. Jungens like yours.'

Zlotnik smiled. Restoring antique clocks was his passion.

Perhaps he had more in common with Dudka than he had previously imagined? 'Time to go.'

The two SBU officers walked to the front door. Zlotnik removed the slippers then replaced his shoes. He held out his hand to Dudka. 'I'll see you in two weeks.'

'Undoubtedly.'

Heathrow Airport, London, UK

Raymond Kennington held the mission brochure in his hand and mentally ticked off the faces as they arrived at the Heathrow check-in area for the BA flight to Jeddah. As the mission leader and secretary of the Trade East Association, he was eager for all his charges to make the flight on time. A former diplomat and Arabic speaker, Kennington had retired from the service eight years earlier, but had found his new life too pedestrian. He had approached the Trade East Association, whom he had liaised with while working for the British Embassy in Riyadh, offering his services. Working part-time, he had for the past few years taken three missions a year to the region, concentrating either wholly on the Kingdom of Saudi Arabia or a multi-leg trip hitting Oman and the Emirates.

He had fallen in love with the desert the first time he had laid eyes on her thirty years before when he had been caught up in the Aiden offensive. To him she was a living, breathing, moving entity, a source of life, a bringer of death. He had been, and was still, in awe of her. Each time he spotted the moving sands for the first time from the window of his plane, he felt as though he had come home. He tried to imagine what it must have been like for Lawrence uniting Arabia. He was a romantic man and felt as though he had been born out of time.

As if to remind him, his mobile phone buzzed in his pocket, a modern annoyance. 'Hello, Raymond Kennington.'

There was static on the end, then an anxious voice explaining he was stuck in traffic on the M25 and when exactly was check-in closing? Inwardly Kennington cringed, but his voice remained his perfectly professional, perfectly calm self. He would ask the BA staff and do all he could to ensure that the 'missioner' – a salesman, ironically, of heart-monitoring equipment – didn't miss the flight.

Kennington ended the call, took a deep breath to compose himself, and headed for the nearest BA desk. He adopted his best smile to match that of the perma-tanned, blue-suited check-in girl.

Snow entered the terminal and again felt for his passport in his shirt pocket. It was in the name of Aidan Mills; his first name had been retained. It wasn't foolproof but then a legend seldom was. For the next week Snow was to be a sales representative for a UK-based manufacturer of designer optical frames. As such he was to have a meeting with a distributor in Jeddah and several with two large optical chains based in Riyadh. Snow's 'employer' was indeed real, and orders could therefore be placed. The MD was on the SIS payroll and Aidan Mills had recently been 'hired' as the new interim Export Sales Manager for the Middle East and Africa. He was home office-based, which explained his general absence from the company office in Richmond.

Snow had taken on assumed identities in the Regiment for intelligence-gathering purposes, but this was the first time he had acted on his own, on foreign soil, as an agent of the SIS. In role he was to move and mix with the other missioners but would take every possible chance to gather intelligence on what he saw. His main priorities, however, were to meet with his contact in Jeddah and then Fox in Riyadh. Snow had found it odd that Patchem didn't want this done by the embassy-based SIS officer in Saudi but made no comment. Patchem was his 'controller'.

Snow joined the check-in queue and was spotted by Kennington. 'Aidan Mills?' It was an educated guess as Snow's photograph hadn't been added to the brochure.

Snow looked down at the wiry, diminutive man in his mid-sixties. 'Yes. You must be Raymond?' Snow knew exactly who he was.

'Must be, yes.' He extended his hand. 'Raymond Kennington.'

'Nice to meet you, in person.'

Kennington smiled. 'Likewise. I'm sorry we couldn't get your picture in the brochure.'

'Not to worry. I hope my products will speak for themselves.'

'Yes, I hope that will be the case. Have you been to the Kingdom before?' Kennington was curious; the passport had been devoid of any Middle East stamps. It had been his duty to liaise with Watergate Travel to get the invitation letters for the visas. As such he had seen the passports.

'No. This is my first time.'

It was true. Snow had just missed Gulf War One and had left the Regiment by the time Gulf War Two had kicked off and SAS units had been sent into Iraq via Kuwait and Saudi Arabia.

'It's an exciting and fascinating place. I hope you get a chance to meet your business contacts informally. You'll find the Saudis to be a very hospitable people.'

Snow nodded. Kennington sounded like an advert for the Saudi Ministry of Tourism, if they had one.

Snow reached the counter and checked in. The majority of the missioners were flying economy, the only exception being the equestrian supplies manufacturer and the artist. Both men were old hands at Saudi and normally travelled on their own. Snow managed to get an exit seat; with his height he needed it. He took his boarding pass and laptop bag, and entered the line for the final security check. There was a two-hour wait until the boarding time and Snow planned to have a quick look at the duty-free shops – he needed some desert boots – before sitting in the executive lounge with a large cognac.

Chapter 8

Crowne Plaza Hotel, Jeddah, Kingdom of Saudi Arabia
Snow's first morning in Saudi Arabia had started with a large, pork-free buffet breakfast, continued with the official mission briefing, and was now to end with his first business meeting as Aidan Mills.

With a head full of 'dos and don'ts' courtesy of the man from the British Embassy, Snow crossed the heavily air-conditioned foyer and exited the hotel as a large Hyundai saloon pulled up. The driver wore a dark maroon suit with mustard-yellow shirt and tie. He looked at Snow down his long, crooked nose.

'Mr Aidan?'

'Yes, I'm Aidan Mills.'

The elderly man extended a bony hand. 'I am Mosbah Fattouh. Welcome to Jeddah. Please get in.'

From Snow's briefing with View Bright's MD, he knew that Mosbah Fattouh took the company's economy range and sold mainly to chemists and other low-end outlets. He had been an agent for View Bright since the Eighties and now, in his seventies, had no thought of retiring.

Fattouh steered the saloon out of the hotel complex and into the Jeddah traffic. Snow noticed that, although clean, the car smelt heavily of cigarettes.

'It is your first time in Jeddah?'

'Yes.'

'What do you think?'

'Hot.'

Fattouh nodded. 'Have you been to Lebanon?'

'No,' Snow lied.

'Much more green and the air so much better. Here is OK for work but not for living.'

They neared a large roundabout and headed further into the city. 'Have you worked here for long?' Snow knew the answer.

'Yes, a long time. I also have a business in Beirut. Perhaps you shall visit me there also?'

'Insha'Allah'

'Yes, Insha'Allah. You speak Arabic, Mr Aidan?'

'No.'

'Better to speak English or French. I am sorry…' Fattouh reached for his mobile phone and started to speak rapidly in Arabic.

Snow looked out of the window at the passing dusty buildings. Along the coast there had been some modern glass offices, what looked like restaurants, and of course several mosques; here in the side streets the buildings were a uniform grey concrete with peeling white plaster. Still speaking, but now in annoyed Arabic, Fattouh brought the car to a halt outside a nondescript six-storey building. 'AJ is waiting; let us go to the office.'

They took the steps to the second floor and entered the office, which had two rooms, a toilet, and a small kitchen. One room had dusty carpets, the others bare concrete. A man greeted them.

'This is AJ.'

AJ held out his hand. 'It is good to meet you, Mr Aidan.'

'You also,' Snow replied.

Fattouh resumed the conversation with his employee that had started on the phone. Admonished, AJ went into the kitchen. Fattouh beckoned Snow into his office. Both men sat. Snow looked around the barely decorated space. One wall had a window with views of

160

other similar buildings, on another hung a large map of the Kingdom, and on another a corkboard with several letters pinned to it.

Fattouh leant on his desk and lit a cigarette. 'How is Mr Mark?'

Mark Farrow, the MD of View Bright, had warned Snow to take everything Fattouh said with a pinch of salt and to promise him nothing. 'Well. He sends his regards.'

'Tell him thank you. When Mr James came to see me, we discussed prices. He raised them. I told him, Mr Mark would never have agreed to this.' Fattouh took a drag on his cigarette. 'Mr Mark and I had an agreement and Mr James changed it.'

Snow frowned. 'Mr James left the company before I joined; I can't really talk about anything he may have done.'

Fattouh waved his cigarette. 'He was no good; Mr Mark would never have raised my prices. Mr Aidan, I tell you, the prices should be changed. My customers, Mr Aidan, are not wealthy; they are the foreign workers who have come to Saudi Arabia. People from Pakistan, India, Egypt, the Philippines.'

Snow nodded. He had been briefed on this. 'Mr Fattouh...'

'Mosbah, Mr Aidan, call me Mosbah.'

'Mosbah, your sales figures have stayed the same even with the increase. So I don't think price is an issue.'

'Mr Aidan, I tell you the prices should be changed.' Fattouh stubbed out his cigarette; he had had his moan. 'Would you like a drink? I have beer in the fridge. I shall call AJ.'

'Thank you. Now what I want to talk about is our new range.'

'Please show me.'

Snow opened his pilot case and spread several frames on the desk. AJ brought in a bottle and glass. Snow read the label. 'Kaliber, alcohol free. I haven't had this for years.'

'We have more in the fridge.'

After three bottles of fake beer and the promise of an order for two hundred pieces, Fattouh deposited Snow back at his hotel.

'Mr Aidan, my sponsor, Mr Hassan Al Rashid, has invited you to his house this afternoon for a drink.'

161

'That is very kind of him.'

'I shall collect you at five? This will give you time for a rest.'

'Five is good for me. I shall see you then, Mosbah.'

Fattouh drove away as Snow headed back into the hotel.

Mentally drained from Fattouh's negotiations, Snow sat in the foyer bar and ordered a 'drink'. He had decided international business wasn't his forte. A large glass of fresh pineapple juice arrived and he drank it with his eyes closed. He still didn't quite understand why Patchem had sent him to Saudi or what he expected him to see. In the day he had been there, as a Westerner he had been constantly stared at by the Saudis and kowtowed to by workers from the subcontinent. He couldn't be any more conspicuous even if he painted himself blue, and sitting in a primitive office with an elderly salesman wasn't going to gain him any intel.

'Hello, Aidan. How are you enjoying it so far?'

Snow opened his eyes to see Raymond Kennington sitting opposite him. 'Fine.'

'Any sales yet?'

'I've just taken an order and I've been invited to the house of my agent's sponsor this afternoon.'

Kennington nodded. 'I always tell my missioners the Saudis are a very hospitable people. Once you get to know them they're some of the nicest people imaginable.'

'I can imagine.'

Kennington smiled, not registering Snow's sarcasm. A waiter appeared and Kennington ordered a mineral water in fluent Arabic.

'You have a real love for the region, don't you?' Snow asked awkwardly, to break the silence.

'I suppose you could say that but I think it's because I appreciate all that the Arab people have done for the Western world.'

'Oh?' Snow had no idea what Kennington was talking about, but was too tired to let on.

'Indeed, the so-called Islamic Golden Age of Learning

happened at a time when we, in the West, were primitives. After the fall of the Roman Empire, we had no learning to speak of. The Muslims kept the works of Plato, Aristotle, and many others alive by translating them and retranslating them. They developed medicine and maths. Did you know that algebra is an Arab word? We could never have had such a renaissance of "Western learning" without the knowledge that the Muslims not only kept alive, but developed.' Kennington folded his arms.

'I see, but if they were so much for the preservation and sharing of learning, why did they develop a religion and society that's become so secretive?'

'You can't have it all.' Kennington laughed.

Snow looked at his watch. 'I'm sorry, Raymond, but I've got some calls to make to the office.' In fact, he still had to file a quick report to SIS.

'Don't let me hold you up. Just remember, I'm here if you need me.'

*

The street had been dusty and the grass sparse, but on passing through the high gates into Al Rashid's gardens, Snow was shocked to see the lawns were manicured and a lush green. As the car came to a stop a man in a white thobe appeared at the door.

'That is Mr Hassan, my sponsor,' Mosbah Fattouh announced. 'Let us get out.'

The elderly Lebanese man exited the car, flattened his tie, and quickly walked towards Al Rashid. 'Mr Hassan.'

'Mosbah.'

'This is Mr Aidan, from View Bright.'

The Saudi bowed ever so slightly and extended his hand. 'It is an honour to meet you, Aidan.'

Snow was surprised by the perfect Oxbridge accent. 'And you also, Mr Hassan.'

The Arab smiled. 'Please, just call me Hassan. Mosbah is an old friend of mine yet he also forgets.'

'Habit, Mr Hassan.'

'No, it is your Lebanese manners, Mosbah. Please let us go inside. You must be thirsty.'

Al Rashid led them into the house, along a white, high-ceilinged hallway, and into a reception room. He gestured to a long leather settee. 'Please take a seat. I have given the staff the afternoon off; I thought it would be more informal if we were on our own? What would you like to drink, Aidan?'

Snow paused; he didn't want to make a faux pas. 'Whatever you're having.'

Hassan nodded; he understood. 'I am having a glass of Johnnie Walker and Mosbah is having a big one.'

'Thank you, that would be nice.'

Hassan walked to the far end of the room and opened a large drinks trolley. Snow made out several different brands of whisky and vodka. Hassan picked up the nearest bottle and a glass.

'Tell me, Aidan. How much does a bottle of Johnnie Walker cost now in the UK?'

Snow wasn't a whisky man. 'I don't know about the high street, but at the airport they were selling two bottles for £22 duty free.'

'What!' Fattouh raised his thick eyebrows. 'So little?'

Hassan held up the bottle as he spoke. 'I pay £80 a bottle here. But then, this is the price I pay, for living in this wonderful country!' As he moved his arms, a trail of whisky fell from the bottle and onto the carpet. 'Oh dear, but no matter… we have much more.'

'If you don't mind me saying so, your English is very good.'

'Thank you, Aidan. I studied at Eton and then Oxford. It is the tradition in my family and one that my son Gafar has continued.' Hassan handed first Snow, then Fattouh, a glass. 'Where did you graduate from?'

'Leeds.' This was true and had been kept for his cover.

'Ah. You know, I miss Yorkshire pudding. I remember having it for Sunday lunch as a student.' Hassan raised his glass.

'Yer not wrong, reit Yorkshire puddin's a poem in batter.' Snow's grandmother had been from Rotherham and it was one of the only accents he could do, with the exception of Moscow.

Hassan smiled broadly while Fattouh continued to drink his whisky. 'What did you read?'

'As little as possible.'

'Me too. Now, Mosbah has been telling me about these new products you have shown him. Very good, I am sure, but we will not talk of that. Mosbah is in charge of his own business. I am just a sleeping partner.'

'I tell Mr Aidan, Mr Hassan, that the prices are too high, but he assures me they will sell.'

'Mosbah, I do not doubt that you are both correct. Now, enough, please, of business. This is your first time in my country?'

'Yes.'

'What is your impression?' Hassan smiled playfully as both he and Fattouh awaited Snow's answer.'

'Well, it's different.'

Hassan stood and refilled the glasses. He waved the bottle. 'No need to try to appease me, Aidan, I know the drawbacks of this "Kingdom". Did you know that, once upon a time, my family ruled Riyadh?'

Snow raised his eyebrows. 'No, I didn't.'

'It was a long time ago. We were angrier then and lost a battle to the House of Saud, who, with the support of the British Army, became the rulers of this land we now call Saudi Arabia.'

'He should be King.' Fattouh pointed with a long, bony finger.

'No, Mosbah, I should not be. It was a large family and I am more than happy with the way things have worked out. Who would want to be the ruler of the home of Islam? Think of the pressure and responsibility that brings? No, I am not an enemy of the state – far from it – but I do disagree with the way it is run.'

'Really?' Snow didn't want to get drawn into politics.

Hassan took a drink then continued. 'There is a fight at this very moment for the soul of the Kingdom. On one side we have the progressives. These are the people the West approves of, those who want the country to be part of a modern international age. On the other side are the fundamentalists. What the West must understand is that the fundamentalists are not all bad. The militant few, the ones who want to get their way using Bin-Laden-type tactics, are very obviously beyond the pale. However, a lot of these people are traditional, simple Saudi people who are scared of change and outside influence. They simply don't like the way the world is going and will resist the erosion of, as they see it, their beliefs and morals.'

Fattouh added his own summary. 'It is these simple people who are naïve. They are impressionable and listen to the extremists.'

'Some may, Mosbah, but not all of them. You see, Aidan, we live in a very strange state. We have to deal with the West because twenty-five per cent of the world's oil reserves are here, yet at the same time we are expected not to want to get to know our business partners. I am sorry; please tell me if I am boring you.'

Snow quickly swallowed his drink. 'No, please go on. I know very little about your country.'

'The oil will, some day, run out, and what then? Are we to sink back into the sand as before? I am a member of a consortium, a group that wishes to emulate the examples of Dubai, Abu Dhabi, and Bahrain by bringing tourism into the Kingdom. By tourism I do not mean religious tourism such as the Hajj pilgrims. I mean real, Western-style tourism.'

Snow was now more interested. 'How will you do that? The visa regime here is the toughest I've seen.'

'True. I still have to sponsor Mosbah here, even though he

has been a dear family friend since I was in my teens. There is a large gorge, a canyon much like the one in Arizona, a few hundred miles up the coast and isolated from all Saudi cities; I won't bore you with exact details. It has been the aim of my consortium to turn this into a self-contained holiday resort, a place where there is no chance any Western tourist could "taint" the Muslim faith. It would need its own airport and infrastructure but, as the environment there is so unspoilt, we believe it would be a very profitable venture.'

'What does the government think of your plans?'

'They are in agreement, in principle, but are, as always, beholden to the fundamentalists. And so, we go around and around in circles. Another drink?'

Fattouh stood. 'If you will excuse me for a moment?'

Hassan watched his elderly business partner leave the room before letting his face grow serious. 'Aidan, let me show you the garden?'

Snow followed the Saudi through the patio doors and out onto a flagstone path. The sun had started to set and the air was still, save for the 'swish swish' of the lawn sprinklers.

'Aidan, I have been asked by Jack Patchem to keep an ear to the ground.'

Snow could not hide his surprise. 'I'm sorry, I don't understand.'

'Aidan Snow, sent here by his controller, Jack Patchem, to learn more about a possible terrorist attack.' Hassan held up his hand. 'Do not try to deny this. I am your contact. Jack and I are old Oxford chums. Did he tell you he "didn't care" for Arabs?'

'Something like that.'

'That is because we once quarrelled over the same woman. I won, but then he married her.' Hassan stared at the rapidly setting sun, as if to remember.

Snow was now tense. 'So what intel do you have for me?'

The Saudi turned to face Snow. 'I, too, have been hearing

more, shall we say, "mutterings" than usual. There are always those who will make threats, but what I have been hearing is new. It is not clear, and I could not press my contacts further, but something is indeed planned for Riyadh.'

'What?' Snow could feel his pulse quicken.

'Some sort of an attack on Western targets and soon. My son has also heard as much from his friends.'

'Do you have anything more specific or a timescale?'

'I wish I knew more but I'm afraid this is all I have.' Hassan shrugged.

Snow finished his whisky. 'I need to speak to London.'

'I understand. Please do come back and visit me again. I have enjoyed meeting you, Aidan.' He extended his hand and shook Snow's. 'If I do learn anything new I shall immediately contact you.'

'I am ready, Mr Aidan.' Fattouh appeared from the side of the house; he had his car keys in his hand.

London, UK

In his study and aided by a glass of single malt, Patchem read again the update from Snow detailing his meeting with Hassan Al Rashid. It had been several years since Patchem had caught up with his Oxford pal. His mind drifted back to the rivalry there had once been between them, when they had both vied for Jacquelyn's attention, Hassan not used to being ignored and Jack not used to losing. In the end, of course, it was Jacquelyn herself who had decided.

Patchem often wondered if her Irish genes, fair skin, and red hair had swung it in his favour. She wasn't fond of the sun, preferring a deep book to a deep tan. Oxford seemed like a life-time ago and indeed, if he were to count the years, it was. He was what now, fifty-four? They had graduated thirty-three years ago and he'd been with SIS for almost thirty. Patchem inadvert-ently caught his reflection in the study window and raised his glass as a toast to himself. Thirty years with Six and here he was, unable to relax on a Saturday.

He read the report for a third time, as if something new would magically appear, but no. The report was professional but brief. It simply stated that Hassan had heard rumours about an attack and that was it. There were no confirmed targets to narrow down the list of British interests and alert them, or dates. It was all innuendo. He poured another large measure into his glass. Something was going to happen, he was sure of it; now if he could only find out what, where, and when.

British Embassy, Riyadh, Kingdom of Saudi Arabia
Now in the Saudi capital on the second leg of their mission, the group had started to bond and were looking forward to an evening of free drinks courtesy of HM Government. As the rest of the group joked about their Saudi experiences, Snow was on edge, supremely aware of Al Rashid's intel.

The Hyatt hotel's shuttle bus came to a halt outside the British Embassy and the members of the Trade East Association Trade Mission de-bussed and passed through security. Snow had sat next to the driver at the front. After his near-fatal car crash in Poland, over a decade before, he always tried to sit in what he felt was the safest place. At least this seat, unlike those behind, had a working seatbelt.

The British Embassy in Saudi Arabia was situated in the Diplomat Quarter, a gated zone five miles from the centre of the Kingdom's capital, Riyadh. It was an area on a slight rise, over-looking the Wadi Hanifa in one direction and the emptiness of the desert in the other. The zone contained most of the foreign embassies to the Kingdom, including the official residences of the ambassadors. All vehicles attempting to enter the area were checked by armed Royal Saudi police officers while calls were made ahead to confirm their appointment with the relevant embassy.

Each embassy had its own compound within the zone, separate from the embassy, which housed diplomats and other personnel. The British Embassy was made up of two buildings forming an L shape, with a courtyard at the front and a swimming pool and tennis court at the rear. A high brick wall several feet thick surrounded the entire place. Even before the attacks of 11th September, all visitors had been subjected to a metal detector and bag check. Now, in the new era of Islamic terrorism, 'the Insurgency' as it was called, body searches were common.

Snow had read that the American Embassy was even more secure, with two rings of walls, a vehicle checkpoint, and armed US Marines. The Americans had vowed to ensure that the events of 6th December 2004, when militants stormed the US consulate in Jeddah, killing five foreign employees, would never be repeated. The consensus was that, with the exception of US military bases, the diplomatic zone was the most secure place in the Kingdom.

Tonight would be another test for Snow travelling as Aidan Mills. He felt confident enough to discuss business with any interested parties and knew enough about the industry. This was important as the embassy's commercial attaché had invited several local opticians and retailers to meet him at this reception evening. Snow's case containing his samples was scanned and he was nodded through. He followed the other missioners around the side of the main building, past the swimming pool and into the single-floor conference and reception room. A table had been laid out for each member of the trade mission. Snow found his had been placed in the corner, as per his request. He smiled to himself as he noticed the large free bar at the opposite end of the room. The embassy might well be located in the Kingdom of Saudi Arabia, one of the world's dry states, but this was British soil and the ambassador, as always, intended that everyone should have a good time.

A white-jacketed Malaysian waiter approached Snow and took his order. In keeping with his cover of Aidan Mills, Snow ordered a drink; in keeping with Aidan Snow, it was a large cognac. As expected, the cognac was French, whereas he much preferred Ukrainian. Within fifteen minutes the guests had started to arrive and, as expected, they included not only invitees but most of the British ex-pats based in Riyadh. Snow shook his head as he saw the world's most obvious alcoholic standing by the bar. He looked to be in his mid-fifties and had a large whisky in his fat hand. His face was florid and his red neck was trying to burst out over the top of his shirt collar, each and every button on his crimson shirt straining under his girth. Over the top of the shirt he wore the ex-pat uniform of blue blazer with the regimental crest on the chest pocket. As the waiter poured him another drink he pushed his bottle-bottom-thick glasses back up his crimson nose.

'I'm surprised he's still breathing.'

Snow turned to see his neighbour Lermitte, the bio-fuel generator exporter, laughing. 'This is the third time I've been here in the past five years, and every time, there he is, standing at the bar.'

Snow left his table and joined Lermitte. 'What does he do?'

'He's a civilian adviser to the Royal Saudi Air Force. Former squadron commander or something.'

Snow shook his head in disbelief

'I know,' continued Lermitte. 'Would you buy a secondhand plane from that man?'

'Maybe they stick him on the runway at night as an emergency light?'

Lermitte grinned. 'A green solution?'

Both men drank. 'So, truthfully, is there actually a market for your products in the world's largest oil-based economy?'

Lermitte shrugged. 'In theory, yes; in my MD's opinion, yes; however, in my personal opinion, no. Why on earth would a Saudi choose to run bio-fuel when, for a fraction of the price, he can support his own economy by running on cheap oil? And if you push them on the environmental issue they take it as a

171

personal attack on their beloved royal family.' He drained his glass.

'So why come? It can't be for the women or the booze.'

'I'm a camel fancier.'

Snow smiled. He liked Lermitte. They had the same sense of humour.

'My MD wants to change the world, convert them all to bio-fuel. I think he feels it's his duty to attack the evil Saudi empire. So he keeps sending me here and I keep saying the same stuff to anyone who cares to listen. Fancy a brochure?'

'I'll pass on that. I run on hot air.'

The 'crimson' ex-pat laughed loudly, getting both men's attention. A Saudi in full traditional dress was shaking his hand while waiting for his own glass to be refilled. Another Saudi was using his hands to make a bird shape in an attempt to tell a joke. Snow had seen some very bizarre things in his time but those present at this reception were the best yet.

'Here comes Brown Owl!' Lermitte nodded at their approaching mission leader, who had been fussing over them ever since they checked in at Heathrow.

'It's a good turnout, isn't it?' Kennington said enthusiastically, gesturing with his outstretched arm.

'As good as last time. I see some familiar faces,' replied Lermitte.

'Ah, yes. Well, these evenings do tend to become something of a social event.' He focused on Snow. 'Have you had any interest, Aidan?'

'My invitees don't seem to be here yet.'

'Well, it is still early. Actually, I've been meaning to ask you myself. Do you think I need a new pair of frames?' He removed his spectacles and held them up for inspection.

Snow gave the mottled brown specs a professional once-over. 'How long have you had this prescription?'

'Four years. Is that bad?'

'Hmm. It wouldn't hurt to have an eye examination; then, if there is a change, you could get some new frames for the new prescription. We have a lightweight, flexible, titanium range now that's perfect for the frequent traveller like you.'

'Really?' Kennington replaced his glasses. 'That's good. Maybe I'll do that. Now I've just seen someone I need to talk to, if you'll excuse me.'

'Loony,' Lermitte whispered as he watched Kennington enthusiastically greet a Saudi in Arabic.

'Why's that?'

'You can't be based here for ten years, as the trade attaché, like he was, and then want to return after retirement, unless you've got a screw loose.'

'Or like camels,' Snow added.

Paddy Fox straightened his tie. Although he had been invited to the reception as an ex-pat, not a potential customer for any of the missioners, he had surprisingly felt the need to wear a pair of chinos, shirt and tie. What had come over him recently, he didn't know. He still, however, wore his desert boots, hidden beneath his turn-ups. The drive in from the compound had so far taken forty minutes through the outskirts of the city. The locals drove like madmen. On the highways they used the hard shoulder as an extra lane and tried to force their way through if you weren't driving fast enough for their liking. He shared the bus with Lordy and Frank; they were good for a laugh, if in small measures.

'Step on it, mate, me Heineken's getting cold.' Lordy, ever the mouthy Londoner, leant forward, instructing their driver.

'Shut it, Si, remember this is a Muslim country.' Frank was ever wary.

'You're right, Franklin. In Allah's name, hurry up, me Heineken's getting cold.'

Their driver, Hatim, just smiled as usual. His English wasn't great and they could have been talking brain surgery for all he understood or even cared.

Fox looked out of the window at the half-built houses and the desert. He was happy in the desert but not here, Saudi Arabia. Even though his employer was a hospitable royal, Fox found the Kingdom in general hostile to Westerners. The sense of antipathy had grown considerably since his last visit to the country. Still, he didn't have much to complain about. He had left his recent troubles behind him thanks to the Al Kabir family, who had made them disappear and given him his new job. In a small way he almost felt bad spying on them for the SIS. As yet, however, he hadn't heard or seen anything out of the ordinary. If the SIS thought he was going to crack a new terror cell, they were barking up the wrong palm tree.

Fox's mind drifted back to his wife and, despite the heat, felt a shiver run down his back. He had loved her and she had betrayed him with, of all people, his boss. Fox relived the millisecond it had taken him to decide to shoot her lover – the moment he had pulled the trigger, sending a piece of white-hot lead into the suited lothario. He had killed numerous men on behalf of HM Government but that shot had been solely for him. It was a pity it hadn't been fatal. He missed Tracey. The way she spoke, her flat, Northern vowels, the sound of her voice had made the old soldier's stomach flutter… and then there was her body. She had the most fantastic pair of tits he had seen and a tight, round bum. He smiled despite himself as he saw flashes of her naked, a mirage reflected off the desert sand.

It had all started to go wrong when Tracey had been promoted above him at work; she started to travel more, leaving him to fend for himself. He hadn't minded at first, actually looking forward to having some time by himself to work on his old Porsche, but then the meetings had become more numerous and he noticed a change in the way she spoke to him, like she was better than him, like she was his boss. Fox had taken this with humour, a trait learnt dealing with the very green 'Ruperts' he had met in the army.

Then there had been his redundancy, engineered, he now believed, by Sawyer; and for her, his 'loving' wife, he became beneath contempt. A useless old man. Fox balled his fist and pressed it hard against the window; seeing his own reflection, he looked like a demon. He had to cut away from the pain of losing her. He had to become strong again. For Fox to move on, his mind had to believe she was dead and not out there somewhere without him. He closed his eyes. She was dead.

'You asleep, old man?' Lordy slapped Fox on the back.

'Just daydreaming.' Fox snapped back to the present.

'What, about men in dresses?' The Londoner laughed.

'Yeah, can't get my hands on any real women out here.' Fox became the jovial ex-pat again. 'I thought I'd try my hand at shirt-lifting.'

The minibus slowed and was waved into the security zone. The driver and the guards exchanged nods. Hatim was well known to the police, having served the royal family for several years as a driver and sometime messenger.

'Might be some nurses there tonight,' Lordy announced. 'Eh, Frank, what d'ya rekon?'

The Geordie whistled. 'I do reckon. Got some tasty bits, at that King Khalid Hospital.'

'Not blokes, you nonce.' All nurses at state-run hospitals were male. 'The birds that take care of the embassy.'

As was usual, most of the banter was concerned with the pursuit of women and the lack thereof. In Saudi this tended to focus on the complete lack of any women. At ex-pat events, any single white female suddenly took on near-mythical status and attracted a hungry pack of predators.

'There is that one bird that answers the phones,' Frank replied.

'Yeah, I reckon she's got a few miles left in her.'

'She's almost sixty, mate. Too old even for Gandalf here.'

Fox shook his head; he really had missed male company since getting married. 'I like older women; they can't run away as fast.'

Lermitte passed Snow another drink. Snow had switched to sipping lager as his head had started to buzz from the combined effect of heat and cognac. He had to stay semi-sharp for the handover. The room was now almost full, as locals and ex-pats alike mingled. Snow had just finished talking to the owner of the Al-Sarakat Optical Group. Sammi, the CEO, had boasted about the number of brands they represented and was eager to add View Bright to the list. He had arrived with an exclusivity contract and had pretended to be shocked when Snow had said he would have to read it first. The fact was that Sammi was a collector of brands. He gained exclusivity and then, under the restrictive Saudi laws, would only sell the products of those who paid him the most. Once in effect, the contract was iron-clad and extremely difficult to break, unless one party paid off the other against future earnings and subsequent loss thereof.

Snow had listened to both his MD's induction and the business briefing at the embassy that morning. In his personal opinion the Saudi businessman was the inventor of the meaningless smile. A smile that was flashed at many but meant nothing; it was simply a tool to improve business. As a businessman, Snow was learning fast. He smiled in return and assured Sammi that he would pass his enquiry directly onto his managing director.

Hatim left the diplomatic quarter and headed back towards central Riyadh. After ten minutes he changed direction and followed a desert track, driving for another kilometre before pulling over and killing his lights. Here he would await further instructions.

Fox sipped the cold beer, his first of the day. Currently the stocks were low, which would account for the large number of ex-pats

176

at the embassy. Fox turned to face the room and almost choked on his drink as he spotted Snow standing at the opposite end of the room, in conversation with several Saudis. The SIS had told Fox he would be contacted in country but not when, where, or by whom. They had instructed him to get on with his duties for his new employer and not to make any waves. Fox had been more than conscientious in this and had started to check out other regional compounds. He had been beginning to wonder if Whitehall had forgotten him. He approached Snow as soon as he became free. 'What are you selling? I'll take two.'

Snow held out his hand. 'Aidan Mills. View Bright. Optical frames. Glasses.'

'Don't wear them myself.'

'I've got some sunglasses too. You'll probably need a good pair stationed out here.'

'True enough.'

'I shouldn't do this, but I don't want to lug all this back on the plane; so here, have a free sample. Latest thing, replace your old ones.'

Snow retrieved a case from his bag. It contained a pair of adapted frames with a row of four-minute microphones, a micro-sized digital video camera, and a transmitter concealed within. The 'frames', with the exception of the camera, were derived from Dutch hearing aid technology and were two generations ahead of what was commercially available. The frames were voice activated and would record both audio and video. When they were put into the case, the device would stream data directly to a transmitter, which would condense and scramble the data before it was sent as a burst transmission. Both units had built-in ultra-long-life batteries.

Fox removed the frames and looked at them. He had been instructed on their use in the UK. 'Plug and Play', the MI6 techie had called them. 'Pop them on, put 'em back in the case, and then we play.' All very James Bond. What was very un-Bond-like was the fact that he'd had to wait until now for a pair. All luggage brought into Saudi was scrutinised for such banned items as alcohol, pornography, and icons or literature that promoted other religions. The frames had been with Snow's samples, which, along with samples for other mission members, been put in the diplomatic bag. It was far easier than filling out the numerous customs declaration forms.

'Thanks.' Fox nodded.

Snow winked. No one else in the embassy knew Snow was with the SIS, not even the intelligence officer stationed there. Patchem wanted to keep this operation on a 'need to know' basis. Snow had no problems working on his own. In his opinion, the more people that knew about any operation, the more likely it was to go pear-shaped or, to use SAS parlance, become a 'gang f###'. This had happened when he and Fox had worked together in The Det. Support staff had heard about operations and this had invariably led to leaks. Leaks had cost lives. In addition to this, in Saudi Arabia, one of the few remaining friendly countries demanding entrance by visa only, British visitors and workers were closely monitored. A new diplomatic passport would, perversely, attract far more attention than that of a member of a trade group.

'So, how long have you been out here then?'

'A couple of weeks.'

Snow smiled. 'It's a bit of a strange place. How are you finding it?'

'Hot and sandy.'

'Have you seen the sights? Anything of interest I should go and see?'

'No. There's not much to do in the desert, apart from count camels and grow a beard.'

Snow understood that he had nothing to report. Several more potential customers approached the table and Fox slipped away without saying another word, his gift carefully placed in his trouser pocket.

*

Hatim must have fallen asleep, for he awoke with a start to a banging on his driver's door. Hatim instinctively reached for his handgun before realising he hadn't brought it with him. A face suddenly loomed at the window; the dark, piercing eyes that made him fear for his life were staring at him.

'Get out.'

Hatim scrambled out of the minibus and stood on the dirt track. A second vehicle had pulled up behind him and several men were standing around smoking. Hatim addressed his leader. 'Khalid.'

Khalid stared back, his eyes showing hatred for the incompetent driver. He spat into the sand. 'I should kill you for falling asleep, but your face is known too well.'

'Thank you, Khalid.'

Hatim had started to shake; the man before him was the person he feared most on earth. There were rumours, which he had no reason to disbelieve, that Khalid himself had been responsible for many abductions and executions of coalition troops in neighbouring Iraq. These same rumours said he was personally known by the man at the top, the world's most wanted terrorist, Osama Bin Laden. Khalid, however, did not appear on the Americans' most-wanted list. A 'clean-skin' Saudi national, he could safely walk the streets of Riyadh or any other capital city.

'How many did you bring, Hatim?'

'Three.'

'British?'

'Yes.'

'Will there be any trouble?'

'No. They will be drunk.'

'Their vices make them predictable.'

Hatim lit a cigarette, unaware of the irony. 'They will be very predictable.' His hand shook as he took a quick drag.

'Bring them here as arranged. Now go!'

'Yes, Khalid.' Hatim climbed back into the minibus and retraced his route towards the embassy.

Fox's head was buzzing and he had, in a strange way, enjoyed himself. His two mates had managed to find the only two unattached women at the reception; however, they were also vying for their attention with the commercial secretary and a very bloated, red-faced ex-pat. Fox had continued to ignore Snow and latched onto another mission member who filled him in on the antics of his beloved Celtic. When they finally climbed aboard the minibus, none of them noticed the smell of cigarette smoke from Hatim's chain-smoking, or his less-than-jovial mood. Twenty minutes into the journey and all three Brits had started to sing football songs and rib each other about which team would stuff whose in a fantasy game. Lordy was convinced his beloved Plymouth Argyle, a strange choice for a Londoner, would be victorious.

Lordy held up his hand and looked around in a conspiratorial manner; Fox and Frank leant in nearer, over the back of the bench seat. From under his jacket Lordy produced a bottle of Johnny Walker Red Label and grinned.

'Yer mad bastad.' Frank snapped his neck in the direction of Hatim. 'If we get caught with that we're buggered!'

'Better drink it then. Here, age before beauty.' He handed the bottle to Fox.

Fox kept the bottle below the driver's eyeline and took a swig. 'Up you and yours.'

Lordy took his own swig before persuading Frank to have one. The minibus bounced over a pothole and Frank spilt the brown liquid over his cream slacks.

'Looks like you've pissed yerself, mate!' Lordy roared with laughter.

Frank gave him an evil stare before smiling and taking a larger swig. They hit another bump, then an even larger one.

'Hatim, drive like a normal shagger, will yer?' Lordy shouted to the front.

Fox looked around. He could see no lights and the road had started to feel worse. His training started to kick in. 'We're not on the road we came in on.'

'What?'

'Probably a shortcut, mate,' Lordy offered.

Fox scanned the darkness outside for any signs of life. 'Hatim, where are we?' The driver didn't reply; Fox could hear him mumbling to himself. 'Oi, Hatim. I said, where are we?'

The driver looked back. 'We go new road. Short.'

'Doesn't feel very new.' Frank looked out of the window.

Fox had a bad feeling. 'I think we're in trouble.'

Lights abruptly appeared from in front and behind them. The van skidded on the sand-strewn track as Hatim applied the brakes.

'What is this?' Lordy tried to open the side door.

'Stay in the van.' Fox grabbed his arm.

'Do as he says, man,' Frank hissed, grabbing the bottle and holding it upside down by the neck, oblivious of the last dregs of whisky pouring onto the floorpan.

Fox moved over his seat towards Hatim. The driver was applying the handbrake. 'Move this bus! Move the dam bu…'

The rear, side, and passenger doors opened simultaneously and men with shemaghs covering their faces pointed guns at them. Frank brought up the bottle and smashed it into the jaw of the nearest assailant. The man fell back and dropped his gun inside the minibus. Fox grabbed the AK47 and applied pressure to the trigger. Nothing; it was turned to safety. As he attempted to flick the switch, rounds peppered the van around him. There was a scream next to him as Frank was hit in the chest. A fist struck Fox in the face; the weapon fell. Before he could react, another fist hit him and he felt himself dragged out of his seat and thrown onto the desert floor. Reaching into his trouser pocket he did something that went against every instinct and bit of training he had; his fingers grasped his passport and wallet and dropped them on the sand. A rifle butt hit him on the side of the head, then everything went black.

Khalid cursed as the remaining two Westerners were pulled out of the bus. One was bleeding profusely and his face had gone grey. The second was trying to protect his face. Khalid ordered his men to hold the second man up by the arms. He then looked him straight in the eye and spoke.

'If you try to escape you will be dead like your friend.' Khalid removed a dagger from his waistband and slit Frank's throat.

Lordy was unable to speak and Khalid was disgusted by the urine stain that suddenly appeared around his crotch. Both Lordy and Fox were moved into a second vehicle.

Khalid approached Hatim, who was standing nervously puffing a cigarette at the front of the minibus, trying to look the other way.

'You have done well.' Khalid extended his left hand to shake the driver's. As soon as their hands made contact, in a swift and powerful movement Khalid pulled Hatim down with his left while drawing the right hand, and the dagger it held, across his neck. Hatim fell to the floor, blood bubbling out of the cut in his neck as he grabbed at it in vain. Khalid turned and walked away as Hatim choked on his own blood. The driver had served Allah well.

Minhal Holiday Inn, Riyadh

The phone rang in Snow's room, waking him from a restless sleep. It had been a choice between a loud air conditioner or the hot desert air. He'd eventually chosen the air. He reached over and grabbed the room phone, his voice croaky.

'Hello?'

'Aidan, Raymond Kennington here.' The mission leader always gave his full name on the telephone.

'Hello.' Snow looked at his watch. It was six; he hadn't overslept.

'Aidan, someone from the embassy is coming here at seven. There is to be an emergency security briefing.'

Snow sat bolt upright. 'What?'

'A man from the embassy is coming to brief us. You will also need to have your things packed and be ready to leave the hotel.'

'Right.'

'Seven, sharp. Sorry, got to phone everyone.' He hung up.

Snow switched on the TV and flicked through the channels, skimming two Arabic programmes, not understanding a word, before finding CNN. He watched for a minute or so before changing to BBC World. The usual stories about Iraq, but nothing new. The man from the embassy Kennington had mentioned would be the intelligence officer. As a former diplomat Kennington would know the protocol too. Snow reached for his mobile and speed-dialled the UK. It would be 4 a.m. there. No. He disconnected before Patchem's line rang and instead dialled the night desk at GCHQ. He was asked for his officer identity code before being put through to the duty officer.

'Has anything been reported overnight in either Saudi Arabia or on the Iraqi border that would affect Riyadh?' He leaned against the window frame and peered through the wooden fretwork at the dusty car park opposite the hotel.

'Let me check for any flash traffic,' a voice replied.

There was a pause as the night officer speed-read the incoming traffic for the shift he was halfway through, traffic taken mostly from the US-managed Echelon network. The officer knew better than to ask why the information was needed or where the agent was calling from.

'A suspected car bomb in Southern Iraq... not near the border... wait... yes... British national found dead on the outskirts of Riyadh. Franklin Glaister. A construction contractor for the Al Kabir Group.'

An alarm sounded in Snow's head. The same company Fox worked for, owned by Prince Fouad – the man Fox had been assigned to watch, the same prince whose life had been threatened. 'I need you to connect me to a number.'

'Go ahead.'

Snow relayed Fox's cell number from memory. The call would be routed through the UK so it was untraceable and could in no way incriminate Fox. Snow waited and dared not breathe as the line first connected, after which an automated voice told him the mobile phone he was trying to reach was switched off.

Snow blinked, ended the call, walked into the bathroom, and stepped under the shower. He ran through the situation in his head. The dead man worked for Prince Fouad; so did Fox. Fox's phone was switched off. Protocol was for it to always be left on and by his side. Was he overreacting? Could he be out of coverage or – a sudden chill hit him – unable to answer the phone? There was no point in getting jumpy. He didn't have time to stand still. This security meeting would perhaps shed more local light on the situation. The mission group was then due to leave the hotel for the King Khalid Airport and their flight to Dammam, the last stop on the three-city tour. Snow dried quickly and dressed in a pair of loose-style cream combats, long-sleeved blue polo shirt, and desert boots – he never wore a suit when travelling – then tried Fox again. No answer.

Arriving in reception at six-thirty-five, he added his cases to the pile already there and saw Lermitte in the breakfast room. The bio-fuel man was, according to himself, 'on the Atkins', so had a huge plate of beef bacon, scrambled eggs, and cheese. Snow grabbed a couple of bread rolls, beef bacon, and eggs. He couldn't let his unease show; as Aidan Mills he didn't have the same access to information as Aidan Snow.

'Morning. How are you feeling?'

Lermitte looked up with red-rimmed eyes. 'Peachy.'

He had drunk far more than Snow the night before and had barely been able to cross the foyer to the lift. The night porter had offered to get him a doctor; however, diagnosing a case of severe 'leglessness' wasn't a wise move in Riyadh. Snow's own head wasn't as clear as he might have wished, but nothing compared to the crazy times of Kyiv.

Snow filled a roll with beef bacon and a fried egg. 'Kennington woke you too?'

'Knob.' Lermitte shovelled a forkful of beef bacon into his mouth. 'What did he tell you?'

Snow shrugged and took a swig of black coffee. 'The embassy needs to brief us about some security issues or something.'

'Maybe someone stole the prince's favourite wife? Or one of our camels is missing?'

Snow smirked although he was in no mood for frivolity.

Kennington entered from the foyer holding a newspaper. 'They've done it again.'

Snow raised his eyebrows. 'Who has?'

Kennington continued, for once showing something other than admiration for their hosts. 'The bloody Saudi state-run media. Just look at this.'

He handed Snow the morning newspaper. There was the official picture taken at the reception the night before (which Snow had managed to skilfully be out of the room for) and a headline that read 'British Investors Gain Partners in Riyadh'. Snow looked up blankly.

Kennington furrowed his brow. 'They won't ever say we're trying to sell to them, no. They always say we're investing. Much better for their image.'

Unseen by Kennington, Lermitte rolled his eyes.

Snow scanned the article and saw he had been misquoted. 'View Bright to open local factory... Oh.'

'Exactly. You clearly said, and I heard you, that you wanted an agent not a manufacturing partner.' Kennington folded his arms and rocked on the balls of his feet.

Lermitte shrugged and took another mouthful. 'So why the wake-up call?'

Kennington looked around in a conspiratorial manner. 'I don't know the details but someone was found dead in the desert this morning. Could be a British citizen.'

Lermitte's fork stopped midway between mouth and plate. 'Shit.'

Snow's mind focused. 'Go on.'

'Look, I really can't tell you much more. I only know this because I'm ex-FCO. But at seven we'll get the full picture.'

Surely this couldn't be pure coincidence? It had to somehow be linked to both his and Fox's mission. Snow felt a mixture of emotions: anger at the death of an innocent man but also helplessness. He was unable to do anything. He wanted to grab a car and charge off across Riyadh to check on Fox, but Aidan Mills couldn't do that.

Fox opened his eyes to near darkness and found he couldn't move his hands. The realisation dawned on him that they were tied behind his back. As his eyes gradually adjusted and his senses returned, he realised he was wearing a hood. He could hear faint voices talking in Arabic. He stayed still, to feign unconsciousness and assess what was happening. He had been in the minibus, then it had stopped, and then... There was a loud moaning near his left ear and then footsteps. Fox held his breath.

'This one is awake,' a voice said in Arabic.

'Sit him up and remove his hood,' Khalid replied.

Fox heard scraping sounds and then the unmistakable voice of Lordy. 'Oh my God... Oh my God... Oh my God...'

'Wake the other,' Khalid ordered.

Fox felt a strong pair of hands drag him to a sitting position and throw him back against a wall. The hood was then roughly removed. Fox kept his eyes closed for a further second or so before deciding that he had to 'wake up'. He looked up into the face of a Saudi with piercing eyes. The man was looking at him but speaking in Arabic to someone else. Fox understood every word but didn't let any recognition show in his eyes.

'Where am I?'

Khalid crouched on his haunches and spoke in English. 'You are in Iraq.'

The shock was obvious on Fox's face as Khalid's own took on a gleeful smile. 'You are a prisoner of the Warriors of Mecca.'

'Oh my God...' Lordy gave out a loud wail.

Khalid sighed. 'Allah is the one true God. It is He whom you should be asking for forgiveness from.'

Fox was lost for words; his head hurt doubly from the alcohol at the embassy and the whack he had taken from the rifle butt. He tried to get his brain to work. He was being held captive in Iraq? His eyes darted around the room as the man looked at both him and Lordy in turn. From his training Fox knew that the best time to escape any hostage situation was as near to the initial abduction as possible. A time at which the kidnappers may not have yet reached a secure location. But he was too late. He didn't know how long he had been out for or how many were holding him. His best course of action was to play dumb, act like a civilian, plead, look pathetic, and bide his time.

Khalid stood and walked away, waving his arm. 'We will bring you water and something to eat. Remember, it is not we who are the barbarians.'

A heavy-sounding door shut and the two men were left in near darkness.

Fox spoke in a whisper. 'You OK, mate?'

'I thought you was a goner, when they hit you with that gun.'

Fox looked around the dark, bare room. 'I've a hard head. Where's Frank.'

Lordy started to hyperventilate. 'Th... the... the... bastard cut... cut... his throat right in front of me...'

'Jesus.' Fox placed his head against the bare wall. It hurt like hell. His captors, whoever they were, had just taken the next step. 'Listen to me, Lordy. We're gonna be all right. OK?'

Lordy nodded but was far from convinced. 'Are we in Iraq?'

Fox thought for a moment. 'It's possible. How long was I out?'

'Dunno, they took me watch.'

Fox realised that his wrist, too, was bare and his pockets were empty. 'Did you see which direction they took us? Can you remember anything about us getting here?'

'They put that stinking hood over me head, and it was dark anyway. Not long after, the road got smooth – not bumpy like when we stopped – and then I dunno... they were dragging me from a van into somewhere. Here I suppose. Then they came in.'

'So I came too, just after we got here?' Fox was trying to figure out how far they had been taken but any estimate would have been very rough. 'Was it light outside?'

'Yes, I could see my feet.'

'How bright was the sun?'

'Err, not very. Why?'

'Early morning. That means they've had us for about six hours or so.'

'Meaning?' Lordy was confused.

'That we can only be six hours away by car.'

'I hate to say it, mate, but you can get to the Bahrain causeway in four and a half if you go some.'

'Right enough.' A thought occurred to Fox. 'We may not be in Saudi but we may not be in Iraq either.'

'That helps.' Lordy tried to regain his composure but was breathing hard.

'Did you hear them talk at all?'

'Yeah.'

'What where they saying?'

'They were speaking Arabic.'

'So?'

'I only know a few basics. You speak it, don't you?'

Fox didn't want to play up his language skills, but he was fluent having taken intensive courses with the Regiment and being deployed in the Kingdom during Gulf War One. 'I know a few words. Not much.'

'Shit.' Lordy leaned back against the wall. 'Can't even pick me nose with me bleedin' hands tied behind me back.'

In the near darkness Fox smiled. 'Don't go asking me for help.'

There were footsteps and the sound of metal grating. The door opened and in stepped Khalid with two other men silhouetted in the sunlight that entered through a second outer door. Fox squinted; he could see that Khalid held a tray in his hands while the others had AK47s trained on their captives. Khalid placed the tray on the floor at the wall furthest away from Fox and Lordy and then moved towards them with a knife. Lordy suddenly started to shake as Fox tried to ready his body for action.

'I'm going to cut the bonds from your hands. You cannot eat like dogs.' He smiled and made eye contact with each man in turn.

The two armed men took a step forward; a rifle was pointedly aimed at each captive. Lordy flinched and screwed his eyes shut as Khalid grabbed his hands and cut the bonds.

Fox relaxed slightly as his turn came. There was no way he could make a bid for freedom without getting ripped to pieces by the 7.62mm rounds from the Kalashnikovs. 'Thank you.'

Khalid nodded. 'You are welcome, James. Now please eat. You too, Simon.'

Fox looked around the room. The light coming from the door was daylight. The room they were in was at the end of a short corridor, a storage building of some sort but new and seemingly unused. The floor was rough concrete, the type usually put down before flooring was laid. Khalid beckoned them again; Fox slowly rose to his feet and crossed the four metres to the other side of the room. He bent, picked up the tray, and returned it to Lordy.

'Bon appetit.' Khalid exited the room followed by the two armed men.

As the door was shut a light flicked on above them. It was a bare bulb with a protective wire cage surround screwed to the coiling.

Fox looked at Lordy. 'Did you tell him our names?'

'No.'

'Then how does he know them?'

'Passports?'

'Yeah, that'll be it, mate.' But it wasn't and Fox knew it; he'd made sure that his had stayed in the desert. He picked up his plate and grimaced. 'I hate lamb.'

'Aren't you sodding scared?' Lordy replied accusatively.

'Course I am, mate.'

'You don't bloody look it.'

Fox nodded. 'My wife told me I had trouble expressing my emotions.'

Minhal Holiday Inn, Riyadh

'Thank you all for being here.' Harry Slinger-Thompson stood in front of the lectern in the lavish meeting room. He looked slightly nervous, as if he didn't quite know how to relate what he had to say. 'Last night we believe a terrorist organisation abducted two British citizens who were with you at the reception.'

There were gasps from the assembled group and some hushed words exchanged. His plummy voice continued. 'A further British ex-pat was murdered and left in the desert...'

'My God!' The perfume manufacturer looked as though she would faint.

'Please, I know it's an awful situation to be in but we mustn't panic. As you are aware, today you were to take an internal flight to Dammam for the last leg of your Saudi visit to Al-Khobar. While we at the embassy cannot force you to leave the country, we feel it would be safer if you did so. That is why you are being given the option of either flying directly back to the UK today or flying to Bahrain.' Slinger-Thompson paused and looked at the faces in front of him. Most were petrified.

'Can you tell me the names of the men who were abducted?' Snow's desire to know if Fox was among those taken was unbearable.

'I'm sorry but I cannot release that information until we have contacted their next of kin. I can say, however, that all three men, who were travelling together, have been identified and worked for the same Saudi organisation. It is in all our best interests if we keep a lid on this until you are out of Riyadh. Please try to refrain from informing anyone else about this situation.'

Snow's heart rate increased and he felt a sick sensation in his stomach – they had Fox. He noticed Lermitte on his left, texting. Lermitte looked up, unabashed, and shook his head slowly.

Kennington stood and started to speak. 'Harry has told me that the Saudi police are to provide us with an escort to the airport. We shall be leaving in twenty minutes. Any questions?'

'Are we really in danger?' Sheila, the interior designer, who had the demeanour of a Victorian headmistress, looked at Slinger-Thompson over the top of her spectacles.

'Yes, we believe so. I'm not attempting to be an alarmist but you're a high-profile group and, as such, a potential target if these kidnappers were to strike again.' He nodded.

She frowned. 'We'd better go then.'

'So, ten minutes at reception to check out, then board the bus ten minutes after that.' Kennington was precise as always.

The group quickly dispersed. Several had started to retrieve mobile phones and were busy dialling. Others were none too steady on their feet.

Snow approached Slinger-Thompson. 'Any idea who did it or what they want?'

The SIS man gave Snow a strange look. 'No, Mr Mills.'

'Was there any suggestion that something like this might happen?' Snow was finding it hard to stay in character.

'None.'

Kennington tapped his wristwatch. 'Right, Aidan, you'd better get to reception.'

Snow nodded. He needed to call Patchem. He left the meeting room and walked through the main foyer and up the stairs to the mezzanine floor. Once he was certain he couldn't be overheard he called his field controller.

In the UK it was 5.35 a.m. Patchem rolled over in bed and

grabbed the phone, which vibrated on his bedside dresser.

'Patchem.' His voice was thick.

'It's Snow. We have a problem.'

Patchem coughed to clear his throat and got out of bed; his wife was still asleep and it was better if she stayed that way. He exited the bedroom and shut the door. 'Go ahead.'

Snow explained what he had learnt from GCHQ and from the SIS briefing.

'That is very unfortunate.' Patchem entered his study to switch on his computer. 'They have no idea where he is, I suppose?'

'No.' Snow's voice was tinny; the line between Saudi and the UK was none too good.

'I'll contact Slinger-Thompson and get him to check up on Fox's compound. Fox could be anywhere so there's no point in you staying in Riyadh. Stay with the mission group, Aidan, and stay under. No one else need know who you are.'

'I'd like to stay here to see what I can do.' Snow didn't want to leave.

'I know you would, but we have no guarantee that Fox is still in the country. Aidan, get on the flight to Bahrain. You may be able to do something there.'

Snow sighed. Patchem was right; at least if he was in Bahrain he was still within striking distance, if needed.

SIS Headquarters, Vauxhall Cross, London, UK

At his Vauxhall Cross desk, forty minutes after speaking with Snow, Patchem was speed-reading the latest update from GCHQ as he dialled his Saudi field officer. He was angry the field officer hadn't personally informed him before addressing the trade mission, a hangover from Maladine's watch no doubt.

'Slinger-Thompson.'

'Harry, it's Jack Patchem.'

Slinger-Thompson was taken aback but didn't let it show. 'Jack, good morning. I take it you've heard?'

'I have the intercepts here from GCHQ, but please, tell me, what's happening over there?'

'It's a worrying situation, Jack.' Slinger-Thompson had worked hard to recruit reliable sources. 'I received a call very early this morning from a contact in the Royal Saudi police to say a British citizen had been found in the desert with his throat slit.'

'How was the man identified?'

'Well, believe it or not, his passport and company identification card were in his pocket. But that's not all. A further British passport was found under the abandoned vehicle in the name of "James Fox". There was also a second body, a Jordanian driver employed by the same company.'

'When were the bodies found?'

'First light. Now this is the strange part; it's incredibly easy to hide a body in the desert, yet these two were left on a road that's used daily by a local farmer. It was the farmer who found them.'

Patchem paused to let his mind process the information. 'So the bodies were meant to be found?'

Slinger-Thompson involuntarily nodded at the other end of the phone. 'I was at an embassy party the night before, as was the dead Briton.'

As was Snow, Patchem didn't add. 'What time did this finish?'

'About midnight.'

'And the bodies were found at first light?'

'About five.'

Patchem paused again. Five hours was time enough to get away with a hostage.

'Jack. There were two others with the dead man at the party, Simon Lord and James Fox. There's no trace of either of them. The local police have asked at their compound, they didn't return last night.'

This was confirmation enough. 'So two British citizens have been taken captive?'

'Yes, it appears that way.' Slinger-Thompson cleared his throat nervously. 'Jack. James Fox...'

Patchem knew what was coming. 'Yes?'

'I tried to run a background check but couldn't get very far. Then I remembered the media coverage. Is this the same James Fox that saved Al Kabir's daughter?'

'Harry...' Patchem paused to emphasise the importance of the admission. 'Paddy Fox is an asset.'

Slinger-Thompson felt his cheeks flush. He should have known about any assets or operations on Saudi soil for risk of him compromising them or them compromising him. He wanted to ask his new boss why he hadn't been told, but held his tongue. He didn't know Patchem well enough yet to trust him.

'If he is being held by an insurgent group we have an unparalleled chance of stopping them. Are we tracking Fox?'

Patchem wished it was so easy. 'No. Because of his actions in the UK he was placed with the Al Kabir family. We couldn't risk giving him anything that could be found and used against him.' This was partly true; there were the sunglasses.

Slinger-Thompson could hold back no longer. 'Is there anything or anyone else I should know about?'

Patchem frowned. The field officer's irritation had not been hidden well. 'Yes.'

King Khalid Airport, Riyadh, Kingdom of Saudi Arabia
Khalid sat in the backseat of the sedan as the taxi left his namesake's airport. He had an AKS-74U short assault rifle on his lap, covered with a spare thobe. The Pakistani taxi driver, another of his men who regularly worked the airport in his normal job, had his own standard '47' Kalashnikov in the passenger footwell. Khalid's eyes were closed as he communicated with Allah. In a matter of a few minutes, His divine will would again decide if Khalid lived or died a martyr. The taxi turned onto the Riyadh highway and left the airport behind.

A further ten kilometres and they would converge with other elements of the assault.

Kennington looked at the itinerary and tutted. He wasn't happy that his schedule had been disrupted at such short notice. Most of the group had opted to continue with the mission, taking the Bahrain option; only two wanted to fly home. They would now arrive at the airport far too early for the next flight, but too late to catch an earlier one. This created what he called dead time, when all he and his group would be doing was sitting, sipping airport coffee, and waiting for their flight to be called. He turned to Thacker, the artist, who was on the bench seat behind him.

'I've arranged that we be upgraded to have the full brunch at Le Meridien. It's really something, you know.'

Thacker nodded, even though he had been to the hotel in Bahrain before. 'That will be nice.'

Kennington continued. 'They put on an impressive spread but there's also an excellent fish restaurant very close by.'

Lermitte sat a further row behind and tried not to look bored by the conversation. All he wanted, with any meal, was a good glass of wine. 'The sooner we leave this godawful dry country the better.'

Kennington looked hurt. 'It's not such a bad place, Tristan. If you were to stay here longer, you might...'

'Jesus!' Lermitte's eyes were wide. 'Get killed on the roads!'

Snow looked back from his usual front seat and saw what Lermitte had. Two vehicles, a white Ford pick-up and a minibus, were drawing level with them. The Ford suddenly swerved towards them. Their driver sounded his horn and waved his arms. The Royal Saudi police cruiser, which was in front of them, switched on its lights. The Ford then accelerated and hit the rear bumper of the cruiser, sending it swerving across the lane and onto the hard shoulder. Dust and dirt were kicked up by its tyres as it tried to stay on the road. The mission's bus carried on past it but the driver started to slow, waving his arms, and sounding his horn. Snow looked around. The second minibus was now also slowing and a window had started to open. Snow caught the gleam of something metallic.

There was a thunderous clap and a flash of light. A tyre exploded. The mission van shook violently. Before the driver had time to react, further rounds impacted the van and he slumped forward over the wheel, blood splattered the screen, and the van swerved ominously sideways. Snow grabbed the wheel and tried to wrestle the van back into the centre of the lane but to no avail. There were now yells and screams from behind as the rest of the passengers realised what was happening; but before they could react fully, the van hit the sandy verge and was thrown onto its side.

Snow heard the words 'Everyone down…' spill out from his lips as the side of the van embedded itself into the sand. His whole body was hurled sideways and then forward, the seatbelt digging into his neck, squashing his Adam's apple. Glass exploded around him and splinters tore at his skin. Something hit his head, and Snow battled to remain conscious as the corners of his vision blurred and became dark grey. There were several seconds of absolute silence as the van came to a complete rest. Voices started to call out to each other.

Khalid leapt out of the taxi and ran towards the police cruiser; his AK had the stock locked and the safety was off. He sighted the first officer and let off a three-round burst before the man saw him coming. The officer crumpled and fell back over his open door. The driver's door opened and the second officer attempted to retrieve his sidearm but Khalid was too fast and, drawing level with the car, shot him in the head. He leapt back into the taxi, which covered the distance to the minibus. Khalid's men were out of their own vehicle; some trained their weapons on the wrecked bus while others manhandled the passengers out and onto the floor.

Snow's vision was blurred and blood ran into his eyes. He undid his belt and fell onto the corpse of the driver. The windscreen had exploded as the front of the van had caved in. He felt the back of his head. No blood, just a large lump, which, when he touched it, sent needles of pain jolting down his spine. There was movement all around now as the working doors were pulled open and hands grabbed. Snow kept still and closed his eyes; with any luck they would leave him for dead. He felt a hand on his shoulder and then a hushed voice. 'Aidan... Aidan.'

Snow opened his left eye and saw Kennington looking down at him; a large, jagged cut crossed his entire right cheek. Kennington's head suddenly jerked backwards as a strong pair of hands pulled him upwards and out of the van. Snow watched as open-mouthed horror registered on the mission leader's face. Arabic voices shouted instructions to each other, Snow shut his eyes again. Arabic voices all around now; Snow didn't speak the language but understood the tone. Orders were being given. A hand grabbed his shoulder and shook him, pain coursing down his back. Then he heard it – a police siren in the distance getting progressively louder. The hand let go and Snow let his body fall back onto the corpse once more.

Outside, Khalid swung his Kalashnikov in an arc to cover the motorway. Traffic on the other side had crawled to a halt as rubberneckers stared at the overturned vehicle and the armed men running around it. Khalid pointed his rifle at the nearest vehicle, a high-sided van, and fired a short burst into the cargo area. The driver got the message and pulled away, pushing the small sedan in front with him. Behind, the road was completely blocked; drivers who were too far away to see what had happened held down their horns as if this would magically clear the carriageway. The nearer motorists cowered in their cars; some had abandoned theirs and run off. Many others were on cell-phones, either making calls or recording videos.

The sirens were getting louder – they had to move now. Khalid shouted guttural instructions to his men and kept his weapon moving back and forth in a steady arc until, moments later, his men had grabbed and dragged the bewildered infidels out of their bus. He saw it now on the opposite side of the motorway, a police cruiser racing towards the scene. They had to go before the army was called in to block the road further south. He fired a short, lethal burst into the front of the cruiser, shattering the windscreen and causing the car to thud into the heavy central reservation. The convoy was ready to move. The minibus pulled away with its cargo of hostages. The Ford tried to move but the engine wouldn't start. The driver waved Khalid away; both men knew they had to make their escape. Khalid nodded and got back into the taxi, which shot up the road to rejoin the minibus.

Snow pulled himself up and gingerly drew his head out of the door. A taxi shot past but the Ford was still there – two men in front speaking animatedly as the engine spluttered. The front bull bars were distorted from hitting the police escort. Without thinking, an idea had appeared in Snow's mind. Now was his chance. He pulled himself out of the bus and fell onto the sand, bolts of pain shooting down his spine as his shoulder hit the ground. His mouth opened in a silent scream, the wind knocked out of him. Nothing, however, seemed to be broken. From behind the overturned bus he could still see the Ford; the passenger was now at the front of the vehicle, banging the bonnet with the butt of his Kalashnikov. The engine started but sounded none too healthy as the armed man got back inside the cab. The large pick-up moved off slowly, tyres fighting to grip the asphalt through the sand.

Snow ran at a crouch through the dust clouds and grabbed hold of the tailgate, pulling himself up and onto the exposed truck bed. The truck accelerated, hard in pursuit of the other vehicles; Snow rolled onto his back, pressed himself flat against the floor pan, and panted. As the truck bumped back onto the highway his back slammed into the steel below, causing him to cry out in pain – whatever he'd done to his back was going to get even worse if he took much more of this. There was no movement from up front and, unless the passenger or driver looked back and directly down at the truck bed, he couldn't be seen.

Snow tried to steady his breathing and make sense of what had just happened. They had been attacked on the way to the airport by an organised group. It wasn't an opportunistic or random act. These militants had to know when the mission was leaving and where it was headed. This meant what? Someone had told them or someone had been watching. Snow closed his eyes to force his mind to concentrate. His head was woozy and his back felt like it was on fire, but he was alive and, for the moment, free.

On the highway now, the ride was much smoother. Snow gingerly reached for his phone and thanked the gods that it was still safely buttoned inside his cargo pocket. He couldn't risk speaking so sent a text message to Patchem. ATTACKED ON HIGHWAY INSURGENTS POSSIBLE FATALITIES HOSTAGES TAKEN AM FREE WILL PURSUE

Snow switched the phone to silent with vibrate off. He then accessed the menu and typed in a code. The modified Nokia now acted as a GPS transponder. The phone would power up and send his GPS coordinates every few minutes to Patchem's receiver at Vauxhall Cross. The SIS would be able to tap into the US satellite feeds and track him.

Khalid's taxi had taken point for the convoy and was now half a kilometre ahead. They passed three patrol cars racing on the other side of the highway but weren't paid any attention to, just one of many taxis ferrying travellers from the airport. Their exit came and the taxi swung off the highway and onto a minor road before reaching a warehouse complex. The taxi entered a large, opened-ended warehouse where their new transport was waiting. The delivery van was painted with the livery of a livestock producer. Khalid allowed himself a smile. It was apt. The infidels were to be lambs to the slaughter.

The minibus, closely followed by the truck, skidded into the warehouse. Men already inside the building moved towards the minibus and pulled the Westerners out, half-dragging, half-pushing them towards the far end of the warehouse. Lermitte had tried to fight back but had been pistol whipped in the face; his mouth had taken most of the impact and his lips were swollen. Kennington held a handkerchief to his face. Blood was still gushing from his cheek and for once he was quiet.

Without any breeze, the heat inside the warehouse was unbearable; Snow painfully rolled onto his stomach and slowly raised his head. He counted the missioners, all there bar two. He could only hope that they, too, had escaped, but knew the chances were slim. In the far corner of the warehouse, several large flags which Arabic characters on them had been attached to the walls and a dozen or so chairs stood in regimented lines in front. A video camera on a tripod sat facing the 'set'. To the left, one of the kidnappers started to place the confiscated passports of the missioners on a table. A tall Arab, the leader of the group, spoke to the hostages in perfect English.

'We do not have much time. You will sit on the chairs and not say a word unless we ask you to.' As if to emphasise the importance of these instructions one of his men kicked Lermitte to the floor. Khalid continued, 'Do what I say and all will be well, Insha'Allah.'

The group was herded towards the seats. At the other end of the warehouse, the minibus pulled back out into the sunlight. In that moment's distraction there was a movement from the group; Thacker bolted for the door. Showing shocking speed for a man of nearly sixty, he reached the Ford pick-up just as Khalid fired a single shot into his back. Thacker was thrown forward as though a giant hand had pushed him. He tried to push himself up but his arms shook. In the second or so that he looked skywards, his eyes locked onto Snow's. He fell forward and blood trickled from his mouth, a large, crimson stain spreading across his cream, Savile Row shirt.

'You murdering bastard,' Snow growled quietly.

Khalid looked down at the remaining hostages. 'He did not listen. Now, if you will all please sit.'

Assault rifles were trained on the hostages to keep them still as other Arabs put on balaclavas to hide their faces. Khalid stood at the back and read from a prepared speech. His face was hidden by a red-checked shemagh that showed only his eyes. Snow felt a cold anger inside. Thacker had been harmless, an artist. A man who captured images of the Kingdom of oil in oils. While the pantomime proceeded, Snow carefully and painfully craned his neck to look around. There was no way he could overcome the kidnappers, no way to guarantee that, even if he could grab a weapon, anyone would escape. It would be suicide. As he watched, the group was pushed violently inside the white, flat-sided van. There were no protests, only whimpering and some tears. The roller door was then shut. The leader banged on the side and the van pulled off.

Snow's chauffeurs dismantled the set before heading back towards the Ford. Snow moved his head lower but his eyes were transfixed by the leader. As Snow watched, the tall Arab put his arm around the driver of the taxi and together they took two steps before his left hand drew a blade across the man's neck. The driver went limp in milliseconds and fell to the floor – a ball of rags. The leader held up his blade and pointed at the Ford. Snow flinched, but they hadn't seen him. The two remaining men shouted something in Arabic and got in. Snow again felt very exposed as the truck pulled away. He held his breath and made himself as flat as possible.

After watching the two vehicles leave the warehouse Khalid picked up a canister of petrol and poured it over the dead driver. He had been useful and had served Allah well. He would indeed go to Paradise. After covering the taxi he dropped a match into the puddle that had formed and moved away. Seconds later the car exploded. He moved towards the body of Thacker and kicked it. To his surprise it groaned. Khalid nodded and collected the video camera, tripod, and a chair. He turned it on and lined Thacker up in the viewfinder. When he was happy with the composition he rolled the man over onto his back. Thacker's eyes snapped open. Khalid put an arm under each of Thacker's and pulled him onto a chair. Thacker felt no pain, only a growing sense of delirium, as his body desperately tried to deal with the fatal wound it had sustained.

His head lolled; he had lost all sense of feeling and could move nothing apart from his eyes. Khalid positioned himself directly behind Thacker, shemagh on again, and spoke quietly but forcefully into the camera. He held Thacker's head with his left hand then drew his blade across the man's throat. The eyes flickered and then Thacker died. Khalid took several more blows to sever the head completely. The Arab turned the camera off, disassembled the tripod, then got into his own car and drove off. He had neglected his two other infidels for long enough.

Chapter 9

British Embassy, Riyadh, Kingdom of Saudi Arabia
The breaking news banner caught his attention instantly. Slinger-Thompson unmuted the television and leant towards the screen. Against a background that could have been anywhere, four armed men wearing balaclavas stood menacingly over a dozen or so dishevelled-looking Westerners.

Slinger-Thompson's eye twitched as it suddenly hit him. The trade mission. He pressed the record button on the DVD-TV combo and sat motionless. The footage ran in a loop, showing the same images again and again. The hostages with armed guards, the leader waving his fist and reading demands from a prepared list, and a close-up of the hostages' passports arranged on a table, open at the photo pages. The British ambassador appeared at the door, a shocked expression on his face, but before either man could say a word the desk phone rang. It was London.

SIS Headquarters, Vauxhall Cross, London, UK
Patchem followed the coordinates Snow's phone had transmitted and traced the route the insurgents had taken. From the Riyadh highway they had moved onto a much smaller and lesser road which would eventually take them towards the border with

Yemen. Patchem shook his head. Even with his relatively limited knowledge of the area, he knew Yemen was potentially as dangerous as Iraq for any Westerner to enter unarmed. It was widely acknowledged in intelligence and security circles that Yemen, in spite of recent covert operations, was becoming to the insurgents in Saudi Arabia what Pakistan was to the Taliban: a safe haven.

Patchem called up a map of the Kingdom and realised that things could only get worse. In the south was an area called Rub al-Khali, the Empty Quarter. One of the largest sand deserts in the world, it covered an area of more than 250,000 square miles, an expanse similar in size to France or, as the 'Russian' expert assessed it, Ukraine. Patchem traced the map with his finger; the Rub al-Khali extended beyond the international boundaries, continuing on into Saudi's neighbours, taking up large parts of Oman, Yemen, and the United Arab Emirates. In essence this meant that border crossings were completely unenforceable. In terms of the fight against terror he assessed it as a 'sodding nightmare', although he would use less colourful language when he addressed both the Foreign Secretary and the Prime Minister. He glanced at his wall clock. He still had ten minutes before he and Knight had to leave for COBRA. Clicking an icon on his desktop computer he watched once again the footage from Al-Jazeera.

Cabinet Office Briefing Room A (COBRA), Whitehall, London, UK
Since the general election defeat of New Labour and the formation of the Tory-Lib government, there had been three COBRA meetings: one to evaluate the impact of the recent outbreak of BSE in Jersey, a second to discuss the raising of the threat level to 'critical' after an attempted terror attack on the Bluewater Shopping Centre in Kent; and the last to discuss the downing of a Hercules transport plane en route to Kabul.

Known by the acronym COBRA, Cabinet Office Briefing Room A was the coordination centre in Whitehall used by the UK government in cases of national emergency or events abroad with major implications for HM Government. It was there that the group of government advisers and senior politicians who formed the Civil Contingencies Committee had secure communications facilities to enable them to obtain vital information about an incident and act upon it if needed.

Flanked at the head of the table by his two most vocal appointees (the Home Secretary and the Foreign Secretary), the Prime Minister, David Daniels, called the room to order. The attendees, in addition to the PM's party, included the Head of the Intelligence Service, the Director of UK Special Forces, the Director General of the Secret Intelligence Service, and Jack Patchem. It was the first COBRA meeting Patchem had been part of under the new Prime Minister, but he wasn't one to be intimidated, even though he was by far the most junior person in attendance. This was a COBRA emergency meeting and, as such, wasn't a full gathering of the Committee.

The Prime Minister pushed a lock of errant, unnaturally dark hair back from his forehead. 'Ms Knight?'

Abigail Knight flashed her perfected professional half-smile. 'Thank you, Prime Minister. Today, at 7.20 a.m. local Saudi time, we were alerted by our field officer in Riyadh that a British citizen had been murdered and that two others had potentially been taken hostage. The men worked for the Al Kabir Group. Just over two hours later, at approximately 9.20 a.m. local time, we learnt that a British trade mission travelling to the King Khalid International Airport with the intent of leaving the Kingdom had been attacked. Twelve more hostages were taken. Two further British citizens were confirmed dead at the scene by the Saudi authorities. Less than two hours after this second event, footage appeared on the Al-Jazeera network.'

Knight nodded at Patchem who pressed play on a remote. At the far end of the room a projector glided into place and a flickering image started to play.

'We have counted twelve British citizens onscreen which leaves one unaccounted for. The missing missioner is one of our officers and a former member of the Special Air Service.'

The attendees knew better than to ask questions until all the information had been presented. The Director of UK Special Forces, however, did half-open his mouth. Knight gave Patchem his cue to take over the presentation.

'We have been tracking our officer by GPS transmitter. He has informed me that he is travelling with the hostage group but that he has not been captured. I believe he is hiding in the second vehicle you see here.'

Patchem held up the remote again and a shot from a US surveillance satellite now appeared on the wall. The image showed, with almost unbelievable clarity, two vehicles – a white delivery van and an open-bed pick-up truck. 'I have every confidence in our officer and believe he will be able to assist us in any assault on the insurgents.'

The Home Secretary raised his eyebrow at Patchem's use of the word insurgents.

Patchem continued. 'The insurgents seem to be heading south towards the Empty Quarter where they will have to change their mode of transport if they are to attempt to cross the desert. There are no roads in this area; it is virtually impassable and its borders completely unenforceable. The Empty Quarter flows over the borders of Yemen, Oman, and the UAE. If we lose contact with our man once in the desert we may not be able to find them without direct assistance from US surveillance satellites. If, however, they decide to continue south-west, there is a road leading via the mountains to Abha. By taking this route they could hide in the mountains.'

'Any questions, gentlemen?' Knight took the helm again.

The Head of the Intelligence Service spoke first. 'You said that the first three British nationals to be targeted worked for the Al Kabir Group? That company is owned by Prince Al Kabir whose daughter was abducted in Brighton.' The Intelligence Service had handled the investigation in the UK, as per their remit. 'So is it just coincidence, or is this another attack on Al Kabir?'

Knight replied to her MI5 counterpart. 'At this stage we can't rule anything out. The Al Kabir group is a high-visibility target. An attack is always a possibility.'

The Intelligence Service Director, Burstow, made a note on his pad. 'So we send a team to Roedean to beef up their royal protection detail.'

'What demands have they made?' Wibly, the Home Secretary, had seen the footage but wanted to be sure.

The Foreign Secretary snorted and folded his arms. 'The usual! Leave Iraq, leave Saudi, convert to Islam, or we'll kill them all. Am I correct?'

Knight didn't like Robert Holmcroft, as he revelled in talking at her, but in this instance he was correct. 'Yes, Foreign Secretary. They have given us until midnight tonight; then they say they will execute one hostage every twelve hours.'

Around the room heads shook and faces became grim.

The PM again fiddled with his hair. 'I'm confused. Are these demands for both kidnap groups, or only the second? Also, have both incidents been perpetrated by the same group? What do we actually know about the insurgents?' He wanted all the answers.

'We don't know if both groups are being held by the same people. The video demands make no reference to the first group.'

'It would be a very bad case of coincidence if they were different groups!' The Foreign Secretary again spoke over Knight.

Knight continued undaunted, ignoring the Foreign Secretary. 'To answer your question, Prime Minister, we know very little except for their video demands. It is a group that is unknown to us.'

The PM's face showed signs of shock. Still new in his position, he had yet to realise or at least accept the limitations of intelligence. He sipped coffee from his cup and touched his hair. Of the seven people in the room, only two hadn't been present at the 'no eyes' meeting: Patchem and Sir Trevor Innes, Director of UK Special Forces. Events had, however, moved on and serious consideration now had to be paid to the very real possibility that these abductions, in an otherwise 'quiet' Saudi Arabia, might be part of the alleged Russian plan.

'Is this linked to the intelligence we received from our Ukrainian source?'

'We have no way to verify that either way, Prime Minister,' Knight replied.

Daniels looked at the soldier. 'General, what assets do we have in place to launch an assault?'

If Innes felt out of the loop, he didn't show it. 'There are some Royal Air Force personnel in Bahrain training the Bahraini Air Force. The Americans have some Marines in their Saudi air bases...'

'Where are the nearest SAS units?'

Sir Trevor cleared his throat. Officially, the British Army wasn't in Iraq any more. 'We have a team currently rotating out of Basra. Their replacements are due to arrive after the weekend.'

'Send them in.' The PM folded his arms to show that he had reached a decision.

The Foreign Secretary started to quiver; he'd had to hold back his bullish PM on other occasions too. 'Prime Minister, as I am sure you are aware, Saudi Arabia is a sovereign state, a friendly state. We cannot send any armed forces in unless we get the express permission of the Saudi government. I am afraid they would never agree on time.'

'I agree with the Foreign Secretary on the last part. We had problems during both Gulf Wars regarding operating rights out of Saudi bases.' Innes frowned. 'The Saudis have their own Special Forces unit and a hostage rescue team. They would, I believe, insist upon using these two units to assault any insurgents. These units have been trained by the Americans, Prime Minister, but they are unproven. I believe we have no alternative but to send in our own unit.'

'Which we cannot do.' The Foreign Secretary pointed with his finger.

Patchem listened and tried not to look annoyed. Precious time was ticking away; it was 10.25 a.m. in the UK, which meant 12.25 p.m. in Saudi. In less than twelve hours an innocent British citizen would be murdered, on camera.

'Prime Minister, we need a decision.' Knight broke the silence in her businesslike manner. 'We currently know where the second group of hostages is. We cannot let the insurgents get away.'

'Agreed.' The PM looked down the table. 'Mr Patchem, isn't it?'

'Yes, Prime Minister.'

'What would be your suggestion?'

All eyes focused on Patchem; the Foreign Secretary glared.

'We send in our own men and assault the insurgents. Once our people are safe, we inform the Saudis and let them take all the glory. Al-Jazeera and the Western media can then broadcast news of a successful hostage rescue attempt by the Saudi military. The Saudis will initially have their noses put out of joint, but once we've explained our reasons to them for acting unilaterally and the kudos they'll gain internationally for taking the credit, I'm certain there will be no repercussions.'

Innes nodded, Wibly furrowed his brow but remained silent, Burstow scribbled notes, while Holmcroft made eye contact with Patchem and shook his head slowly. Knight remained a passive observer; her pit bull was challenging the PM's.

'You have my agreement. General, contact Hereford and task the SAS unit with drawing up a hostage rescue plan. Liaise with Ms Knight. The sooner we can get our men on the ground the better.'

The decision taken, the meeting was called to an end. The PM exited the room followed by both the Home and Foreign

Secretaries. He took Holmcroft to one side as Wibly continued along the corridor towards the lobby.

'Robert, I know this isn't a course of action you approve of, but we have no other choice. I'm counting on you to smooth things over with the Saudi ambassador.'

Holmcroft sighed. 'He won't like this one bit.'

'Could you not offer our assistance in looking for those who kidnapped his brother's employees or perhaps offer to send over SAS directing staff to train his men?'

The PM was making sense but Holmcroft didn't want him to think that he knew best. It was no secret that Holmcroft had coveted the party leader position as his own, challenging all comers – including Daniels – but losing. He hadn't wanted to be Deputy PM and was glad he hadn't been asked. The Foreign Office was where the real power and prestige lay. A place where he spoke to the wealthy and influential, and didn't have to deal with the drudgery of day-to-day domestic politics.

'I think, David, that I might be able to persuade the ambassador to let us help him, but he will surely ask about the second kidnapping. Shall I lie to him and say we don't have any leads?'

The PM looked perplexed. 'Well, yes. Isn't that what you're meant to do, Robert? Lie on behalf of HM Government if it protects our citizens?'

'Of course.' There was a moment of silence. 'I shall phone the ambassador from my office and arrange to see him.'

'No, Robert. You'll call him now from a secure line; we can't waste any more time.'

'Of course, Prime Minister'

'Good, good.'

In room A, the general was already patched through to Basra via Hereford and relaying orders. At the other end of the table a live feed from a US satellite was displayed on the screen showing the two-vehicle convoy slowly moving along a metalled road that skirted the desert. Patchem sat and spoke to Vauxhall Cross.

'So why is Paddy Fox in Saudi Arabia?' Burstow asked Knight. 'Coincidence?'

The interservice rivalry had subsided somewhat in the post-9/11 years. Banter had now replaced boasts and secrecy.

'He was offered a job as a security adviser to the Al Kabir Group by Prince Fouad. We felt it would be a good opportunity for all if he took it.'

Burstow shrugged. 'We really don't have anything on these people, do we?'

Knight shook her head. 'If the insurgents gain a foothold in Saudi…'

She let her words trail off. Both directors knew what turmoil would ensue. The Saudi authorities would launch an all-out war, a crackdown on anyone suspected of being a militant or insurgent. The Mabahith, the Saudi secret police, would make arrests in the hundreds and use torture freely. It would split the nation in half: those who tolerated the presence of Westerners in the Kingdom and those who believed that the presence of infidels in a country housing two of Islam's most holy sites, Mecca, where the prophet Muhammad had been born, and Medina, where he was buried, was sacrilege.

The House of Saud would be caught in the middle, having to appease those who were anti-West and, at the same time, look out for their oil revenues from sales to the West. The insurgents believed the monarchy were puppets and had to be removed. In short, a civil war would ensue, one that would attract every Muslim fighter from around the globe to defend Islam. Oil supply would stop and, unless another source could be found, or US troops went in, the West would in effect be crippled.

'We're going to lose the satellite in about an hour.' Patchem turned in his seat. 'We could ask the Americans to retask it but there would be some explaining to do; at the moment we're just lucky it's covering the Riyadh and central Saudi area.'

'We could use their help but I'd rather keep this HM at the moment. '

'If you need me I'll be at the office.' Burstow stood and held out his hand. Knight shook it with her firm, professional grip.

The heat had been building all morning and Snow could feel his skin burning through his clothes, but he had no choice other than to stay lying on the truck bed. He had slowly turned over a couple of times to lie on his arms, protecting them from the worst of the sun. For the last forty minutes or so the two-vehicle convoy had slowed as it moved along an ever-worsening road. Snow had been bumped and banged more and more; the pain in his back, however, had become a dull ache as his body had become stiffer, the muscles contracting, while all the while his ears had been treated to the best Arab pop the Ford's radio had to offer. He pulled his mobile from his pocket and read the screen; he had two bars of reception left. If they headed any further into the desert he would lose contact with the network and, more importantly, anyone tracking him. It was now or never. He dialled Patchem's number.

He felt the phone vibrate before the ringtone had a chance to kick in. 'Patchem.'

'Jack, can you hear me?' Snow's voice was low and faded.

'Yes.' Patchem held the handset tighter to his ear. 'We have you visual on satellite.'

The pick-up hit a boulder and lurched; Snow rolled to one side as he tried to keep hold of the phone. His head hit the bulkhead and he let out a silent gasp.

Oblivious to Snow's agony, Patchem continued. 'We're going to lose visual in less than an hour. What is your situation?'

Snow hung onto a cargo hook and pressed himself even flatter. In as few words as possible, he gave Patchem a sit-rep. The number of men he had seen, a description of the leader, the murder of Thacker. Knight listened as Patchem put the phone on speaker, Snow's voice sounding ever fainter.

'I'm losing the signal.' Snow cursed that the phone wasn't an Iridium, but then Aidan Mills wouldn't have brought a satellite handset into the country.

'Stay with the insurgents; we're sending in a team.'

Another bump. Snow winced. 'Team?'

'Regiment.'

The line went dead.

There was a moment of silence before Patchem moved to a computer terminal and brought up a map of Saudi Arabia and the surrounding Gulf on the wall.

'We know they're here now.' He circled the area with a light pen. 'The only possible route for them to take with the vehicles is here.'

Knight nodded. 'If they stay in their vehicles.'

The road the kidnappers were on led them out of the Nejd, the Kingdom's central plain skirting the Empty Quarter, and up into the mountain range of the Jabal al-Hejaz before descending towards the administrative capital of Abha. It was at Abha that the Saudi government had taken its first steps towards tourism. Almost all vehicles, especially commercial traffic, entered the town via routes from Jeddah, Mecca, or Taif. However, it wasn't unknown for some to take the older and more arduous route preferred by the Bedouin. It was for this very reason that the insurgents had chosen this road where they would encounter only a handful of trucks.

'If they stay in the vehicles, we can estimate that they will have reached this point by nightfall.' Patchem indicated an area at the foot of the mountain range. 'Once here they'll be untraceable should they "de-bus".'

Knight let out a sigh. The mountains, although not particularly high, could hide myriad caves, a potential Saudi equivalent of the Afghan 'Tora Bora' complex. 'But on foot, wouldn't they be very slow?'

'Very slow.' Patchem echoed her words as an answer.

'Impossible isn't easy.' Innes joined them by the screen. 'But possible.'

'General?' Knight frowned.

'May I?' Innes took the light pen from Patchem. 'HMS *Tipperary* is currently here.' He made an X in the Persian Gulf. 'We can get our boys from Basra to there in a helo. No problem, just moving personnel around.' He drew a line. 'However, the interesting part is getting our team from the ship to the target area.' To demonstrate further he drew another line. 'This means cutting right across Saudi territory undetected and not having enough fuel to return.'

All three stared at the map as if to will a solution to appear.

Innes cleared his throat. 'The other option would be an HAHO insertion.'

'HAHO?' Knight frowned again.

'It's a parachuting term meaning "High Altitude High Opening". The men would be released at a high altitude, to reduce threat of the delivery aircraft's discovery by radar. We could fly a C130 out of Basra, down the Gulf, arc into Saudi, high over the drop zone, then return to base citing engine problems.' Innes could feel his fingers tingling. He wished he could be out there again.

'Which option is fastest?' Knight asked.

'HAHO is much faster than any HELIOPS – using a helicopter.'

Knight smiled. She knew what it meant, she wasn't completely clueless. What are the risks?'

'The helo would have to ditch in the desert; not enough fuel to return, so we'd have to explain that away. With HAHO the same risks as any night jump, but with the added complication of navigating into the unknown. The desert is quite featureless so they would have to rely one hundred per cent on GPS, but without visual way points.'

'Neither option is perfect but HAHO it is. We have to get your men there ASAP.'

'We can have them up within the hour.'

'I'll inform the Prime Minister.' Knight took a deep breath and picked up a phone.

The Desert, Kingdom of Saudi Arabia
With blurred vision Snow looked at his phone in disgust and put it back in his pocket. The engine note of the Ford changed as the incline of the road started to increase. Summoning all his strength he raised his head and could now for the first time see the shimmering peaks of mountains in the distance. He imagined the air getting cooler and fresher. Throughout the day his head had throbbed as the relentless sun bore into it. Without water, and exposed, he had become dangerously dehydrated and sleepy. Dehydration was by far the biggest cause of death in the desert. Snow's only hope was that they would stop soon and that he would find both water and shelter. If not, he was likely to pass out, never to wake.

Snow squinted in an attempt to clear his vision. Up ahead he made out figures emerging from the desert, as though painted with watercolours, their forms blurring into the sand. They waited at the side of the road. As the vehicles drew nearer Snow could see that these men, too, were armed and had with them several camels. It was a scene as ancient as the distant mountains but as foreboding as the automatic rifles they held close to their robed bodies. The vehicles slowed and stopped next to them. The driver of the truck jumped down and hugged the first Bedouin. The men in Snow's vehicle also stepped out and stretched. One walked to the other side of the road and down a sand berm where, unseen by all except Snow, he urinated. The Arabs, when it came to bodily functions, were modest.

Snow dropped slowly down to the scorching road surface and made his way around the blind side of the Ford. Both doors to the cabin were open. Thoughts flooded through his head of gunning the accelerator and ramming the insurgents, but he knew that wouldn't save the hostages. Instead he saw something that would mean the difference between life and death: his life or death. A bottle of water. He grabbed it and retreated back from the cab and towards the rear of the vehicle. The head of the 'relieved' Arab started to show above the sand. Snow crawled under the pick-up, behind the wheel, and lay still. The Arab passed the truck and moved to the van; Snow crawled back out and crouched. The Arab was met by two Bedouin, who helped him open the rear doors. Out stumbled several missioners overcome by heat and exhaustion; unlike Snow they had been protected from the sun by a steel roof; this, however, had raised the temperature even further. Lermitte and Kennington clambered out, helping the perfume manufacturer and the interior designer, who fell almost on top of them. One of the Arabs laughed and kicked one of the fallen women. Snow was disgusted but again unable to react. Lermitte, however, was not, and as Kennington complained to the man in Arabic, using his outraged diplomatic tone, Lermitte rose, swung his fist wildly and hit the Arab in the jaw. The Arab fell sideways – his thin, robed body knocked clean off his feet. Every muscle in Snow's body tensed as he saw the rifle land at Lermitte's feet.

Time seemed to stop as the other Arabs looked on astonished. Kennington was the first to speak, babbling faster than ever in Arabic. The Arab grabbed the rifle and pulled the trigger – but the safety was on. Snow felt himself move forward, ready to run at the group. A single shot rang out – fired skywards – and all eyes turned to the Bedouin by the side of the road. He held a pistol aloft and spoke softly. The Arab nodded his assent and hit Lermitte in the chest with the rifle butt, knocking him back. The remainder of the Bedouin and the kidnappers then herded the Brits out of the van and marshalled them in the desert at the side of the road.

Snow took a deep breath and relaxed. He sipped the water from the half-empty bottle slowly, savouring the warm, plastic-tasting liquid in his mouth. It was no way enough to rehydrate him, but was better than nothing. From Snow's viewpoint, crouching at the back of the truck, he saw the hostages being led onto a track that stretched away towards the mountains. It was hard to estimate the distance in the glittering desert heat but he gauged that, although the peaks were still distant, the actual range started no more than three miles or so away, where the sand started to give way to rocky outcrops. Even that relatively short distance would be torturous to all but the locals. The Bedouin with the pistol exchanged hugs once more with the driver of the livestock truck and gave a signal that his men should move off. The Arabs shut the van doors and climbed back in. Snow scrabbled off the road and lay in the burning desert sand just below the berm as the engines of the van, then the pick-up, started and the vehicles moved off.

Snow crawled up the berm and looked over the road. The Bedouin were frogmarching the Brits along the track at a speed which caused them to stumble and trip. Snow pulled out his phone and hoped against hope there would be a signal, but before he had even focused his tired eyes on the screen he knew he was wasting his time. With his GPS signal gone and the satellite probably lost too by now, Snow was on his own until the promised Regiment team arrived. *If* they arrived and could find the hostages, he mused bitterly. He let his face fall forward into the burning sand; he was exhausted, dizzy, his head still throbbed, and his back was impossible. But his mind was clear. He had no idea when the satellite feed had been lost or whether Patchem would drop a team onto an unconfirmed target. He raised his head. He had no choice but to follow the column, track them, and then try to rescue the missioners.

Embassy of the Kingdom of Saudi Arabia, London, UK
Prince Umar rose from behind his desk and raised his right arm to greet the British Foreign Secretary.

'Robert, my dear friend. What can I do for you today?'

Holmcroft noted that the prince was dressed in an impeccably tailored suit but today wore an expensive silk replica of their old school tie. The school they had both attended as boys forty years before.

'We have a lead on the men who kidnapped your niece.'

Umar kept hold of Holmcroft's hand. 'You have?'

'We believe they have now kidnapped a group of British citizens in Riyadh.'

Umar released the hand and waved his visitor towards the settee. He had a faraway look in his eye, Holmcroft noted, almost as though he was trying to calculate something. The men sat. Umar took several seconds then spoke.

'Tell me, what has happened?'

Holmcroft recounted how, first, the three employees of the Al Kabir Group had been taken, and then, the next day, the British trade mission. 'We have no concrete proof that both these abductions are the work of the same group but it would seem to be too much of a coincidence to be otherwise.'

Umar waved his hand in a dismissive gesture. 'It is not a coincidence, of that I am certain. And the lead is?'

'We have been tracking one of our men, an SIS officer who was with the trade mission but who was not captured. We know where the hostages are and we, HM Government, want the approval of you, the Kingdom of Saudi Arabia, to take them back.'

Umar leant back and folded his arms. The British Foreign Secretary had not only confirmed that British Intelligence had been working covertly in the Kingdom, but now also wanted to use their forces on his sovereign soil. It was a very blunt and shocking request for the Saudi.

'You have not been honest with me, Robert, regarding this agent. Who is he and why is he there? Of the Al Kabir employees, I have been told one man is dead, two are missing. One of these

218

is Mr Fox. Am I to presume that he, too, is an SIS agent? Has he been sent to spy on my own family?' There was a pause as the nostrils of the usually composed Saudi prince flared.

Holmcroft tensed, tried to speak. 'I know that...'

'Don't.' Umar held up his hand, took a deep breath. 'Stop. Robert, we are old friends, which is why I am listening to you. You wish to seek my agreement to use British Special Forces in a hostage rescue capacity on Saudi soil? Correct?'

'Correct.'

'This I will consent to. '

'Thank you. We would, of course, want Saudi Arabia to take full responsibility for any successful rescue operation.'

'Do not try to appease me, Robert. It is not I who needs his ego stroked, although I am certain the Crown Prince would be most pleased with any praise the Royal Saudi Army were to receive.'

Holmcroft was silent.

Umar stared at him. 'I will make a call to the Saudi Ministry of Defence; they will in turn expect a call from whoever is running your operation. I do not need to know the details. I just need to know that, if these really are the same people responsible for abducting my niece, they will be eliminated.'

Umar rose and returned to his desk. Holmcroft paused for a moment before he headed for the door.

'Robert.'

Holmcroft turned to face his childhood friend.

'We will talk more of the implications of what you have told me today at a later date. You have greatly disappointed me.'

Before Holmcroft could apologise an aide opened the door and he exited.

Umar sat motionless for a moment as he tried to form the words in his head that he needed to say to his younger cousin, the head of the Saudi Ministry of Defence. He felt anger that his family were under surveillance, supreme anger that they were being targeted by terrorists, resentment that HM Special Forces were best placed to rescue the hostages, and humiliation that he had to order his own regiment to step aside. A thought flickered across his mind. Had Jinan's abduction been staged in order to insert Paddy Fox? He dismissed it. No. Fox was a man of honour and Umar still owed him a debt of honour. Umar would allow the rescue to go ahead if that would mean Fox was rescued and his debt to the man repaid.

Riyadh, Kingdom of Saudi Arabia
In the Riyadh hotel room Khalid read the text message. All was in place. He closed the flip phone and looked across at the Chechen. 'The Bedouin have the hostages. Now can I have my money?'

Voloshin nodded and spoke in accented Arabic. 'Of course, my brother. I, too, am a man of my word.' He picked a pilot case up from the floor and placed it on the wooden desk. 'Please.'

Khalid stood and opened the bag. Inside, bundles of $100 bills filled it to the brim. He was astonished. 'And you had no problem bringing this into the Kingdom?'

Voloshin waved away the question; it had been in a diplomatic bag. 'Such things do not concern me.'

Khalid stood. 'Until we need you again, my brother, I must take your leave.'

Voloshin bowed and Khalid left the room. He was booked on an internal flight to Dammam where he had unfinished business.

Voloshin waited until the Arab had walked away from the door before putting the chain across. He didn't trust the man any further than he could spit. He opened the drinks cabinet and swore again at the lack of alcohol; he desperately needed vodka but instead opened a Coke. As the noisy air-conditioning unit broke the silence, he shut his eyes and visualised the next step of the operation in his mind. This, the most dangerous, he would undertake on his own. It was an act of potential suicide.

'The team are ready to go,' Innes announced with a tone of determination.

'And we've lost the target.' Patchem folded his arms in exasperation and leant back heavily. 'The satellite feed has gone and Snow's phone is still dead.'

Knight sipped her green tea and thought. 'General, what would be the likelihood of us finding the target based on starting at their last known location?'

Innes frowned. 'Not high. If they're still on the road, we could follow. If not, they could have moved off in any direction. We need a definite target for a rescue mission; for a recon mission, things are different.'

Knight nodded. Even moving as fast as they had, HM Government had not been fast enough. 'Options?'

'We go ahead, send in the team, then extract them if they can't find the hostages.' Patchem didn't want this to stop here.

'How long do they search for? A day? Two?' Knight shook her head. 'We do need a target otherwise we'll have to change our plan.'

'Involve the Saudis?' Innes didn't like the sound of that.

'If need be.' Knight took another sip. 'Or the Americans; this impacts them too.'

'If we want more satellite coverage I can't see any other alternative.' Patchem leant forward. 'So, "C", you need to call the PM.'

Knight nodded. Much as she hated the idea, she knew that to involve either the Americans or the Saudis would need Number Ten's permission. She just hoped the PM would make his own decision and not be swayed by the Home Secretary.

Patchem's Blackberry vibrated in his pocket. He pulled it out. 'Patchem. What? Yes, send it to me.'

Knight raised her left eyebrow.

'That was a technician from the Arab Desk. We have some footage taken by Fox's sunglasses.'

'I don't understand?' Innes waited for an explanation.

As Patchem hastily connected his Blackberry to the nearest computer and uploaded the file, he explained the device to both Innes and Knight. They waited as the footage was opened on the computer screen. The image was jumpy but showed a desert road, the outskirts of a town, and then more desert. The last few seconds showed three concrete, single-storey buildings and then, tantalisingly, the inside of a minivan and two figures slumped on the floor between the rows of seats. The footage stopped as the corner of a beard appeared in the frame.

Knight spoke first. 'We need to know where that is. Get the tape analysed frame by frame.'

'That's already underway.'

'Why did it stop?' Innes asked. 'The recording?'

'Presumably the wearer took the glasses off. Also, remember we only get an upload when they're placed in the case.'

'Hmm, I normally leave mine on the dashboard.'

Patchem nodded. 'No piece of equipment is perfect.'

Doha, Qatar

The courier sat and drank his sweet coffee. As requested, he had dropped off the tape at the head office of the television channel. However, contrary to instructions, he had unwittingly picked up a tail and was at this precise moment being watched by an agent of the Central Intelligence Agency.

From their headquarters in Langley, Virginia, the CIA had kept tabs on the network for the past nine years, ever since it had shown the first tape from Osama Bin Laden. The channel knew they were being watched. As the most transparent broadcaster in the Gulf, they knew they had nothing to hide, but were still, rightly so, highly protective of their sources. On numerous occasions the CIA had attempted to infiltrate the station but somehow it had never happened. However, routine surveillance of anyone entering or leaving the building had been kept up, especially when packages were delivered. The station boss knew about this.

Ayman Qasim (real surname Johnson), the son of a Sudanese mother and African American father, stood across the road, leaning against his taxi, lazily reading a paper. The CIA field officer spoke Arabic as a native speaker, which worked for his cover as a migrant worker. Keeping his eyeline just above the paper, he watched the man wearing the red Saudi headscarf who had visited the broadcast office. The man had seemed tense on entering the building but his body language had changed as soon as he re-emerged. Sitting in a café, not more than fifty metres away, he looked as though he hadn't a care in the world. Johnson had a photographic memory for faces and was certain he hadn't seen this one before. His cellphone rang via a Bluetooth headset.

'Nam?' He answered in Arabic, using the word for 'Yes'.

The caller spoke English with a Southern drawl. 'Our friends just aired some breaking news. Footage of a group of Brits, taken hostage in Saudi Arabia.'

Ayman's heart beat a little faster as the caller asked, 'Have there been any deliveries in the last hour?'

'Nam.' Ayman was looking at the only person to enter the building that morning who didn't work there.

'You got it covered?' The voice knew Johnson was watching the entrance.

'Nam.'

'Good. Don't lose him.'

Johnson ended the call.

The way footage was delivered didn't differ from any other television station. It could be sent electronically via email, the internet, or physically in the form of a DVD, memory card, or USB stick, either in person or by courier. Thanks mainly to the belief that the United States could see all and hear all online, certain organisations had now switched back to the low-tech,

223

simple, analogue delivery methods, such as the one sitting opposite, drinking sweet coffee.

There was, of course, no proof that the man under surveillance had delivered the hostage footage; that might have come from any number of other sources or the branch office in Dubai. But Ayman had a gut feeling. The same feeling that had got him through the Academy. As he watched, the man stood and hailed a cab. Ayman had no choice but to let his colleague, a real taxi driver higher up the rank, take the fare. As they pulled, off Ayman followed, making sure he wasn't following too close behind. The courier was returning to the airport, the journey barely a twenty-minute ride away from downtown Doha. Ayman let the passenger pay and leave before he opened his own door and spoke to his fellow driver.

'Good tipper?'

The older man shook his head. 'Awful. He didn't give me one.'

'Where was he going?'

'Riyadh – he called his wife. Why are you interested?'

Ayman shrugged. 'We live on tips; I don't want him in my cab, that's all.'

'Huh.' The man grunted and pulled away.

Ayman removed his headset and put his phone to his ear, partly obscuring his face, and swiftly walked into the airport. The suspect had joined a line for the Saudi Arabian Airlines flight to Riyadh. He made a note of the flight number.

'Yo?' The voice with the Southern drawl picked up.

'He's getting on the Saudia flight to Riyadh.' Ayman gave the number.

'Understood.'

Ayman lingered until he saw the suspect enter passport control then returned to his taxi; luckily it had not been ticketed.

In Riyadh, a cellphone rang. 'Hello?'

'Got one coming your way,' the voice said. 'The Saudi Arabian

Airlines flight arriving at 5.20 p.m. I'm sending you a photo now.'

The phone bleeped to advise the user a multimedia message had arrived.

'OK.' Muhammad Khan closed the phone. A CIA field officer of Pakistani descent, he would continue surveillance in Saudi Arabia.

Embassy of the United States of America, Riyadh, Kingdom of Saudi Arabia

'This is Vince Casey.' The lazy-sounding Southern drawl hid an agent who was far from it.

'Vince. What can I do for you?' At the other end, Harry Slinger-Thompson cradled the phone between his neck and right shoulder as he typed an email.

'That's a strange question, Harry. I was wondering what we could do for you?'

Slinger-Thompson paused mid-keystroke.

Casey continued. 'It seems to me you got a problem there with some of your nationals.'

There was no point denying it; the footage was all over the 24-hour news channels and he himself was personally shaken by it. 'Yes, a problem indeed, Vince. A trade mission was attacked this morning and twelve British citizens have been taken hostage.'

'I know. MI6 called Langley, so that's why I'm calling you, Harry.' There was silence except for the sound of breathing at the end of the line. 'Do you have any idea where they are?'

'Yes.' He replied too quickly and immediately realised. 'No. We had a GPS location but then we lost the satellite.'

'Harry, you wouldn't be planning anything that would worry our beloved hosts, would you?'

Slinger-Thompson sidestepped the question. 'Vince, finding the hostages is my main priority, so anything you have would be greatly appreciated.'

'OK, email me the last known fix. Also, I may have something, maybe nothing. We have a man under surveillance who visited the Doha office of a TV network this morning. We're going to follow him and see what we get. This so far, Harry, as the French say, is "entre nous".'

Given far greater budgets than the SIS, the CIA amazed Slinger-Thompson with the sheer number of agents and other assets they seemed to have.

'That's all I wanted to say to ya, Harry. I'll keep you in the loop.'

Casey brought up a file on his desktop and traced the coverage circles of all US satellites covering Africa, the Middle East, and the Pacific Rim. Unless he tasked one of the birds, there would be a six-hour gap between passes. He brought up another file and entered a password. A further three birds appeared – these showed up on no other chart or record. Bird number two was stationed in a geo-stationary orbit above the Middle East. At its southernmost reach lay the Yemeni coastline. He shook his head; even with this classified CIA spy-bird, it would be like looking for a needle in a haystack, blindfold.

In the British Embassy, Slinger-Thompson was ill at ease. The Americans knew HM Government was planning an assault. He tapped his fingers on the embassy-issue desk. Something had been worrying him and it was starting to become clear. It was something Casey had said – a phrase. It was nearly there; an idea in his mind but not quite, not yet. He leant back and ran his fingers through his schoolboy-like floppy hair and stared at the water stains on the ceiling caused by the faulty air conditioner. What was it? What had been niggling at him?

'Under surveillance'. That was the term Casey had used. The trade mission was under surveillance – someone had been watching them to see when they left the hotel and where they were going; or, even more chilling, had made the mission leave the hotel early. He sat upright and slammed both palms onto the desk. The attackers had known the embassy would evacuate the trade mission and had planned to intercept it all along. Therefore, the first attack, which had left Glaister dead and Fox missing, had been a diversion. The full horror of what he might have been partly responsible for registered. He had ordered the evacuation; he had gone along with the kidnappers' plan. His hands started to shake. But wait, he told himself – this was just a theory not confirmed by any evidence or facts.

He took a deep breath and called his contact within the Riyadh police. He asked him to check the employee records of the mission's hotel. Were any of the employees acting suspiciously? Had any of them gone home sick or taken the afternoon off? Were any of them new? Also, the taxi company that serviced the hotel – the same questions. Could they get the surveillance tapes from both the hotel lobby and entrance?

His contact happily took down the list of requests and immediately started to act upon them. A promotion would be on the cards for anyone who found the missing Brits and he wanted to be that person.

Next, Slinger-Thompson called Patchem and relayed his theory to him. Patchem, still in the COBRA, listened and did not dismiss the idea. In Slinger-Thompson's opinion, the man on the ground generally knew best.

Unknown Location, the Arabian Desert
The kidnappers had been humane so far, giving Lordy and Fox more water than they could possibly drink and leaving them unchained. They had been led, one at a time, out of their cell and along the corridor to a smaller, empty room with a dirt floor that they had been instructed to use as a toilet. Fox had tried to sneak a peek outside but had been gently reminded by a tap to the temple that he was not to do so.

Lordy sat with his head in his hands. 'I can't take this, Paddy.'

'Mate, we've been here less than a day. Course you can.'

In truth, Fox was worried about the usually jovial Londoner.

He had cracked up and gone into shock after seeing his mate murdered in front of him. Fox sometimes forgot that not everyone could cut away, compartmentalise the mind. Now he was focused on survival and would think about the death of Frank Glaister only when he himself was safe. Fox recited the old saying in his head, 'Once Regiment Always Regiment', the mock greeting he and his mates had said to each other at Hereford piss-ups. It gave him a strength that could never be taken away, reminded him of who he was and would never cease to be.

Fox stood and leant against the wall. 'Right, you get up.'

Lordy looked up blankly. 'What?'

Fox held out his hand. 'Up.'

Lordy shrugged and Fox pulled him to his feet.

'Now, the best way to relieve stress is through gentle exercise.' It also distracted the mind, he didn't add.

Lordy's face was still blank. 'What, have a wank?'

Fox dropped to the floor. 'No, you silly sod. Copy me.' He did ten quickfire press-ups before getting back to his feet. 'Your turn.'

'You're a loon,' Lordy grumbled, but he copied none the less.

Fox led the pair of them through a routine of press-ups, sit-ups, and stretches before they both sat back against the wall. 'Better?'

Panting, Lordy nodded. 'Yeah. You're fit for an old codger.'

Fox smiled. He could feel his body becoming alive and felt some of his aches lessen as more blood pumped around his system. 'We do this three times a day and, by the time we've finished, you'll be able to pull all the nurses you want.'

Lordy managed a smile then became serious. 'How long do you think they'll hold us here for?'

Fox shrugged. 'Couple of weeks, perhaps. Look, it's not Beirut. We're not going be here for years like John McCarthy.'

'Wasn't he one of the Beatles?'

It was now Fox who became serious. 'From what I can see there are about five or so of them holding us. We're going to get out of here; it's just a matter of when.'

Lordy nodded and didn't question Fox's statement. Fox, for his own part, didn't either. If he could grab a rifle he was sure he could take some of them out – especially with the cover the building gave him. He noted the way they held their weapons; they had little or no training.

The door opened and two men carried in a heavy metal table while another held an AK pointed at the two Brits. Once the table had been placed in the middle of the room the men retreated and returned with three metal chairs. Lordy held his arms around his chest and looked on. Fox felt the hairs on the back of his neck stand up; something told him this wasn't good. The men returned again for a third time, but now carrying what appeared to be jump leads and car batteries. It all became clear: the water, the metal furniture, the leads, and now the batteries.

'What's all that for?' Although quick-witted, Lordy hadn't a clue, and Fox wasn't going to be the one to break it to him.

'Perhaps they want to run some more lights or a camera.'

'Oh, yeah,' Lordy replied weakly, nodding. 'They make tapes of hostages, don't they?'

Fox didn't reply; he focused on the man with the gun who lifted up his balaclava. He had a young face covered with a straggly beard and arrogant eyes. Why show your face now? Fox didn't like the answer he reached; if they were to die it wouldn't matter whose face they saw.

The man spoke in English. 'Get up.' He pointed his finger first at Lordy, then at Fox. 'Up now!' His accent distorted the words.

Fox stood slowly and stuck his hand out to Lordy, who held it and pushed himself up.

The man shook his head in disgust and spoke in Arabic to the two others. 'That one acts like a woman.'

Fox didn't let his face show he understood as the man nearest the door replied, 'She is a woman, Salah.'

The three laughed in a strange manner. Fox didn't find any humour; it must have been an in joke between 'bum chums', he decided. The man at the door reached back around the frame and produced two orange bundles. He threw them at Fox and Lordy.

Salah, the one with the exposed face, spoke again. 'Put these on.'

'W… why?' Lordy stammered

'Put these on.'

'He doesn't want us to see his knickers,' said the third man in Arabic, sniggering. The trio started to laugh again but their mood swiftly changed when they saw Lordy's tattoos.

'What are those?' Salah demanded.

'They're just tattoos,' replied Fox.

Salah pointed his bony finger at Lordy. 'What are those?'

'Tattoos,' Lordy said in a voice that almost broke.

Salah rushed forward and grabbed Lordy's right arm. He stared, his eyes full of fury at the large, inky cross that covered the entire side of his upper arm. Lordy tried to pull his arm away but the grip was firm. Fox's hands were in his jumpsuit, pulling it up. As he freed them, two rifles were aimed at him. Salah span Lordy around to inspect the rest of the tattoos. Another much larger cross rose from his lower back and spread across his shoulder blades; on his upper left arm was a small Union Jack with the words 'Green Army' written underneath.

'You are army!' Salah accused Lordy, pushing him violently against the wall. 'You are army!'

Arms free, Lordy held them up to protect his face. 'No.'

'You are army!' Salah kicked him in the stomach.

'No, I'm not army. H… he… he's…'

The vein in Fox's head throbbed and his body tensed for action. The two rifles, however, remained pointed at him, ready for an excuse.

Before Lordy could give away his secret, Paddy spoke. 'It's football. It's a football team.'

'What?' Salah turned his head. 'Army football team?'

'No, just football. Like Manchester United.'

Salah's eyes flickered. 'Which team?'

'Plymouth Argyle.' Lordy's voice was raspy.

Salah took a step back. 'What division are they in?'

'The Coca-Cola league championship.'

The Arab's face was confused. 'I have not heard of this team or this league. They must be very bad? Perhaps they are women?' He translated this into Arabic and it apparently became funny as the two kidnappers holding the guns started to laugh.

Lordy didn't like the insult but remained quiet.

Salah pointed at the overalls again. 'On, woman football.'

As Fox continued to dress he felt the mood in the room change; below the balaclavas he could sense that serious faces were now on. Three of them in the room now meant there were two more outside, maybe more. If he moved quickly he could get to one rifle and perhaps pull the trigger, but no, there wasn't enough space.

'Sit on the chairs.' Salah's eyes looked cold.

'Come on, mate; be nice to sit for a bit.' Fox helped Lordy to his seat.

Without warning, Salah picked up the bucket of 'drinking water' and threw the contents over the two captives. He then took a roll of duct tape and secured their arms to the table before taping their legs to the chairs. Lordy was too scared to resist and Fox too wise. Next came the electrodes. Lordy fainted as the first was placed on his chest. Fox tightened his jaw. The voltage initially wouldn't be fatal, just painful, very painful. Salah took the second bucket and tipped it over Lordy's head, making him regain consciousness with a jolt.

'Time to start.'

The man by the door tightened the connectors on the batteries and bolts of pain shot through the two men. Fox clenched his jaw as his body tried to pull away from the seat but was stopped by the tape. Lordy's tongue lolled out of the side of his mouth and blood trickled along its length. Salah turned his back to speak to the others.

Fox looked at Lordy. 'Put your tongue inside your mouth and clench your jaw or you'll bite it off!'

Two more shocks followed in quick succession before they were allowed to rest. Steam rose from the cotton overalls.

'What do you want?' Fox's voice sounded weaker than normal.

Salah's eyes narrowed. 'To see how long you will live.'

Fox's heart beat faster. The man was a sadist – he wasn't after anything. Fox took a deep breath. He had to give them a reason to keep him alive. 'Look, I'll tell you anything; just let me know what you want.'

Another shock hit him and he fought to keep his jaw clenched.

There was a noise at the door and their leader entered. 'Salah! Stop!'

'Khalid! I was trying to see what they know.' His voice grew higher and took on a pleading tone.

'About what?' Khalid hadn't given any such orders.

'I thought they might…' The sentence was cut short by the back of Khalid's hand hitting the youth's mouth.

'Do not do anything unless I tell you. Is that clear?'

Salah held his mouth – he tasted blood. 'Yes, Khalid.'

Fox listened to the Arabic then spoke in English. 'What do you want from us?'

Khalid placed a video camera in Salah's hand. 'Set it up.' He looked at Fox. 'What I want is for your government to leave this country, to stop persecuting peaceful Muslims!'

'But if the British government leaves Saudi, who will ensure peace?'

'We will!' In his anger, Khalid hadn't noticed Fox's deliberate use of 'Saudi'.

So they weren't in Iraq, Fox thought. 'But we are here to help you.'

Khalid leant forward and Fox got a close-up of his dark eyes.

'You being in the country, breaking Islamic law, is an insult to Allah. All you infidels must leave!'

The camera was ready; Salah and a masked kidnapper took a large flag and taped it against the back wall of the room. Khalid positioned himself behind the two hostages and spoke into the camera in Arabic.

'You have not heeded our warnings; you have not followed our orders. Your Christian crusaders are still in Iraq and your devils mock Allah in the Kingdom. Because of your arrogance and inaction these two British men will die! We will electrocute them the way you do your prisoners in America. The Warriors of Mecca are upon you! Allah Akbar!'

The other insurgents present joined the chant. 'Allah Akbar... Allah Akbar... Allah Akbar... Allah Akbar... Allah Akbar... Allah Akbar.' Their eyes seemed to glaze as they chanted.

Lordy started to squirm as he thought he was about to die. 'NO! D... don't do it! Don't... P... Please don't KILL ME!'

Another shock hit Fox and Lordy; it was longer and felt more painful than ever, causing both men to pass out, the manic chant still ringing in their ears.

When Fox awoke he found himself lying on the floor in the foetal position, still dressed in his orange jumpsuit. The set had been pushed to one side and two more buckets of water were present. Fox had never felt this way before; his nerve receptors were on fire, his body hot with pain, his muscles cramped. He tried to stretch as his body shook, every movement agony as though his body was ripping apart. To his left Lordy was still out. Fox stubbornly forced himself through the pain to perform a push-up, then another. As he did so his body relaxed slightly as the muscles warmed and more blood pumped. He stood and slowly hobbled around the room. Could he believe what their leader – the one they called Khalid – had said? That they would die? What about their demands? Had these been issued recently or before the kidnap? It didn't make sense. Why make demands but not give enough time to carry them out? Why make threats so soon?

As Fox paced his mind started to work. If they had been taken for money, then their safety could be bought; Al Kabir would pay. But global demands like theirs, 'leave Saudi', were unrealistic. He knew it and he felt pretty sure Khalid knew it too. As Lordy started to groan it hit him. He and Lordy, once captured on tape, were dispensable; the footage could be shown at any time regardless of whether they were actually alive or dead. Fox sat next to Lordy and let the back of his head bang against the wall. That was it. He had to escape.

Olaya District, Riyadh, Kingdom of Saudi Arabia
The taxi brought the courier directly to Riyadh's Olaya District, the commercial heart of the city. The route took him past the Kingdom centre, one of Riyadh's major landmarks, and deposited him outside another, the Al Faisaliyah Centre. The courier paid the driver and entered the building.

Muhammad Khan left his own driver and discreetly followed the courier towards the Al Faisaliyah complex. As Khan watched, the courier marched directly into a men's outfitters. Khan edged closer and stood looking into a window in the boutique opposite. He studied the reflection behind him; the courier was greeted by a shop assistant and then shown to a rack of Western business suits. Khan cursed not having a parabolic microphone handy; he had a mini version especially designed for listening in to urban conversations. The quality wasn't great but indoors it improved. He could not lose contact with the courier, so swallowed, said a silent prayer, and entered the shop. The assistant was still showing him the suits so Khan walked towards a rack of ties. He was himself dressed in slacks and a short-sleeved shirt, perfect for buying a tie. He positioned himself so he was at a right angle to the courier and, while studying the designer silk ties, listened to the conversation occurring in Arabic.

'This is a Chanel suit and is made in Paris. You will find that the quality is extremely high. It has a ventless back, which is very contemporary and flattering for the thinner man like yourself.' The assistant held up the suit and smoothed the lapel with his thumb and forefinger.

Khan listened to every word, searching for any code or hidden meaning.

'Is it the latest line?' the courier asked.

'Yes, it came from a small shipment that arrived today. Very exclusive, only two in this colour,' replied the assistant.

'May I try it on?'

'Why, of course you may. Just through the curtain there.' The assistant beamed and the courier entered the fitting room.

Khan concentrated on the nearest tie; this, too, was Chanel and he had to admit it was very elegant. Burgundy, with a dark-blue stripe and a very subtle repeated Chanel logo. 'This is very nice.'

'Why, yes, sir, it would be a very good match for that blue shirt you are wearing.' The assistant glided forward and dripped obsequiousness. 'Is it for business wear?'

'Yes,' nodded Khan. 'I couldn't help but notice the suit you showed the other customer. I also like that.'

The assistant's eye flickered briefly. 'I am afraid that is the only one in that particular line.' He smiled. 'But there are others that would "suit".'

Khan wanted to stay in the shop until the courier left. 'No, that is OK. I think I shall take just this tie; that is unless…'

The assistant's eyes flickered again. 'Unless what, sir?'

'Unless you can convince me that there is another tie I might also like?'

He clasped his hands together, dollar signs all but visible in his pupils. 'Why, of course.' He gestured with the palm of his hand. 'Here we have a very distinctive tie by Hermes. It depicts a repeated interlocking chain on a burgundy background, or this one has a delightful skylark pattern.'

Both Hermes ties were too fussy for Khan's liking. As he pretended to consider them the curtain fluttered open and the courier reappeared.

The assistant moved away. 'If you will excuse me for one moment, sir?'

The courier held up the suit. 'I shall take this.'

'Very well, you have excellent taste.' He scanned the price tag. 'That will be 3,026 Riyals.'

The courier didn't flinch at the price, merely handed the assistant a credit card. The assistant studied the card. 'There is a slight handling fee for American Express.'

'No problem.'

'Very good. If you could sign here?'

The courier signed the credit slip as the assistant packed the suit into a Chanel suit carrier. The canvas carrier seemed to hang slightly as though it wasn't empty. Khan walked towards the counter brandishing the Chanel tie. There was no point in trying to hide his face from the man; it would only make him look more suspicious.

The courier picked up his suit and left the boutique.

The assistant took the tie and read out the price. 'Six hundred and seventy-two Riyals.'

Khan tried not to show his shock but handed over seven hundred Riyals and willed the man to give him his change quickly. As Khan left the shop the assistant bade him a cheery farewell. Outside on the pavement the courier put on a pair of sunglasses and stepped into a taxi. Khan followed the direction of the taxi and stepped into a car.

'I think we have something.'

'You think so?' replied the driver, a CIA field officer by the name of Mahdi.

'Yep.' They now spoke in English. 'I think he was given something at the shop.'

'Follow that car?' mused Mahdi.

'Yep, just like the films.'

The CIA Toyota followed the taxi at a distance, always keeping at least two cars in between them. The route took the two cars into the old part of the city, Al-Bathaa, known for cheap lodging and shopping, where the courier got out. Mahdi stopped the car further along the road and watched as the courier entered a building that purported to be a hotel.

'We can't stay here for long.'

Khan agreed. 'But we need to find out what he was given. We'll have to go in.'

'I'll find a place to park; you stay here and keep an eyeball on the hotel.'

Khan nodded and exited the car.

As Mahdi moved away Khan entered the hotel. As he asked the desk clerk for room prices he scanned for a back door. To his relief he couldn't see one. Once furnished with a rack rate quote he crossed the road once more and sat in a nearby café, ordered an Arabic coffee, and focused on the front of the hotel. He would wait there until he got further instructions from Casey. In an hour or so Mahdi would swap places with him. It would be difficult for just the two of them to keep a constant watch, but without any further proof more agents wouldn't be allocated.

Embassy of the United States of America, Riyadh

'Casey.'

'Mr Casey, you asked me to keep an eye out for anything unusual...' The monitoring clerk, another Southerner, was nervous with excitement.

'Yes, Doreen?' Casey sat up straighter at his desk.

'Well, Echelon just picked up a message from that sat phone we found before in the Saudi desert.'

'That's great, Doreen, send it over.'

'Right away, Mr Casey.'

His desktop played the clicking clock from the TV show *24*, a simple thing he had installed to amuse himself and to alert him to any new high-priority emails. He clicked on the icon and opened the message from Doreen Wilson. The call that had been intercepted by the keyword recognition software of the Echelon monitoring system wasn't in itself alarming; rather it was the combination of phrases, that had been identified as in use by Al-Qaeda.

Two sentences stood out:

Caller: 'Greetings, my brother, your friends have arrived safely. When shall we commence the celebrations?'

Receiver: 'My brother, I have been delayed by one hour and will not be able to be with you until morning.'

It was an old code, one he hadn't seen for over a year, but a ping none the less. The analysis of the conversation, which Casey didn't need to check, was attached:

Caller: We have the hostages. When shall we execute the first?

Receiver: Delay for twelve hours.

The code was simple, effective, but broken. The location of the call had been triangulated, the caller staying on the phone for just long enough. Casey tapped the coordinates into the desktop and immediately an area in the Saudi mountains was pinpointed. A large smile creased his tanned face.

'We got your boys, Harry, we got your boys.'

Casey's hand hovered over his desk phone before going back to the keyboard. He tapped in a quick message and forwarded the coordinates to Slinger-Thompson. He then brought back up the spy-bird and zoomed in on the coordinates. He'd keep an eye on this development but his real goal was the man at the other end of the conversation. The man who had been under surveillance since he first started to deliver packages to the TV network. The man who, Casey also believed, relayed messages from the top. The number was tracked and, as expected, was the same Saudi cellphone. The courier had become sloppy, underestimating the reach of Echelon and the CIA itself. No name or billing address was registered for the number. Casey, however, got a location from the call: Riyadh. The location was in the Al-Bathaa quarter. Was it as simple as that? Casey rang his two field officers from his cellphone and called for his car. They would grab the courier and his phone, a bit of 'friendly rendition' for the Brits. The courier would, he hoped, lead them to his 'sheikh' and, in turn, the wider network of insurgents operational in and between Iraq and Saudi Arabia.

Unknown Location, the Arabian Desert

The door opened again. Lordy cowered in the corner as Fox readied himself for attack. The two guards had returned. Fox held a bucket in his left hand and, just as the second man entered, threw it. It hit the guard on his shoulder. He dropped his weapon. The first, stunned, stood motionless. Fox pounced and grabbed the AK from the first guard. Both men slipped on the wet floor and went down. Fox rolled on top and held the rifle against the man's throat as the trigger finger pulled. On fully automatic, rounds leapt out of the barrel of the Kalashnikov and impacted into the concrete walls. Both Fox and the guard were momentarily deafened. The weapon started to come loose when there was a sudden sharp blow to the back of his head. Fox's hands lost their grip as stars burst before his eyes. His body was limp before he hit the floor.

Khalid slapped Salah in the face with the back of his hand, a second time. The insult and loss of status in front of his men hurt Salah as much as the blow. He bowed his head, humiliated for the second time that day.

'You fool.' Khalid whispered the insult. 'What if he had managed to escape? You would have been ridiculed, an affront to the Prophet.'

'Khalid, I am sorry.' Salah's pleading tone hid his rising anger at himself. 'I will ensure that they pose no further threat.'

'You will keep them bound and you will not kill them unless I directly order it so. Is that understood?'

'Yes.'

Khalid placed his hand on Salah's shoulder; he had used the stick, now he would use the carrot. 'My brother, when the West sees our footage, they will tremble at the might of the Warriors of Mecca.'

Salah looked up at Khalid with pride.

Khalid smiled. 'I am to leave now and give further instructions to our brothers.'

Alone, Salah watched as Khalid exited the building, climbed into his German-built SUV, and headed for the city. Salah returned to the cell. Both the infidels had been tied to the chairs once more. The older one was still unconscious but the other was awake and shaking. Salah told the men to attach the electrodes while he, once again, switched on the camera. He was proud that Khalid had chosen him; he would now show him what he was capable of.

As though through a fog, Fox's eyes started to focus. Before they could distinguish any definite shapes he felt tepid water being poured over him. Suddenly everything was once again clear. He could hear Arabic from behind him. He had no choice but to speak. 'My name is James Fox and I came to Saudi to help the Saudi people…'

'BE QUIET!' a voice yelled in Arabic.

'I came to help the people of Saudi Arabia but these…'

'QUIET!' Salah shouted again, this time in English.

The two guards didn't move; they were being filmed but the infidel was shouting in his own language. Salah fired his rifle, the sound bouncing from the concrete walls. He grabbed Fox's chair and pulled it to the floor. Fox tensed and his neck took the torque, preventing his head from slamming into the floor.

'My name is James Fox and I am a friend of the Saudi people…'

A rifle was thrust into his face; he tried to turn his head as it bit into the flesh of his cheek. The muzzle was warm from the single shot and stung.

240

'You will be quiet now.' Salah barked an order 'Shoot him.'

Time stopped as Fox saw the end. Images of his parents and Tracey appeared in his mind's eye. He closed his eyes, not because of cowardice but because he didn't want the manic face of Salah to be the last thing he saw. Tracey's face was there smiling, one of those smiles he hadn't seen since she'd left him. She was the only person who had mattered to him. He smiled now too. Sod it. None of it mattered any more. Despite himself he could feel tears form.

A single shot rang out, a scream. Fox opened his eyes. His chair was yanked upright, then turned to face Lordy. Blood was seeping through the stomach area of his jumpsuit and his crotch was wet. Salah prodded the area with his rifle as the others laughed.

'I told you to be quiet.' He placed his rifle on the table and produced a curved blade dagger. He held it against Fox's chest. 'You have caused this.'

The stomach wound wept more blood. It would be fatal if not treated. Fox closed his eyes again, willing it not to happen, bound to the chair, unable to do anything to stop it. He heard the three Arabs in the room start to chant.

'Allah Akbar... Allah Akbar... Allah Akbar...'

'Paddy...' Lordy's words were cut short by a scream.

Fox's eyes flicked open and widened in horror as Salah drove the dagger deep into Lordy's heart. The Londoner's body shook as his life left it. Salah removed the dagger and held it aloft, the chanting continuing. He was toying with him, the murdering bastard. Fox's blood ran hot. Killing Lordy was one thing but, somehow, taunting him was another. His arms flexed and he felt the bonds move ever so slightly, but move they did. A wave of pain jolted his body as the current was sent racing through his system. He felt his heart pound and clenched his teeth. The lifeless corpse of Lordy jerked, reanimated by the current. Fox looked past the Londoner and fixed his gaze at a point on the wall, willing his body to ignore the pain, all the while his heart being forced to beat faster.

More duct tape was bound round his legs as he was cut from the chair then kicked to the floor. His body went into spasm and he curled up. There was laughter above as the voltage continued to be sent through Lordy, now causing the skin and hair to singe. The smell of burning flesh mixed with the fetid air.

'Enough.'

Salah uncut Lordy and let his body fall next to Fox. The three torturers left the room.

Saudi Arabian airspace

High above the desert the huge doors of the C130 transport plane opened, causing all inside to be buffeted by the ferocious howling winds. The loadmaster stood on the brink, patiently awaiting the signal from the pilot that they were over the correct drop zone. Behind him stood six members of G Squadron, 22 Special Air Service Regiment, dressed in high-altitude compression suits and oxygen masks, their bergens held between their legs. Through the Perspex of his own mask the loadmaster saw the light switch blink from red to green. He motioned the team forward and yelled above the noise. 'GO GO GO!'

Unable to hear his voice, but seeing his sign, the stick of men shuffled forward and within ten seconds had disappeared into the swirling darkness below. The doors of the C130 closed. Inside became calm once again and it headed back to Basra.

Falling at a terminal velocity of 120 mph the SAS troopers shot towards the drop zone. Following the blinking green light of the man in front, each relied on the other and ultimately the team leader for direction. Hitting 27,000 feet they deployed their chutes and instantly decelerated. From here on in they would rely on GPS way points and terrain features to navigate; however, in the sands of Arabia these were few. Six black specs against the desert night, they were all but invisible. Sergeant Richard Lewis guided his men towards the mountains and the last-known contact location: the intercepted splash from the Iridium phone flagged by the CIA, confirmed by GCHQ.

They would land in the desert and then move covertly into the mountain range. They had their own satellite-linked communication equipment that they would use to communicate with Hereford.

Rub al-Khali, Kingdom of Saudi Arabia
Darkness fell quickly in the Saudi desert. Within half an hour the raging sun had been replaced by a desert moon, which cast an eerie glow on the increasingly rocky terrain. This added to the impression Snow already had, that he was on the moon. The temperature had started to drop and a wind had risen from nowhere, blowing cold against the sweat which had clung to his body all day. Snow started to shiver. It was nothing compared to his winter days in Kyiv, but took his weakened body by surprise. Ahead of him the path led up between the mountains and out of sight.

He had tracked them for three hours now, first across the plain and then into the unforgiving mountains, having to check continuously that he hadn't been spotted. Snow was following at an erratic pace, moving in bounds, lying flat against the sand then darting forward to the next bit of cover. The Bedouin were masters of the desert, having roamed for generation after generation. They were perfectly adapted to this hostile land, but even they needed water. Snow had to hope that their tracking skills wouldn't help them to detect that they were now the ones being tracked.

The moonlight cast long shadows across the rocks, which were now increasing vastly in size. Snow strained his eyes to make out the route ahead, in a world of contrasts: pitch-black, grey shadows and almost blinding moonlight. He tilted his head so the rod receptors at the side of his eyes would pick up the detail his main receptors missed, but even so it took him all his concentration to keep his footing. His head had again started to ache, a cocktail of eye strain, exhaustion, and dehydration. He hadn't eaten since breakfast and, apart from the water stolen from the insurgents, had had nothing to drink. He was running on less than empty and could collapse and fall into unconsciousness at any moment. The only thing that kept him going was willpower.

Snow had lost sight of his quarry five minutes earlier when the path veered to the right behind the start of the rock face. This was the most dangerous part of all; he was being forced onto a narrow cutting between sheer rock. The perfect place for an ambush.

Snow crept forward, stopping every other pace to listen. The noise of the wind whipped around the rocks, with its banshee-like whistle. He reached the cliff face and stood stock-still, listening for a minute. It was now that he was entering the killing zone. Snow steadied his breathing and opened his mouth in an attempt to further enhance his hearing. His heart started to beat faster and he would have sworn it could be heard over the wind. With one further calming breath, he pushed himself flat against the rock and eased his head around the natural bend. He now saw that the path rose again and disappeared in a pool of darkness not eighty feet away. If he was being watched he was dead; if they had night-vision goggles he was dead.

No shot came, no sound of men readying weapons, or the glint of a blade. Snow pushed forward and was illuminated for a moment by the moonlight, before plunging back into shadow. Here the sound of the wind had vanished and his heart seemed to beat louder than ever. He paused halfway and listened again. There was a rustling noise at his feet. He flinched as a snake passed not more than a foot away. A second sound, this time a camel up ahead, then another accompanied by some calming voices in Arabic. He was getting nearer to them, the missioners. With more caution and trepidation than before, Snow continued to follow the path. It climbed before the ground dropped away and he found himself looking down at a water hole some fifty feet distant.

Caused by the desert rains running off the mountains above, the oasis stood in a natural hollow, unaffected by the worst of the relentless sun during the day and the howling winds at night. The camels lapped at the water while their masters tugged at the packs they had been carrying. Two more Bedouin crouched over a pile of kindling and attempted to light it. The missioners sat furthest away from the entrance with their backs against the rock face; three men stood in front of them cradling Kalashnikovs. Snow carefully lowered himself flat onto his stomach and counted the Bedouin. Four with the camels, two lighting the fire, three guarding the hostages, and another two who were talking at the farthest edge of the hollow – eleven in total and all armed. The odds had just got worse. Snow noticed that their leader, the one who had fired the pistol round at the roadside, was having a heated discussion with what appeared to be his second-in-command.

The leader waved his arms dismissively and moved away. He reached into his robes and produced a light-grey object. Snow squinted. He instantly recognised the shape but couldn't believe he was correct. The Bedouin extended the antenna and dialled a number into the Iridium handset. Snow shook his head slowly. How many Bedouin had sat phones? Whoever these people were, they seemed to be well organised and were not acting alone. Snow's mind went back to the Arab he had seen make the video; the Arab who had shot Thacker. Was he the one in control? More importantly, where was Fox? Did he have him?

The Bedouin's conversation lasted just over a minute before he closed the antenna and put it back under his robes. The missioners were now being given water. They were all there. Lermitte sat as straight as he could and tried to be defiant while Kennington thanked his keepers profusely for the water. Some of the missioners whimpered but none spoke, the life all but bleached out of them by the desert sun. It had been more effective than any torture their captors could have inflicted. Snow could see the hostages but could not rescue them; could see the phone but could not take it; could see the water but could not drink. He clenched his fists in anger; he hated not being able to do anything.

Surprisingly, there was no guard at the entrance they had used and from which Snow was now observing. The Bedouin were obviously satisfied that no one knew they were there. This, however, couldn't hold for long and, sooner or later, a man would be sent up as sentry, to check on the perimeter. That would be his chance. With the fire starting to burn, casting hypnotic shadows against the rocks, Snow felt his eyelids grow heavy and his head start to drop, white specks flashing before his eyes. He battled to stay awake, to remain conscious, again the lack of water muddling his brain. He shook his head violently in an attempt to stay sharp, to stay awake, and instantly regretted it as pain surged through his neck. He was alert again, however, until eventually his head dropped once more.

Eyes snapping open, Snow didn't know how long he'd been out: seconds, minutes, hours? Suddenly he felt it, an almost imperceptible change in the air pressure behind him, the faintest of scrapes of gravel. Snow tried to turn but felt a heavy gloved hand grip the back of his neck and force his face into the sand. A knee pushed him in the small of his back. Warm breath in his ear, then a whispered voice.

'Identify yourself.' The words were in English, accented. Welsh valleys.

Snow tasted sand and had to spit. The voice spoke again.

'Identify yourself.'

'Snow, Aidan.'

'Which Squadron?' the voice persisted, pressing down harder.

'D Squadron, Boat Troop.'

'Correct.'

The pressure left his neck and Snow was pulled up and backwards by his shoulders, away from the vantage point. In the darkness he could now make out the SAS team in full desert fatigues with NVGs. One slid on his belly and retook Snow's vantage point while the rest hugged the shadows in the dead ground.

'Had to be sure you weren't a raghead. We're the cavalry.' The Welshman held out his water bottle.

Snow took it and drank greedily. 'We've got eleven X-rays and ten hostages.'

Sergeant Lewis nodded. 'OK, anything else I should know?'

Snow took another swig. 'They think they're secure. The leader's got a sat phone. He's the biggest.'

'Loney's our tail end. Charlie, stay near him.'

Snow wanted to be involved in the hostage rescue but was in no state to use a weapon with the accuracy demanded. He moved back down the path further into the dead ground and was patted on the shoulder by several team members. He sat down heavily in the shadows next to a crouching trooper, Loney. The SAS man ripped open an electrolyte sachet and poured the contents into his water bottle, replaced the lid, shook it, then handed it to Snow. Too tired to thank him, Snow undid the lid and drank in sips – he already felt nauseous from gulping down the first bottle. Loney handed him a high-calorie 'power bar', the type weightlifters and athletes used. Snow bit into the gooey, chocolate-flavoured, synthetic block.

'Just like Mum used to make,' Loney said with a straight face, half to himself.

As Snow ate, the rest of the team stood in silence, not needing to say anything, leaving the lookout and team leader to check on the camp. It felt good to be with the Regiment. Snow wished he hadn't been forced to leave a decade before. Lewis, the Welsh team leader, rejoined the group and traced a quick circle on the ground with his gloved index finger.

'Davies, you're lead sniper; Jim, take the opposite arc. Sight your targets. Kyle and Steve, work your way down into the camp. I'll illuminate if I can. I'll toss two flash bangs in as soon as any X-rays return fire. Davies, Jim and I will cover you. Loney, you stay tail end but ready to take on any opportune targets, or runners – there may be an exit we can't see. Questions?'

The planning session, although hastily convened on the mountain floor, was a version of a well-rehearsed drill. In theory it would all be over in under a minute. Maximum surprise, maximum aggression. The team got into their ready positions, the air around each man buzzing with adrenaline. Davies joined Jim, who had been lookout, but moved to the left of the ridge, taking his pre-assigned arc. Kyle and Steve belly-crawled over the lip and into the shadows towards the camp. Their comms units switched on, Lewis spoke into his throat mic.

'Davies, do you have a shot?'

Davies did not give a verbal reply, rather depressed his pressel switch in the affirmative.

'Jim?'

Another squelch of static.

'Kyle?'

Squelch

'Steve?'

Squelch.

'Stand by… Stand by… GO… GO… GO!'

Two rounds in quick succession left the rifles of Davies and Jim respectively, the bullets hitting the targets before the sound had time to ricochet off the opposite side of the mountains. The two Bedouin nearest the hostages dropped, instantly becoming sacks of skin and bone. The third spun and grabbed for the AK slung over his shoulder, but before he could put both hands on it was propelled back against the rock face by at least three rounds hitting his torso and head. Kyle and Steve opened up with their assault rifles, firing controlled bursts at the nearest Bedouin. The

248

camels reared up from the ground, frantically trying to loosen their cobbled hind legs as the men who sat by them were drilled with rounds. The nearest camel broke its legs free and stood, only to be hit by a fully automatic burst of 7.62 rounds from the Kalashnikov of its owner, who was cowering behind it. The camel bucked and fell back, crushing the Bedouin against a large boulder.

Through the green of his night-vision scope, Lewis could see that the hostages had started to move. He had to keep them still.

'Flash bangs in,' he ordered into the mic.

Kyle and Steve dropped and shut their eyes, and so did the rest of the team, as Lewis hurled two deodorant-sized grenades into the camp. Designed for room clearance, their effect would still be considerable in this enclosed rocky bowl. Boom – night fleetingly turned to day as the white phosphorous burnt, momentarily disabling all those who hadn't known it was coming. Night vision completely destroyed, balance affected and hit by pressure waves, the Bedouin staggered, fired wildly, or just fell over. Eyes back up, Davies and Jim took easy targets, dropping the two men still illuminated by the fire, one falling onto the burning wood and impersonating a bonfire Guy Fawkes. Kyle and Steve moved further into the camp trying to locate the surviving tangos. Kyle went down as, from behind a rock, an AK opened up.

'Man down! Man down!'

Lewis snapped off a volley of rounds at the muzzle flash. Steve bounded forward and put rounds into another Bedouin. Lewis scanned the area for the leader and suddenly saw him crouching in a corner tapping furiously into his handset. He steadied his breathing and took the shot. The leader seemed to sense something as he looked up and shifted to the right. Too late. The high-velocity round skimmed the underside of his jaw and exploded into his shoulder. Instantly the phone fell from his hand. The leader slid down the rock face and onto his side, feeling more pain than he'd ever thought imaginable. One Bedouin was still unaccounted for; all eyes and muzzles searched the killing ground. Suddenly he popped up, a sword held aloft in both hands, and ran at Steve. Briefly losing the target, Lewis and the snipers didn't shoot. Steve held his rifle in front of him. The Bedouin got nearer.

'Allah Akbar!' he yelled at the top of his voice.

'I agree, but you're not!' Steve applied second pressure to the trigger and a dotted line of lead punched its way across the Bedouin's chest. The swordsman folded, almost cut in two.

'Clear.' Lewis was on the net.

'Clear.'

'Clear.'

'Clear.'

'Clear.' Each member confirmed except for Kyle.

The team moved into the camp; Jim crouched next to Kyle. The rounds had made a mess of his thigh but not hit the artery. He might not be able to fight again but he was alive. Jim, who also doubled as the team medic, injected morphine, applied a trauma pack, and immobilised the leg. Steve moved to the hostages and stood over them, M202 raised as Davies made them lie flat on their faces, fingers crossed, and hands on the backs of their heads. It was usual practice until all the missioners could be identified; it wasn't unusual for kidnappers to attempt to pass themselves off as hostages or even for the hostages to shelter them. There was, however, no risk of 'Stockholm syndrome' here. Davies frisked them, just to make sure, for weapons or potentially any concealed IEDs. Snow, now having found a new energy, bounded into the camp with Loney and made directly for the missioners.

'You know them, mate. Down to you.' Davies spoke, his West Country accent sounding very out of place in the desert.

Snow looked at the rescued mission members. He didn't need to check their faces; he had been eating, drinking, and 'surviving' Saudi hospitality with these people for the past week. 'Clear.'

'Sure? OK, you can get up.'

Davies helped the nearest woman to her feet. Her body shook with terror. Jim arrived to check for any injuries.

Lermitte rubbed his eyes and struggled to his feet, his voice raw. 'Aidan? How the... we thought you were dead.'

Snow now handed Lermitte a flask. 'What, die before ordering my bio-fuel generator? Couldn't let it happen.'

'But... how?'

'I'll explain later. Check the rest are all right for me.' Snow slapped Lermitte on the back.

'Over here, Jim.' Lewis called the medic. The Bedouin leader was losing a lot of blood; not that the Welshman cared, but the 'Spook' would probably prefer him alive. Jim's hand was about to plunge a morphine-filled syringe into the Bedouin.

'Wait, Snow will want him talking. Just stem the blood flow.'

'OK, boss.' The trauma pack and white bandage all but glowed against the grime-encrusted dish-dash.

Snow joined Lewis.

'One leader. Check. One sat phone, secondhand but service-able, check.'

Snow took the phone. It had been brand-new, the latest model in fact, but was now scuffed and encased in dirt.

'I need to check the numbers, upload them if I can. The same people may have Fox and the other missing Brit.'

'Stay still, you amateur transvestite!'

Snow and Lewis turned their heads. The Bedouin leader, robes stained crimson by his blood loss, was trying to push Jim away.

'Allah Akbar... Allah Akbar... Allah Akbar...' Although weak-ened and in shock he was putting up a fight.

'Who were you calling?' Snow kicked him in the stomach.

'Allah Akbar... Allah Akbar... Allah Akbar...'

Snow placed his boot on the injured shoulder, and the man screamed. 'Who were you calling?'

Through gritted teeth he yelled, 'Allah Akbar... Allah Akbar... Allah Akbar...'

Snow transferred his entire body weight to the bloodied shoulder. There was a crunching noise as broken bones scraped together, sending red-hot flames of pain to the Bedouin's brain. The Arab passed out. Jim looked up, shocked. Snow knew the question. 'We've got the number. No morphine. He'll talk.'

There was a distant sound of rotor blades. Snow looked skywards. 'Ours?'

'Yep, but we had to do a deal with the Saudis. We were given an hour to get in and get clear before they arrived with their own HRT and the state media – Foreign Office instructions.' Lewis shrugged. 'Another place we never were.'

'And the hostages?'

'The Saudis insisted on debriefing them, and on filming their safe rescue.'

'Shit. We can't let the insurgents know we've got them!'

Snow looked at his watch; it was almost ten in the evening. They had two hours until the first deadline arrived. Would Fox now be executed in place of one of the missioners if the other kidnappers learnt of the raid? He had to move and fast.

'I'll take charge.' Kennington had found his voice.

Lewis gave Snow a questioning look. Kennington held out his hand. 'Raymond Kennington, late of the FCO, now mission leader. You SAS lads get out of here. They'll be fine with me.'

COBRA, Whitehall, London, UK
Patchem let his head fall back and exhaled deeply. The team were safe aboard the RAF Chinook. Snow had, following instructions from an SIS techie, downloaded data from the Iridium phone. Several messages had been sent by the Bedouin with the compromised code. They had Fox. The dialled numbers were being examined and their locations triangulated. The last number dialled also belonged to the same Iridium phone that had received the messages. The location was the oil refinery port of Dammam. At a push the Chinook could just make it.

'We have a potential fix on Fox.'

Back in her own office Knight sipped her green tea and listened. 'Go on.'

'I want to divert the SAS team to get him out.'

Knight looked at the clock. The midnight deadline was drawing ever nearer. 'We don't have time to get it officially sanctioned.'

'Not if we involve the Foreign Secretary and the Saudis.'

'Is this your idea or Snow's?'

'He wants to go in and the team have agreed.' There had been no hesitation in agreeing to the second insertion. Fox was Regiment.

'I see.' There was a pause. 'Do it. My call.'

Patchem hastily called Slinger-Thompson, who got hold of the British Trade Office in the neighbouring town of Al-Khobar. An LZ was agreed upon; the compound was owned by a British Oil company.

AB Oil compound, Al-Khobar, Kingdom of Saudi Arabia

Clouds of sand swirled up from the AB Oil compound as the Chinook touched down. Snow was first off, running at a crouch towards cover, quickly followed by the rest of the SAS team, minus Kyle. The Chinook was to take off and immediately RTB before anyone had time to learn of its visit.

The company canteen had been given over to the team, the local staff told to go home. A white-haired, portly ex-pat in a light-coloured suit strode purposefully towards Snow and Lewis.

'Aidan Snow?' He didn't wait for an answer. 'This is all a bit of a fastball. I'm Bob Knowles. I'm with the British Trade Office here in Al-Khobar.'

'We haven't come to buy or sell,' Lewis replied without humour.

'Indeed.' Knowles spread out a map on the table in front of them. 'Everything we have is on here.' The map showed the oil refinery town of Dammam. A red circle had been drawn around the surrounding area. 'This is where the signal emanated from. A sat phone used in an open environment like this is easy to trace. This area is deserted, an unoccupied piece of land that was once the property of a local Saudi family before they sold it to AB Oil. I've checked with the company; there are three outbuildings and nothing more. I've also cross-checked the buildings with images I've received from Vauxhall Cross and there is a match.'

'How far away is this from here?' Snow traced his finger on the map.

'Eight miles, give or take.'

'And how do we approach?'

Knowles smiled. 'Helo. I've twisted the arm of AB Oil; they've kindly agreed to lend us one of theirs. It should raise no suspicion as they make several flights a day in the same direction; they own land both here and at the target. This isn't Iraq. Any military transport raises suspicion, especially foreign military. There are eyes everywhere.'

'OK. We'll take the AB helo and put down at a safe distance.' Snow felt dizzy and had to steady himself against the table.

Knowles grabbed his elbow. 'You OK?'

'I'll be fine.' Snow sipped his water. 'Carry on.'

Knowles placed several enlarged photographs on top of the map. 'These were taken a while back during an aerial survey. I'm sorry we don't have anything more on the schematics of the buildings.'

Lewis called over the rest of the team, who crowded around the table. The three buildings he logically designated by numbers ONE, TWO and THREE. He then divided the men into three teams: ALPHA, BRAVO and CHARLIE. ALPHA and BRAVO for the assault and CHARLIE to act as a sniper.

'Snow, you're CHARLIE with Davies. Once the hostages are secure you'll go in.'

'No. I need to go in.' Snow stabbed his finger at the map. 'Look, we've got three target buildings and two teams. We have to move together.'

Lewis shook his head, his light-brown eyes flashing. 'You're in no fit state to take part in an assault – and you know it.'

Snow knew the SAS team leader was right. He'd stay with the sniper.

Lewis continued. 'ALPHA, you take ONE; BRAVO will take TWO. It's a risk but THREE is by far the smallest target and looks to be a storage hut of some sort. Agreed?'

As was the culture in the Regiment, all men on ops, regardless of rank, were equal and had the right to speak.

'Agreed. When we get in range we'll scan each target with the thermo; if there is anyone in THREE we'll see them. So, once more, we'll put down here, fan out and approach from the south and west. CHARLIE eyeballs the target as we approach. We then take our assigned targets. Until we thermo, we've no idea of the size or strength of the X-rays or if they know they've been compromised. I don't need to tell you that we want to stay covert for as long as possible, but when we go noisy, we go noisy. Fellers, this is one of the most dangerous things we've been asked to do. Let's not turn it into a "Gang F###". Lives depend on us.'

Twenty minutes later the depleted team of six, five SAS and Snow, were aboard the AB Oil helo. The pilot, an ex-Indonesian military AB Oil employee, kept the bird steady and on an arched course before dropping to within fifty feet of the desert floor and heading for the drop point. Now, with lights off and flying on a loaned pair of NVGs, the pilot brought the bird to a hover within six feet of the swirling sands and scrub before the team dropped into the night. As he sped away, back onto his normal heading and Dammam, the team fanned out and listened for any sign of company.

Lewis gave the all clear and took point, leading the team towards the target, a mile away across the sand. Without even a cursory recce, this was the most dangerous time. Noise travelled uninterrupted for miles in the desert and the chance of compromise was high. Reaching a natural sand berm at about the hundred-metre point, Davies and Snow, as CHARLIE team, took up their positions, scanning the target through night scopes. Given the go ahead, in the green haze Snow watched ALPHA and BRAVO continue towards their target. BRAVO moved silently in the dead ground past ONE and reached their position at TWO. As ALPHA took up their position, there was movement through Snow's scope and two armed figures appeared outside ONE, the ends of their cigarettes flaring.

'Stop. Stop. CHARLIE has two X-rays at ONE.'

More light flares streamed out from under makeshift blinds at the window but the two X-rays constituted the only immediate threat.

'I have.' Davies applied first pressure to the trigger of his high-powered rifle. In a matter of milliseconds both X-rays could be taken out.

A door opened. NVGs and scopes flared wildly, and Snow screwed up his eyes. A third X-ray exited ONE, turned left, and urinated into the desert. Snow again relayed what he could hear via the comms network. Lewis, with Loney, team 'BRAVO', looked through the thermo at TWO. Inside the building he made out five heat sources, three of them standing. An X-ray outside ONE dropped his cigarette and stared in the direction of BRAVO. He moved forward, inclined his head, and squinted into the desert. He shouted in Arabic and waved his AK. The second X-ray now brought his weapon to bear on the same piece of desert. Loney and Lewis pushed themselves flat behind a low dune and dared not breathe. The AK went down as the second X-ray slapped the first on the back. Both X-rays turned, walked back to ONE, and became unsighted inside.

Now aiming the thermo at TWO, BRAVO relayed to ALPHA what they could see. At distance the image wasn't clear, but a further possible three heat sources could be seen. Two seemed to be seated while a third stood over them. Lewis cursed. He now had two targets who could equally be holding the hostages. 'CHARLIE. Update.'

'X-ray one and two still unsighted. X-ray three is pissing for Saudi.'

Snow smiled in the darkness. Davies was professional but this didn't stop him from cracking a joke. Snow trained his night scope on TWO. A figure appeared at the window. 'Window TWO. X-ray.'

'I have.' Davies changed targets.

Lewis studied ONE again, squinting his eyes involuntarily to focus. Two of the heat sources were static, lying on the ground. One was now standing up and three more seemed to be in a different room. 'Stand by... Stand by...'

There was a shout in Arabic. White light flared in Snow's night sight as the door of TWO was thrown open. An AK opened up. Without tracer, the rounds flew invisibly through the desert air. Crosshairs fixed on the centre mass of the X-ray even before he left the doorway and Davies applied second pressure to the trigger of his rifle. The X-ray was propelled backwards into TWO. It had gone noisy. A muzzle flash from the window as another X-ray opened up. Davies shot again. There was a yell and the firing stopped.

'Go... Go... Go!' Lewis gave the order for the assault.

Another X-ray, weapon up, charged through the open door of TWO, shouting and firing wildly into the desert. He was cut down by rounds from ALPHA.

As CHARLIE gave covering fire, ALPHA took up positions at either side of the door before tossing in flash bangs and then bomb bursting into the building.

'Clear!'

Inside, the first room was empty; they quickly moved down the corridor into the second. A robed figure cowered in the corner and babbled in Arabic. He had something in his hand... a grenade.

'Grenade!' An ALPHA member delivered a double tap into the X-ray's centre mass before retreating back into the first room. In the confined space, the explosion sounded like thunder and

257

brought down half the exterior wall. Ears ringing and covered in cement dust, ALPHA pushed on before declaring the target secure.

Hearing this over the network, Snow trained his scope on ONE. Flashes erupted from both windows of the single-storey building. Lewis swore. He was pinned down.

The comms hissed, as Snow spoke. 'Two X-rays at the windows of ONE.'

The crack of high-velocity rounds pierced the air inches from his head. Shit. Snow flattened himself into the sand. 'They have NVGs! Repeat, X-ray in ONE has NVG.'

Before ALPHA could reply there was a scream and a hiss of static. 'I'm hit. Repeat, I'm hit!' Loney's voice was raspy.

'BRAVO, we are on our way.' ALPHA would now skirt the target. Lewis covered his face as a round passed through the thermo, showering him in glass and broken optics. He rolled to his right and leopard-crawled towards Loney. The injured trooper lay on his back and was breathing raggedly. Under fire and without cover there was nothing Lewis could do.

'X-ray neutralised.' Davies's voice.

'Cover me.' Snow got to his feet and ran at a crouch towards ONE.

Davies let off rounds at ONE as Snow zigzagged as best he could in the sand. He landed next to Lewis with a thud.

'I told you to stay back!'

'I did.' Snow looked on as Lewis inspected Loney. His eyes rolled up into his head as his boss injected him with morphine.

Lewis took Loney's MPK 5 and handed it to Snow. 'On me.'

Snow nodded his assent.

'All call signs. BRAVO to assault TWO. Covering fire.'

'Have that.' Davies let fly with another round.

'Roger.' ALPHA now replied.

Under a shield of rounds, Snow and Lewis ran at the target, throwing themselves against the wall on each side of the main entrance. Lewis held up his fingers, 3… 2… 1… He hurled a flash bang into the dark interior. Both men pressed fingers firmly into their ears and shut their eyes. As with the earlier assault, night turned to day. Two lifeless bodies were illuminated. Now, opening their eyes, Snow and Lewis entered the room, tracing an arc with their weapons, searching every corner.

'Clear,' Lewis hissed. The room was long and narrow with three doors leading off. Snow nodded as Lewis indicated right. They moved to the farthermost door and once again stood on each side.

The pair waited and listened; there was a strange silence broken only by a faint scraping somewhere beyond. Very carefully Lewis pressed his hand against the bottom of the door. It moved almost imperceptibly before being restrained by the lock. When stealth was needed, a mirror or mini fibre-optic cable could be pushed either underneath or through the lock, but now, with the element of surprise gone, speed was what was needed. Lewis reached inside his ops waistcoat and retrieved a small-shaped charge. He carefully placed it on the lock before mouthing 'Ready?'.

The explosion tore through the door, closely followed by Lewis. The room was empty save for a hole in the floor and a sink. Silence fell again, broken only by ALPHA informing them that there were no more visible X-rays.

An explosion sounded as a dull thud. Fox pulled against his bonds, looking for the tiniest amount of give. Lying almost nose to nose with the corpse of Lordy, his anger was willing him to break free. Salah – 'the sadist', as Fox had christened him – stood in the corner. He had taken great delight in the sight of Lordy's body convulse with electrical current. There was a wild look in his eye and he was staring at the door. His two most trusted men were now by his side, the last three remaining servants of Allah.

A second explosion shook the room and Fox braced himself. If they were going to kill him, now was his only chance. Yet Salah remained still and a smile started to crease the grimy face underneath the straggly beard.

'They will speak of me for generations!' The words were in English but the accent thick. He moved towards the video camera and pressed the record button on the Sony, covering both Fox and the door.

With sudden realisation of what he had in mind, Fox found a new strength and managed to move his hands. There was a noise at the door and now the Arab brought up his AK. Fox's hands snapped free and he rolled towards the still-upturned metal table. Incensed, Salah's trigger finger jerked and the barrel of the AK, on fully automatic, spat a storm of lead. Rounds impacted the table and bounced off at obscene angles. Fox curled into the foetal position, holding his hands to his face.

Within seconds the magazine emptied and there was a frantic series of clicks as Salah's finger hopelessly pressed against the trigger. As the door to his cell was blown off its hinges, Fox shut his eyes, his training taking over. Through his eyelids the room suddenly became bright. Lewis and Snow exploded into the room, hitting the two X-rays with multiple rounds.

Salah, stunned by the flash bang, fell to cover behind the table, inches from Fox, his Kalashnikov tumbling away. From somewhere inside the need for revenge took over and Fox heard himself yell.

'Stand down! Stand down! British national! This one's mine!'

Fox rolled clear of the table and slowly stood, his hands raised. Two assault rifles were trained on him. Fox met Snow's eyes. 'Aidan, he's mine!'

There was the briefest moment of silence as the two SAS assaulters took in the lifeless orange-jumpsuited body of Lordy. A glint of steel as Salah leapt up and screamed, his left hand like a claw, his right holding a knife. Lewis's finger quivered as instinct told him to drill the remaining X-ray, but Snow pushed his muzzle aside. The blade slashed forward wildly at Fox, who calmly stepped back and into the centre of the room.

'As I thought, you are no more than a boy. A true warrior would not need to use a knife.' Fox spat the Arabic at Salah with disdain.

The Arab froze as his eyes widened at hearing the infidel speak the language of the Prophet. 'You dare speak Arabic...'

Fox stepped forward and kicked him between the legs. As Salah doubled up, Fox grabbed the hand holding the knife and threw him to the floor. Following him down, knee to chest pinning him, he held the knife at the boy's throat. 'Too easy. Has Allah really sent a woman to fight me?'

Fox drew the knife across the neck, cutting through the outer layers of flesh, causing pain but not yet death. Fox stepped away as Salah wailed, hands frantically holding his bloody neck.

'Fox! That's enough!' Lewis moved forward.

Fox pointed with the blade. 'Thanks for saving me and all that, but you can piss off now.'

Snow moved in between the pair and stared at the cold blue eyes of Fox. Snow said nothing, knew nothing he could say would make any difference.

'One minute.'

'What?' Lewis was shocked.

Snow grabbed Lewis's arm and hustled him back to the door. He had seen that look in Fox's eyes before. 'We give him one minute.'

Fox shut the door. Salah was on his knees. Fox dropped the knife, took a step forward, and kicked the boy in the face. Salah fell back, blood flew from his nose, and there was a sickening crack as his head hit the concrete floor. Fox pulled him up to his feet by the hair and looked into his bloodshot eyes.

'You are a piece of pig shit. No fornicating with virgins for you in Paradise.'

The mouth of the once cocky Arab quivered. 'I am a servant of Allah... you infidels will all die...' He swung wildly, hitting Fox in the kidney.

Fox grunted but didn't release his grip; rather, he hit him in the face with his right fist, his left still holding his greasy hair. The nose broke.

'Once I've killed you, I'm going to take your body to the nearest farm and feed you back to the pigs.'

Suddenly real fear flashed in the Arab's eyes. To die for Allah was glorious but he would not be accepted into Paradise if his body had been defiled. Fox hit him again and his lower lip split, his front tooth pushed through the upper. Fox felt the body go limp as he passed out. Dragging him towards the bucket still half-filled with water, Fox thrust the youth's head under the surface. Arms suddenly flailed and legs kicked, feet beating an obscene beat rhythm on the concrete floor. Fox stepped back and let the boy roll onto his back, choking.

'You killed my friend and you were going to kill me. Now, what should I do? Should I kill you and then feed you to the pigs or should I break all your limbs and then throw you into their pen?'

'No, no, please…'

Fox laughed and switched back to English. 'You ignorant piece of shit. Did you stop when Lordy was begging you?'

'I am a servant of Allah… there is but one God… Allah…'

Fox's laughter rose. 'You thank your god for living like an animal? For the glory of shitting in the sand? I've known plenty of Muslims, men I was proud to call friends. You're not a real Muslim. You're nothing but a brainwashed camel-shagger. Now, get up. Get up!'

Salah slowly pushed himself to his feet. Blood streamed from his mouth and nose; his hair, now plastered against his scalp, made him look even more pathetic. Fox pointed towards the chair. 'Sit. If you don't want me to turn you into pig food, you're going to speak into the camera and apologise to the family of the man you murdered. You are then going to tell the camera everything you know about your boss.'

*

Snow leant against an exterior wall, the let-down after the adrenaline of battle suddenly overcoming him. He stared at the sky and shivered; the first rays of morning sun wouldn't arrive above the horizon for several hours yet. Lewis took a gulp from his flask to wash away the cordite-tainted sand.

'How do you know Fox won't kill him?'

'I don't.'

Lewis passed him the flask. 'I hope you know what you're doing, Snow.'

'Haven't got a clue. Thanks for everything.' He held out his hand.

Lewis took it in a tight grip. 'Don't thank me. I may need your help when I leave the Regiment.'

'Believe me, you don't want my help.'

Lewis looked around at the carnage they had created. 'Maybe you're right.'

Fox appeared. 'Tied him to the chair. He's gonna sing like a prize canary.'

Snow noted the half-grin on Fox's blood-speckled face. 'You OK?'

Fox grabbed the flask. 'Fine as rain, boy. Their boss was here, I saw his face. He made a video of us. He said he was off to give further instructions to the "brothers". We've gotta move fast.'

'Hang on. I'm here to get you both out, then get you debriefed.'

'We don't have time.'

'Orders are orders.' The sound of the RAF chopper tasked with extracting the team hit their ears. 'Stay put.' Lewis joined the rest of the team who were standing by Loney.

'What did their leader look like?'

Fox described him. '…And a nonchalant nobber to boot.'

'Sounds like the bastard I saw kill a hostage.'

'Shit.' In the moonlight Fox for the first time noticed the state of Snow. 'What the hell happened to you?'

Snow shook his head and winced; he'd almost forgotten about his whiplash. 'You think you've had a bad day?'

Snow brought Fox up-to-date with what had happened since he'd been kidnapped. Glaister's body found in the desert, the ambush and abduction of the missioners, the execution of Thacker, the tailing of the Bedouin, and finally the hostage rescue.

Fox nodded thoughtfully. 'So they sent the ice-cream boys in to rescue me. What the hell is going on?'

Lewis approached, sat phone at his ear. 'Yes, sir, I understand. I'll put him on.' He offered the handset to Snow.

'Aidan, it's Jack. Can you give me a sit-rep?'

'Fox is alive but we lost the other hostage, dead before we got here. One assaulter down, all X-rays eliminated except the one who tortured Fox. He's going to give us some intel. Fox saw their leader; sounds like the same Arab I saw execute Thacker.'

'These attacks were well planned. Did the group use any name?'

'I didn't hear one. I'll ask Fox. Paddy, do you know what the X-rays called themselves? Did they have a name?'

Fox looked skyward, to recover his memory. 'The Warriors of Mecca.'

Snow relayed the intel to Patchem.

'Probably a name of convenience. Anything else you can tell me now before I debrief you?'

'The leader has a video of Fox and was en route to a meet with a group he called "the brothers". Could be another cell?'

'OK, I'll look into that. Now get on that helo and I'll see you both in Bahrain.'

The line went dead. 'Patchem's debriefing us personally in Bahrain.'

'I could think of worse places.'

Lewis laughed. 'You haven't seen the Bahraini barracks!'

'Loney?' Snow became serious.

Lewis looked down. 'He'll make it, just.'

Knightsbridge, London, UK
Knight kicked off her slippers and popped her feet on the leather

pouf. Swirling the tumbler of single malt before taking a long, slow mouthful, she shivered slightly as the whisky slid down her throat like liquid fire. The stress of the day started to leave her body, replaced by a growing sense of tired contentment. BBC, Sky News, ITN, CNN and Al-Jazeera had all led with the same story – the successful rescue of eleven British hostages held by Al-Qaeda in Saudi Arabia. The Saudi Interior Ministry spokesman, General Mansur al-Amin, had stated that the kidnappers were 'linked directly to Al-Qaeda and had attempted to launch terrorist attacks within the Kingdom of Saudi Arabia'. The reports piggy backed on the footage released by the state-run TV channel, Al Ekhbariya, which showed various types of weaponry, said to have been buried in the desert and discovered by Saudi Special Forces after the hostage rescue. This included plastic explosives, ammunition cartridges, handguns, and rifles wrapped in plastic sheeting. Al-Amin then continued to praise the Saudi police and military.

Knight closed her eyes. She was the little Dutch boy plugging the dam. Today it hadn't burst but one day it would unless… her glass fell, splattering the last drops of malt across the rug. Shit. She shook her head and sat up in the chair. Falling asleep here would do her no good at all. She picked up her tumbler, clicked off the TV, and made her weary way to her bedroom. The free world was safe – for at least seven hours, she hoped.

In Moscow it was three hours later and the drink was vodka. Maksim Gurov nodded to himself. It made no difference to him whether the British hostages lived or died, were rescued or not. The outcome was the same. The oil-reliant nations of the world had seen that Saudi wasn't a safe place to be in, or to buy from. The Saudis had rescued the hostages but they had been taken in the first place.

It may have played out better if the British nationals had been killed, but it made no odds. He raised his glass in a mock toast to the brave men of the Saudi Special Forces. The cold vodka hit his throat and heightened his senses. He picked up his encrypted mobile phone and speed-dialled the number in Saudi Arabia.

'Da?' an alert voice answered before the second ring.

'Davai.' A one-word instruction: 'Go ahead.'

Gurov ended the call and poured another measure. The militants in Saudi Arabia were about to launch a retaliatory attack.

Chapter 10

After being at his desk all night, Harry Slinger-Thompson was expecting a call from Patchem, but it was another familiar voice that greeted him.

'It was quite a night for you fellows, huh?' Casey's voice was too perky for the time of day.

'Yes, Vince, it was. I'm just happy our hostages were rescued and that the Saudi security forces carried out such a professional job.'

'Huh. Well, I hope your black-op boys are "getting the bevvies in". They deserve them.'

'I don't follow you, Vince.'

'Sure, play it that way. Listen, I've got a lead for you. The sat phone that was pinged at both rescue locations… You interested?'

'Go on.' Slinger-Thompson picked up a pen.

'It received a call from Doha – our friend we had under surveillance. We tailed him back from there to Riyadh, then invited him to join us for an informal Q&A session. You want the transcript file?'

'Please.'

'OK, it should hit your inbox about now. Oh, Harry, before I go, pass my regards to Jack. It's been too long; tell him to call me before he leaves Bahrain.'

'He's not in Bahrain.'

'No? OK – my mistake.'

The call ended. Slinger-Thompson furrowed his brow. Casey was being very cooperative but how did the damn Yanks know so much? He opened the email and started to read. And how did the damn Yanks get so much intel? He clicked 'forward message' and sent an encrypted email to Patchem.

Dammam Seaport, Kingdom of Saudi Arabia

Konstantin Voloshin swam slowly towards the giant hull of the tanker. It was the largest thing he had ever seen in the water, larger still than the boats they had trained on, those that had approximated NATO warships. Reaching out ahead, he placed his hand against the barnacle-encrusted steel to stop his forward momentum. He paused and looked around. He had good visibility in these warm waters; the powerful lights of the port illuminated the uppermost metre of the sea and lights from the deck above spilled over the side of the towering hull. This, however, meant he had to be extremely vigilant. Reaching down to his pouch he retrieved the first of the magnetic satchel charges and secured it to the hull. He had four in total and would place them in the pre-assigned stress points. They were time-delay PE4.

With his tanks perilously close to empty, Voloshin kicked away from the ship. The blackness of the Gulf night would conceal him long enough to make good his exfiltration.

Shaikh-Isa Air Base, Bahrain

Outside, the sun attempted to burn away the tarmac; inside, the coffee and prescription painkillers were just as strong. Both Fox and Snow had been given a thorough check-up by an SIS-vetted doctor before being advised to take several days of R&R, bed rest if possible. Now, after a few hours' sleep, both men were to be debriefed in person by Patchem.

With his own red-rimmed eyes, the SIS section chief also

looked as if he had had a restless night; which, of course, napping on an HM Government jet, he had.

'I'll get straight to the point. We have intelligence that leads us to believe someone is specifically targeting British interests in Saudi Arabia in order to erode international confidence in the Kingdom. This is the first time we've seen kidnap videos emanating from Saudi Arabia posted on Al-Jazeera. It's a worrying development…'

'You think so? Try being the star of the show!' Fox stated without sarcasm.

Patchem frowned. 'Quite. The group, the "Warriors of Mecca", is hitherto unknown. Before the attacks we'd seen no chatter whatsoever using this name. The man who tortured you, James – Salah Mahmoud – is a university student from Medina. He has given us a name: Khalid. The man who recruited him and probably the same man you both saw. It seems that this Khalid has something of a fearsome reputation among Mahmoud and his fellow "believers". He allegedly was responsible for beheading a coalition soldier in Iraq and is known to the very highest levels of Al-Qaeda. None of this can, of course, be taken verbatim. In my opinion, all terrorists are prone to boast, but whoever this man is he must be caught. However, if even a fraction of what Mahmoud said is true, Khalid could be a tier-one player.'

Snow massaged his neck with his right hand. 'There was another X-ray taken alive, the Bedouin leader. What have the Saudis got from him?'

Patchem pursed his lips. 'A signed confession, taken under extreme physical duress, that he was responsible for the kidnappings.'

'And?'

'Nothing more. He died shortly after. I believe it was because he stopped talking.'

Snow shook his head. The Saudis weren't known for their gentle approach, especially when it came to insurgents. 'Videofit?'

Fox grunted. 'How many bearded men are there in the region?'

'So, who's interrogating Salah? Not the same Saudis, I hope.'

'No, Aidan, not the Saudis.' Who it was, he didn't want to admit. 'So...' Patchem paused and reached into his trouser pocket. 'Sorry, bad manners and all that.'

The encrypted Blackberry flashed to show a new message. Thumbing the scroll button, Patchem opened the email from Slinger-Thompson and started to smile. 'Gentlemen, it appears that someone is on our side, maybe even Allah himself. I've just received new intelligence: full name, photograph, and possible whereabouts.'

'Where?'

'Dubai.'

Fox felt his adrenaline surge. 'Mr Patchem. He killed a man in front of me in cold blood. He's an animal. I want him. I want you to let me find him for you.'

'James...'

'It's Paddy.'

'And I'm Jack. Paddy, you've been very valuable so far but SIS can't possibly let you continue.'

'Jack, I've seen this wanker up close. What better way to identify him than have us meet again? I see him, he gets ID'ed or he pings me and reacts, then he also gets ID'ed.'

'That does make sense, but Paddy, can I trust you?'

'Ask Aidan.'

Snow ignored Fox and sipped his drink; he, too, had been witness to a murder committed by Khalid. 'Jack, how recent is this intel?'

'Fresh.'

'Then unless we move immediately he may not be there anymore.'

'I believe the Americans have him under surveillance.'

'Then send us to Dubai. I promise to make Paddy behave himself.'

'Agreed.'

Patchem read from his Blackberry. 'Khalid Al-Kazaz. A Saudi national educated in chemical engineering at Oxford. In short, a British-trained bomb maker.'

Patchem held the device up. Fox and Snow saw the face they had seen the day before peering back at them from the screen.

Fox snarled. 'That's him.'

Patchem continued. 'He has his own consulting firm in Dubai.'

'And a sideline as a murdering bastard?' Fox clenched his fist.

'So how does this Oxford graduate become an Al-Q player?' Snow asked.

'There's a seven-year gap between his graduation in '82 and any further records of him in Saudi. We can take an educated guess that, after graduating, he spent time in the Stans.'

All three men knew the pattern. For a believer of that generation, the call for jihad against the Russians has been great. Many young, idealistic Muslims flocked to the CIA-funded training camps of Pakistan before being let loose on the occupying Soviet Red Army in Afghanistan. In the early Eighties this had included innumerable Saudi nationals, including a young believer by the name of Osama Bin Laden.

'And now he's shitting on his own doorstep?'

Patchem frowned and rubbed his chin, which, unusually, had two days' growth of salt and pepper stubble. 'That's one way of putting it, Paddy. He's now being funded and supplied by a very powerful third party.'

Chapter 11

Westin Hotel, Dubai, United Arab Emirates

The room was on the top floor of the Westin Dubai and overlooked the Dubai Palm, with the newly opened Atlantis Hotel at the far sea end, a mile away. Vince Casey leant against the balcony railing looking back into the room at Fox and Snow. A warm breeze swept in causing the curtains to flutter. The sun was setting.

'Gentlemen, for political reasons the Agency cannot be seen to be operating in the UAE, which is why we're not and you will be. Jack and I go way back, hence you've been "borrowed". To business. We believe the suspect is in a suite on the fourth floor.'

Snow looked at the photo in his hand; taken by a concealed camera, it had blurred edges but a sharp centre. He shivered. 'That's him.'

Fox craned his neck. 'Aye, that's the little shagger.'

Casey's faced creased into a large smile. 'That's the British spirit! We don't know how long he's going to be here for or what he's doing. Heck, he'd be a great target for a surveillance operation, but given his actions to date, and the pressure both our governments are exerting, we're going to snatch him. Any questions so far?'

'So, exactly what backup have we got?' Snow wanted it to be clear.

'We have two men in the hotel. Our agents have an eyeball on his room and the foyer. If he moves, we'll know it. We're going in tonight. We need him alive, but if he shoots, shoot back.' Casey pointed to a case on the dresser. 'In there are two 9mm Glocks with suppressors. Untraceable. When this is over they go in the drink. However, we would rather you used this.' He held up a syringe. 'It's a muscle relaxant with a little added "fun".'

'So, we just prance in there, happy as you like, ask him to stand still, and stick him with a needle?'

'That's one idea, Paddy. Aidan, you and Paddy will enter the hotel grounds at 22:00. Meanwhile, one of our operatives will trigger a small incendiary in the ventilation system. The hotel fire alarm will kick off; all guests will evacuate, including the suspect and you two. At this point, Paddy, in the confusion outside, you'll stick him with the needle. There'll be a boat moored nearby on the Palm. Take it and him to the coordinates programmed into the onboard GPS and I'll have someone pick you up.'

Casey made the snatch seem simple, but Snow had his doubts. 'And if we get stopped or he gets away?'

Fox spoke before Casey could. 'We won't and he won't.'

Casey's phone bleeped. Without a word he retrieved it and looked at the screen. His face hardened as he read the incoming message. 'There's been another attack in Saudi.'

Fox's nostrils flared. 'On whom?'

'*The Texan Lady*. She's a supertanker, registered in Portland. She's been scuttled in Dammam Seaport.'

'I thought those tankers were meant to be safe?'

'They are unless you know exactly where to place underwater explosive charges.' His phone rang displaying Langley's number. 'Gentlemen.' Without another word Casey left the hotel room.

Snow stood and walked to the balcony edge. The sun had now set and the sky was turning from a dark orange to black. The sea breeze, however, was still warm. 'You think Khalid Al-Kazaz is responsible for the tanker?'

The older man joined him outside and handed him a weapon. 'You're the expert, you tell me.'

'He'd need technical help.'

'You'd need to be a frog to do something like that.' Fox referred to the SBS.

'Or Spetsnaz.'

'What, you think the Russians did it? Sank a US tanker in Saudi?'

Snow shrugged; it sounded too far-fetched. 'Who gains most from destabilising Saudi, apart from Al-Qaeda?'

'Israel.'

'True. Who else?'

'We're back to Russia, because they export oil? So all this is about business?'

'Or national pride. Look, before '91 the Soviets were a super-power, and for "Soviet Union" read "Russia". No one dared do anything against them. Now? Ukraine refuses to pay them for gas and Georgia dares fight them. They've lost face. The West thinks they're an irrelevance.'

'You swallowed a history book?'

Snow half-smiled. 'I've just got a thing about the rise and fall of empires. Look, if Russia is relied upon to supply oil, they become relevant.'

Fox looked at the darkening sky and the lights of the Atlantis flickering out to sea, like a mirage in the desert. 'Never liked the Saudis much, nor the Russians.'

Atlantis Hotel, The Palm, Dubai

Voloshin sat in Plato's Bar, just off the hotel's lobby. He sipped an Arabic coffee. The menu described it as part of the 'connoisseur's collection', but to him it looked and tasted like brown sludge. His meeting with Khalid was to be their last. The mission had been deemed a success. For the next part, different contacts would be relied upon to make any link between Minsk and Saudi all the more tenuous.

Dressed in the Western attire of polo shirt and cream slacks, with freshly trimmed beard, Khalid looked like any other wealthy guest as he smiled at the waiter and placed an order. On seeing the Chechen his eyes narrowed slightly although the smile remained. The Chechen finished his drink and left the bar. Khalid cancelled his order and followed.

Outside on the terrace both men stood, a pair of business travellers in the warm evening air. Khalid looked at the Palm as it spread out before him. A man-made monstrosity that mimicked the natural beauty of the region. Many found the view from the balcony impressive; he found it an affront to the true believers. This had been constructed for the oil-fat Westerners who had raped his country and insulted his God, the one true God. However, it served His divine purpose that he, Khalid Al-Kazaz, make use of this place tonight.

The Chechen spoke. 'You have accomplished more than we ever expected of you, my brother.'

'The Westerners were rescued and my brothers killed.'

'Your brothers were martyred.'

Khalid grunted. 'They did not kill enough infidels.'

'They proclaimed the message, our message. The taking of the hostages so easily…' It was a disaster for Khalid, Voloshin knew, but for him their purpose had been served. 'You have posted the executions, the first such to happen in the Kingdom. It will make all who would seek to insult the Prophet by working in the Kingdom think twice.'

Khalid's eyes flashed with rage. 'We mustn't simply deter the infidels from entering my country; we must drive those who are in it out!' He turned to face the man who had funded him. 'I do not think you know who I am or what I have achieved. I have never before failed. Not when fighting the Soviet sons of whores in Afghanistan, and not when killing the Americans in Iraq.'

Voloshin nodded an outward assent. The man was a savage

and he had no respect for him. 'Your reputation is well known, my brother, and you shall be rewarded.'

Khalid sneered and once more looked out over the Palm.

The car dropped them off fifty metres west of the hotel entrance on the Palm's Crescent Road, out of the reach of the security cameras. Both Snow and Fox had their silenced Glocks concealed beneath light suit jackets. The suppressors made the weapons longer and heavier but in the darkness their shapes were hidden well enough. They walked into the hotel complex unchallenged by the security guards; two suited Westerners worried them little. They found a table away from the lights and waited for their signal. Most guests would now be frequenting the main outdoor bar area or one of the terraces. Here they were unmolested and undetected.

The noise of a siren erupted into the night sky. Voloshin involuntarily flinched. Khalid spun and looked back at the hotel. Voloshin released his grip on the railing, ready for action.

'Fire alarm,' a waiter called out across the terrace. 'All guests are to use the stairs and congregate in the car park at the sea end of the hotel.'

'Let's hope it burns to the ground,' Khalid said without any sarcasm as he made for the external stairs.

Voloshin gave no reply but instantly started to look for any signs of either a fire or a snatch team. In his experience fire alarms were usually set off by someone for a reason. A rush of annoyed, intoxicated or worried guests pushed towards the fire exit from the lobby, restaurants, and the terrace.

The small earpiece in Snow's ear crackled and an American voice said: 'Target acquired. He is foxtrot. You will have visual in approximately thirty seconds. Repeat, three-oh seconds.'

Snow looked at Fox, who winked. The pair of 'deniable operatives' waited as the hotel's rich clientele made their way towards the fire-assembly area. In the distance the sirens of the fire service could be heard. Khalid moved past their table, unaware he was being watched.

'Have eyeball.' Snow spoke into his concealed mic.

Snow and Fox stood. Unseen in the shadows, Fox balled his fists; he'd rather use them to knock the target out than some chemical.

Fox grunted. 'Let's do this.'

Voloshin froze. He had seen them, two men dressed almost identically, moving with purpose after his contact. One turned around and their eyes met. The Belarusian fought the urge to look away and carried on walking.

The harassed-looking hotel management stood, attempting to placate angry guests as the fire brigade de-bussed and entered the hotel foyer. Several members of staff had been issued with clipboards and were asking guests to confirm their names and room numbers. Khalid noticed that the Chechen was no longer with him. He had expected nothing less. They could not be seen together. Not now, not ever. Suddenly he felt a white-hot pain in his left leg. It buckled and, before he knew what was happening, he collapsed to the floor, a wave of cold sweeping over his body. His head hit the tarmac and momentarily his vision blurred.

Snow saw his target fall, a second later realisation registered in Snow's eyes. Their target had been shot. He turned and searched for the would-be assassin and met the eyes again of the man walking no more than ten feet behind them, his own suppressed weapon raised, firing. The rounds passed millimetres from Snow's head.

Snow threw himself into the cover of the shrubbery lining the path and drew his Glock.

Voloshin saw the speed with which both men had reacted and at once knew they were professionals. The younger one had moved into cover quicker but the older had drawn his weapon faster and was now firing at him. Kill or be killed. Voloshin dropped heavily to the ground and removed the suppressor from his weapon. He ignored the burn this caused to his palm and returned fire. The unsuppressed sound of gunshots had the desired result as guests froze, then suddenly panicked. His own escape was instantly aided by a fat woman who was dragging a much smaller man back into the hotel. Their view blocked by this unlikely coupling, the men, whoever they were, wouldn't dare shoot. Voloshin sprang to his feet and sprinted across the gardens to the exterior wall. He vaulted over it and onto the Palm's Crescent Road.

Snow pushed himself up and moved towards Khalid. Blood had pooled behind his leg. The Arab was conscious, however, and his eyes stared at Snow uncomprehending. Snow had no idea how bad the injury was and had no time to wait around and find out. A hotel porter tried to help. Snow looked up and shouted, 'Get back, I'm a doctor.' He removed the syringe and plunged it into Khalid's thigh. 'Call an ambulance and tell these people to give me some space.'

Fox reached Snow's side and grabbed the Arab's arms. 'We've got to move.'

Ignoring protests from onlookers, Snow and Fox hauled Khalid up and dragged him away. Whatever was in the syringe had worked, for there was a strange smile on the man's face despite his gunshot wound.

The Arab looked at his abductors. 'You…' His voice trailed off and a laugh started to rise in his chest.

It was all Fox could do to suppress his urge to throw Khalid to the ground and put a round through his skull. They turned the corner back into the shadows and were lost in the confusion.

More sirens in the night air, this time police. The boat, a small outboard-powered cruiser, was no more than fifty feet away in the shallows of the man-made 'Royal Beach'. It had been moored there five minutes before by the other Agency man. He was now long gone. Snow and Fox dragged the Arab through the light-yellow sand. There were shouts from behind and Fox picked out commands in Arabic: 'Stop, halt, this is the police.'

'We've got company.'

As they readied the boat, Snow looked back and saw officers running in their direction. He shook his head. 'Lay him down and hang on.'

As a former member of Boat Troop, Snow was more at home on the water than Fox. He started the outboard and the cruiser lurched away violently. They would have to go the entire length of the crescent before they broke free into open water. Snow throttled up to maximum and held on. The beach fell away, as did the shouts. Snow looked down and switched on the GPS. The course was pre-plotted and would take them away to their rendezvous point.

Snow frowned. 'The RV's in the middle of the sea.'

Fox looked up; he was leaning against the gunwales. 'Anywhere's better than here.'

'How's our guest?'

Fox shrugged. 'Can't tell, too dark, too choppy.'

Snow frowned again. They couldn't slow to patch him up, but if they didn't he'd... 'See what you can do.'

'Aye.' Fox looked down. Khalid's eyes were open but glazed; the drug-induced smile was still there. A limp arm came up to hit Fox. He grabbed it like a child's and carried on with the assessment. Khalid was unable to fight. The first and only round to hit had smashed the left fibula, lodging itself in the tibia. Most of the blood on the Arab's green polo shirt had come from the lacerations to his head. 'Looks like he'll live.'

They reached the end of the sea wall and turned north out into the Arabian Gulf. According to the GPS their RV point was a further three nautical miles away. Fox, who had now made sure that Khalid's arms and legs were bound, joined Snow at the controls. 'I could murder a beer.'

'The shooter was white, European or American.' Snow directed his words at Fox but kept his gaze fixed on the horizon.

'You still going with this Russian theory then?'

'You got a better one?'

'Aliens.'

The adrenaline had started to ebb away but they couldn't yet relax. Snow cut the power to idle as they neared the RV. With nothing but blackness in front, stars above, and the lights of Dubai on the horizon behind, they stood in the open boat. In the darkness there was the faint noise of what seemed to be an electric motor. Then the sound of something breaking the water. In front of them a large, dark shape slowly rose. The conning tower of a submarine. Unseen by Snow and Fox, NVG goggles checked them out.

Fox whispered to Snow. 'Aliens.'

Jumeirah Beach Hotel, Dubai

The hotel had been a longtime favourite with Russians and, as such, Voloshin felt that, hiding in public, he would have less chance of being noticed. He would stay there for a couple of days until he could safely return to his villa on the Palm and retire. He sat in a corner of the hotel bar and took a shot of vodka. He had sent a secure email to his KGB handler's address in Minsk. It read:

'Contact taken by opposition. What are my orders?'

In Minsk, Sverov had read the document he was to send in reply more than once and was still shocked by its content. Although safe in his apartment, he was sick with fear. Killing a traitor was one thing, and kidnapping British businessmen had pushed him to his limit; but this new task was definitely beyond comprehension. Shakily he clicked 'send' and an encrypted file was immediately forwarded to Voloshin's modified smartphone.

Sverov stood and grabbed his coat. He had to get out, get

away. He'd get his car and leave the city, go to the woods. The fresh air and cold would clear his head; perhaps even cleanse him in some way?

The Russian prostitute at the bar, whom he'd had before, was attempting to make eye contact. Voloshin closed his eyes. Why did the Russians love this chunk of sand so much? His phone vibrated before he opened his eyes and noticed that the woman was now with a fat man in a tight shirt. Easy come, easy go. He removed the handset from his trouser pocket and read the message. He took another shot of vodka from the extortionately priced bottle and re-read his orders. No, he hadn't been mistaken.

CIA Interrogation Centre, Undisclosed Location, Arabian Peninsular
'I've never read the Koran personally, but then I have no desire to.' The American pronounced the word 'Koo-ran', his lazy Southern drawl making the holy book seem all the more alien in his infidel hands.

Khalid sat motionless, ankles and wrists shackled to the metal chair, and stared into the American's eyes. He hadn't spoken, not given them the chance to hear his perfect Oxford English. The accent his family had paid so much for him to acquire.

The American continued. 'The one biggest cause of suffering in this world is… religion. Pure and simple. Christians fighting Jews, Jews fighting Muslims, Muslims fighting Christians, Muslims fighting Muslims… you get the picture. I personally do not have a religion. I do not worship an idol or an "almighty" and that in my opinion, makes me a free man.' The interrogator paused; Khalid still stared back without emotion. The interrogator smiled. 'Now, I ain't no dummy. I know you can understand me so I'll just continue…'

Khalid remained impassive. Thus far, they, 'the Americans', hadn't asked him a single question apart from his name, which of course he had not answered. He had no idea where he was or how long he had been held. He guessed that the infidel who sat in front of him was from the CIA but he hadn't introduced himself. As though Khalid cared.

'Now I mean no offence, but to me your religion seems made up. A fantasy. Let me explain. Five times a day you have to kneel on the floor and praise Allah, saying how great "He" is an' all. Oh, mighty Allah, oh, great Allah, oh, humble Allah… My question to you is why? Why, if "He" is so mighty, so great, so humble, would you have to tell him? Surely "He" knows? I mean to say, if "He" is God and created the world and all, why would you personally have to remind him five times a day? I can understand you thanking him once in a while, if you believe he's responsible for the world, but surely constantly thanking him makes you a sycophant? He must get tired of it? Millions of sycophants every day saying, hey, Allah, you're great! Great job, we love you!'

Khalid tried to remain composed, tried to block out these blasphemous words, but they were making him boil inside. In any other situation the American would already have been dead, his throat cut. His right hand twitched involuntarily, a movement that wasn't missed by the American who was pacing around the small, metal-walled cell.

'Pork.' The American spun and pointed like a quiz show host. 'You Muslims can't eat pork. Hey, that's fine by me; you and the Jews together on one thing at least, and the Hindus with the Sacred Cow and all that? All a matter of taste. But here's where it gets a bit peculiar again for my liking. Alcohol. Now, according to the Koo-ran, what I've been told – remember, I've never read it – is that you Muslims can't use drugs or stimulants. Correct? Now, as far as I know, when the Koo-ran was written, the full effects of caffeine, tannin, and nicotine on the body weren't known. Of course, now we know these are stimulants – drugs if you like. So my question to you is: surely the Koo-ran must be revised – a second edition if you will – to reflect this new knowledge? As a Muslim is it not wrong for you to pollute your sacred body with such things?'

Through the anger, Khalid's mind tried not to agree with the logic of his interrogator. The American smiled sincerely and continued. 'And I don't understand your holy martyrs. Now let me see if I've got this straight, and please, by all means, correct me if I'm wrong. To kill another human being, a non-believer, in the name of Allah is glorious; again, it's a way of saying "thank you" for being so great an' all? What, really? But then if the... holy warriors, let's call them... get killed in the process, they become martyrs. They go to Paradise where they're pleasured by virgins. Now I'm no party pooper – hey, I've had my share of virgins in the past – but it seems to me that Allah is running a brothel and the cover charge is... what? Your life?'

Khalid's hand twitched more and was joined by a clenching of the jaw as he battled to control his fury.

The American saw this and sat. 'Seems to me like your Allah and I would get on just fine, long as we could come to some financial agreement over the cover charge.' Another pause.

'Now, just a question. What about the martyrs that are women? Do they get pleasured in Paradise by men? If so, are they also virgins? Because no woman wants a man that doesn't know what to do with it. Or do they get pleasured by women?' The American sat back in his chair and raised his hands behind his head. 'Do you have any sisters or perhaps a wife?'

Both hands trembled and Khalid shut his eyes. This man would die and burn for eternity. The American looked at Khalid, who had steadied himself once more. He placed his hands on the metal table. 'That's my take on the Muslim faith. I have views on a lot of things. It's a darn pity we don't have the time for a real debate, an exchange of views, because I'm eager to learn and willing to apologise if I'm wrong, but we don't. It's now time you answered a few questions for us.' The American smiled; Khalid stared back defiantly. 'Hey, I know you're a man of strong beliefs and would rather die than give up any information on your Muslim brothers if you had the choice. But you don't. In

283

fact, you'll be singing like Britney Spears – "oops, I did it again" – but it won't be your fault. You won't be able to control yourself. So please don't feel bad. Allah, or whoever, will forgive you.'

The door opened and a thickset man with a metal attaché case entered the room. Khalid sneered. He had endured torture at the hands of the Russians. What could these feeble fat men do to him? Inside his head he prepared himself for the pain that would surely follow, but he would not speak. He would die and so would his secrets. He would be a martyr.

The case was placed on the table and the man opened it. The fat man removed a syringe and then a bottle that he plunged into the top, drawing up a greenish liquid. He tapped the syringe and let the bubbles out via the needle. Khalid's eyes widened slightly.

'Like I said, you won't be able to stop yourself.' The interrogator tied a leather strap around Khalid's left arm, tight, until he could see the vein bulge. 'Don't tell anyone about this; it's against the Geneva Convention.'

Panic struck Khalid as the realisation hit him of what the American had meant. That whatever he did he wouldn't be able to keep his secrets. He would shame his men and his God. Allah forgive him!

The thickset man plunged the needle into Khalid's arm. 'Good evening,' he said jovially.

His job done, Casey left the room and headed towards the mess. He had lied about the Koran; he had read it, albeit an English-language translation. Although he'd been brought up an atheist, Casey felt dirty after insulting the Muslim and his 'maker'. He hated ridiculing the beliefs of others, even if he didn't believe then himself, but if it wasn't him doing the dirty work it would just be someone else. Casey sighed and ducked through a door and into the mess.

'What type of sub is this?' Fox asked.

'I can't tell you,' replied Casey with a smile.

'Classified?'

Casey shook his head. 'No. I can't tell you because I don't know. I'm not into subs.'

'Whatever it is, it's rendition class,' Snow said with irony.

'Ah, that British sense of humour.' Casey reached inside his jacket and pulled out a hip flask. He opened it and poured a measure of rum into three metal mugs. 'Naval ration, something you Brits invented.'

They drank.

Casey pulled a face. 'I'm a bourbon man; this stuff is too goddamn sweet.'

Snow looked into his mug. Waves of fatigue had started to hit him. It was over.

Fox grunted. 'Where are we headed?'

'Classified but we'll drop you off. You'll be back in London by tomorrow night.'

'And laughing boy?' Fox was referring to Khalid.

'He'll be telling me a whole load more funny stories, you can bet.'

Riyadh, Kingdom of Saudi Arabia

Despite security concerns raised by the Russian Embassy to the Saudis, the state visit had been completed without a hitch. The press stood a respectable distance back from the red carpet. The President of Chechnya waved cordially as he proceeded towards the Russian Aeroflot plane. He had been the guest of the Saudi King and as such had brought a message directly from the Russian President. During the years of unrest, Chechnya had been viewed as a front line by Islamic militants waging jihad against Russian forces. Thousands of the faithful had poured into the region to continue their fight against the godless Russians, who were preventing Chechnya from becoming an independent Muslim state. Many of these fighters were battled-hardened from years of guerrilla warfare against the mighty Soviet Union in Afghanistan.

Eventually, and after two separate wars, a full and lasting cease-fire had been declared. Parliamentary elections were held and the Moscow-backed candidate, Ramzan Shamil, announced President.

Shamil had been a Grozny warlord but had seen the wisdom of entering the political ring. He, like all real Chechens, wanted true independence, but knew that, without further unimaginable loss of life, this wouldn't be possible. However, there were those who wanted to fight on at any cost, those who would pursue ruthlessly the goal of an Islamic state in the Caucasus. Those who would seek to oust Shamil. These included the men, Saudi believers, who had fought in Chechnya. The visit to Islam's place of birth was therefore significant. Shamil had to gain the support of Saudi Arabia and its King if he was to prove himself a worthy leader of the Chechen people. He had to make them see that Chechnya was already a Muslim state and respected abroad.

During his four-day trip the Chechen leader had visited the holy city of Mecca to perform the 'Umrah', a pilgrimage recommended to all devout Muslims and second only to the Hajj in importance. He had also become the first ever Russian to take part in the traditional ceremony of the washing of the 'Kaaba', the cube-like black shrine that Muslims faced in daily prayers. In short, as a devout Muslim, Ramzan Shamil had acted as though on a pilgrimage and not a diplomatic mission. His association with the Saudi royals had given him validation with his countrymen. His high-wire act had, in effect, become much easier.

He reached the steps and turned to wave once more before he entered the plane and the door was shut. The private Aeroflot charter began to ready itself for take-off.

Voloshin lay still on the rooftop, covered with a dark tarpaulin, the American-manufactured Stinger missile at his side. The Russian airliner lifted off the runway and started to bank away from the airport. Voloshin said a quiet prayer, for superstitious rather than religious purposes, and stood up, hoisting the Stinger onto his shoulder. The fat outline of the airliner gave an all-too-easy acquisition target for the surface-to-air missile and almost immediately the reticule of the launcher alerted Voloshin that the missile was locked on. He took one deep breath then depressed the trigger switch.

The missile raced out of the tube and shot towards the plane. The Aeroflot captain registered a small flash on his starboard side, but before his brain had time to interpret the image, the plane shuddered, dipped, and then exploded.

Voloshin dropped the launcher and ran back down the steps and out of the building. He had three minutes to escape or he would be of no further use. On the ground, the remaining film crews who had filmed Shamil's departure from the Kingdom of Saudi Arabia had also filmed his departure from the land of the living. Instantly the footage raced towards newsrooms. Frantically the Saudi Information Ministry attempted to stop it.

Chapter 12

The Prime Minister tapped the report he'd received from Knight that morning. He had called a second emergency COBRA meeting to discuss the further developments in Saudi Arabia. 'How was this information obtained, Ms Knight?'

'Our assets apprehended the suspect but the Central Intelligence Agency are responsible for the intelligence.'

'Where is Khalid Al-Kazaz now?' Holmcroft wanted to know.

'In custody.'

'Where?'

'I'm afraid I don't have that information.'

'Afraid? Yes, I'm afraid too. Your men snatch a Saudi citizen from a third country and hand him over to the Americans, to do God only knows what to, and now you don't know where he is!'

'With respect, Foreign Secretary, this is neither the time nor the place to be discussing the morality of the CIA's methods. The intelligence speaks for itself. Someone has used an old KGB network to sponsor terrorist acts in Saudi Arabia.'

The PM held up his hand before an angered Holmcroft could speak. 'I agree with Ms Knight, Robert. From where I'm sitting the evidence looks pretty conclusive.'

Holmcroft all but exploded. 'But it's circumstantial, that's what the Russians will say. A Chechen meets with a former KGB asset? No links to the Russian government. The Belarusian KGB Director has a conversation with an unknown man who we believe to be the Russian PM's adviser, whom we can't identify? No substantiated link to the Russian government.'

The PM coughed and looked at Burstow, the Head of the Intelligence Service. 'What did the Russians have to say?'

'The Russian PM is renowned for his secrecy. He is surrounded by members of the old-guard KGB he served with prior to '91. Beyond this, our contacts said no one really knows who these inner circle advisers are.'

'So what are we expected to do? I've got a call with the US President in an hour. The markets are in turmoil, oil prices are rising, the Saudis are about to implode.' Daniels ran his hand through his hair.

'Ask the Russians to stop.'

All eyes looked at Patchem. The PM spoke. 'What?'

'If this is a plot to enable Russia to step into the oil-supply vacuum caused by the disruption in Saudi, we simply hand Russia a copy of our evidence and ask them to stop.'

'And risk World War Three?' Holmcroft verbally flew out of his seat.

'Please explain, Mr Patchem.' Daniels was becoming annoyed by his Foreign Secretary.

'We simply explain to the Russian President that we have acquired some rather toxic intelligence that suggests a rogue element in their government has been involved in the attacks on Saudi Arabia.'

Wibly, the Home Secretary, spoke for the first time before Holmcroft could interrupt. 'We give them the chance to deal with this "rogue element", as you put it?'

'In a nutshell, yes.'

Daniels frowned. 'So, the US President and I call the Russian

President and say just that to him? We have no reason to believe either you or the administration is directly involved but we have evidence that…?'

'How bloody simple, Mr Patchem. This isn't the school playground.'

Patchem looked at Holmcroft; the man was a buffoon. 'But we do have the "big boys" on our side.'

'Prime Minister.' Knight broke the tension. 'I feel that this is the best course of action open to us. We can't definitively prove the Russian government is behind this and we have no way of levering anything out of Belarus without risking this whole situation becoming public.'

'Why?'

'They don't want our trade or investment and would publicise any approach we made to them.'

'But what if the Russians deny it? What if they don't wish to cooperate?' Daniels was still struggling to accept the proposal.

'Russia has long wanted to be treated as a superpower once more, but with "super" power comes "super" responsibility. Russia wants the West to see them, and treat them, as equals. What is the one thing that insults them the most?' Knight asked.

'The missile defence plan?'

'They still haven't been appeased by the Black Sea option.'

'Black Sea option?' The Home Secretary frowned.

Holmcroft quickly stepped in. 'The US plans to scrap the proposed Polish site in favour of systems located on US Navy warships potentially located in the Black Sea.' It had been in one of the plethora of briefing minutes he had had to read.

Knight continued. 'If the defence system were to include Russian warships or land-based units they would have less cause to refuse.'

'I doubt we can link the two things together, Ms Knight.' Daniels looked down at the report.

Holmcroft had now calmed a little. 'We have to show our

continued support for Saudi Arabia, Prime Minister. We must demonstrate to them that we will continue to buy their oil and wish to trade further with them.'

Daniels nodded. 'I agree. If we're seen to accept these incidents for what they are, terrible but isolated attacks, and continue to trade as usual, the effect on Saudi Arabia will be lessened. Ms Knight, can we expect any more attacks?'

This was the one question that had been haunting her. 'The members of Al-Kazaz's network, which he used for the two kidnappings in Saudi Arabia, have been either killed or apprehended. He has himself confirmed this much. Al-Kazaz had no knowledge of the Russian airliner, however. We must therefore conclude his wasn't the only cell funded by his contact "the Chechen".'

'It was a Stinger missile, if I am correct?'

'Yes, Prime Minister. The launcher has been traced back to a batch that was "given" to the Mujahedeen in the Eighties by the CIA.'

'By whom?' Holmcroft again jumped in. 'Who's traced the serial number, the Americans? Highly unlikely.'

'No. The information was leaked by an unknown source but has since been confirmed to me.'

'I don't follow. Does it matter who leaked or traced the missile? The fact is that a US missile was used by a terrorist to bring down a Russian diplomatic aircraft.'

Knight nodded. 'I agree with you in part, Prime Minister, but that particular Stinger was from a batch that suffered from battery-pack degradation. It should have failed to launch. If that particular missile was in fact used, then it was refurbished by someone with a lot of ballistic technical knowledge and access to specific equipment. This is not the profile of the average extremist.'

The PM closed his eyes. 'So there is at least one more cell operating in Saudi Arabia?'

'We can't say definitely either way. If the effects of the attacks aren't severe enough, presumably there will be more. We also can't rule out the possibility of other groups carrying out copycat attacks in solidarity.'

Holmcroft was ashen-faced and making notes on a pad. With the exception of the scratching of his nib the room was silent.

Daniels smoothed his hair. 'Right, I have to somehow formulate a course of action and either sell it to the Americans or hope they've independently reached the same conclusion.'

'Don't forget the Ukrainians, Prime Minster. Without their help this would have never come to light.'

Daniels nodded at Patchem. 'Yes, of course, but they also must follow our line.'

'Have you agreed this with their President?' Patchem asked and wished he hadn't. Holmcroft gave him a dirty look but the PM answered.

'Not as such. You are correct. I will need to speak to them.' He stood. 'Thank you all for your time and input. Now, if you'll excuse me, I have a phone call to make.'

The meeting at an end, the Prime Minister left the room to make his way back to Number Ten. Wibly rose and was followed by Burstow. Holmcroft stood but didn't move. He stared at Knight and Patchem, a cold anger in his eyes.

'We need more on this "Russian adviser", otherwise we've got nothing. He's the key to it all. I want you to get it for me. Don't tell me how.'

Knight raised her eyebrows but remained both seated and silent until the Foreign Secretary had left the room. 'Any ideas?'

Patchem shrugged. 'How do you ID anyone? Photographs? We search all images taken of the Russian PM for the last ten years for any unknown faces that crop up?' It was the proverbial needle in a haystack.

'And then who do we ask to look at the photographs?'

Patchem had a sudden look of mischief on his face. 'The Director of the Belarusian KGB.'

Knight burst out laughing and leant against a wall. 'Of course we do, and he'll say yes, I did attack Saudi Arabia, and this is the man who told me to do it.'

Patchem was surprised by his Director's flippancy. 'You sound like Holmcroft.'

'He's my role model, didn't you know?' She shook her head. 'Sorry, I've not been getting much sleep.'

Neither had he, what with his recent return from Saudi. Patchem stood, placed his hand on her shoulder, and stared into the eyes of his old friend. 'Look, it won't hurt to put a suspect list together at least. Agreed?'

Knight nodded. 'Agreed. Get a list of faces and then we'll see.'

Presidential Dacha, Minsk Region, Belarus
The open fire was lit in the presidential *dacha*. The weather had become wintery. Sverov looked across the table at the man from Moscow and noted how shadows cast by the flames danced on his face. Perhaps this was how he should be seen, a devil? Sverov had done many things to protect his motherland but shooting down a Russian diplomatic airliner was too much.

'The debt has been paid in full, Director, thanks to the services of the KGB.'

Sverov shivered, not because of the temperature. 'So that is the end of this business?'

Gurov's mouth smiled but his eyes did not. 'Yes, business is now concluded. My Prime Minister is extremely grateful to Belarus.' He stood abruptly and held out his hand. 'Goodbye, Director.'

Sverov mimicked the gesture. 'Goodbye.'

The Russian left. Sverov turned off the light and caught his reflection in the mirror. Now the flames danced over his face.

SIS Headquarters, Vauxhall Cross, London, UK
'Voilà.' Patchem handed Knight a sheet with a row of eight photographs printed on it.

'Russians?'

'Our facial-recognition software narrowed it down to these possible suspects.'

Knight was impressed. She studied the sheet. 'That is, of course, if our man has been photographed with the Russian PM.'

Patchem shrugged. 'Exactly. It's all we have to go on. You know there's only one person who can narrow this down even further.'

Knight looked up. 'You're wrong. There are two.'

Patchem frowned. 'You mean ask their PM?'

'Not quite. We get them to ask their own PM. We send a copy to the President and say we have reason to believe that one of these men is the agent provocateur.'

It wasn't something he would have thought of. 'You'll suggest this to Holmcroft?'

'Of course.' She dialled a number on her desk phone and pressed the speaker button. The line went directly to the Foreign Secretary.

'Yes.'

'Foreign Secretary, it's Abigail Knight.'

'Yes, I know who it is. What do you have?' Holmcroft's irritation boomed from the speaker.

'We have a list of suspects for the second man on the tape and feel we should pass this information onto the Russian President.'

'You what? Are you completely out of your mind?'

Knight smiled and Patchem had to look away. 'Does that mean you object to the idea?'

'Yes, I bloody well do object! Ms Knight, I asked you to find a way to get me a name, not a way to further insult the Russian government!'

Knight remained calm. 'So you'd like me to find another solution?'

'Yes, and don't bloody waste my time with the details. All I want is a name.'

'Thank you, Foreign Secretary. You have been most helpful.'
She ended the call before Holmcroft could say another word.

Patchem frowned but this time with amusement. 'You put the phone down on him, you cut him off.'

Knight sipped from her cup of lemon and ginger tea, her mouth curling. 'I also got you the all clear to get creative.'

Patchem shook his head as realisation dawned. 'I defer to your knowledge and wisdom, Madam Director.'

Queen Mary Gardens, Regent's Park, London
Regent's Park housed both the London Central Mosque and Winfield House, the residence of the US Ambassador. This fact wasn't lost on Vince Casey.

'This is all very clichéd, Jack.'

'Thanks for coming at such short notice.'

'You were lucky to catch me, you know, as a tourist, just passing through.'

'Tourist.' Patchem rolled his eyes; the word had a different meaning in CIA parlance. 'My request. Can you do what I've asked?'

'Here.' Casey handed his SIS partner a folded piece of paper. 'Contact details. Safer than email.'

Patchem put the paper into his coat pocket. 'Thank you.'

'Jack, I don't need to tell you, but I will anyway, that this is serious shit. Dubai was a friendly city. If they get caught this time, just remember we don't know 'em.'

'I have faith in my men.' The intelligence the operation would produce was critical.

Both men were silent for a moment as a pair of real tourists stopped to admire the national collection of delphiniums.

Once they were out of earshot Casey spoke. 'So, our elected leaders have spoken to the Russians. Let's just say that *their* elected leader didn't respond well to his government being accused of sponsoring terrorism. He did, however, say he'd look at the evidence we presented to him, meaning he'll call in his "Premier Minister" for a chat and together they'll decide what to do. Of course we told them that if anything else were to happen in Saudi in the interim, we'd blame them.'

Patchem had known Casey a long time and his security-clearance level never ceased to amaze him. 'Although without proof we can't tell anyone else about it, or even threaten to.'

Casey pointed at Patchem's coat pocket. 'Then we need to provide the proof.'

'We'll get it.'

'See you around.' Casey walked away in the direction of York Gate.

Moscow, Russian Federation

From his apartment window, Maksim Pavelevich Gurov watched the Moscow River as a tourist launch passed in front of the Kremlin. The meeting which had taken place in an FSB *dacha* outside Moscow had been the inner circle only, Gurov and his peers. The President of the United States and his lapdog, Daniels of the UK, had called their leader that afternoon. The President had expected the call to express sympathy and support to Russia following the assassination of the Chechen President, but no. The West, they were told, had made unfounded allegations against the Russian government. This meeting was to provide answers. Both the Russian President and Premier Minister wanted to know why.

A copy of the allegations and evidence presented by the Americans had been given to each man to study. Gurov had given his opinion: that the Americans had engineered the entire situation to make Saudi Arabia more dependent upon them. He argued that it was a gambit to allow the Americans to maximise both their political and military presence in the area. This view was supported by another who suggested it would make a future invasion of Iran all the more plausible. Yet another asked if the assassination of the Chechen President had been planned or funded by the US, for indeed, a US surface-to-air missile had been used. But, someone asked, why point the finger at Russia? For this there was no logical answer. Were they to be a scapegoat in case the plan became public?

Theories and ideas were debated but the conclusion was a shocking one. For reasons unknown, the West had accused Russia of something she had no part in. It was decided that the Russian government would vigorously rebuff all accusations and threaten to publish the allegations to the United Nations Assembly in New York. In the meantime, the US, British and Saudi ambassadors to Russia would be warned that any further allegations would result in their expulsion. Russia would also lodge an official complaint over the shooting down of her airliner to the Saudi government via the UN.

Gurov opened his balcony doors and stepped out into the late-afternoon Moscow air. Had he been responsible for the world's largest act of sabotage or was it realpolitik? Was there a difference? Was he, too, to be regarded as a Renaissance man like Machiavelli, for both had been state servants concerned only for the interests of their nation? What drove Gurov on wasn't the desire to be recognised but the desire to save Russia. In a matter of days the man above him, the man hailed as the post-Soviet saviour of Russia, his Prime Minister, would be implicated as a sponsor of terrorism and ousted from office, an international enemy of the people. Worldwide condemnation would follow and President Melnikov would step out from under his predecessor's shadow and flourish. A wounded Russia would recover with more respect and dignity than ever before, as a nation willing to finally stamp out all corruption.

Russia once more, could stand tall, an equal, if not better, to the West. Gurov's actions, however, were to be unknown and unrewarded. The plan, a decade in the making, was now almost complete. He nodded as the sun started to slip below the skyline to the west. In forty-eight hours or less a new day would dawn for his Russia.

Central London, UK

There was a buzzing in his ears, Snow felt as though his head had barely touched the pillow yet he had slept for ten hours. It was just after 9.00 p.m. and it wasn't his alarm. He swung his legs out of bed and looked at the video intercom. It was Patchem. He buzzed him up. He'd barely had time to throw on a T-shirt and splash water on his hair when there was a knock at the front door.

'Evening.' Patchem stepped into Snow's Central London crash pad and marched into the lounge, where he sat without waiting to be asked.

'Evening.' Snow followed and sat opposite him.

Patchem picked up the half-empty bottle of cognac from the glass-top table in front of him to study the label. He wasn't surprised it was Cyrillic. He looked at the former SAS man. 'Sleep well?'

Snow held his neck and tried to massage out a crick. 'Better than on that dam sub.'

'I need you to go to Belarus.'

Snow blinked; he still wasn't with it. 'When?'

'You're booked on the Austrian Airlines flight to Kyiv via Vienna. It leaves from Heathrow at 6.05 a.m. That will give you plenty of time to drive into Belarus before nightfall.'

Snow continued to massage his neck. Having been back in the UK for less than a day he was now off again. 'OK, what's this about?'

Patchem gave Snow a long stare before answering. His operative now had a right to know. 'We believe that what happened in Saudi was orchestrated by the Russians. We've found links to Belarus; we now need to confirm the link from Belarus back to Moscow.'

Snow's theory had been confirmed. 'So what exactly do you want me to do?'

'Carry out an interview in Minsk. You'll be a two-man team.'

'And the other member is?'

'Fox, if you think he can handle it? I've chosen you two as you're already involved. This is a non-attributable operation.'

'Black op?' Snow frowned. No record and no support if it went tits up. 'Who do you want us to interrogate, President Lukachev?'

Patchem ignored the sarcasm. 'No. The General Director of the KGB.'

Snow blinked and waited for Patchem to smile. He didn't. 'You're serious?'

'His voice is on a recording we have. He was responsible for carrying out the attacks but you need to ask him who he was taking his orders from. We know it's one of the Russian PM's closest advisers. We don't have a name and without a name we can't pin it on the Russians.'

'No pressure then?' Snow took the bottle and considered having a shot. 'I'm not an interrogator.'

'But these men are.' Patchem retrieved the piece of paper Casey had given him and placed it on the table along with a new British passport and an envelope. 'Aidan, if anyone gets wind of this there'll be severe consequences all round. You know this. HM Government will deny all knowledge of both of you and I'll be powerless to help. I wouldn't ask you to do this unless I knew we had no alternative. Travel to Kyiv as Aidan Mills; the cover hasn't been compromised. Once there you'll use a Ukrainian passport in the name of Andrei Shamanov. He's ethnic Russian.'

Snow could pass for Russian or indeed ethnic Russian, but Fox?

Patchem read his mind. 'Fox will be Irish. Twice.'

Snow thought about the innocent men and women who had been killed or injured so far in the attacks in Saudi and the desire he had for revenge against those who had perpetrated them. He had felt cheated when ordered to hand Khalid Al-Kazaz over to Casey, but the intelligence he had given far outweighed their right to revenge. The desire for revenge, however, still burnt. 'I'll do it.'

'I know you will.'

Chapter 13

Jumeirah Beach Hotel, Dubai, United Arab Emirates

The old man sat at the bar next to the very attractive Russian girl. He showed her the photograph. 'So, my dear, have you seen this man?'

The prostitute shrugged, non-committal. Her accent was sharp, Muscovite. 'I have seen many men here.' She looked away, uninterested. He wasn't going to pay her for sex.

He took her hand and placed a $100 bill in it. 'Are you sure?'

She faced him again. Money without sex? 'Yes. I've seen him. He always orders a bottle of Smirnoff Black.'

'Always?'

'He is not a tourist. He comes here to get Russian girls.' She lit a cigarette and looked away again, feeling a little ashamed explaining herself to this old man, who looked like her grandfather.

The old man noticed. 'I am his uncle. It is very important that I find him.'

'Oh?'

He pretended to be saddened and looked into her eyes. 'Do you often see your mother, my dear?'

The girl became slightly defensive before answering. 'Not for three years. Not since I came here.'

301

'I am sorry to hear that. My sister, this man's mother, is very, very ill. She may even…' He let his voice trail off and drank a little of his beer before continuing. 'He is her only son and… well, I am sure you understand.'

She touched his hand. 'I can tell you where he lives. I have been there.'

The old man smiled appreciatively. 'If he has enjoyed your company, my dear, then he is really a very lucky man.'

The girl was embarrassed; she sensed he was being sincere. 'Have you got a piece of paper and a pen?'

Boryspil International Airport, Kyiv, Ukraine

Snow had enjoyed breaking the speed limit on London's ring road, the M25, to get to Heathrow. He cared little for speed cameras or police patrol cars. The police had a list of all SIS vehicles that they were not to attempt to stop. Snow wasn't a big music fan and as usual was listening to BBC Radio 4, the news and current affairs channel, as he sped towards one of the world's busiest airports. The news of the Russian diplomatic airliner shot down over Riyadh with a SAM was still a newsworthy story. Reactions from various parties were discussed and pundits were talking about the implications for the future of air travel safety. At Heathrow itself, security had once again been tightened up. The UK took terror threats seriously.

Once onboard the flight, the passengers had been jumpy, understandably so as Al-Qaeda had boasted other airliners would soon follow. Snow's flight, first to Vienna and then to Kyiv, however, was uneventful. He sat in his business class seat, which was marginally larger than economy class, a row behind, and annoyingly sipped water, as he was on duty. As the plane lost height and approached Boryspil Airport Snow looked out of the window at the city below, which he had once called home, and then the rows of *dachas* nearer the airport. It was the first time he had returned to the country where he had been shot and almost died.

Still sipping his bottled water, Snow showed his 'Aidan Mills' passport to the Ukrainian immigration officer before walking through customs and out to the crowded concourse full of both licensed and unlicensed cabs. He was accosted by local men saying 'taxi'. He shook his head and gave the reply he had always given: 'I'm an English taxi driver.' Once outside the terminal a familiar face stood beside a black Audi saloon. Snow stepped in through the open rear door and the diplomatic car pulled away.

'Aidan, good to have you back and actually working for us now.' Vickers smiled at the man sitting next to him and grimaced, his jaw still sore. 'Fox is being collected by car.'

Patchem had told Snow the bare minimum about Sukhoi's assassination and Vickers's involvement. The physical appearance of the once-debonair SIS officer nonetheless surprised him. 'You OK?'

'Nothing a few pints of Guinness wouldn't cure.'

'Really?'

Vickers shrugged, then looked out of the window before speaking. Sukhoi's death had affected him more than he wanted to admit. It was the first time anyone he had been responsible for had died. An SIS enquiry was underway, as was a Ukrainian police investigation. Sukhoi would have been the highest-ranking defector of any country for over ten years. It was only his own boss's actions that had stopped Vickers from being suspended until the investigation had been completed. Patchem had said that Vickers was 'a vital component in the ongoing operation' and therefore his suspension would be both 'a nonsense and counterproductive'. Vickers, however, remained despondent and considered his future.

'I failed, Aidan. A man died. Any pain I'm in is justified.'

Snow knew how Vickers felt. Unable to help, unable to stop the inevitable from unfolding before his eyes. His own nightmares had haunted him. 'This is ironic coming from me, but take the counselling, Alistair. It helps.'

'Maybe.' Vickers closed his eyes and pinched his nose. One of the headaches he'd been getting since the attack was coming, and he'd forced himself not to take the tablet for fear of becoming drowsy. 'So what did Jack tell you?'

'Drive to Belarus and ask a man a few questions.'

'Aidan, you know this operation is blacker than black?'

'Is that term still PC?'

Vickers tried to smile but didn't manage to. 'If you'd asked me two weeks ago, I would have said this op was too much, but not anymore, not after what they did to Sukhoi and those innocent people in Saudi Arabia.'

'You don't have to tell me, I was there.'

Vickers squinted as if a light had gone on. 'Ah, I see. I didn't realise. I knew about Fox.' He paused to again massage the bridge of his nose. 'Look, what I'm saying is that if this goes tits up, you'll be on your own. The embassy in Minsk knows nothing of the op, won't be able to help, and I'll be in Kyiv.'

'Alistair, I've no intention of joining the Tits Up Club.'

The car pulled off the Boryspil-Kyiv Highway and into the car park of a roadside restaurant. The lunchtime customers had left and only a few cars dotted the bays.

'I'm going to need your Aidan Mills passport.'

Snow handed it over.

'Thanks.' Vickers nodded at a white Lada Riva estate. 'That's yours. The passports are in the glove compartment. Good luck.'

Snow was joined at the Lada by Fox as the two diplomatic saloons pulled off to leave the former SAS men with the battered Soviet car.

'Welcome to Ukraine.'

Fox looked around and noticed an eight-feet-tall cartoon-style bear made of painted concrete on the other side of the highway. '1980 Moscow Olympics?'

'Misha was the emblem. Some of the sailing events happened here.'

'Before the road was built?' Fox said without a trace of sarcasm.

Snow shook his head. 'Get in the car.'

Snow opened the glove compartment and studied the Ukrainian passport. It was real and bore his photograph as well as several stamps for entry and exit into Russia, Turkey, and Bulgaria. Holidays and business trips.

Fox flicked through his own. 'They could have given me a better name.'

'If I were you I'd have asked for a better face.' Snow smirked.

Al Sefri, The Palm, Dubai, United Arab Emirates

Voloshin stood on his balcony and looked back at mainland Dubai, a mile away. The Arab had been right: this place wasn't natural. But unlike the Arab, he had now started to appreciate all it had to offer. A man could go mad living in a place as artificial as this but he wasn't such a man. His retirement had started and this villa on Al Sefri, the Palm's fourth branch, was his payoff. His cover had been blown by the British diplomat he hadn't killed. But he bore the man no ill will, nor had he borne any malice towards those he'd killed in the line of duty, for that is what it had been. He hadn't been the 'plaything' of businessmen; he'd been an instrument for Belarus and had served his country with both honour and pride. He shut his eyes and felt the heat linger on his eyelids. He didn't miss the abysmal weather of his homeland... Something hit his cheek. Instinctively, he touched it and felt a cut. There was blood on his hand and then the window behind him exploded.

Voloshin threw himself to the ground as a white-hot searing pain erupted in his chest. He hit the wooden-decked concrete, a wave of cold sweeping over his entire body. He saw the quickly darkening sky above and knew his time had come unless he moved. He tried to sit and, on the second attempt, managed to raise his head just in time to see a large figure emerging from his beach steps in front of him. He pushed his arms with all his effort and slid backwards into the villa, smashing the back of his head against the patio rails. Now his feet worked and he pushed faster, his shoulder hitting a chair. Wildly, he grabbed at the chair legs and managed to roll into a kneeling position. He scrabbled forward until there was a dull thud and he felt a sensation like a hot poker bursting through his upper back.

Voloshin fell forward, smashing an ornate glass table. Needles of pain dug at his face. But still, as stars erupted in his head and blood burnt his eyes, he moved on, desperately trying to get away from his assassin. Summoning the remainder of his strength from a fading body he pulled himself up onto an armchair.

'That's enough.'

He recognised the voice, but it was out of place. He turned and fell into the chair. Voloshin's eyes bulged. Across the broken table, a man sat down. Director Dudka of the Ukrainian SBU.

'That's far enough.' Dudka had a silenced pistol aimed at the Belarusian. Voloshin's bare chest was a wet, red mass. His cream linen trousers had become dark with blood.

'You, old man? It is you who would kill me?'

Dudka said nothing.

Voloshin spoke again. 'You herd me into the house like a wounded animal to finish me off?'

'I was aiming for your head. I missed several times.' He stared into the eyes of the man who had destroyed an entire family, his friend's family that he had loved as his own. 'Why did you kill my friend?'

'Orders.'

'His daughter?'

Voloshin thought back to the pretty girl in Belarus. That act had been harder. 'Orders.'

Dudka ran his tongue over his lips. They had gone dry. 'So you admit to killing them both, Director Sukhoi and Masha?'

Voloshin hadn't known her name. 'I was following orders. Like you I was an instrument of the state, Dudka, that is all.'

Dudka saw a bottle of expensive imported vodka on a side unit. 'I need a drink.'

'What?'

Dudka stood and placed the bottle on the table along with two glasses that had stood in a set next to it. Voloshin tried to move but found he couldn't. He now noticed that the Ukrainian was wearing surgical gloves. Dudka poured two measures. He held one up to the light and peered at it.

Voloshin's mouth formed a sneer. 'What now, Dudka? Are you so weak? You need a drink for courage?'

Dudka downed the shot. 'No. I'm toasting absent friends.'

Before Voloshin could reply Dudka pulled the trigger. Voloshin's head snapped back.

Dudka stood and kicked the body with all his might as tears now formed in his eyes. Reaching inside the pocket of his summer jacket, he removed a copy of a photograph of Leonya and Masha. It had been taken at his *dacha* one of those summers so many years ago. He kissed the photograph before placing it over the face of the corpse.

Ukrainian-Belarusian Border Crossing Point
Having left the small town of Skytok, the battered Lada bounced over the potholes on the approach to the border crossing between Ukraine and Belarus. Fox and Snow had their passports ready. Fox, the Irish travel writer William Burke, and Snow his Russian interpreter, Andrei Shamanov. Both passports were the work of experts and could not be faulted. Without a single coherent word of Russian, Fox felt nervous. Meanwhile Snow, with his Moscow accent, pretended to be at ease.

'You know how many words I know in Russian?' said Fox.

'No.'

'Five. Babushka, vodka, da, niet, and Kalashnikov.'

Snow smirked as he slowed for the checkpoint. 'You'll be fine then if you get into a firefight with a bunch of drunken grannies.'

The Ukrainian border guard waved the car to a halt and approached the door. Snow wound down the window and became Russian. 'Good afternoon, officer.'

'Good afternoon. Your passports, please.'

Snow placed the documents into the hand of the border guard.

The guard gave Snow's passport a cursory glance before taking more time to look at Fox's. After checking he had a visa for entry into Belarus he returned them. 'All OK.'

Snow thanked the guard, started the car, and drove towards the Belarusian side.

'That was easy enough.'

'The Ukrainians will spend more time checking us when we come back. They don't mind us leaving the country but getting in is another matter.'

There was a line of traffic ahead, three cars waiting to be cleared before them.

Fox craned his neck. 'Have I missed something? Has Belarus become the new Club Med?'

'Actually I saw a documentary on National Geographic the other day, *The Bearded Ladies of Belarus*. Right up your street, after Saudi.'

Fox cast Snow a sideways glance. 'Yeah, and I saw one you'd be interested in. *The Mincers of Minsk*.'

It was their turn to be checked. Once again Snow wound down the window and handed over the passports.

'Please step out of the car, both of you.'

Fox felt his pulse rate increase as Snow translated. Both men got out. A second border guard was standing at the side of the road watching.

'Open the boot, please,' the first guard, passports in hand, asked in a reasonable tone.

'Of course, officer.' Snow had nothing, except his identity, to hide.

The second guard now joined the first and peered into the open boot.

'You Irishman?' the first asked Fox in English.

'Yes, officer, I am that.'

'Guinness, very good,' replied the officer, with a thumbs up.

Fox smiled back. 'Ah, I hear Belarusian vodka is also very good!'

The guard laughed and pushed the boot closed. He thrust the passports back into Snow's hand and once more switched back to Russian. 'You are his interpreter?'

'Interpreter, driver.' Snow shrugged.

'OK. Come to the office and we will stamp his entry visa.'

Out of the guard's earshot, Fox spoke. 'I personally think Guinness tastes like shit.'

Snow furrowed his brow in mock incomprehension. 'How would you know?'

KGB Headquarters, Skaryny Avenue, Minsk, Belarus

Sverov looked at the emailed report he had been sent from Abu Dhabi. An anonymous caller had telephoned the local police stating that a known Belarusian assassin, living in Dubai, had just been murdered. Due to the very odd nature of the call, the police had thought it was a hoax until they had arrived at the address and discovered a body. The houses on both sides were empty investment properties so there had been no eyewitnesses. The police had then decided to contact the Belarusian Embassy in Abu Dhabi on the strength of the photograph found beside the corpse and a piece of paper giving the dead man's name, nationality, and KGB identity number.

The embassy liaison officer stated that Belarus knew nothing of the deceased, but the police had insisted they be given a copy of the information so they could check their records. The photograph of the corpse was now on Sverov's screen along with a copy of the image found with the body. Sverov studied the two images and felt sick. It was a message. Voloshin had been assassinated by someone who knew of the plot; why else would they have placed the old photograph of Sukhoi at the crime scene? His hand hovered over the desk telephone until he forced himself to make the call.

'Yes.' It was answered on the second ring.

'We have some worrying news.'

'Who is this?'

'Sverov.'

'Why are you calling me?'

'Voloshin is dead.'

'Who?' The line was cut.

Sverov looked at the phone in disbelief. Did the Russian not care for his safety? Sverov dropped his head into his hands and took comfort in the warmth of them on his face. He couldn't think; his mind had simply stopped working. If the assassin knew what Voloshin had done to Sukhoi, they also knew why! And if they knew why, they would know about him. Sverov sat up straight. No. No! He had done nothing wrong. He had been acting in the best interests of the nation of Belarus. He was Director of the KGB. He was feared, not fearful.

In Moscow, Gurov knew the Belarusian Director was a weak link, but the trail would stop there. In Minsk, in his KGB headquarters, Sverov was safe from any foreign investigation regardless of what evidence they had. Besides, Sverov had no information about him, didn't even know his real name, and the number he had called would become inactive tomorrow. For Sverov to accuse him was impossible. No, much better that Gurov himself leak information later to implicate his Premier Minister and the Belarusians. Although not his own doing, Voloshin's death had been timely. Gurov once more played the covert and purposefully jerky footage he had taken of their meeting at the *dacha*. The meeting at which the Director of the Belarusian KGB had received orders from a close adviser to Russian Premier Minister Privalov. An adviser who did not sound at all like Gurov.

Chapter 14

Minsk, Belarus

After crossing the border the two former SAS men drove directly to the GPS reference they had been given by Patchem. This turned out to be in a forest near the outskirts of Minsk. They arrived just before midnight. Snow guided the Lada down a rutted path and into the woods. Once he was sure the car couldn't be seen from the main road he switched off the engine. Snow stood guard while Fox set about finding the dead drop. As Snow looked back down the path he heard the occasional Scottish curse from behind.

It took ten minutes of searching with a torch but Fox found the cache. It was in a DPM holdall hidden under a pile of leaves. It contained new number plates for the cars, a couple of bottles of mineral water, a syringe of 'sedative', two silenced pistols with ammo, a few Belarusian banknotes, and another set of GPS coordinates, the drop-off point. Fox heaved the bag towards the car and set about unscrewing the Ukrainian number plates and fitting a pair of Minsk-region, registered ones.

The plan was simple. Snow and Fox were to lay up in the car and then drive into central Minsk around noon, just another car on the capital's streets, and find a place to park near to Sverov's flat. They would then wait until an unseen contact sent a text message indicating that Sverov was on his way home from the office. By snatching the Director in the evening, they hoped his disappearance wouldn't be noticed until mid-morning the next day. This would give the interrogators perhaps twelve to fifteen hours before any alarm was raised.

Snow opened the tailgate and removed a heavy woollen blanket. 'You sleep, I'll take first stag.'

'You saying I need my beauty sleep more than you?'

Snow stretched; the upright driving position hadn't done his back any good. He chucked the blanket at Fox. 'Shut up, ugly, and get your head down.'

Fox made no attempt at any further banter. The truth was he wasn't twenty-five any more, he wasn't even thirty-five any more, and he was buggered. He climbed into the back and curled up as best he could on the back seats. They'd sleep two on and two off, each getting six hours sleep, in theory. Snow had no illusions that, come first light, both of them would be knackered but unable to close their eyes.

*

In Minsk, Sverov was called into a meeting with the President of Belarus and ordered to explain how it was possible that a deniable operative, Voloshin, had not only been assassinated but publicly named as an agent of the KGB. The President was furious that the Arabs were accusing him personally and Belarus secondly of conducting espionage on their soil. The millions of dollars in potential trade between the two nations could not be put at risk. Like all meetings with the President, Sverov's opinion meant little if it did not tally with that of his superior. The President, who was still livid his ambassador to Ukraine had been so unceremoniously expelled, wanted to know if Sverov thought the Ukrainians might be responsible. It was a paranoid thought from a paranoid man but Sverov gave his opinion that this might be possible. This was readily accepted by the President, who vowed to make their meddling southern neighbours pay. Sverov simply nodded. He was used to his leader's hollow threats.

After joining the lunchtime traffic into Minsk, Snow and Fox parked their Lada on a street several hundred metres from Sverov's apartment building. Just out of the city centre, there were no parking restrictions. Their unremarkable car hadn't attracted the slightest bit of attention. Minsk did not seem, to Snow, that much different to Kyiv. Some of the words on signs had different spellings, Russian, Belarusian and Ukrainian all being distinct languages, and the people seemed to lack some of the sophistication that Kyivites, eighteen years after the fall of the USSR, had accumulated. That was it, Snow realised; time had certainly not stood still in Belarus but definitely slowed. Keeping his observations to himself he went to get some lunch from a Gastronom while Fox pretended to be asleep in the passenger seat. The fact that Fox did nod off while Snow was gone, he kept to himself. Boredom was a factor in all operations but all the more so when the options were limited.

They moved the car twice, each move to a new location a similar distance to the target address. In between, both men made a pass of the target apartment checking on security personnel, signs they had been compromised, and parking spaces. Darkness came at not long after 3.00 p.m., bringing with it a light rain. Rush hour came again and the streets were bright with myriad taillights. Then, at a quarter to six, Snow received a text message on his single-use phone.

'Here we go. We've got forty minutes.'

'Jolly good.' The reply from Fox came with much sarcasm.

They were going in half-blind. The only information they had about the apartment was what had been left for them at the dead drop. It gave the address, a rough floor plan, and the combination for the alarm, which might or might not have been changed.

*

It was early evening when an exhausted Sverov arrived at his apartment. He removed his overcoat and jacket and placed them on hangers. He then took off his highly polished shoes and swapped them for a pair of slippers. It was only then that he noticed the door to the lounge was ajar. He tutted at himself for not shutting it and entered the room.

'Good evening, Director Sverov.' The masked intruder was sitting in his leather armchair as though it was a job interview.

Sverov involuntarily froze. The door was shut behind him. He span round.

'Sit down.' The language was English, the man large.

Sverov remained standing. 'You are both making a big mistake.'

Snow continued in Russian. 'And you have made a bigger mistake, but we are here to give you the chance to repent.'

Sverov's eyes darted around the room. Snow continued. 'We switched off your alarm; we didn't want to be disturbed.'

'Who are you?' Sverov demanded, disdain masking fear.

'Friends of Leonid Sukhoi.'

'The traitor.' Sverov spat the word but the fear rose inside. It was his turn; they had come for him.

'The man behind you is an animal. He was an interrogator for the IRA. You wouldn't like it if I were to leave you alone with him.' Snow shook his head then switched to English, but kept the Moscow accent. 'Mr Matthews, hit this gentleman for me.'

Fox stepped forward and swung a haymaker at Sverov's jaw. Shocked, the Belarusian made no attempt to deflect the blow and dropped like a stone to the wooden floor.

'What do you want?' His voice was coloured with pain as he shuffled towards the coffee table.

'Your confession, the truth.'

'Fools!' With speed, Sverov grabbed something from under the table and brought it up, a Makarov pistol. If he was quick, he could get them both. His trigger finger pulled. A click. He pulled again. Click… Click… Sverov stared at the weapon as if not quite believing it had been emptied.

'Would you be so kind now as to take a seat?' Snow's words were condescending.

Sverov held up his hands in a manner that was half-surrender, half-placatory. 'OK… OK.' He sat on the settee facing Snow's chair and held his jaw. 'Who sent you?'

'We sent ourselves, Director. We know it was you who ordered the assassination of our dear friend. Now, if you would be so kind as to tell us, in English if you will, who it was that ordered the terrorist attacks in Saudi Arabia?'

Sverov went rigid. He was shocked. Finding out about Sukhoi was one thing; in fact, it was almost to be expected. But establishing that they knew about Saudi Arabia had confirmed his worst fears. Killing the old man had been in vain, as he had attempted to tell the Russian it would be beforehand. Had there been a leak?

Regaining some composure Sverov snorted. 'Let me remind you who you are addressing and where you are!'

Fox stepped forward and used his Irish accent. 'We're talking to a piece of shit in a shithole.'

Sverov jerked his head as the meaning of the insult hit him.

Snow pretended to scratch his own chin; it was an attempt to hide a smirk.

Sverov was livid. 'I am the Head of the KGB and you are in the sovereign state of Belarus!'

'Bela-shite'.

Sverov's eyes narrowed. He had never been insulted like this; it had not been in any KGB training session.

'Just tell us what we want to know. Then me and my Russian friend over there can get the hell out of here and go somewhere where the beer is fresh and the women don't have beards!'

Snow laughed; he couldn't help it. 'My Irish associate has a very good sense of humour, no? But we are not joking.' He placed a recording device on the coffee table along with a contact sheet containing the photographs of eight men. 'Tell us what we want to know and there's no reason for you to get hurt any further.'

Sverov's eyes caught the face of the man who'd given him orders, the man whose name he didn't know. He felt a strength inside and stood defiantly. He couldn't tell them his name. 'I have been highly trained in both interrogation techniques and resistance. I will not tell you anything!'

'You will, Director – this is not in question. What you now need to decide is where you will talk and how much of yourself you wish to lose.'

Sverov's fears suddenly became physical; he could feel them grabbing at his throat. This whole series of events had overstepped the line and he was going to pay for it. But he was a patriot. He swallowed hard and mustered his courage. 'I will die before I betray my country!'

'You'll die afterwards.' Fox hit him in the stomach, causing the wiry Director to fall back onto the settee. 'Shall I start?'

'Yes, Bernard. This man has wasted too much of your energy.' Snow fixed his eyes on Sverov. 'You will find Mr Matthews very persuasive'

Sverov started to inhale deeply as though he was about to dive into a pool.

Fox pulled a lightweight Glock 19 from his pocket. 'Don't do anything we would consider aggressive or I'll shoot you in the kneecap. I've had plenty of practice.'

Sverov flinched, a look of hatred creeping onto his face.

Snow retrieved a small package from his coat and opened it to show a loaded syringe. He advanced.

'You think drugs will make me betray my country? I pity you for even thinking that I would be receptive to such a thing!'

Sverov held no fear of any truth serum; they didn't work. He should know – the Soviet KGB had invented many of them. At best these fools would achieve either his death by heart failure or his loss of consciousness. He could think of no more noble way to die than defending his country. But he didn't want to die. His legs started to shake.

'Mr Matthews, will you please help our friend remain still?'

Fox pushed the Glock into the Belarusian's head, pinning him back against the settee. 'My pleasure, Mr Brezhnev.'

Now fear gripped Sverov as never before in his adult life. 'You are wasting your time. I will never talk… You seem like well-trained men. There could be a place for you in one of my units?'

Snow thrust the needle into Sverov's bicep. Almost instantaneously the tension in the Director's body lessened.

'This is a waste of tiiii…' Sverov became unconscious.

Snow and Fox laid him out on the settee and began to search him for anything that might contain a transponder. There wasn't one.

Fox wiped his brow with the back of his hand. He'd been sweating. 'I'll check the exfil route.'

He stepped into the bedroom and carefully looked at the small courtyard that was formed by the space behind Sverov's building and two others. A small, fenced, grass play area was in the middle. Their Lada was adjacent to this.

'Clear.' Next checking the hallway, Fox put his eye to the spyglass. 'Clear.'

Snow pulled Sverov to his feet as Fox roughly forced him back into his overcoat. Carefully checking they had left no visible trace of their visit, the two operatives exited the flat, propping up Sverov. Two friends helping a third. In the lift, then out into the courtyard towards the car. An elderly woman, depositing rubbish into a dumpster, looked scornfully at the trio.

Snow smiled in response. 'Birthday.'

The woman snorted and carried on with her chores. At the Lada they eased Sverov into the backseat. Fox sat next to him, Snow taking the wheel. The Russian-built estate car coughed into life and pulled away. Now was the time they would be challenged;

now was the time they would hear shouts, rounds fired... Nothing.

Snow followed the access path onto the main road and joined the Minsk traffic. Heart rate slowing, his eyes met Fox's in the rear-view mirror. 'Mr Brezhnev?'

Fox wiped a bead of sweat from his brow. 'Bernard Matthews.'

Both men allowed themselves a moment to alleviate the tension.

The rain became heavier as they followed the Majakovskogo road south out of the Leninski region of Minsk towards the suburbs. The wipers rubbed the screen each time they moved, making smudges rather than cleaning the rain away. The traffic started to slow. Snow peered through the ever-increasing rain and saw the last thing he needed.

'Militia checkpoint up ahead. They're checking the cars leaving the city.'

'You think they already know he's gone?'

Snow was tense. 'Can't say.'

'I've got the whisky. OK now, nice and easy. Remember we're just friends on a drive.'

Their turn came. Snow edged the car forward before stopping next to the roadside Militia box. As he wound down the window, rain blew in.

'Documents, please.' Water dripped from the brim of the officer's cap.

Snow handed him the Russian passport.

'And theirs?' the officer asked as he flicked through the red booklet.

'My friend has left his at home, which is where we are heading now.'

The officer's eyes looked up from the passport. 'Then I will have to arrest your friend.' He peered into the car. 'Do you not know that it is an offence not to carry one's documents?'

In the back, Fox's hand tightened on the concealed Glock as

318

he furrowed his brow in ignorance. He didn't understand a word but knew what was being said.

'Officer, do you not know who the man in my car is?' Snow had to take the chance. 'This is Director Sverov of the KGB. We are his friends and, as you can see, he's not feeling well.' Snow handed the officer Sverov's identity card.

'What is wrong with him?'

'He is, how can I say this, "tired".'

The officer looked harder at the card, then at Sverov, who lolled against Fox's shoulder. 'Tired?'

Fox slowly passed the bottle of Johnnie Walker to Snow, who handed it to the man in uniform. 'Please, officer; this could be a very embarrassing situation if his wife were to find out. I'm sure Director Sverov would appreciate your discretion.'

Eyes falling on the bottle, a smile formed on the officer's lips. 'I understand.' He returned the documents to Snow, who placed the bottle in his outstretched hand.

'Thank you, officer.'

'Go.' The officer skilfully put the whisky bottle into the pocket of his oilskins, turned, and pointed at the next car.

Snow gently pulled away and rejoined the traffic as both he and Fox breathed out heavily.

CIA Interrogation Centre, Undisclosed Location
'Let him have it.'

The agent nodded and plunged a needle into Sverov's upper arm. Immediately the KGB Director opened his eyes.

'W... where am I?' he asked in Russian.

'Sorry, Mr Sverov. I don't speak Russian but I hear you speak pretty good English?'

Sverov stared at the American. 'Who are you?'

'You can probably guess. Now, I have a few questions I'd like to ask you.'

'I am the Director of the KGB and I order you to release me.'

319

'You are free to walk out of here, if you can.'

Sverov tried to stand but his legs wouldn't move. What had they done to him? 'You'll learn nothing from me, Mr CIA.' He tried to spit the words but his mouth was still not quite working. He sounded drunk.

'Bravo, Director, good guess. I am "Mr CIA" and you are in Langley, Virginia.'

Sverov's mouth fell open. He tried to make sense of what the man had told him and moved his head to look around the room. There was a CIA plaque on one wall and a wall planner in English on another. On a small table, next to the wall, stood a couple of cans of Coke.

'But this cannot be. I demand you release me immediately.'

'Well, Mr Sverov, I will do that. I'll release you directly to your embassy. No doubt you'll want to lodge an official diplomatic complaint after you've answered a few questions for me. I need to find someone and I know you can help me.'

Sverov suddenly felt as though he was floating and his mind wasn't quite his own. 'You're wasting your time. I don't know his name.'

Casey pulled up a chair and sat in front of the Belarusian. 'Whose name, Director? Did I ask you for a name?'

Sverov was aware that he was thinking and that his thoughts were being verbalised and that he couldn't stop it. 'The man you want to find. The Russian. I can't tell you his name because I don't know it.'

Casey nodded. 'Well, I'm sorry about that but I'm sure we can work around it. Just so I don't get confused, are we talking about the same man? I want information about the Russian who gave you orders to attack Saudi Arabia. The man who ordered you to plan the kidnapping of British citizens.'

'That is the man I meant.' Why was he talking? 'Why am I talking?' He couldn't stop.

Casey nodded. 'Well, it does no harm to talk. Seems to me,

if our leaders talked a whole lot more, we could solve the problems of the world. Now, I have a few pictures here I'd like you to look at. Can you tell me if the Russian you met with is any of these men?'

Sverov looked at the sheet and his eyes went wide when he reached the third image. 'Yes. That is the Russian.'

SBU Headquarters, Volodymyrska Ulitza, Kyiv, Ukraine
Dudka sipped his first work coffee of the day and looked at his mountain of post. Two weeks away had been too long. He'd spend the rest of the day clearing his backlog. His office door opened and Zlotnik entered, holding a file. He sat without offering a greeting.

'Did you murder Investigator Kostyan?'

Dudka was impressed that his boss was being so blunt. 'No.'

'Are you sure?'

Dudka sipped his coffee. 'Yes. I did not murder Investigator Kostyan as he does not exist. I murdered Konstantin Voloshin.'

Zlotnik's face went red. 'You assassinated a Belarusian agent!'

'And they say there is no justice.'

Zlotnik was lost for words. He had thought he had made his message clear to the old fool, but Dudka had done the unthinkable and not only located the killer but eliminated him. 'I don't know what to say.'

'Then say nothing.' Dudka took more coffee. 'Biscuit?'

'What?'

'Would you like a biscuit?'

'What I'd like is to arrest you for murder. But I'll settle for your immediate resignation, Dudka.'

'No.'

Zlotnik started to shake. '*No?*'

'That's right. No. I am not going to resign and you cannot make me.'

'You murdered a Belarusian national!'

'You, General Director, aided a Belarusian assassin in the murder of a Belarusian national.'

Zlotnik's mouth opened but he managed to hold his tongue. It was true. He had assisted Kostyan when he thought he was a real investigator. He regained his voice. 'You... but you...'

Dudka stood. 'No, don't thank me. I have a lot of work to catch up on, so if you have finished, I would appreciate it if you left my office.'

Zlotnik pointed his finger at Dudka and snarled. 'You have gone too far.'

'And you haven't gone far enough. Go away.'

Balling his fist and unable to speak any further, Zlotnik left the room and slammed the door.

CIA Interrogation Centre, Undisclosed Location

The pain in his head woke him. A hammer blow, that seemed to strike with each heartbeat. Sverov opened his eyes and shut them quickly. The light in the room was blinding. He opened them again, this time shielding his brow with his right hand. Sverov sat up and realised he had been sleeping on the floor. He blinked and found that his vision was blurred. He was suddenly nauseous and managed to turn his head just in time before he vomited.

Rolling away, he steadied himself against the wall and stood up. The hammering in his head intensified. The room slowly came into focus. He suddenly remembered where he was. In the CIA headquarters, Langley... His hands shook and he moved along the wall until he reached a small table. On it there was a can of Coke. He opened it and drank half of it in one long gulp. The two men in his apartment had injected him with something and he had woken up here. An American had then questioned him about... He almost fell. He had given them everything. Voloshin's name, the Russian orders, the payment schedule from Russia, and he had also identified the Russian's face. Sverov shook with fear. He, Director Sverov of the Belarusian KGB, had turned traitor.

He retched again and brought up the Coke. This time it splattered on his feet. Slippers? He was still wearing his slippers? He wiped his mouth on his shirt sleeve and drank the remainder of the Coke, an acrid taste in his mouth. There was a noise from beyond the door. Something that shouldn't have been there, a car horn… He frowned. Something was different about the room, something was wrong. But what? He then realised that the CIA crest had been removed.

Warily he moved towards the door and tried the handle. It opened easily. He took a deep breath and walked through. Darkness. There were no CIA agents, no long corridor, and no walls. He was standing inside a large, empty apartment. A rumble of traffic came from outside. Sverov opened the apartment's front door and moved down the hall towards the exit. He opened the communal front door and the noise of traffic hit him. He stepped outside and was on a Minsk city street staring at the morning rush-hour traffic.

Chapter 15

American Embassy, Minsk, Belarus

'Ms Knight, it's a pleasure to finally meet you. I have, of course, heard a lot about you.' The secure link to SIS in London was up.

'And I you, Mr Casey.'

In London Patchem rolled his eyes. Given half a chance Casey would wine and dine Brezhnev's own mother. 'So, Vince?'

'We have a name to go with the face Director Sverov gave us. Maksim Gurov.'

'Why don't we have anything on him?' Knight raised an eyebrow.

'Because, Ms Knight, he's been cold in the ground since the mid-Nineties. We don't tend to tail the dead.'

'So either he's not our man or he's not dead.'

'Those are the only two options, Jack.'

Patchem ignored the sarcasm. 'So, what do we have, Vince?'

'Well, I'm sure SIS has its own image database, but on ours he's been seen with old Vladimir on a dozen occasions in the last five years. Each time, either alone or in the presence of Privalov's known close associates.'

'Who is Gurov, Mr Casey?'

'We don't know who he is now, but we know who he was.

He was in the First Chief Directorate of the Soviet KGB. Within that he commanded a clandestine Special Forces group called Vympel.'

Patchem thought back. Vympel had been a name whispered during Soviet times. What little intelligence 'the West' had about the unit was alarming. It suggested that Vympel cells would be activated in time of war for acts of sabotage, covert action, and espionage to be carried out on enemy soil. In other words, state-sanctioned terrorists. Even among Spetsnaz units, Vympel was a name said with fear. 'I thought it had been disbanded?'

'It was, as they say in business, "reorganised to meet market needs" around 1995 and became a police unit known as Vega. Apparently the majority of the officers resigned. This was just after Gurov was reportedly K.I.A. in Chechnya.'

Knight looked puzzled. 'Why would the KGB want to hide its personnel?'

'I've thought about that. My theory is, as Yeltsin was responsible for their disbandment, the KGB wanted to form a more secretive group that was loyal to itself, or in this case the next President, Privalov.'

'Vince, have we got any proof of this?'

'Absolutely none whatsoever except that Gurov appears to be alive, well, and counselling the current Premier Minister.'

'So let's cut through this.' Knight hated getting sidetracked. 'Do we have our link to the Russian government? Is this something we can take to them?'

'We have intelligence gathered with... err... unconventional methods that links the Russians to this.'

Knight looked at Patchem; she knew no details of the operation in Belarus and, for reasons of plausible deniability, didn't want to. 'Jack?'

'Take it to the Foreign Secretary. The Prime Minister can then be honest with the Russians. Present them with the facts: that we've identified the other voice on the tape as Maksim Gurov, and believe he's not acting in the best interests of the Russian government.'

Knight nodded. 'Agreed... but I still...'

In Minsk there was a sudden knocking on the door. Casey turned around, surprised, as an embassy staffer entered with a note.

'Excuse me.'

Casey moved away from the camera and read the note. The link was silent for a minute or so as Casey could be seen working at a computer terminal. His face registered disbelief. He then returned to his seat and spoke into the camera.

'Someone has posted video footage of the Sverov-Gurov meeting on the internet and it's been picked up by the major news networks.'

Patchem raised his eyebrows. 'What?'

Casey continued. 'Your GCHQ will have it, no doubt, as will the BBC and Sky News. I've sent you the link.'

An email arrived on Patchem's desktop. He clicked. 'Video? But the tapes only had audio.'

Knight and Patchem watched the footage in London as Casey did so in Minsk. The video, clearly taken with a concealed camera, jerked as the cameraman entered a room and shook hands with Director Sverov in front of a large fireplace.

'Stop. Did you both see that? Vince, rewind your copy to eleven seconds.'

Knight squinted; she should really wear glasses. 'What are we looking at?'

'This.' Patchem rewound their copy and put his finger on the screen. 'A reflection in the mirror.'

'I see it too, Jack.'

Knight now found it. The face of the cameraman appeared momentarily in the mirror above the fireplace. 'Gurov?'

Knight's mobile phone rang. She retrieved it from her bag and saw it was the Foreign Secretary. She didn't pick up. 'So what does this mean?'

'It means that, in addition to the audio recordings, the other party made his own video.'

'That's not Gurov!' Patchem stared at the frozen image. 'It looks like Valentin Nevsky; he's a Deputy Director of the FSB.'

'How certain are you?'

'Abigail, he's my opposite number. I've met the man; he's very close to the Russian Premier Minister.'

There was a pause, then Casey said adamantly, 'This tape is a fake.'

Knight looked up at the screen showing the CIA officer. 'Can you be sure?'

'Absolutely. The method we used to get the intelligence from Director Sverov has a one hundred per cent success rate.'

Knight held up her hand. 'OK, Mr Casey, please don't tell me anymore. If we're presuming our intelligence is correct, then we know this tape to be a fake. Someone wants us all to accept this tape as genuine. Setting these authenticity issues aside, what is their motive for releasing this tape?'

'To get the Russians to stop?' Patchem was still peering at the screen.

'What if we've been looking at this whole situation from an entirely incorrect perspective?'

Casey shrugged. 'Which is, Ms Knight?'

'Well, what if the primary objective of the attacks weren't to destabilise Saudi Arabia but to discredit, and in doing so destabilise, Russia? The release of this tape squarely points the finger at them.'

Casey leant back in his chair and let out a deep sigh. 'That's a big assumption.'

'Mr Casey, thank you. Jack, make sure our lab analyses a copy of this tape – specifically, checks the voices against the existing tape and also cross-checks against any audio we have of Nevsky.' Knight's phone rang again. 'I'll have to take it this time.' She stood and left Patchem's office.

'Shit happens, eh, Jack?'

Patchem stretched. He was mentally and physically drained. 'Regularly, Vince.'

Ukrainian-Belarusian Border Crossing Point

Snow and Fox had spent a tense night held up in the woods until rush hour, when they had driven back the way they had come to the border with Ukraine. It was early afternoon by the time they reached the crossing to leave Belarus. The Ukrainian number plates had once again been attached and the relevant passports were on hand. To his relief, Snow noticed that the same two border guards were on duty as when they'd crossed from Ukraine.

'Good afternoon, officer.'

The border guard looked at the occupants of the car. 'Passports, please.'

Snow once again placed the documents into the guard's outstretched hand.

The guard looked at them. 'Please step out of the car, both of you.'

Snow again translated the request into English. Both he and Fox got out.

The second guard now joined the first. He recognised the pair and nodded at Fox. 'It is you, the Irishman?'

'Yes, officer, it is me.'

'You try drink, Belarusian vodka?'

'I did.' Fox gave a thumbs up.

'Next you must try Belarusian girl!'

The first guard gave his colleague a stern look and said something in Belarusian before speaking to Snow.

'OK. Come to the office and we will stamp his exit visa.'

They left the car and walked to the two-storey concrete building. A third border guard, their superior, was sitting in front of a computer. He had a telephone to his ear. The first guard held up the passports then put them on the desk before returning to the road, leaving his younger, more talkative, colleague to stand with the foreigners.

Fox looked around the office. It was hardly impressive, with a garish calendar on one wall of a woman in Belarusian national dress, a portrait of the President on another, and several badly photocopied 'wanted' notices on a large, white-painted, wooden noticeboard. Steps at the far end led up to the first floor.

The chief guard replaced his handset. 'You are Irish?'

'Yes, I am, sir.' Fox used his best smile and accent.

The guard tapped his keyboard and checked the passport numbers. He then pointed at Snow. 'You are his interpreter?'

'Interpreter and driver.'

'You wait a moment, please.' More tapping then the guard spoke quickly in Belarusian to his junior. Fox tensed; he recognised the tone. 'Your passports have not been registered.'

'I don't understand?'

'It is a requirement for all foreigners to register with the local police when they book into a hotel. A Xerox copy of your passport is taken for registration.'

'I'm sorry. We were in Minsk for two nights. Perhaps the system is a little slow?'

The senior officer looked up at Fox, his expression showing he'd heard it all before. 'No. All registration happens immediately. It is the law of Belarus. Which hotel did you stay at?'

'The Hotel Minsk.'

'You must wait there while I call the Minsk.' The officer pointed at several seats by the stairs.

They sat, with no choice but to wait and hope the registrations had been taken care of by one of Casey's assets. Snow saw the body language of the chief guard change as he spoke in quickfire Belarusian on the antiquated, light-green, Soviet-era desktop telephone. Snow nudged Fox as the expression of the younger guard changed. The guard looked at Snow and Fox before quickly looking away, too quickly. His chief said something and he nodded.

The chief guard made eye contact with Snow. 'There are some irregularities. You will have to stay with us until they have been investigated.'

'What type of irregularities, officer?' Snow slowly rose, but, as he did so, saw the younger guard, eyes fearful, start to reach for his sidearm.

'An officer from the KGB is on his way to question you.' This sentence was said in English.

Feigning ignorance, Fox stood. 'KGB?'

'There is a security alert. You will wait here. It is the law.'

Snow saw his chance and moved. His left hand grabbed the forearm of the advancing young guard as the pistol left its holster and he twisted. Meanwhile, with his right foot he kicked the man in the groin. The guard's legs buckled and he fell, leaving the pistol in Snow's hand. Fox now reacted, slamming his fist into the chief guard. The man fell from his chair and hit the floor with a jolt. Fox advanced for a second blow, but as he did so there was a flash and an ear-splitting roar. Time seemed to slow. Cordite fumes rose from the chief guard's weapon and Fox stumbled backwards. Another two roars, this time from behind, as Snow returned fire, sending a double tap into the guard's chest.

Snow looked down with horror. He'd had no choice. The guard had shot first. Fox hit the concrete floor. Snow grabbed him by the collar and scrabbled back out of the building and towards the Lada. All was silent until a siren went off and then rounds flew overhead from the remaining guards. Snow heaved Fox into the car's backseat and was about to clamber into the front when the barking of a Kalashnikov joined the fight. Snow dropped into the damp grass, pinned down as heavier 7.62 rounds thudded into the Lada. He shouted through the open door. 'Paddy, Paddy! Can you hear me?'

'Aidan, get out of here,' Fox wheezed

'I'm not leaving you, you dopey sod.'

Snow popped his head up and sent two quick rounds back

over the bonnet at the building. Their options were limited. Driving on was madness; the Ukrainian side of the border would now be closed. They could only drive back down the two-lane highway and hope they didn't run into any Militia coming in the opposite direction. The shooting stopped and Snow scrambled into the seat. As he did so a loudhailer opened up.

'American agents. Put down your weapons and give yourselves up. You cannot escape.'

'Leave me… just go…'

Snow gritted his teeth. 'Sorry, you'll have to put up with me a bit longer.' Key still in the ignition, he started the car.

'Put down your weapons,' the loudhailer ordered again. 'This is your last warning…'

The windscreen smashed as the Kalashnikov started up again, Snow felt a piece of glass nick his forehead. He slammed the car into reverse and attempted a J-turn. The Lada bounced off the tarmac, briefly sliding on the wet grass before momentarily coming to a halt facing the opposite direction. Into first gear, they lurched forward. Snow risked a glance in his rear-view mirror as it was shot away.

'Just keep your foot down!' Fox's voice was distorted by pain.

'Paddy, where are you hit?'

Fox lay spread out on the backseat, his left hand braced against the driver's seat, his head knocking the door insert. 'In the chest… I can't breathe…'

They rounded a bend and left the border post behind. Snow was under no illusions that, unless they could find another route away from the border, their chances of escape were slim. The wind whipped his face, causing his eyes to stream as they powered on. Hitting 100 kilometres, the Lada started to judder. They couldn't outrun anyone in this heap, Snow was certain. The road they were on, the E95, went north to the town of Gomel before intersecting with the M10 West, leading eventually to Brest, then Poland, and the M5/E271 north-west to Minsk. Both routes were main arteries for Belarus and would have roadblocks being set up. Snow saw a sign to the right for the village of Novaya Guta and took the turning. At least they were off the main road, but unless they kept moving it would only be matter of time until they were found.

A dense forest on one side of the road straddled the border, extending over a mile into Ukraine. It would be too much to hope for, that they could find a route through. Straight ahead, to the east, thirty miles or so would take them to the border with Russia. But could they cross? The road worsened, giving out to potholes, and the Lada's suspension groaned.

'Paddy, you still with me?' Snow shouted.

'Where else would I be?' Fox managed to wheeze back.

Above the noise of the wind in his ears, Snow heard a sound that made him tense. Sirens. Looking over his shoulder he could see a Militia vehicle tearing down the road after them. It was a 4x4 Niva and, as such, oblivious to the potholes. Snow pushed his foot flat to the floor and hoped the Lada would respond. Up ahead were farm buildings and the beginning of the village. Shots were fired from behind and the Niva started to gain. Snow urged the car on, knuckles white, gripping the wheel.

There was a blur to his left and something large lurched into his vision. From a concealed junction, an ancient Soviet tractor pulled out. In a millisecond, Snow had reacted and turned the wheel hard right. It was almost too late. The car clipped the side of the much heavier farm vehicle and was pushed onto the grass before it spun and came to a halt facing back the way they had come. The tractor shuddered to a halt and blocked the road ahead. The Niva stopped, now no more than thirty feet away. The passenger gingerly climbed out, his sidearm trained on Snow.

'I take it we're in the shit?'

'Paddy, stay still, and shut up.'

Snow raised his hands and climbed out of the car, all the while keeping his eyes on the advancing Militia officer.

'Don't move or I'll shoot!' The officer's voice was shaky.

'OK.' Snow saw the uncertainty on his face. 'Please don't shoot me.'

The officer straightened slightly, emboldened by Snow's pleas. 'Turn around.'

The officer changed the grip on his weapon from double- to single-handed and pushed Snow in the back with his left hand. Snow pivoted, grabbed the officer's outstretched arm, and threw him to the ground. Before he had a chance to realise what was happening, Snow was holding his pistol. 'Tell your friend to get out of the jeep.'

The voice was jittery. 'Igor, get out. Please! Igor!'

Snow pulled the frightened officer to his feet and held him by the neck, with the end of the handgun still pressed firmly against the man's temple. 'Tell Igor to take his shoes off.'

'Wh… what?'

'Tell him.' Snow dragged him to the side of the road.

The officer shouted the order to his colleague, who, having warily climbed out of the Niva, now undid his laces.

Snow hit the officer in the back of the head with the Makarov pistol. Unconscious, the man fell to the ground. Snow now covered the remaining distance to Igor. 'Where is the key?'

'In the car. In the ignition. Please don't hurt me. I've got a mother.'

'Strip.'

'Sorry…'

'Take your jacket off. Have you got a mobile phone?'

Igor nodded and reached into his pocket. He held it out, his hand trembling.

'Thank you. Now go and lie down next to your friend.'

Igor's eyes widened. 'Please, no…'

Snow rolled his eyes; he had no time for dramatics. 'Just do it or your mother will lose a son.'

As Igor walked slowly to his colleague and lay in the muddy

grass, Snow heard the tractor groan into life and pull away. The farmer didn't want to get involved. Snow started up the Niva and positioned it next to their Lada. With the engine running he jumped out and opened the back of their estate car.

'Can I talk now?' Fox eyes were red with pain.

Chapter 16

Gurov sat back in his chair and watched the international news reports via satellite. He couldn't have wished for a more successful response to his tape. What had initially been placed on the internet with links sent to international news agencies was now global headline news. The Director of the Belarusian KGB and the Deputy Director of the Russian FSB on tape, discussing how to destabilise the sovereign state of Saudi Arabia, was explosive. Some were proclaiming it the story of the decade; others, whom Gurov had toasted, said it was the most shocking story to arise in living memory.

He finished his ice-cold vodka and poured another shot. His work was almost done. Nevsky, the man who had the position the PM had promised to him, would be ruined. It was a promise made by the man he had once trusted all those years before, a deal that had been reneged upon, a betrayal he had pretended to accept and forgive. Now the Premier Minister, too, would be ruined, for how could he not know that his chosen man, Nevsky, had planned this? President Melnikov's only real rival for re-election would be vanquished. Gurov would then be able to slip into the shadows again, a happy man, as Russia rose from the flames.

For Gurov, revenge was something which commanded no upper price.

Unknown Location, Belarus

Snow eased the Riva into traffic and tried to steady his breathing. Wearing the uniform jacket and cap of the Militia officer he drew no attention. A line of cars and trucks had started to build up, heading towards the now-closed border crossing. Snow kept his head still but constantly used his eyes to scan for signs of danger. He had secured the Militia officers with their own cuffs to the battered Lada estate, but knew it wasn't a question of 'if' but 'when' they were discovered, at which point he would have to ditch the Niva. At that point he had no idea how he would move Fox.

Slumped in the back, Fox was wheezy. 'So where do we go now?'

'Pripiatsky National Park.'

'You want to take me on a picnic?'

'The Pripiat marshes cross the border, and so can we, via the exclusion zone.'

'The Chernobyl exclusion zone?'

'Yep.'

'You want to irradiate me, turn me into the bloody Ready Brek man?'

Snow looked at Fox in the rear-view mirror. Fox's face was grey. 'It would save on light bulbs.'

Fox coughed. 'Aidan... I don't know how much longer I can hold on.'

Suddenly serious again, Snow nodded. Fox would die without medical intervention. 'Paddy, you can make it. Just try to keep breathing.'

'What... you think I'd rather stop?'

Snow reached down for the Militia officer's Nokia. Slowing the 4x4 slightly, he tapped in a number from memory and placed the handset to his ear.

In his office at the British Embassy in Kyiv, Alistair Vickers picked up his mobile phone. Looking at the screen he didn't recognise the number. 'Yes?'

'I need help. We've been compromised. I have a casualty.' Snow spoke in Russian, a language both men understood fluently.

Vickers recognised the voice. The line wasn't secure; he couldn't use the man's name. 'There's nothing I can do.'

Snow tried not to lose his temper. 'We need an out now, today, or my friend will die. Do you understand me? Call me back on this number in thirty minutes, that's three-oh minutes.'

'I can't...'

The line went dead.

The operation was deniable. Vickers, representing HM Government, could officially do nothing. His hand shook; he balled it into a fist and slammed it on his desk. He ached: his neck, his jaw. He knew it was mainly psychosomatic now, that the fear he had felt, fighting for his life with the Belarusian, had stayed with him as the physical pain lessened.

He was a wreck. The pain medication had him hooked but he was going to fight. He shut his eyes, took a deep breath, opened them, then stood. There had to be something he could do to get Snow and Fox out.

There was one person he could ask, one person for whom this whole operation truly meant something. Vickers picked up his phone and dialled.

10 Downing Street, London, UK

David Daniels was both mentally and physically drained. The call was possibly the most important and delicate of his political career. He had never felt such pressure before in his life and was now regretting having sworn off the bottle a year before. Daniels had organised a conference call between himself and the Presidents of both the United States and the Russian Federation.

The Russian Premier was in a foul mood and could barely

contain his anger at his so-called Western partners. The US President, backed up by Daniels, had stated categorically, via a translator, that they had not released the new tape, and that they believed it to be wholly or in part manufactured. The Russian was slightly placated by this, as to him the very idea that a Director in his FSB would plot such a thing was unthinkable.

SIS had sent, via a secure email, the laboratory report on the video. It concluded that the data had been recorded with either a cameraphone or a device with a similar quality lens. In essence the images, in particular the face of Valentin Nevsky, couldn't be verified. The quality of the lens wasn't good enough. However, the audio could be verified with a higher percentage of certainty and had been compared with the first tape. The voice on the original tape was a 98% match to that of Director Sverov, and on the second 92%. It was, however, the other voice that was interesting. On the new tape there was a 78% match with Nevsky, but the original recording, made on an HD device, produced only a 36% match. The laboratory had therefore concluded that the second tape, while containing the same voiceprint for Sverov, had been altered to enable the second voice to sound more like Nevsky's.

Daniels looked on as the young Russian Premier thought about what he had heard. As he did so, a man entered the screen from the side. Unknown to both Daniels and the US President, Nevsky himself had been in the room and listening.

'Prime Minister, Mr President. Can I confirm that you do not consider me responsible for this?'

Daniels was stunned but tried his best not to stutter. 'Director Nevsky, that is certainly our opinion.'

'Who do you suspect?'

Daniels cleared his throat and wished his glass didn't contain water. 'Maksim Gurov, a former colleague of yours.'

Nevsky blinked. 'He is dead.'

'Director, we know that's not the case.'

'Who has given you this information, Prime Minister?' President Melnikov now asked in perfect English.

'I'm afraid the source is classified.'

The Russian frowned and turned to the FSB officer. They conversed for several seconds in hushed Russian that neither Daniels nor his American counterpart could understand or indeed hear.

The Russian Premier then addressed both his counterparts. 'Gentlemen, was this name given to you by Director Sverov of the Belarusian KGB?'

The shock on Daniels's face couldn't be hidden, but before he had a chance to speak, the American took over, his Bostonian tone sounding quite commanding.

'Mr President, the name was indeed given to us by Ivan Sverov.'

'So it was you who kidnapped him?' Melnikov laughed.

Daniels felt his toes curl. He didn't know how they had persuaded the Belarusian to give up the name. 'No, that is not something HM Government or the United States would do.'

'Officially.' The Russian held up his hand. 'Prime Minister Daniels, although I laugh, this is no little matter. Someone has represented my government abroad without due authority and has attempted to implicate us in a series of terrorist attacks. As we speak, I am informed that protesters have gathered outside my country's embassies in London, Washington, Paris... These protesters are blaming me for this situation and demanding not only my resignation but, in addition, that of Premier Minister Privalov! My ambassador to the Kingdom of Saudi Arabia has been summoned to the royal palace and will, I believe, be expelled. But most of all the image of Mother Russia has been tarnished.'

Daniels felt a chill of fear, even though the face and voice came to him via satellite from Moscow. 'I of course regret what has happened, Mr President...'

'Regret? What are you going to do to help with this situation?'

There was a silence. The Russian's eyes remained fixed on Daniels.

'I have an idea,' the American President said.

'I am listening.' The Russian President folded his arms.

KGB Headquarters, Skaryny Avenue, Minsk, Belarus
'This is Deputy Director Dudka of the Ukrainian State Security Service. Please connect me to Director Sverov.'

There was a pause before the secretary in Minsk spoke. 'He is not in his office today. He is unwell.'

'Then give me his home number and I will call him.'

'No. I mean no, sir, I cannot hand out such sensitive information. Perhaps I can take a message, or is there someone else who could help you?'

'Very well. Put me through to Deputy Director Maltsev.'

'I will see if he is available. Can I take your name again?'

'Dudka, he knows me.'

Maltsev was old guard like Sukhoi had been. He had, however, been a lifelong irritant of both Dudka and his late friend, an extremist whose belief since 1991 that the Soviet Union should be reconstituted was shared by the Belarusian President. There was a brief silence and then a faint humming on the line before a gruff voice spoke.

'Director Dudka. What does Ukraine want now? To further insult the nation of Belarus by making abusive telephone calls? Is it not enough to expel our ambassador?'

'Director Maltsev. I am calling to offer an olive branch to Belarus. I will come to Minsk to speak with you personally about this.'

'You will, will you?'

'Ivan Fedorovich, we are both too long in the tooth to waste our time with politics. Let us discuss this in person. I will travel today so we may meet tomorrow morning.'

'Hmm. Agreed. You will be met by a car at the airport.'

'Thank you but I intend to drive. I no longer have any faith in air travel.'

'As you wish, Dudka.' Maltsev put the phone down. He would enjoy arguing with and humbling the old Ukrainian idiot.

Moscow Oblast, Russian Federation
Flakes of snow clung to the shoulders of the Russian Premier Minister as he entered his private *dacha*. His protégé, the President of the Russian Federation, fresh from his conference with the Americans and British, had arrived first and sat in a thick winter coat in front of an unlit fire.

The Premier Minister spoke. 'You wanted to see me?'

Melnikov gestured to a spare chair. 'Vladimir Vladimirovich, tell me about Maksim Gurov.'

'What would you like to know?'

'We agree that he is responsible for the current situation with the Arabs, but I would like to know why he has perpetrated these acts.'

'Gurov has been a trusted servant of the state for as long as I have. Lest we forget his dedication to the service and the sacrifice he made.'

'Living as a dead man?'

'In part.' The older man's eyes narrowed momentarily. Only he knew the true extent of Gurov's clandestine past. 'He is a man who does nothing without reason.'

'Am I to presume he has been "turned" by an enemy of our country?'

'No. I can think of no greater patriot, ourselves included.'

'What then?'

Privalov remained silent for a moment. 'I have no answer, but I should.'

'We need to know his reasons.'

'He must be interrogated.'

Unlike his mentor, Melnikov did not have a background in the KGB and talk of such things made him mentally flinch. 'My thoughts exactly.'

'Nikolai Denisovich, I know that I do not need your sanction to make this man disappear, but I feel for both our sakes that he should do so.'

'We are certain of his guilt?' The President needed reassurance.

'We are,' the Premier Minister replied.

Melnikov looked at the man seated next to him, the man responsible for rebuilding post-Soviet Russia. The man responsible for his presidency, who would be President again. 'Then it shall be so. What of the madman in Minsk?'

Privalov cracked a seldom seen smile. 'The President of Belarus has been informed that he and Director Sverov have been hoodwinked and that they will not be receiving any type of payment from us.'

Melnikov shook his head. 'Why did that fool ever believe we would approach him with such a scheme?'

'He has been the biggest fish in his pond for too long. Besides, Gurov is a man of much persuasion and influence.'

'That is why he advised you?' Melnikov's anger momentarily surfaced.

'Yes.'

The President stood. 'Let us hope that this has not tarnished Mother Russia's international image for ever.'

From the veranda, Privalov watched the presidential limousine pull away.

Nevsky entered and nodded. 'Vladimir Vladimirovich.'

'You were with him at this meeting?'

'Yes. The evidence against Gurov is quite damning.'

'I am aware of that. What was the mood of the British and Americans?'

'They were very eager that we should accept their findings.'

'That is to be expected. They are too weak to be dishonest.'

Moscow Oblast, Russia
The meeting had been expected and planned for. Indeed, Gurov

342

was only surprised it hadn't been called sooner. Heavy snow had started to fall as he manoeuvred his Mercedes out of a Moscow December and hit the highway. It was a hundred-kilometre journey to the secluded *dacha* his Premier Minister always used. Gurov did not see the point in building a glorified wooden hut an hour's drive from the city. Even more so in this weather, with the roads slowed by falling snow. In this respect, he mused, he was not Russian. No, once this was all over he would retreat to a villa for a holiday, though perhaps not Dubai as that had become rather dangerous. He had always wanted to visit the Maldives. Yes, that was it. On a far-flung beach he would take a month to sip imported vodka and read the news of his mighty nation's recovery. Until then, however, he would play his part, either way.

Gurov saw his turning and left the highway, immediately having to slow to account for the snow-laden rural road. The snow had got progressively thicker. He wished he had ordered the 'M' class jeep with its four-wheel drive and not the sleek executive saloon he was now perilously piloting. But such things were now immaterial. He looked up; the sky was clear.

Privalov stood on the veranda. Impervious to the swirling snow he watched Gurov bring his car to a halt. He signalled his security detail to ready themselves as Gurov exited the Mercedes and moved swiftly up the stairs.

'Vladimir Vladimirovich.'

Privalov did not shake hands. 'We should go inside.'

In the seconds it took Gurov's eyes to become accustomed to the dark interior of the *dacha* he felt a pain in the back of his left leg as an unseen boot pushed him down. Before he could react, two pairs of strong hands dragged him across the floor and pushed him into an armchair.

'What is this?'

'Your chance at redemption,' Privalov replied in an even tone.

Gurov's eyes settled upon Nevsky. 'Why is that traitor here?'

Nevsky stepped forward. 'You have nerve; even now you protest your innocence. It is you who is the traitor!'

'That is enough, Director.'

'Yes, Vladimir Vladimirovich.'

Privalov spoke again. 'Why?'

Gurov fixed his Premier Minister in the eye. 'You made a promise to me, Vladimir; you gave me your word as an officer of the KGB. A man's honour should mean something but yours was worthless. You broke your promise.'

'What is he talking about?' Nevsky edged forward.

'He gave you my job, Nevsky. You then aided him in destroying my motherland.'

'So, Gurov, it has come to this? It is you who has tarnished the name of Mother Russia and ended countless lives. And over what? A broken promise?'

Gurov's eyes were still burning into Privalov. 'Your lack of honour has caused our country to become a laughing stock. You have guided us backwards while our former republics flourish.'

'You overestimate your own importance, Gurov, if you really believe that things would be different with you heading the FSB. As President I raised this country from its chaotic market experiment. The bandits were banished and...'

Gurov sprang to his feet. 'The bandits flourished under your FSB!'

Privalov's bodyguards grabbed Gurov before he could advance.

Privalov stared at the man he had betrayed, the man who had once been a trusted ally. 'Take him outside and shoot him like a dog.'

Gurov looked at Nevsky, then back at Privalov. 'May the people of Russia one day forgive you, for I will not!'

He didn't resist as he was taken away.

There was a silence. Nevsky dared not speak, but his boss did. 'We should return to Moscow.'

There were shouts outside then an explosion. The window

imploded and Nevsky fell. Privalov spun as a round tore through his wool coat. He hit the floor and scrabbled for cover. He heard the thud... thud... thud... of rotor blades. The heavy sound of .50 calibre rounds. Then all became still except for the wind, which blew in through the broken window. Footsteps started to crunch in the snow, and Nevsky groaned. Privalov cautiously stood and looked outside. Gurov had gone. One member of his detail was down, his blood staining the snow; the others had their hands raised above their heads. Gurov had not been alone. At least one sniper had been covering him the entire time in addition to an attack helicopter. Gurov was away and clear.

Vladimir Vladimirovich started to laugh. Gurov had let him live. Live to face a humiliation he believed was worse than death. But Gurov had miscalculated. He had been identified. Sverov had confessed all and, as such, the Premier Minister of the Russian Federation was blameless. The world would now have to accept the tapes as the fabricated lies of a traitor who had funded Islamic extremists. A man who had just attempted to assassinate the architect of new Russia.

Nevsky sat up, holding his arm. 'What happened?'

Privalov looked down at the FSB Director. 'I doubt if anyone will ever know.'

Chapter 17

Pripiatsky National Park, Gomel Region, Belarus

The Volga with Ukrainian SBU number plates came to a halt next to the Lada Niva with the Militia livery. Dudka turned off the headlights and stepped out into the Belarusian night. The forest around them was filled with many strange noises, but none of them manmade.

'Director Dudka, I cannot thank you enough for coming.' Snow shook the old man's hand.

'Aidan Phillipovich, I am still indebted to you for what you did last time we met.'

Blazhevich extended his own hand. 'Aidan.'

'Vitaly.'

Dudka took a deep breath. 'We can waste no time. I am expected in Minsk by morning, which is why we shall be in Kyiv. So we must get back to the border. Vitaly, help Aidan Phillipovich with his associate. I shall keep watch.'

'Yes, Gennady Stepanovich.'

While Dudka looked down the road, Blazhevich helped Snow ease Fox into the Volga. The large backseat was much more forgiving than that of either of the Ladas. Fox had become very weak and barely managed to acknowledge the SBU officer.

'We have a helicopter on standby at the border to take Mr Fox to a medical facility.' As ever, Blazhevich's English was precise.

Snow spoke in Russian. It was the first time he'd seen the SBU officer in almost two years, and he wanted this to be between him and Blazhevich. 'Vitaly, I never got a chance to thank you.'

'For what?'

'Saving my life, in Kyiv.'

'I only stopped you from bleeding to death.' Blazhevich shrugged, a half-smile on his face. 'You'd do the same for me.'

'I hope I don't have to.' He held out his hand.

'I hope so too.' Blazhevich took Snow's hand and shook it.

*

Dawn had broken as they reached the tailback of vehicles waiting to cross the border. Closed earlier than normal and without notice, due to a security situation, the truck drivers had had no choice but to wait the night. Now eager to get on, a group was protesting that the crossing should be opened early to let them pass. Having driven past the waiting traffic, Dudka stopped the SBU Volga in front of the customs building. A border guard appeared and walked towards the car with a perplexed look on his face.

'You must wait in line. You can't park there.'

Dudka held up his SBU shield. 'I don't intend to park here, officer. I intend to go home. Now please raise the barrier and let me through.'

The guard peered at Dudka's pass. 'It will not be opening until later.'

Dudka looked up at the uniformed cretin. 'I have telephoned ahead and the Ukrainian side has been opened. If I do not relay another order to close my side, where will those people go? They will come here and then you will be forced to take action!'

'The border will not open until later today.'

'Just raise the barrier.'

The guard became flustered. 'I will need to check your vehicle and your customs declaration.'

Dudka exited the car. 'I am Director Dudka of the Ukrainian State Security Service. As such you will accord my vehicle and I diplomatic status. Now, unless you would like me to telephone either Deputy Director Maltsev or Director Sverov of your KGB and lodge an official complaint, I suggest you raise the barrier.'

'Who is your passenger?'

'He is another SBU officer, officer.'

'I'm going to have to speak to my superior.'

'You already are. Now raise the barrier!' Dudka retrieved his mobile phone and held it purposefully in the air.

'Very well.'

Dudka got back into the Volga and drove out of Belarus.

Volodymyrska Street, Kyiv, Ukraine

The wind blew furiously down the steep incline of Volodymyrska Street as the first blizzard of winter hit Kyiv. The usually busy city centre boulevard was all but empty except for the parked cars, which were gradually disappearing under white coats. The few passing pedestrians who were out paid no attention to the shabby-looking figure battling upwind against the elements. He crossed the road and shuffled into the entrance foyer of an apartment block. Inside, the building's concierge, an elderly woman paid to be the gatekeeper, looked up with a frown.

'*Dobrey Dehn.*' Good afternoon. Russian, with a deliberate British accent.

'*Dobrey.*'

'Alistair Vickers?'

The woman's frown lessened as she realised that the intruder had come to visit the polite British diplomat.

The visitor used the stairs, arrived at the top floor, and pressed the doorbell.

'Aidan?' The surprise on Alistair Vickers's face was evident.

'Is this the Tits Up Club?'

'Come in.'

Vickers shut both inner and outer security doors before looking at his fellow SIS officer. As Snow removed his coat and boots, Vickers gave him a summary of events, including the internet video. 'You may not agree with me, Aidan, but the op was a success. Sverov gave us everything we needed. We took the intelligence directly to the Russians.'

They entered the lounge. 'So what went wrong?'

'I don't know. Sverov raised an alert. Drink?'

'Several.'

They sat. Vickers placed a bottle of Tavria cognac and two shot glasses in front of them. He poured; they both downed the drink in silence.

'I'm sorry, Aidan.' Vickers refilled their glasses; Snow noticed that the SIS officer's hand was shaking. 'It's the tablets, the ones they gave me for the pain.'

'Do you have any more?' Snow's body had finally given up on him.

'Lots.' Vickers rose, crossed to a wall unit, and removed a bottle. 'Here.'

Snow took two of the large pills and washed them down with more cognac.

Epilogue

Royal Palace, Riyadh, Kingdom of Saudi Arabia
Daniels waited patiently with the other world leaders for the Crowned Prince of Saudi Arabia to lead them out of the royal palace. According to the press release, the summit had been called to discuss 'new strategies' against international terrorism in the Arab Peninsular.

The media, by various agreed channels, had been advised to interpret the summit as a show of strength against the so-called 'fabricated' internet-based allegations that Russia and Belarus had been responsible for the recent terror attacks in the Kingdom of Saudi Arabia. Allegations, Daniels reminded himself, which could have potentially caused incalculable damage to international relations.

Daniels had watched nervously as pundits from every major news network had given their views on the power of the 'citizen journalist' and how that power was unchecked. In addition to this he had made sure disinformation had been leaked to the BBC and CNN, to further erode the credibility of what were being laughingly referred to as the 'Sandgate Tapes'. While there were those who believed it all to be spin, an attempt to hide what in fact was genuine, these views were gradually being marginalised and their authors mostly ignored by the mainstream media.

The focus now had switched to the success of the Saudi Intelligence Service in preventing further attacks, and the beheading, literally, of Al-Qaeda. Indeed, only three days before, the Saudis had released footage of the questioning of the alleged leader of Al-Qaeda in the Gulf Peninsular.

Amidst extremely heavy security, the summit group exited the royal palace and posed for the invited international media. The Saudi Prince took centre stage, flanked on either side by the President of the United States and the President of Russia. Daniels stood beside Melnikov, while the President of Belarus stood next to the American. At either side were positioned the rulers of the Gulf States.

Behind his white-toothed smile and jet-black moustache, the head of the House of Saud was still incensed by the attacks on his Kingdom. He wasn't party to the truth; if he had been, the Belarusian President wouldn't have been leaving the Kingdom.

This was a photo opportunity only. All attending journalists had been specifically warned not to attempt to ask any questions at this time.

As they headed back into the palace, Daniels glanced at the Belarusian President. The man's smile was fixed. He had shown no sign of unease. If anything, he had acted as though he were now being accepted as a member of the world's most exclusive club. Which, by default, he was. His price of admission, however, was still unknown.

Dear Reader,

Thank you for buying *Cold Black*. I hope you have enjoyed reading it. I certainly enjoyed writing it. It is said that writing is a lonely business and without your support it certainly would be.

I have been asked how much of myself is in the character of Aidan Snow. Well, we have lived and worked in the same places and speak the same languages, but I was not in the SAS. Aidan Snow and I both have a passion for Ukraine and our adopted home, Kyiv. I write the type of books I love to read, about places and people that have struck a chord with me, so if you're reading this note, I hope they have for you too.

Please let me know your thoughts and any comments you have. You can follow me on twitter: @alexshawhetman or Facebook: alex.shaw.982292

I do reply to all my messages and would love to hear from you.

Warm regards,

Alex Shaw

Dear Reader,

Thank you so much for taking the time to read this book – we hope you enjoyed it! If you did, we'd be so appreciative if you left a review.

Here at HQ Digital we are dedicated to publishing fiction that will keep you turning the pages into the early hours. We publish a variety of genres, from heartwarming romance, to thrilling crime and sweeping historical fiction.

To find out more about our books, enter competitions and discover exclusive content, please join our community of readers by following us at:

🐦 @HQDigitalUK

📘 facebook.com/HQDigitalUK

Are you a budding writer? We're also looking for authors to join the HQ Digital family! Please submit your manuscript to:

HQDigital@harpercollins.co.uk.

Hope to hear from you soon!

Read on for a sneak peek at *Cold East*,

the next book in the Aidan Shaw series…

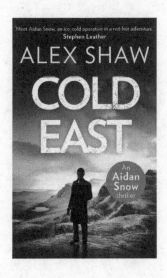

Prologue

Donetsk Region, Ukraine

'I can't see them yet.'

'They'll be here soon, he said so.' Vitaly Blazhevich peered into the distance towards the besieged city of Donetsk. Smoke rose from tower blocks on the outskirts, the result of early-morning shelling by Russian-supplied Grad rockets. The ceasefire agreement between the Ukrainian government and the Russian-backed insurgent organisations of the Donetsk People's Republic (DNR) and the Lugansk People's Republic (LNR) had been in operation for several months, yet attacks continued. The men around Blazhevich were a mixture of regular Ukrainian infantry and young, hastily trained members of a volunteer battalion. Despite the cold, the Ukrainians kept their spirits high as they rotated manning the vehicle checkpoint, cooking, and resting. Blazhevich had nothing but respect for the volunteers who, until recently, had been carrying on normal lives as university students, mechanics, bus drivers, doctors, and businessmen. Every now and then the group would spontaneously start singing Ukrainian folk songs or old Soviet tunes in Russian. They were Ukrainian and what mattered to them most was one country, not one language. The checkpoint was to the north of the small town of

Marinka and straddled the road towards Donetsk. The adjacent flat fields of fertile black earth had been left barren in the conflict zone. A click away, the road forked and the treeline started.

'Here.' Nedilko handed Blazhevich a mug.

'We should be doing more to help him,' Blazhevich replied to his SBU colleague before sipping the bitter-tasting army coffee.

'He likes pretending to be Russian.'

'That's true.'

Blazhevich saw movement ahead. He put his drink on the ground, raised his field glasses, and focused on the road. A white Toyota Land Cruiser appeared from the treeline. As it neared, the blue flag and markings of the Organisation for Security and Co-operation in Europe (OSCE) became visible on its paintwork. The Ukrainian soldiers manned their weapons, ever wary of a surprise attack. The checkpoint had changed hands several times so far; the men were taking no chances.

Nedilko's phone rang. 'Hello? OK.' He pointed at the SUV. 'It's him, or at least he's is in the vehicle.'

'It's four-up,' Blazhevich replied.

Nedilko removed his Glock from its holster. 'What's the saying? "Plan for the best, prepare for the worst"?'

'Something like that.'

As the Land Cruiser came to a halt, just short of the checkpoint, a series of rumbles rolled across the fields. The DNR were shelling again. A thin man, wearing a blue OSCE vest over a grey, three-quarter-length jacket, stepped slowly from the front passenger door. He held his arms aloft as a pair of Ukrainian soldiers advanced, weapons up. The rear door now opened and out climbed an Asian man followed by someone both SBU agents couldn't mistake: Aidan Snow.

'"Who Dares Wins",' Blazhevich said with a smile.

Snow led the trio towards the checkpoint. The man in the OSCE vest held out his hand to Blazhevich. 'Gordon Ward, OSCE monitor. You must be from the Security Service of Ukraine?'

'That's correct, the SBU,' Blazhevich confirmed, shaking hands. 'Things getting busy back there?'

'Hairy is the word for it. The DNR are systematically violating the ceasefire!'

'We heard,' Nedilko stated.

'Well, here they are, safe and sound.' Ward turned to Snow. 'Don't make a habit of this, will you?'

'I'll try not to.'

Ward flashed a swift smile, turned on his heels, and got into the Land Cruiser. The Toyota crabbed across the road before quickly heading back towards Donetsk and the rest of the OSCE monitors.

'Vitaly Blazhevich, Ivan Nedilko, may I present Mohammed Iqbal,' Snow said.

'It's Mo, to my friends,' Iqbal added.

Snow was in Ukraine to facilitate the repatriation of Iqbal, a British citizen held captive for several months in Donetsk. Iqbal was one of many foreign students studying medicine at Donetsk University, but unlike the others he had been kidnapped by the DNR, who took exception to the colour of his skin. The news of Iqbal's plight had come from a bizarre post on the DNR's 'VKontakte' page. They used the Slavic copy of Facebook to inform the Russian-speaking world of their latest proclamations and 'successes' against the Ukrainian forces. Via VKontakte, Iqbal had been labelled 'a black mercenary' and 'a spy' by the self-appointed Prime Minster of the DNR. Iqbal was subjected to intimidation, beatings, and starvation by his captors. It was only after much negotiation that his release had been brokered and an agreement reached to hand him over to the OSCE. At least that was the official story, and the one that made the DNR look like humanitarians, but Snow knew otherwise. He still had the bruises and an empty magazine to prove it.

'Incoming!' A shout went up as a shell whistled overhead.

Snow grabbed Iqbal and threw him into the ditch at the side

of the road as another shell flew past them to land with a thunderous cacophony further down the road.

'Bloody twats!' Iqbal's Brummie accent grew thicker with his annoyance, as he spat out a mouthful of cold mud.

'Stay down!' Snow ordered. He looked up and saw the source of the shells. What he took to be a Russian armoured vehicle, possibly a BMP-2, had appeared from the fork in the road. Too far away to return fire, the Ukrainians took cover as best they could. Still visible, Snow watched the OSCE Land Cruiser skid around the tracked vehicle and take the fork in the other direction. Then, just as quickly as it had started, the shooting stopped. The BMP-2 turned and followed the Toyota towards Donetsk.

'Nice of them to give you a sendoff,' Snow said as he pulled Iqbal to his feet.

'I'd have preferred a box of chocolates.'

Snow smirked. 'Come on. We need to catch a ride back to Kyiv.'